PUSHING DAISY

THE CLOCKWORK CHIMERA BOOK 2

SCOTT BARON

"It is not only the living who are killed in war"
- Isaac Asimov

CHAPTER ONE

The hard rubber of the heavy-soled boot caught Daisy square in her chest with bone-crushing force. The impact was great enough to send her sliding backwards on the ceramisteel floor before she managed to dig in her feet and stop herself just short of the hard metal wall.

She flashed a little grin.

"Is that all you've got?" she said, taunting the burly woman with the menacing steel-alloy cybernetic replacement arm, who was circling her like a hungry shark. Daisy shrugged off the piercing pain, acting as if the blow hadn't fazed her one bit. She wouldn't give Tamara the pleasure of seeing her wince.

"I think she cracked a couple of ribs, Daze," Sarah said.

Gee, ya think? Daisy silently replied to the woman living in her head.

The disembodied voice of her deceased sister had been a constant companion ever since Daisy accidentally downloaded her entire consciousness into a partition within her own brain. At first, they had both thought the voice in her head was merely Daisy's way of coping with Sarah's untimely death when a malfunction aboard their ship blew her into space. It wasn't long thereafter that it became apparent she was something more.

She was a ghost in the shell, but in the *wrong* shell. It was quite the revelation, learning that while she may have been dead, she was far from gone, and it was one secret the pair had decided not to share with the others on the base. Not yet, at least. Not while it could be an advantage.

"Look at her shoulder dip. She's going to do that fake high kick–low switch trick she loves," Sarah warned.

Thanks, I see it.

Sarah had eventually settled into her new home riding shotgun with her sister. She learned to become a second set of eyes, seeing what Daisy saw, but also able to disconnect and scan the entire picture while Daisy focused on the task at hand. It had been proving to be a rather useful partnership.

Daisy moved to block Tamara's feinted high strike, then quickly jumped aside, leaving the vicious follow-up kick swinging through empty air.

"Not bad, Swarthmore," the sweating woman grudgingly conceded, then launched a fierce attack at twice the speed.

Daisy blocked and counter-struck as best she could, but Tamara was too fast. Too strong. Too angry.

The anger—that was her edge over Daisy, though Daisy couldn't really fault her for it. After all, she had blown Tamara out an airlock and left her for dead, drifting in space, only four short months ago.

Crossed wires, mixed messages, none of that mattered, though she still believed it had really seemed like the right choice at the time. Tamara, however, held a grudge. and their daily sparring sessions were as much about taking out her anger as they were about training Daisy to be combat-ready.

Tamara feinted a hook, then slapped her with an open palm —which was quite unexpected. She used that momentary shock to switch her attack from hard style to soft, sliding in close and throwing Daisy through the air with a modified AikiJutsu move.

Daisy crashed into the ground at an awkward angle, the wind knocked out of her from the impact on her aching ribs.

"Yup. Definitely cracked."

Shut up, Sarah. Not helping, she shot back at her mental ride-along.

"Come on, Swarthmore. You were built for this! Stop pussy-footing around and fight!" Tamara punched a command into the small panel embedded in her metal arm and lunged at Daisy again.

The gravity in the room shifted, allowing the thickly muscled woman to angle her attack from a new trajectory as she jumped to the ceiling, then redirected down toward her target. Daisy scrambled aside, narrowly avoiding the boots she had become all too familiar with.

Fortunately, she had overcome her dislike of low and zero-g environments, and had been secretly using the modified gravity in her daily meditation practices. Tamara thought she was gaining a tactical edge, shifting things like that. It was an overconfidence, one that Daisy pretended had her on the run. But that was far from the case.

Daisy shifted and spun through the low-gravity air and landed a quick series of blows before deflecting off to the side and landing near the far wall. Tamara shook them off easily, but nonetheless gritted her teeth at her opponent making that much contact.

The thing about low-g fighting is that it doesn't favor the strong so much as the quick, and where Tamara was used to relying on her brute strength, Daisy could utilize her lithe frame to outmaneuver her. Also, if you hit someone too hard in low-g, you ran the risk of the transferred force rebounding you right into a wall.

SCOTT BARON

The two women locked eyes, then pushed off into the air on a collision course.

Oh yeah, I've finally got her this time, Daisy thought as they rapidly closed in on one another.

Mid-flight, Tamara quickly tapped another command into her arm panel, and just as the two impacted, the gravity shifted once more, sending them plummeting to the ground with a painful thud. Tamara sat atop Daisy, her mechanical arm pulled back and ready to deliver a debilitating blow. But, despite her grudge, she held off.

After four long months of training, Daisy was nearly undefeatable, and none but a single one of her sparring partners could best her. Tamara, however, fueled by her simmering anger, was unstoppable.

"Yield?"

Daisy reluctantly accepted her defeat. "Yeah. Yield."

The two slowly got to their feet in the now-doubled gravity of the room.

"Sneaky trick," Daisy grumbled.

"You have to be ready for anything," Tamara replied as she tapped the command into her arm's control pad to return the room's gravity to normal. Ever the soldier, that one, even though she hadn't been active as one for some time.

"*Real* fighting is reaction, not thinking, Daisy. Repetition. You've got all this amazing skill stored in your brain, but until your body is ready, you'll never be able to access it. Theory is one thing, but muscle memory always wins out."

Annoyed at yet another loss, Daisy nevertheless knew she was right.

"Okay, enough for today. Go get cleaned up. I know you've got a session with Fatima after lunch, and she won't be happy if I send you to her too bruised up," Tamara said over her shoulder as she exited the room. "See you tomorrow. Same time."

· · ·

4

Daisy sat quietly on a crate in the empty sparring room, replaying the mistakes she had made over and over in her mind. She still couldn't quite beat her metal-armed nemesis. Not yet, anyway, and now she would have to put her mental play-by-play on hold for a bit and redirect her attention to the day's next task: an altogether different type of training.

Her next session with Fatima.

The silver-haired woman was an enigma. A Yoda-esque mentor, she had been picking through her psyche ever since she first arrived on the secret base hidden away on the dark side of Earth's moon four months prior.

Fatima wasn't like the others Daisy had met there. Not by a long shot.

Commander Mrazich, the ranking officer on Dark Side Base, with his buzzed hair, metal jaw, and cybernetic eye, was a battle-hardened leader of few words. His trusty soldiers, Shelly, with her shiny pair of rebuilt arms, and Omar, who sported two hip-down leg replacements, were both happy to follow his lead. As for Donovan, the base's pilot, he was a bit of a rascal, but he fell in line when it was required.

But Fatima? She was different. Calmer than the rest. Wiser. More open to thinking outside the box, and possessing an uncanny way of seeming to know what was going on in your head. If she didn't know better, Daisy would almost believe she was psychic.

Fatima was also the oldest resident of the base.

Oldest by far.

She'd been stranded there during one of the earliest failed attempts to reclaim Earth from its alien conquerors. The experience had left her not only injured and alone on the moon, but also suffering irreparable damage to the minor AI embedded in her head, rendering her forever unable to utilize a cryo unit without frying her brain.

So it was that she had been stuck on Dark Side Base, living

out every hour of every day for more years than anyone would care to count. Her aging, however, was slowed to a trickle by radical gene therapy of her own design. It was that, along with a stem cell replacement regimen, that kept her telomeres healthier, and far longer, than a woman anywhere near her age should possess.

Fatima had coped with the years of hardships and loneliness by learning to focus deeply inward in times of stress, and in her early days in her new home, there had been plenty of that. By this point, she had been at the whole thing longer than any yogi ever had, and it was this mastery of meditative inner calm and control that she had been attempting to teach her impatient pupil.

Of course, she also loved to throw in often-frustrating, and seemingly random projects just to keep Daisy occupied, always reminding her that her exceptional mind held immense potential.

"If you just learn to focus, Daisy, you could harness the power of your mind and use it in ways no human has ever dreamed possible," she would often say.

Or perhaps that was just an excuse she used to send Daisy off on random tasks solely for shits and giggles. At least, so it seemed to her often-frustrated student. Especially as she still had one more task to complete prior to her post-lunch training session.

The interesting thing was, despite Fatima being mechanically altered, and thus not entirely human, Daisy nevertheless found herself growing quite fond of the older woman, in spite of herself.

Daisy shifted on her makeshift seat, her limbs feeling a bit weak after her lengthy sparring practice. Her ribs were aching with every breath.

"Oh, yeah, that's gonna leave a mark," she said, examining her sore flank with a pained chuckle.

"Hey, we really should get to the mess hall," Sarah urged.

"Gotta finish up Fatima's latest torturous busy-work first," Daisy grumbled in her outside voice. Fortunately, no one was present to hear her.

Her metabolism was above average by normal human standards, as one would expect with it supporting her rapidly strengthening musculature. But it was having Sarah's piggybacked mind running at full-capacity in tandem with her own that *really* burned up the ATP and glycogen in her body at an alarming rate.

Too much dual-processor time with her sister revving on all cylinders, like during an all-out sparring match with an angry, metal-armed woman, for example, and Daisy could find herself drained, and with a nasty headache to boot. Such were the drawbacks of accidentally loading her dead sister's entire consciousness into her head.

"Daze, come on. You need to eat."

I know, I know, Daisy grumbled, pulling a few tubes of energy gel from her pocket and gulping them down. *There. Happy? I'll make a proper lunch after I finish Fatima's little project,* she said, slowly rising to her disconcertingly unsteady feet.

"Good girl. You've gotta recharge those glycogen stores. Wouldn't want you running on an empty tank."

Yeah, I do feel a bit wiped out, she admitted. *Thanks for keeping an eye on the old fuel gauge, Sis.*

"Hey, we share the same engine. You know I try to conserve energy whenever I can."

It was true. Sarah, for her part, learned early on how to pull back and hang out in the periphery to help save their valuable resources. It was a neat trick, and one Daisy was quite grateful for.

She cracked her neck slowly, then opened the heavy door

and stepped out of the sparring room, her damp clothes already drying to her body.

She was making good time down the long hallway, but stopped at a thick window to gaze out over the barren surface of the moon.

That was her next destination.

Fatima, always looking to push her limits, had taken quite a liking to having her perform tasks in the bulky annoyance of a space suit in the difficult environs of reduced gravity.

Oh joy, she grumbled to herself.

Daisy was exhausted, but at least her ribs were already beginning to feel a bit better, she noted, as she surveyed the rocky landscape and destroyed outer buildings of the moon base. Now she just had to suit up and get out there.

"Fuuuuck," she said with a long sigh. "How the hell did I wind up in this place?"

This was it, like it or not. This was home, and it certainly wasn't what Daisy had expected when she made a run for Earth all those months prior.

Dark Side Base, it was called. A lone, secret outpost hidden on the shadowy side of the moon. Daisy had arrived hoping the secret lunar refuge would be her salvation from the ship full of cybernetically modified humans she had believed were out to get her. Funny how far from the truth that had proved to be.

The machines weren't trying to harm her. Far from it.

After mankind had been wiped out by a genetically-designed alien super plague, the AIs had managed to *save* humanity, sending a fleet carrying the last traces of viable human DNA far out into the depths of space to restore the species.

Daisy was their crown jewel, and she had been created, not born. A prodigal child sprung from one of the few salvaged cell lines that was immune to the alien plague.

It was a hell of a lot to take in, learning that she had been grown in a lab, was over a hundred years old, thanks to decades in cryo stasis, and that all of her memories of Earth had actually been implanted during the decades-long flight.

The reality was, the entire population of the planet was long dead, and the only traces of the former inhabitants she had come across during her brief escape to the surface were an eccentric AI named Habby, and his dapper cyborg friends, whom she had only happened upon by blind chance.

Daisy had also stumbled upon *other* inhuman things in the city.

Fleshless, crazed cyborgs. Damaged ones. The ones who had gone mad, infected with the alien computer virus, their minds scrambled by the malicious code spread by the invading creatures. And what terrifying monsters those invaders were.

The Chithiid, she learned they were called. Four-armed aliens with a second set of eyes toward the back of their head, affording them a nearly three-hundred-degree field of vision. The bipedal creatures stood on two powerful legs, nearly a full head taller than most men, and sported skin as tough as a rhino's hide.

Daisy had a brief skirmish with them before being forcibly dragged back to the moon, and that was where she'd been cooped up ever since. Just her and a dozen modified humans, a pair of AI-controlled ships, and the AI-run base itself.

All of them helping her train. All of them carrying the belief that she was created specifically for this task. All of them waiting for her to live up to her potential, whatever that was.

She was *special*, apparently.

Special, Daisy mused grimly. *What a laugh.*

"Well, you do have a dead girl riding along inside your head. That should count as special, right?"

Awesome pep talk, Sis. Really, don't quit your day job.

"My day job is basically cruising around in your noggin, and believe me, I'd quit it for my old one if I could."

Daisy chuckled.

The thing was, she actually *was* special. She'd been built that way. Genetically engineered. Stronger, faster, tougher. Her bones, cracked by Tamara's kicks, were already healing, and the rest of her body was just as sturdy. Designed to endure far more than a normal human could. More importantly, though, she was still one hundred percent organic, and that meant invisible to Chithiid scans.

The aliens on Earth's surface had one key weakness in their monitoring systems. Having killed off the indigenous people hundreds of years prior, all they monitored for now was non-organic movement. The occasional cyborg survivors foolish enough to brave the surface were typically picked off in short order, their metal parts setting off the alien detectors. Daisy, however, was, by her nature, a sort of walking stealth unit.

Now if only she knew what exactly it was that she was supposed to do.

Gently rubbing her sore ribs, she snapped out of her fog and picked up her pace to gear up for the last thing on her plate before she could break for lunch.

Barry and Ash, the two resident cyborgs, greeted her as they approached from the opposite direction.

"How was your combat sparring today, Daisy?" Barry asked as he neared.

He didn't seem to hold any grudge against her for frying him with an EMP grenade when she made her escape from her old ship, the *Váli*, several months prior.

"Fine," she answered.

"I see you have a scrape on your elbow," Ash noted. "May I offer you a bandage? Or perhaps you'd like me to escort you to the medical unit?"

Ash still creeped her out, even months after her arrival. At least Barry's body was reasonably close to human. A false-man with a freaky cyborg endoskeleton hiding beneath his lab-grown flesh.

Ash, on the other hand, was a much earlier model, and he just felt *off*. Something about the older cyborgs; they looked human but had some strange element to their speech and motion that put some people on edge. People like Daisy.

"No thanks, Ash. I'll be fine. Gotta get out there and finish clearing the mess outside Hangar Three before lunch."

"Ah, yes, another project to complete before this afternoon's meditation and acuity training with Fatima," he said with a warm smile. "Very well, then. We shall leave you to it."

Without another word, the two mechanical men walked off, leaving Daisy alone with her thoughts, however troubled they might be.

CHAPTER TWO

Moving around on the surface of the moon wasn't all that bad. Once you got used to the funky gravity, that is. It was the bulky spacesuit that made things difficult, but Daisy figured that was a minor inconvenience compared with the rather serious discomforts of freezing, suffocation, and death.

"Stupid thing," she grunted as she struggled to heave another piece of reclaimed scrap onto the pile accumulated beside Hangar Three's massive doors.

It was bound to have happened eventually, a rock slide occurring as part of the crag above the base gave up the ghost and came a-tumbling down. The only problem was it had gathered more than a few friends along the way.

While the reduced gravity of the moon lessened the impact, the rock slide had managed to not only scatter the spare parts Daisy had been so meticulously removing from the collection of bits salvaged from the debris field surrounding Earth, but it had also strewn boulders and spare parts alike in front of the hangar doors.

"Yeah. You were right. Damn thing is all jammed up in the door's track," Sarah said.

Just my luck, right? Daisy replied. *Two weeks of work, all strewn about, and now I've gotta get the door cleared to boot. At least this looks like the last one.*

She grunted as she hefted a salvaged comms coupling back to join its brethren in a small stack under a rocky overhang. It had taken her most of the prior afternoon, and much of the current morning to get doors clear and the last of the pieces back where they belonged. All that remained was a final cleanup of any remaining rocks that might still interfere with the door's action.

Looks like it's mostly clear. You think those smaller ones over there will be in the way?

"Nah, they look fine to me."

Oh, thank God. I am so ready to get out of this stupid suit, Daisy silently replied as she keyed on her comms.

"Hey, Sid. Would you please open Hangar Three's doors when you can? I think I've finally got them cleared."

"Of course, Daisy. Just give me a moment to ensure no one is currently in the hangar. I will open them once it is clear and depressurized," the base AI replied.

"Thanks, Sid. Standing by," Daisy said. She knew it would likely take a minute or two before the massive doors would rumble open.

*Get this done, get back inside, grab a bite of lunch, and I should still have plenty of time to spare before our—*Daisy noticed something poking out of the dust. *Hey, does that look like a piece of an AI cradle to you?*

"I see it. Not sure, though. Might be."

I didn't know we had any of those in with the salvage out here. Figured the big brains would want to keep any high-value components like that tucked away inside.

"Might have been in the last load Donovan and Bob dropped off. Maybe it was just covered by dirt and got overlooked."

Daisy sighed. *Well, I'd better go get it.*

She trudged out in front of the hangar doors, making her way to the mostly buried device. She knew she was well clear of the doors themselves, so their cycling open was of little concern to her.

Yep, it's part of a cradle, all right, she commented as she pulled the unit free from the dusty soil. *There. That wasn't so hard. Once in a while, things actually go my way.*

"Always tempting Murphy, aren't ya, Daze?"

Yeah? What can he possibly do to me that's any worse than being stuck out here?

"Um, you're in a near-vacuum at sub-freezing levels, two hundred thirty-eight thousand miles from Earth. You really want to ask that question?"

Daisy laughed as she began dragging the AI cradle back to her pile of salvaged parts.

"All is clear inside, Daisy," Sid informed her over the comms. "Hangar Three will now cycle open."

"Copy that. Thanks, Sid."

"My pleasure, Daisy," he replied as the massive doors began to move with a low rumble she could feel through her boots.

"Oh, and guess what? I found a partial AI cradle. It must've somehow come in with the last salvage load."

"Interesting," Sid replied. "It would be useful to have some extra componentry on hand as backup parts, should the need ever arise."

"Yeah, I thought you'd——"

"Daisy, dive left!" Sarah shouted in Daisy's head.

She trusted Sarah completely, and knew far better than to pause for even a second to ask why. Dropping her cargo, Daisy dove as hard to the left as she was able, landing at an awkward angle as she roll-bounced and tried to scramble to her feet. Behind her, rocks were tumbling down from above.

She ran as best she could in the awkward gravity, trying to

get clear. It was like a nightmare, one where no matter how hard you tried, your feet felt like they were trapped in sucking mud.

"Daisy, I sensed a geological disturbance. Are you okay?" Sid asked.

Heart pounding loud in her ears, she turned and looked back at the relatively small mass of rocks that had shaken loose and come tumbling down when the door's rumbling disturbed them.

Thanks, Sis. You saved my ass just now.

"*I saved both our asses, technically. But you're welcome.*"

Daisy turned and began walking for the airlock.

"I'm okay, Sid. We had another rock slide out here. Nothing too big, but how about you have Donovan do a few flyovers and hit the hillside with his engine wake to shake free anything else that's loose up there so we don't have any more issues."

"Of course. I'll have him do that when he heads out on his next drift run."

"Thanks. I'm calling it a day out here."

"Understood. I will request that Barry and Ash clear the new debris as soon as they are able."

"Sounds good to me," she replied.

I did my part. All the salvage is back where it should be. Fatima can't give me any grief about not completing her task.

Daisy looked at the newly fallen pile of rocks.

Aw, shit.

The AI cradle—at least what was left of it—was sticking out from beneath the debris at all sorts of wrong angles.

Better it than me, she figured.

"Hey, Sid. Sorry, but the cradle got smashed up pretty good in the rock slide. I don't know if anything is salvageable."

"Understood. While regrettable, what is important is that you are safe."

Her heartrate slowly lowered back to normal as she made

the long trek back to the welcome warmth and relative safety of the base.

Exiting the airlock into the base's fresh air, blissfully free of the restrictive bulk of the space suit, Daisy took a quick whiff of her sweatshirt as she walked the quiet corridors of Dark Side back to her quarters.

I suppose a shower would be the polite thing, she considered.

"No need to assault Fatima with your post-labor BO." Sarah chuckled in her head.

"Not to mention Tamara's funk rubbing off on me from earlier," she said with a laugh.

"Eww, you did not just go there."

"Totally did."

"You're such a freak, Daze."

"Says the disembodied ghost of a genetically-engineered planetary savior."

"Okay, you got me. Point taken."

"Don't sweat it, Sis. They still push that 'chosen one' crap on me too. Being dead, you're the lucky one in that regard. At least they leave you alone."

"In their defense, they don't know I'm here. And excuse me? I'm lucky being dead? Screw you, Daisy. I'd trade with you any day just to be able to enjoy a meal, or go for a run, or take a really good dump."

"Jeez, Sarah. Really?"

"You never know what little pleasures you'll miss until they're gone."

"Any other classy gems or insights you want to share?"

Her sister went silent, but Daisy could almost hear her gleeful giggle in the recesses of her mind as she walked to her quarters.

Unlike the somewhat restrictive living spaces she had been accustomed to aboard the *Váli*, Dark Side Base was like a resort by comparison. Not exactly a resort, perhaps, but it was a much more spacious and comfortable living arrangement at least, one aspect of which were the private showers in each crewmember's quarters.

When the base had been fully manned, only the officers and science crew were afforded private rooms in the safer confines of the rock-ensconced technical buildings. Now, housing barely a dozen humans total, the inhabitants had their pick of lodging.

The facilities that had not been hidden under the moon's rocky surface were rendered empty shells when the alien invaders bombarded them to oblivion as they passed on their way to Earth. In the aftermath, the remaining intact structures, safely tucked under rocky ledges, briefly housed the few dozen survivors out of a base of hundreds.

They had thought they'd somehow miraculously escaped unharmed.

They were wrong.

The remaining habitable spaces soon began suffering catastrophic decompression one by one when the aliens' horrific AI virus was released, sending the powerful mind of Dark Side Base spiraling into insanity and collapse. In the span of but a few hours, it had vented nearly every chamber to space before melting down into a spasming chunk of fused neuro-circuitry as the virus overloaded its core.

The handful of remaining survivors who had been lucky enough to have had access to space suits before decompression found themselves alive, but unable to power up the base without a viable AI operating system.

They even pulled the fried, half-meter-cube of the AI brain from its docking bay and attempted to override the safeties manually. It was a valiant effort, but the base was military in origin, and top secret at that.

The security protocols originally designed to keep anyone from disabling the AI to take over the base had ultimately resulted in those poor souls suffocating in their suits as they ran out of oxygen, unable to restart the scrubber network that provided them an endless supply of fresh air.

Daisy tried not to think of the long-dead bodies Fatima had slowly dragged out of the facility when she came to live in it all those years ago. It must have been horrific, but she had done that, and far more.

In fact, over the decades, Fatima had somehow accomplished the seemingly Sisyphean task of rebuilding and restoring most of the facilities and hangars not directly impacted in the attack.

One by one.

By herself.

She had restarted the organic materials food replication processors and air scrubbers first, followed by the water system that tapped into a deep ice field hidden far beneath the moon's surface. The breaking of the hydrogen/oxygen bond provided the base both a source of combustible fuel in the form of hydrogen, and a clean oxygen supply indefinitely.

The hangars took a bit more work, and it wasn't until nearly a decade later that she managed to get the first of them fully functional. From there, she spent the next few years repairing a small utility ship, and once that was finally flight-worthy, she set to work, drifting in the debris field, maneuvering using only her compressed air thrusters in order to stay off Chithiid scans as she slowly accumulated useful parts from the destroyed fleet scattered in orbit.

It wasn't much of a life, but at least it was *life*.

"At long last," Daisy said with a sigh as she stepped into her quarters. She reached into her shower compartment and spun the knob, a steaming blast of water beckoning her to join it. Daisy stretched high, then twisted from side to side, feeling her cracked ribs twinge uncomfortably as she did.

"Not quite healed," Sarah commented.

18

"Nope. Not yet. Apparently, even *I* don't heal *that* fast, it seems."

"Bummer."

"I'll survive," she replied with a little laugh as she stripped out of her funky workout attire and stepped into the beckoning hot water.

CHAPTER THREE

Daisy's hair was still damp as she walked the corridor to the mess hall, her stomach rumbling loudly, as if to urge her on faster.

Despite her abdomen's vocalizations, a patch of expertly-welded wall made Daisy stop in her tracks, as it had more than once since she'd taken up residence there. She ran her finger admiringly over the perfect seams, lingering as she traced across the one, and only, tiny imperfection in the weld.

All by herself, she did this. Dragged the metal here, sealed the breach, welded it all together. And the whole time without a single human to help her.

Daisy shuddered at the thought. The loneliness must have been unbearable, yet Fatima seemed the most tranquil and at peace of the entire crew.

Who knows? Maybe her training actually will be useful, Daisy pondered as she wondered if it might even help her calm her mind and accept this unexpected new life.

She continued on her way, her footsteps quietly echoing off the walls. Up ahead, she noticed the research lab's door was open, faint music drifting out into the hall.

"Hey, Chu," she called out as she passed the open door.

The technician looked up from his work and flashed a warm smile.

"Hey, Daisy. Dang, you look pretty beat up. Training with Tamara again?"

"You know it."

"Well, if you break anything, let me know. I'm pretty sure I can get the medbot to fix you up in no time." He laughed and returned his attention to the microscope in front of him.

Chu, she had learned, while looking human, actually possessed an impressive array of artificial organs, as well as several ceramisteel replacement bones. She never did ask him what happened to him to require such invasive repairs, and figured he likely wouldn't want to relive whatever necessitated them.

He was one of the resident crew Daisy got along with easiest, and she saw no reason to sour that relationship. Besides, the uncomfortable fact was, *all* of them were modified to at least some extent, though some, far more than others.

Tamara had served as her ship's botanist, and her mechanical arm, though designed for combat, also accommodated a variety of attachments, allowing her to swap out accessories for her gardening work as needed. She loved that arm, and Daisy doubted she'd take an organic replacement even if Mal grew her one.

Finn, their chef-slash-apparent former commando, also had a partial metal arm, as well as several replacement fingers on his other hand, acquired after an incident during the flight to Dark Side Base.

Gustavo, the ship's navigator, possessed a cybernetic eye, along with a chunk of skull that had been replaced. He was massively enhanced, fine filaments running from his brain to the AI connection in his head, allowing him to plug directly into the ship and help navigate the vessel when Mal needed assistance.

Doctor McClain and Captain Harkaway each sported a mechanical leg, though Harkaway's was far older and slowly showing signs of wear and age. Reggie, the *Váli's* co-pilot, sported a shiny metal left hand, five replacement ribs, a ceramisteel femur, and a bunch of other mods, all required by some ailment that had ravaged his body.

Then there was Vince. Oh, Vince. The times they had shared still made her warm inside. She had been so in love with him. Then she saw the scans revealing the almost undetectable enhancements to his body. Reinforcements, to joints, filaments of metal fused to bones, and a small AI mounted in his brain.

The shitty thing was, she had truly loved him up until that revelation. The revelation that her boyfriend was a machine.

That particular discovery had hurt her much more than the others, though, in all fairness, it was Vince who actually felt the pain far more tangibly when Daisy, having just learned his true nature moments before, abruptly sealed a door on him, cutting his arm off at the shoulder.

He had survived the trauma, his limb reattached in their ship's medical unit, and only sporting a thin scar for the ordeal. Not only that, he had shortly afterward both saved her from Earth's hostile surface, as well as forgiven her for what she had done to him. All in the same day, no less. It was more than a little bit of a mind fuck.

Don't think about that, Daisy chided herself as she walked to get some chow. *Get your shit together. There are plenty of people here who aren't entirely human.*

"*Yeah,*" Sarah muttered. "*All of them.*"

Stop reading my thoughts.

"*Stop making them readable. It's your choice, you know.*"

Yeah, yeah.

She knew it was true, though. She just needed to focus

better. Also true was the fact that the other inhabitants of the base, those who had survived attempts to retake Earth and failed, only to wind up stuck on the moon, were enhanced and repaired as well.

Each and every one of them.

Daisy really was the only entirely organic person in the entire base. It could be a lot to handle, and her odd mentor did her best to help her cope, though that wasn't exactly in her job description.

Fatima was essentially the mother hen of Dark Side Base. She was not just older in pure calendar years, but her unique medical status, which kept her out of cryo, meant decades upon decades of actual up-time. She didn't look *old*, per se, not with her custom gene therapies, but while the rest of the team had cycled in and out of cryo for decades while they awaited the next assault to retake Earth, Fatima passed the time the old-fashioned way. One day at a time.

As a result, she had slowly adopted a worldview that was a bit unconventional, but who was to tell her otherwise? At the end of the day, whether it was her decades spent on her own with only a genius AI for company, or her modified neural status, Fatima just saw things differently than others.

Maybe that's why she took me under her wing, Daisy mused. *Another mind-fucked freak show to keep her company.*

"That you are," her secret mental passenger chimed in with a laugh. *"And she doesn't know the half of it."*

Whatever the case, she had taken to training Daisy in a multitude of non-combat skills over the past several months, leaving the martial ways to Tamara and the others.

Aside from Tamara, there was just one other person who could likely give her a run for her money sparring. But whatever terms Daisy had come to with her ex's not-entirely-organic status, she just couldn't bring herself to engage in that much physical contact with him.

It was really Vince's AI-enhanced brain that freaked her out the most. She couldn't help wondering, was it the man or the machine she had thought she was in love with? Add to that her deep-seated dislike of mechanicals in general, and it was a recipe for heartache, but no matter what she rationalized with her mind, it still hurt a little bit every time he was near.

So, while Daisy and Vince may have finally re-established something of a cautious friendship once more, she still refused to spar with him. It was a big step on its own that they had recently begun revisiting their old habit of watching select gems from Captain Harkaway's video collection, and even that was still a bit awkward. Unlike in the past, and despite the visceral urges that sometimes flared up—in defiance of Daisy's logical mind—they no longer curled up against one another as they once had while they watched the videos.

Except for rare incidental contact, they essentially never touched at all, but at least they could watch programs together and enjoy each other's company, however unconventional the situation may have become.

Nice of Harkaway to have loaded all those old videos, she mused.

Once she knew how old they all *really* were, Daisy had realized that each and every one of the captain's cherished movies and television programs, stored away on all those memory chips, was technically a classic. The last remnants of a planet long-dead.

Good thing I didn't get hooked on a show with a cliffhanger, she thought with a grim chuckle. *With the end of the human race, the next season would be a long time coming.*

CHAPTER FOUR

The mess hall was empty when Daisy entered. In what was a rare occurrence, the sound of Finn's knives slapping against the cutting board did not fill the air.

It was actually a bit refreshing, cooking for herself in silence, and was something she wished she found time to do more often.

Time wasn't exactly the issue. More like a lingering sense of discomfort around the base personnel. The same personnel who were almost always filtering in and out of the mess hall. Everyone was great to her, that wasn't an issue. They treated her well—even better than that—but the lingering gazes as they watched her go about her day could be exhausting.

They were waiting for *it*; whatever *it* was. She was *special*, and somehow, Daisy was supposed to be the key to reclaiming Earth.

It could be more than a little bit exhausting.

She opened a crisper drawer in the nearest refrigeration unit and began digging through the selection of vegetables available to her. A bit of fresh produce could make life on the moon a tad more bearable.

Since landing at Dark Side, Tamara's botanical pods had

been carefully relocated and attached to the base. The *Váli* wasn't going to be making any lengthy flights requiring freshly-grown foodstuffs, so those units were networked and tacked onto one of Dark Side's smaller empty hangars.

Conveniently, Fatima had spent years infusing nutrients into the soil she had manually hauled into the unused hangar. With an essentially limitless water supply on hand from the vast subterranean ice field, she and Tamara had delighted in expanding the gruff woman's horticultural works into the new setting.

Tamara may have been a soldier, but her gardening skills were second to none, and she genuinely enjoyed her time tending the crops sprouting up in the freshly-seeded soil. Two months after they had arrived, the first crops had taken hold and were growing nicely. By month four, there was more fresh produce than they knew what to do with.

Especially zucchini.

Everyone was growing quite tired of zucchini, actually, and even Finn was running out of new ways to use the prolific vegetable. Fortunately, an entire hangar full of row upon row of growing vegetables meant that nearly every variety of seed that had been carefully stored for the flight was now represented in some quantity, though some more than others.

Tamara enjoyed doing the garden work by hand and would spend hours in quiet contemplation as she tested the soil, culled problem vegetables, and pulled up the occasional weed that had somehow managed to sneak in with the other seeds.

She didn't kill them, though. Those weeds, in her eyes, were survivors, like her. Kindred spirits, of a sort, although vegetable in nature.

Instead of meeting an untimely demise, Tamara had other plans for the little invaders. A short distance from the farming hangar, off in a separate and sequestered outbuilding, she had set up a small grow room of its own, designated a safe haven for the unwanted intruders in the garden patch.

A weed sanctuary of sorts.

Just when you thought you knew her, Tamara would do something like that and force you to reassess her yet again.

Daisy eyeballed the pile of produce spread out in front of her.

Okay, what have we got in here? she mused.

"You going veggie on me? I think we need something a bit more substantial after all of today's activity."

Don't worry, it won't be entirely veg. But something on the lighter and healthier side does sound kind of nice.

"All right, but remember, we need to get some serious carbs and protein back in here."

Don't worry, Sarah, you know me. A rabbit-food eater, I am most certainly not, Daisy replied with a little chuckle.

She carefully arranged her ingredients around her work space. There were zucchini, of course, which she would quickly roast, then chill, joined by some cauliflower and carrots. After a moment's thought, she added a couple of pieces of celery, some tomatoes, and a red pepper.

Yeah, that's a good start.

Julienned, the firmer vegetables would make for a nice vegetable-based pasta, to which she would add a lightly seasoned piece of replicator-produced protein. Turkey would be today's option, diced and sautéed with some nice, fresh tomatoes and herbs.

A loaf of hearty bread added some much-needed carbs to the mix. Sarah was right. After her time with Tamara, and with the added burn of her ride-along's help during their sparring session, she could really use them.

There wasn't enough room to grow a space-intensive crop like wheat on the base, but the organics replicator had no problem producing a steady flow of fresh flours, from which Finn would bake a multitude of bread varieties regularly.

The *Váli*, safely tucked away in Hangar Three at the moment, could replicate far more complex foods, but its galley wasn't really designed for baking. Dark Side, though hundreds of years older, had, however, taken creature comforts into consideration, realizing that much like Submariners of old, a well-fed crew was a happy crew. For the men and women stuck living way out on the moon, morale was a very big deal.

San Francisco would be proud, she thought as she took a bite of the tangy sourdough. *They actually saved their starter.* The thought brought a smile to her face.

"Replicated it, technically," Sarah corrected.

Yeah, but genetically, it's the same as the sourdough mother they saved when they fled into space. You can search the world, but the best sourdough was always from San Francisco.

"You've never even been there. And I have those same memories, but neither was I. Those were all implanted in your head, just like they did to me," Sarah reminded her.

I know, but that doesn't mean they weren't based on reality. Someone did go to San Francisco in all the panic of the invasion and somehow saved a sample of the starter to the AI network. I mean, in the face of an alien invasion, it's an almost inconceivable set of priorities, but I don't think they realized just how serious things were until it was too late. Or maybe they did, I don't know. Whatever it was, without them, the replicators would never have had that master sample in the Váli's catalogue.

Daisy took another bite, as she prepared the veggies, savoring the tangy flavor.

I had hoped to someday go back to San Francisco. Now even that's no longer an option.

"Well, technically, you had never actually been there."

Yeah, I know, but the memories still feel so real.

"Which, again, was their designers' intent."

Yeah. I had almost hoped that one day I'd at least see *the city, even if it is devoid of human life.*

She sighed as she picked a sharp knife from the rack and deftly twirled it in her hand, then began rapidly chopping, a small mountain of julienned vegetables steadily growing on the cutting board. It was more than one person would eat, but that was the plan.

Vince opened the pressure door and stepped into the mess hall, smiling bright when his eyes met hers. Daisy felt her heart quicken a little, but forced herself to ignore it. No, they were no longer an item, nor could they ever be one again.

He wasn't real. The AI tied into his brain meant he could never truly be in love with her. He was simply enacting protocols according to a series of lines of code. At least that's what she told herself. Sarah, on the other hand, had her doubts.

"Hey, you, whatcha got cookin'?" he asked, snatching up a slice of bread from the counter, relishing its crunchy crust.

"Doing up some veggie pasta with protein. Light tomatoes and herbs to round it out."

"Why do you insist on calling it protein? Just say chicken, or turkey like you used to."

"But it's not, Vince. No matter how much we want to believe it's real, it is just a computer-designed copy. A fake, made to simulate the original in every way."

Vince knew she wasn't only talking about food but let it slide.

"So, how'd it go with Tammy today?"

"You know she hates it when you call her that."

"Precisely why I do it," he said with his trademark mischievous grin. The one that still made her heart flutter ever-so slightly.

Why couldn't he be a real man? Daisy quietly lamented.

"You know she'll kick your ass one of these days," she chided him.

"Nah, I think I can take her." He paused. "Well, maybe we'd fight to a draw." He thought a moment longer. "Okay, maybe I wouldn't get hurt *too* badly."

Daisy chuckled and tossed a carrot at him, which he deftly caught and began munching like a live-action Bugs Bunny. Their friendship was still solid, if somewhat strange, despite whatever uneasiness there may still have been.

It had taken a while, but Vince was simply not willing to let it go. Plus, they saw each other every day, whether she wanted to or not. He had been persistent, and eventually, with good-natured ribbing and a healthy dose of laughter, he wore her down, and the two of them finally began spending more time together once more.

It started with the occasional shared meal, much like the one she was currently preparing. From there, it was easy to slip back into old habits. Chatting about the day's work over coffee and snacks, wandering the base, appreciating the lunar landscape through one of the remaining observation windows, and occasionally settling in to watch old movies together again. Daisy even found herself nestling into his warmth one exhausted evening as they watched some old animated Japanese program.

She had jumped up with a start when she realized what she was doing, pulling away from the comfortable pillow of Vince's shoulder that she knew so well. Instinct drew her to him, but her mind made quick work reminding her what he really was. Not entirely mechanical by any stretch, but not entirely human either.

Part of the difficulty was their shared plans, hatched during their honeymoon phase aboard the *Váli* as they flew toward Earth. The near-disaster that had woken the crew from their cryo sleep early had thrown them together in a crisis situation, and it was that spark of adrenaline that had started the whole affair in the first place.

The sex had been amazing, no doubt, and Daisy felt an ache deep in her gut when she let herself reminisce, but it was the conversations after that had truly bonded them. Talks of trips they would take, places they'd visit. All things they would do together when they were back on Earth.

Only that wouldn't happen. Earth was barren, and Vince had known it the entire time. Sure, it was part of his neuro feed input that had been set in place years before hers, but that was just because he was an older variant, placed in the grow tanks before Daisy's completely organic cell line had been perfected.

"I think he really wanted to go there with you, Daze," Sarah had consoled her. *"Even if he knew it wasn't possible. The neuro-stim fed him info telling him it was home for all those years, just like us."*

The technology that fed their growing minds and kept them not only current on training, but also sane over years and years of inaction, had indeed installed a visceral love of Earth, but it wasn't real. No matter how much data was pumped into her brain, none of it was real, and that hurt. She had dreamed of going home, made plans, talked for hours with Sarah about sitting on a sunny beach drinking margaritas and watching hot men in swim trunks walk through the waves.

Not real.

It was all implanted, and Vince, unlike Daisy and Sarah, had already received the Earth file update that detailed what the true status of the planet was. The AIs figured it would make them readier to fight for the planet if, deep in their bones, it still felt like home, even though they had never touched its soil.

But he knew what he was, Sarah. What I was. What had happened. And he didn't tell me.

"Captain said no one was allowed to speak of it until we neared Dark Side. You just got things rolling a bit early when you jumped ship."

That she had, and Daisy had nearly ruined centuries of planning with her impromptu escape to Earth's surface.

31

She put that thought far from her mind, at least as best she could, and focused on the conversation at hand. There was plenty of time to dwell on the past later, and that, she knew she would do whether she wanted to or not. For now, she'd enjoy a nice meal with a cute boy who, sadly, could never again be anything more than a friend.

CHAPTER FIVE

Daisy had left the mess hall earlier than expected, having accepted Vince's offer to clean up after the meal. It was a typical Vince move, being considerate like that. Of course, she *had* done the cooking, so it made sense, but coming from him, the courtesy just seemed so, well, *him.*

Reasons aside, Daisy wound up with a few extra minutes before she had to trot off to meet with Fatima for yet another afternoon of mental training and whatever other strange regimen was planned for the day. She had used that unexpected free time to relax and pre-game her overall Zen state.

They always started their sessions together with a centering routine, but with her overactive mind, it was a deceptively easy-seeming task that Daisy found consistently challenging. A little extra preparation would make things begin a little bit easier, and Daisy would take every bit of easy she could get.

One thing was certain, she would never be bored in Fatima's training sessions. The fact that Daisy found herself forced to adapt to the unexpected and think on her feet more often than not made their sessions almost enjoyable.

"Concentrate, Daisy. You're daydreaming again," Fatima said.

"Sorry."

"It's okay. Letting your mind wander is a natural reaction—for beginners. But you're beyond that now, wouldn't you agree?"

"Yeah, I suppose," Daisy agreed, reluctantly.

"Then let's get back to the lesson. Breathe. Be silent within yourself. Don't force it. Remember, *soft is strong*. You already meditate, but I want you to go further. Focus your mind even as you relax it. Now, let's begin again. Breathe."

Daisy did as she was told and found herself pleasantly able to slip into the proper mental state after but a few minutes. It had taken a while to begin to understand her new brain wiring after she overloaded it with an untempered neuro-stim info dump, but with every session she was able to get it a little bit more under control.

Fatima had been right. She would get nowhere if she fought to grasp her power. She had to relax in order to embrace it.

She would have liked to simply use the neuro-stim to load the skill faster, but she had tampered with that device one time too many and was well aware of where it got her and the risk any accelerated use held. Her recklessness had already given her a ride-along in her mind, and with it, an inability to run anything but the tiniest streams as she slept. At least for the time being.

The funny thing was, much as she disliked artificially-altered humans, Daisy had filed the neuro-stim in a sort of gray area of acceptability. Once she had managed to rationalize its use, she had embraced the device. Now, as she struggled to learn new things the old-fashioned way, she found herself rather missing it. Even though she disliked mechanically modified humans, she had relied on the neuro-stim, which left the uncomfortable question: What had that made her?

"Daisy? You're zoning out on me, aren't you?"

"What? Oh, yeah. Sorry, Fatima, I was just kinda thinking about stuff."

"Think later. The key for now is to not think. Just be. Flow within yourself."

"Now you're almost starting to sound like Doc McClain."

Fatima chuckled.

"We both know that's not true, though if I'm not mistaken, isn't today your weekly session with her?"

Daisy groaned.

"Yeah. Every week, more of the same. Can't I just play hooky?"

"It's your call, Daisy, but I think if you put aside your natural aversion to therapy, you may realize she is actually helping you more than you realize. Now come on, we have training to get on with."

Daisy clenched her teeth and shut her eyes.

"Relax, Daisy. Let the tension go. Just breathe."

Daisy tried her best, but found herself unable to slip back into the proper state of mind now that her pending psych-eval was on her mind. She was not fond of having the resident shrink poking around in her head, and she was certainly tired of hearing her opinions.

"Okay, it looks like you're having an off day. Let's run you through the new physical acuity course instead. We can revisit your centering work afterward, for a change."

Slowly, Daisy rose to her feet and followed Fatima to the far end of the converted storage facility they trained in.

"Check it, Daze. She's changed up the course again."

Great. Just when I had all the moves pretty much dialed in.

"Well, she does keep you on your toes," Sarah said. *"Actually, look at that small platform next to the crimp-wall. I think she may literally keep you on your toes this time."*

Indeed, Fatima had added a fresh series of difficult physical challenges, apparently more than one of which included utilizing the farthest extremes of her digits for balance. As always, whatever the physical task, Fatima would push her mentally as well. It could be downright exhausting, all told.

I tell ya, Sis, some days I just wish we were still in cryo.

"*Wake-me-when-its-over Syndrome, eh?*"

Something like that.

"*Sorry, to say, no such luck. Now stop griping and get through this. If you make good time, maybe we can get some downtime before the head-shrinker has at it.*"

"Ugh. Not looking forward to that," Daisy muttered.

"What was that?" Fatima asked.

"Um, I just looked at the new course, is all," Daisy lied.

"Uh-huh. Well, get a move on. You have a lot of work to do."

Reluctantly, Daisy climbed up to the opening move of the reconfigured course and began making her way through the new moves. It didn't take long for her to forget about her pending psych-eval once she got into it. Unfortunately, that would only last so long.

"You've got such potential, Daisy, but your stubborn reluctance is holding you back." Doctor McClain crossed her legs, the metal one's ankle shining at the cuff of her trousers. "Why won't you open up to me and let whatever is troubling you off your chest?"

The ship's doctor and resident head shrinker had been trying to help Daisy "adjust" to the notion that she was something special ever since moon-fall, but found herself frustrated by her stubborn patient at every turn.

"Look, Doc, I appreciate what you're trying to do here. Really, I do, but everyone keeps talking about my potential and how I'm supposed to be this amazing, I don't know, *thing*, that can save Earth, but all I am is just a test-tube baby stuck on a base full of half-people." She eyed McClain's metal leg. "No offense."

"None taken, Daisy," the doctor replied. "But you have to accept the fact that you *are* unique. You've even seen the readouts. Your physiology is enhanced. And look what you were able to do with your mind. All the data you retained. That should have been impossible. Whether you like it or not, you *are* special. We just need to find a way for you to tap into your potential."

"Sure, I did download a bunch of stuff and access some abilities I didn't know I had tucked away in my noggin, I'll give you that, but how does knowing a few coding tricks and basic shuttle mechanics make me this '*chosen one*' you keep going on about?"

"No one calls you the chosen one. Have you been watching that old, '*There is no spoon*' movie with Vincent again?"

"You know what I mean. I'm supposed to be amazing, but I feel average. Okay, maybe a teeny, tiny, little bit above average, but you know what I mean. I hate to disappoint you all, but you've got the wrong girl."

"But the genetic––"

"Maybe it was Sarah who was supposed to be the golden child. You ever consider that?"

"Oh no you don't. Don't drag me into this!" Sarah objected.

You were grown just like I was. Maybe you were supposed to be their super messiah savior girl, she silently argued. *What do you say to that?*

Sarah didn't bother to reply.

Doctor McClain studied her a long moment, then sat back in her chair.

"All right, Daisy, let's go with your theory for the moment. Even if you are just a normal woman, don't you want to grow as a person?"

"I was grown in a tube, Doc, and no amount of therapy is going to change that. All I want to do now is just live as normal a life as I can."

"Here on the moon?"

"Yeah, here on the moon. I've accepted that I'm never going back home, because that home never existed at all. I've just got to make the best of a shitty situation and get on with my life."

She rose to her feet and headed to the door.

"I do appreciate your efforts, Doc, but I think I can be of far more help here than I'd ever be on Earth."

Daisy walked out of the room, leaving Doctor McClain jotting notes on her tablet. A minute later the shrink reached for her comms unit.

"Harkaway here," the captain answered.

"Captain, would you please arrange a meeting with Commander Mrazich and Fatima? I think we need to talk."

CHAPTER SIX

Deep in the shadows of the moon, a series of flashes briefly flickered against the inky darkness.

"Commander, Bob has just signaled us. Reggie and Donovan have returned from their drift," Sid's disembodied voice informed Commander Mrazich. "I am opening Hangar Two for their arrival. It also appears, in addition to a successful scanning run, they have managed to retrieve a few pieces from the debris field in the process."

"Excellent. Thank you, Sid. Please have them upload their data to your systems once they're safely inside, and inform Chu and Gustavo that we have some new information for them to review."

"Certainly, Commander. My pleasure."

"And let Shelly and Omar know there's some componentry to be offloaded."

"Of course."

The base AI clicked off the comms and set to his tasks while Commander Mrazich watched the beat-up, but very functional, recon ship as it drew close to the base. Bob, the ship's AI, steered it expertly into Hangar Two, then powered his flight systems down to standby mode.

Fifteen minutes later, Chu and Gustavo were poring over the newly gathered data in the communications lab as Commander Mrazich and Captain Harkaway looked on.

"Anything, Gus?" Harkaway asked.

"Hang on just another minute, Captain, there's a lot of interference in this scan. I was wondering if maybe they could maybe drop lower next time and take readings clear of the debris field—"

"You know we can't do that," Donovan said as he and Reggie entered the room. "Commander Mrazich. Captain." The pilot nodded to the men in casual greeting.

"No difficulties, then?" Mrazich asked.

"Nothing we couldn't handle. We hit a particularly dense patch of wreckage, so it took us a bit longer than usual to maneuver through the field with our air thrusters. Tacked an extra forty minutes onto the flight."

"Beats showing up on the Chithiid scans," Chu said.

"True, that. Anyway, once we settled in, we picked up a fair amount of comms noise, but as usual, it was garbled gibberish. I don't know if it's a scrambler or what, but Bob couldn't make heads or tails of it."

"Nor can I, Commander," Sid chimed in. "Mal is running a parallel scan on her systems, but feels similarly that this will prove fruitless yet again."

"We did send another focused ping directly at Los Angeles to the region where Daisy said she encountered that massive AI presence, as you suggested, but we've been doing that for months now, and there still hasn't been a single reply."

"You think she was hearing things?" Chu asked.

"I don't know," Donovan admitted. "I mean, it's entirely possible that the only reason the AI stayed intact this long was by entirely cutting itself off from external comms. Tactically, it makes sense. If they severed all comms links in order to seal off any possible access point of the AI virus, they'd be sitting blind."

"Blind, but alive," Captain Harkaway mused as he scratched his stubbly chin in thought. "Alive and able to operate their city defense systems. That would explain why the Chithiid are still steering clear of so many cities. The intact ones. But we still don't have any proof, and it's far too risky to plan a full-scale mission based on just a hunch."

"Agreed, Captain," Sid said. "The cutting of all comms would certainly keep the AI clean of the virus, but it would also mean that it could not even so much as hear our transmission, let alone reply to it. Of course, it's all speculation at this point. Once Daisy returns to the surface and re-establishes contact, then we'll finally know what the city's status really is."

"You know she's dead-set against going back there, right?" Vince said as he stepped into the room. "I mean, maybe you'll find a way to talk her into it, but knowing how stubborn she can be, I find the idea highly unlikely."

Harkaway grunted his agreement, or perhaps it was his annoyance, or maybe it was a healthy bit of both, then glanced once more at the results of their fly-over scans, his brow furrowed as he read the data.

"Good lord, look at all the craters where those cities used to be. They've stripped them bare, like goddamn locusts. Reggie, you were reading the monitors real-time, are you sure there wasn't a single sign of any activity from any other intact region?"

"Negative, sir. No communications chatter whatsoever."

"Any surface activity?" he asked. "Besides the usual small transport ships moving their loads to the main warp ship docks, that is."

"Well," Reggie began, then hesitated. "There was something going on in the periphery of Beijing that seemed a bit out of the ordinary. Weapons fire and some smaller salvage ships going down, but we're pretty confident it was just the Chithiid probing the automated defenses again. It looks like they've pretty well stripped the surrounding areas of usable resources, and Chu and me, well, we thought they were probably just testing the city, just in case they could dig into that rich vein rather than have to relocate their deconstruction operations to another developed area."

"Good thing those alien bastards don't know which cities possess nukes and which don't," Mrazich said. "I'm pretty sure that uncertainty is the only thing keeping the majority of them from being overrun."

"So, status quo, then. Have you made any progress in figuring out how their large cargo ship warp device works?" Harkaway asked.

"Unfortunately, the tech behind their warp drive still remains a mystery to us," Chu replied. "If we could perhaps capture one of their ships, then we might have a chance of figuring out how it works. Reverse engineer it, as it were."

"You know that's not an option."

"I know, but we're stuck observing from afar. For now, all we know is it seems to form a tiny skin of a compressed warp bubble around the nose of the ship just prior to its jump. The power signature is quite low, and Sid and Bob and I have long theorized that it's more of a hop device than a true warp. Given that, we all agree that they most likely have to perform a lengthy series of smaller hops in order to reach their fleet."

"Why is that?" Vince asked.

"Well, for one, the power signature seems to be far too low to indicate a significant space-time event. That makes sense looking at the limited area affected by the ship's movement, whereas a large-scale warp would form a proper warp bubble of much greater magnitude. Unlike their current method, that type of larger event would allow for a single jump to their destination."

"So, given how far away the fleet must be by now, we're thinking what? A few months of travel? Days? Years?"

"We really have no way of knowing, but if we figure in the speed at which their main fleet left the solar system several hundred years ago, and the distance they would have covered by now, it is quite likely that even with these tiny hops, it still would take at least a year, if not two, for the ship to reach the fleet. Of course, we don't know if they left our solar system and simply found a new conquest nearby, but given the size of the galaxy and rarity of planets with Earth's resources, it seems most likely that they traveled quite a distance before discovering another suitable planet."

"Agreed," Sid's disembodied voice said.

"Okay, so we probably have a little bit of a cushion between us and their fleet. What do you think, as someone who has been watching this planet for years? Is there a realistic likelihood that L.A. is still active despite the lack of response?" Harkaway asked as he scrolled through the contact map, looking for signs of anything other than alien crews deconstructing the planet.

"Sir, if I may," Sid interjected. "While Miss Swarthmore's recounting of her time on the surface seems a bit fanciful, I would remind everyone that fleshless cyborgs were indeed seen by the rescue unit when they retrieved her and brought her back to Dark Side. Many of her other claims have proven to be true as well. I do not think she was misleading us, nor do I believe she possesses the mental structure of one who would make something like that up. She believes what she reported, and minus proof to the contrary, I feel we must take her at her word."

"Agreed," Harkaway said after a moment's consideration. "But if that's true, then we're going to have to find a way to make contact, with or without Daisy's help."

Chu looked up from his workstation.

"Um, Captain? I think I may be able to help with that. And Daisy will even lend a hand, though she won't exactly know it."

. . .

43

The next afternoon Chu was hunched over a large pile of parts spread across the table in the mess hall, sipping his coffee as he studied the machinery. Daisy, as was her usual routine, stopped in to pick up a snack to top off her energy stores before heading to train with Fatima, but Chu paid her no heed.

"Hey, Chu," she called out.

He ignored her.

"Chu!" she said, louder. The technician looked up as if he hadn't heard her come in.

"Oh, Daisy, hi. Sorry, hang on, I think I've almost got it."

"Got what?"

"Nothing, just a reverse engineered wireless—never mind, you wouldn't understand."

Daisy bristled ever-so slightly as she strode to his table, nudging him aside as she plopped down next to him.

"Uh-huh, wouldn't understand, eh?" She scanned the device and parts spread before her. "So you've got a long-range encrypted comms transmitter piggybacked to an RF modulator with a MK-V uplink filter running tri-band firewalls. Sound about right?"

Chu laughed.

"Damn. How do you do that? You've never even seen this thing, but you know what it does in just a glance."

"Call me special," she joked.

"Now you're starting to sound like the others."

Shut up, Sarah, she silently replied.

"So, what's the issue, Chu? Seems like a solid enough system you've got set up."

"For comms shielded by the moon, perhaps, but we have no way to contact our drift ships while they're in the scanning range of Earth's orbit. They're on their own, and we just sit here, waiting to see if they make it back in one piece. But what if we had a way to communicate with them, all the way into Earth's atmosphere, but in such a way that the Chithiid wouldn't detect it?"

"Seems like an easy fix. Just use a low-frequency encryption and deliver with an asynchronous pulse rather than traditional. That would work."

"Yes, it would, but Bob is running that ship, and his AI brain would be exposed and run a risk of the Chithiid AI infection every time he used it."

"Shit, I see what you mean," Daisy said. "Hmm, gimme a second here." She furrowed her brow in concentration as she looked at the communications device and the assortment of parts on the table.

"Hang on, do you have any of the old DM-15s lying around?"

"We've got a few crates of them, but those things were antiques when they first built this place. Why?"

"I have an idea," she replied with a cocky grin. "Your concern is not only staying off of Chithiid scans, which your system seems to accomplish, but also to transmit in a manner that would protect Bob—and Sid by extension—from running the risk of AI virus infection. So why not overlap a set of two-factor authenticated wireless signals from the DM-15s?"

Chu's eyes went wide as he realized what she was proposing.

"You mean re-working the old units to transmit with actual radio waves, verifying with a super-outdated authentication? Like waaaay back in the old days?"

"Why not?" she said. "The Chithiid, from what I can tell, are so busy focusing on high-tech attacks and defenses, they'd never even notice something so simplistic as a random terrestrial-style radio signal. All you would need is some masking signal to hide the transmission in. Hell, that's easy enough. Then, once it runs through your filter, it would be all but unreadable to those four-armed freaks, while you'd be able to communicate with Bob and the boys easily."

"But what about the radio delays?" Chu asked.

"Come on, Chu, you're a scientist. Sure, the distance to somewhere far away would make for difficulties processing the signal, but the moon won't take ten minutes like it would for radio waves to reach Mars. I'd think at most, and this is if Bob is orbiting on the far side of the Earth from Dark Side, you'd still only have maybe a five-to-seven second delay. Factor that into the algorithm and you should be able to have relatively stable comms, no problem."

She smiled as he processed what she said, proud of her impromptu design work.

"Holy shit, Daisy, that's amazing. Thank you so much!"

"You got it. You need anything else? 'Cause I've got to get to my session with Fatima if you don't."

"No, I'm good. You go."

"Cool."

She got up and headed for the door.

"And, Daisy, thank you for this."

"My pleasure."

The door slid shut behind her, leaving Chu alone once more. He picked up his long-cold cup of coffee and dumped it in the sink, then keyed his comms.

"Commander, I think I got us something we can work with. If I understand it correctly, it should easily be able to handle our needs."

"Excellent. Rustle up the others and meet us in the comms lab. Daisy's off with Fatima for at least an hour, correct?"

"Yes, sir, that's her schedule."

"All right, then. See you in five."

CHAPTER SEVEN

"Breathe, Daisy. Just breathe." Fatima watched her impatient pupil as she led her through a mental warm-up before getting to the day's challenges. "Remember, soft is strong. Just relax. That's it, be mindful, but let the tension and worries go."

"Am I the only one getting sick of this yogi, guru, routine?" Sarah griped.

Go away, Sarah, I'm trying to concentrate.

"Something on your mind, Daisy?" Fatima asked.

"No, I'm fine. Just got distracted for a minute."

"Mm-hm," Fatima said with a faint smile.

For the next ten minutes, Daisy followed the older woman's lead and let herself gradually shed the stresses and worries of the day. When the real training began, she would be an empty cup ready to be filled.

Metaphorically, of course. The fact was her head was so jammed full of information, she would never be truly empty ever again.

"Good, Daisy. Very good. Breathe. Quiet your mind. Sense all that is around you and stay aware, even as you let your mental walls slowly come down."

"I know how to meditate, Fatima. Sarah taught me almost a year ago when we were back on the *Váli*."

Her teacher grinned. "And I am quite thankful for that. She saved me having to go over the basics with you, which certainly gave you a head start on your training. But those skills were merely the first steps. Yes, you've done far more than scratch the surface, but you still have a very long way to go, yet." Fatima took one of the alloy cups from the table and poured herself a helping of tea as her pupil continued to slowly inhale and exhale.

"Good. And again, breathe and open your mind to yourself. Relax into it."

Daisy actually felt herself sliding into her comfortable meditative state, though she'd never done so in quite this fashion. Her eyes slowly began to close.

A lightweight alloy cup clanged off her forehead.

"Ouch! What the hell, Fatima?"

"I said to relax. I didn't say to let your guard down."

Daisy concentrated on lowering her surging adrenaline levels.

"Tough love, huh?" Sarah mused, but Daisy just ignored her, focusing instead on her breathing as Fatima calmly paced in front of her.

"You have great powers locked away in your mind, and you've begun to realize how to tap into them, but you cannot let that remove you from what is happening around you at the same time. Submerge within yourself, but do not lose sight of the world around you." She sipped her herbal tea and observed quietly for a moment.

"Situational awareness and inner awareness can work in tandem, Daisy. Like Yin and Yang coexisting as one. If you practice long enough, eventually you will learn to wield the powers of your conscious and subconscious together. When that happens, you'll be unstoppable."

A few minutes later, their warm-up exercise was complete, and Daisy allowed herself a little smile.

Time for the fun part.

Another small obstacle course had been arranged in the cavernous work room, a smattering of unusual challenges for her to overcome. The tasks were always changing. Fatima made sure to keep her on her toes.

One week she would be focusing on speed, recognizing probable paths and executing her moves with as much speed of both body and mind as possible. The next week the course might morph into a series of tiny, technical handholds, forcing her to slow to a crawl and focus all of her mental powers on determining the best route forward, be it balancing on a step the size of a deck of cards, or hanging from a beam by merely a finger as she attempted to traverse the room.

All the while, Fatima would chat with her.

At first, Daisy had found it distracting, but that was the point. Multitasking. Achieving objectives while forced to handle other stimuli. Within a few weeks of beginning her training, she had found herself able to carry on complex conversations while simultaneously working her way through Fatima's obstacles, and she had only gotten better at it.

"So, tell me again," she said to the silver-haired woman. "I've been trying to figure the logistics. You actually dragged Sid all the way into Dark Side on your own, despite having four broken ribs, a fractured humerus, and a massive concussion?" She looked at the slender woman. It just didn't seem possible.

Fatima paused a moment before replying.

"Yes, Daisy, I did, though I must admit it was not one of my most pleasant experiences."

"That woman is way tougher than you'd ever guess."

I know, right?

Daisy continued across the chamber, hopping from one

wobbly step to the next, her route suspended by cables several feet from the floor.

"So you somehow found Sid, got him out of his pod, where it crashed after he was ejected from his command ship, then dragged him across the moon's surface and into the facility? But how did you get him plugged in? It seems like you should have run out of air long before then."

Fatima got a far away look in her eyes as she remembered that day.

"Of course, you're right, Daisy," she said. "I should have run out of air long before I could get Sid installed and the oxygen scrubbers fired up."

"So what happened?"

A slight shadow flashed across the woman's face, but was gone in an instant.

"I..." she began, haltingly. "I scavenged the dead."

"But I thought they used up their suit air," Daisy said.

"Inside the base, yes. Outside the base, they had died from traumatic injuries, mostly. Ruptured organs from the shockwaves of the attack, or shattered helmets, or shrapnel cutting them down. But once their vital signs ceased, their suit oxygen shut off."

"But the suits aren't designed to swap oxygen units in a vacuum. It's a safety thing."

"Indeed, but the moon isn't *quite* a true vacuum," she noted. "Rather than existing with a complete lack of atmosphere, it possesses what is known as a surface boundary exosphere. It's still far too thin to sustain life, and is more or less equivalent to the outer rings of Earth's atmosphere, where each cubic centimeter contains just a minute fraction of the molecules as sea level. Nevertheless, it was enough to allow me to override the lock-out protocols to a degree."

Daisy took a cautious step, then lunged across a gap to

pinch-grip a narrow ledge as she hugged her body to the rough-textured climbing wall Fatima had installed for the day's drills.

"So, you tricked the safeties into letting you swap out your oxygen unit with theirs. Pretty ingenious."

Fatima's smile faltered.

"Yes, it would have been, but the tank couplings on their suits had frozen from all those years on the surface of the moon. Oxygen was there, but I couldn't reach it."

"But you did, eventually. Otherwise you wouldn't be here telling me this story."

"Yes, I did, by dragging the deceased to the barely functioning wreck of my ship. I had just enough power to fire the engines for a few seconds, but that was enough. I know there's no way I could have smelled their burning flesh through my helmet, but it's an odor that I sensed nonetheless."

"Oh my God. That's horrifying," Sarah said. *"No wonder she survived as long as she did. Fatima is a total badass."*

A set of rungs awaited Daisy, and with a powerful lunge, she threw her body upward, one rung at a time, her fingers barely reaching the widely spaced metal bars.

"So that's how I thawed the couplings and got the tanks free. But that still wasn't enough. I had almost gotten Sid plugged in when my last oxygen unit ran out. All I had was the air in my suit, and no way to power up my wrecked ship to salvage any more tanks. That's when I had the idea."

"What was that?"

"I breathed as shallow as I could and retrieved the nearest bodies whose suits were intact. They had died from the concussion of the attack, you see, so the air in their suits was still there. I only needed a few more minutes to install the AI I'd found on the surface. Of course I had no idea if it was even a viable unit at that time, but it was my only hope. Once it was connected, the presence of a viable AI would activate the base's emergency systems automatically, sealing the doors to the exterior and repressurizing any compartment with vital signs."

"But you said you couldn't get to the oxygen in those suits."

"No, Daisy, I said I couldn't get their oxygen units. What was inside those suits, however, was there for the taking."

A mental image began to form, and Daisy was not liking it one bit.

"Fatima," she said as she slid hand over hand across a slender rope, "what did you do?"

"I think you know, Daisy," she replied, casting an odd look her way. "I gathered my tools and fixed a mental snapshot in my mind, then I took my last, deep breath of stale air and took off my helmet. Oh, it was cold. So very, very cold, but I closed my eyes tight and stabbed a sharp piece of metal through the wrist seal of one of the dead crew's suits. As soon as I felt a hiss, I sucked air from it like from a mama's teat. It tasted horrible, of course. Decades of cold had stopped any decay inside the suit, but nonetheless, it had left the air foul and funky all the same. Anyway, thanks to the low-g gravity, I was able to drag the body with me, holding the arm to my mouth with one hand while finishing my work with the other."

"And you did it? With your eyes closed?"

Again, Fatima paused.

"Obviously. I'm alive, aren't I?" she said, looking at Daisy with an odd expression. "But it took three suits worth of air to finally get Sid plugged in, and for a second, it looked like he wasn't going to integrate with Dark Side's network. But then, just as my air was about to run out, he linked into the base's systems. The doors sealed shut, and the command chamber flooded with oxygen. I've been here ever since."

Daisy completed the last segment of the course and hopped to the ground, looking at Fatima with a newfound awe.

"You survived without a helmet for minutes! Nobody does that. It's utterly amazing."

"Yes, perhaps," Fatima replied. "But it took over a year of skin grafting and stem cell therapy in the med lab to fully recover from the deep frostbite. I was pretty delirious by the time the air scrubbers and heat came back on. My AI boost was damaged, but nevertheless, it was probably the one thing that kept me functional as the rest of my body threatened to shut down from the cold," she said. "Anyway, enough storytelling. Come on. Back to one, Daisy."

Daisy walked back to the beginning of the obstacle course, climbing the four steps to the elevated starting position.

The lights went out.

"Hey, what are you doing?"

"You know the course, Daisy. You've run through it dozens of times. You don't need your eyes to tell you what you already know."

Silence.

"Well? What are you waiting for?"

Daisy hesitated, then dug deep, visualizing the course in front of her.

"Ah, fuck it," she finally said, then stepped out into the void.

The crashing impact with the floor hurt her body far less than her pride.

Fatima flipped the lights back on and assessed her with a disappointed look.

"Okay, maybe something easier for now. Here," she said, pulling out a plastic bin containing roughly twenty parts to a 3-D model of a very basic transport ship. "No instructions. Put this back together."

The image of the ship was printed on the box, but that was all Daisy had to go on.

Great, another mental acuity test, Daisy lamented, picking up two pieces and trying to figure out which went where.

"I don't see why I need to keep doing these, Fatima."

"The designers had these models created so they could

better visualize the ships they were working on in a three-dimensional setting outside a computer screen. It was to help them learn how every aspect functions and connects without having to run a real ship through an energy-sucking reconstruction cycle. Of course, it's different in the case of combat emergencies, where pods need to be hot-swapped on the fly, but until the invasion happened, it was all theoretical, so they had the time to do it right. Now you're the one who has the time, so get to it, Daisy."

Daisy grumbled as she reluctantly started the process of figuring out which bit went where. It was like a jigsaw puzzle, only more complex, in three dimensions, and with pieces that would only fit in a few specific configurations.

"Couldn't I just use the neuro-stim to learn all this stuff? I mean, why the puzzle game?"

"You know the limitations the override you used placed on your system. Yes, you can still use it as a supplement to help reinforce new material, I know, but there's a risk in running anything beyond a slow drip of data. We can't take chances, not until Chu and the AIs are able to figure out what exactly you did to your mind, and how your new neuro-wiring will react to a larger data stream. I mean, there's no telling what another information spike might do. It could lobotomize you for all we know."

"Well, I do have some pretty vivid dreams now," Daisy admitted.

"Like what?"

"Some of them are about things I don't even remember knowing. Like, I had one that I was a farmer, out working in the fields, and then these Chithiid suddenly dropped from a ship right in front of me, and I had to fight for my life."

"Sounds like one of Tamara's nightmares, to me. Daisy, you may have inadvertently tapped into some of the other crewmembers' files. The *Váli* was supposed to have all of that firewalled, and Mal was there to make sure everything went smoothly, but I don't know. The impossible seems to follow you, doesn't it?"

"Follow me? Sure. Maybe I had a quick surge of know-how right after I accidentally downloaded the whole freakin' universe, but since those first few days with all that stuff running around my head, it all seems to have tapered off."

"More like gone away, if you ask me."

Way to be supportive, Sis.

"Well, it's true. After that neuro spike, you seem to mostly have returned to your old self."

Except for the neural clone of my dead sister living in my head, yeah, I'm totally normal, she shot back.

"Daisy?" Fatima was staring at her. "You just zoned out on me there. Are you okay?"

"Yeah, fine."

"Well, as I was saying, I think there's a whole lot more in there, just waiting for you to learn to control it. How to utilize it."

Yeah, and monkeys might fly out of my ass, she grumbled to herself.

"Your potential is just waiting for you to unlock and embrace it, Daisy," Fatima said with a smile as she glanced at Daisy's project.

"Will you people stop saying that? I keep telling you, I'm not special." She looked at her hands. The small ship model was complete.

Huh. How did I do that?

"Don't ask me. You're the one running the hands."

Daisy looked over the model again. Indeed, it was correctly assembled.

"So, what now?" she asked.

"Over here," her mentor replied, leading her across the room.

Fatima had her stand a few meters in front of a wall as she

rolled what looked like a potato cannon a slight distance in front of her.

"Um, Fatima? What's that?"

"Something I rigged up to help you work on your reflexes and build your motor skills."

She powered the machine on. It hummed menacingly for a moment, then, without warning, launched a beanbag projectile at Daisy's stomach. Daisy, while not expecting it, nevertheless managed to dodge it at the last second.

"Not bad, Daisy. Let's go again."

"Hang on a second. I don't think that's a good—"

The machine fired two beanbags, one at her head and one at her waist. Again, she dodged them.

Hey, I'm pretty good at this.

"So what's going on with Vince?" Fatima asked, distracting Daisy, resulting in a beanbag to the thigh.

"Ow!" She scowled. "There's nothing with Vince. We're just friends. Or whatever he is."

"But you loved him, didn't you?"

Another beanbag, but this time she was ready, easily dodging it.

"Good. You didn't let yourself react emotionally," Fatima said with a smile. "But Vince is all about emotions, isn't he? Obviously, he loves you. Anyone can see that. But you love him too."

"I don't."

"You do. Or at least, you did, didn't you?"

"No. I mean, yes. But there's that thing in his head. He's a machine, so it was all bullshit."

"Am I a machine too?" Fatima asked as Daisy narrowly avoided a pair of beanbags.

"I suppose you are."

"Daisy, the mechanical parts of our bodies do not define our humanity."

A quick dodge to the left, then a duck and dodge to the right.

"No. That's not true. An AI in your brain? That means it's a machine doing most of the thinking in there, and how could I ever love a machine? He's just a meat puppet with his strings pulled by a computer."

Fatima hid her annoyance well, but the flurry of beanbags that pummeled Daisy spoke her true feelings more clearly than words. She eyed her difficult pupil, then made a decision.

"Okay, that's enough for now. Meet me back here in three hours."

Daisy brushed herself off and moved for the door.

"Oh, and Daisy," Fatima added with a grin the look of which left Daisy feeling a little worried. "Make sure to have a hearty snack. You'll be needing the energy."

CHAPTER EIGHT

"You shouldn't have said she was just a machine."

Daisy ignored Sarah's all too accurate observation and continued with her arduous task. Fatima had been right to recommend a snack. She would need all the energy she could muster.

I didn't say that. Not exactly, anyway, she lamented as she ran the deceptively simple-looking route around the periphery of the base. Naturally, she wore a suit. To do otherwise would mean certain death, and a very unpleasant one at that.

Fatima had sent her outside with a sneaky little smile on her face. Daisy should have known by the tell-tale helmet hair she had been sporting that Fatima had arranged something torturous for her.

"Come on, Daisy, clock's ticking!" she heard in her helmet's comm link.

Hurry, Daisy. Come on, Daisy. You're special, Daisy, she griped. *Shut up with that crap already!*

She didn't dare voice that out loud, of course, lest Fatima send her on an even more sadistic training run. This one was bad enough as it was, and Daisy had her hands full—literally—

as she raced around the perimeter of the base, searching out the scattered bits of another model ship.

This one, however, was over forty pieces, and strewn about a half-square kilometer area. The real challenge, besides collecting and reassembling it, would be making it back to the airlock before either the clock, or her air, ran out.

Fatima wouldn't put me in that much danger, though, would she? Daisy wondered.

"I don't know. There's something lurking under that serene exterior. I wouldn't count on it, if I were you."

I was afraid you'd say that. Well, keep a lookout. I've got almost all of the pieces, but without those last few, I won't make the cutoff.

"Is it that important?"

No, not really. But you know how competitive I can be.

"Noted," Sarah replied. "This would be so much easier if you had super-cyborg legs like Omar—Hey, is that one over to your left at eight o'clock? Thirty meters out."

Indeed, it was, and Daisy moon-bounced her way over to it in loping strides. She scooped the piece up and added it to the bag containing the others she had collected. The ones she was desperately trying to assemble as she also ran a basic search grid.

Nice catch, Sis.

"Why, thank you."

"How's it coming out there, Daisy?" Fatima asked from the comfort of inside the base. To add insult to injury, she was probably sipping a nice warm cup of tea while Daisy toiled in the low gravity.

Daisy keyed on her comms.

"Fine," she answered with a gasp. "I don't see why I have to do this, though."

"The captain wants me to challenge you with your training, that's all. And I'm happy to comply. Now get moving, your clock is running out."

Daisy checked the readout on her suit's heads-up display and realized she was right. If she wanted to make the cutoff, she'd have to hustle. She took off at a run, or at least the closest thing to a run you could achieve in low gravity.

One would think that running and moving obstacles to retrieve pieces would be easy in the reduced gravity, but Fatima had ensured that Daisy would have to stretch and strain every muscle if she hoped to finish her task on time.

Interestingly enough, after all the months of training, from sparring with the crew to her sessions with Fatima, Daisy's strength, agility, and endurance were greater than they had ever been, by far.

"Maybe there's a method to her madness," Sarah suggested. *"I mean, you are kinda kicking ass out here."*

Not enough, though. I still have three missing pieces, and I'm almost out of time.

"But what about all the other progress? Maybe you really do have super powers in here."

You're the one living in my head. If I did, you'd see them, right? I mean, normal sisters borrow clothes, or steal boyfriends. You borrowed a piece of my brain. So, what is it? You see anything 'special' in there?

Sarah paused.

"Well, no. But that doesn't mean there's nothing here. I just might not be able to see it, is all."

Daisy barked a little chuckle.

No, I'm not some chosen one. And another thing, I'm sure as hell not going back to Earth to be hunted and killed by some four-armed freaks and robots with fedoras.

"Technically, they were cyborgs with—"

Can you still call a cyborg without the meat part a cyborg? I mean, really, Sarah, they were fleshless metal men. Sounds pretty much like a robot to me.

"Okay, no need to get snippy."

I'm sorry, it's just, you've seen the scans. There are no signs of human life. No signs of anything down there. The only reason to go back is some stupid pie-in-the-sky quest that will just get me killed, and you know what? I choose to live. It doesn't matter what I was supposedly designed for. I control my own destiny.

In her haste and frustration, Daisy lost her footing as she skirted a small crater, her boot crunching through the loose crust at the rim, sending her tumbling over the edge.

"Shiiiiiiiitttt!" she cried out as she slid the fifteen meters down into the pit.

The impact was minor—the gravity on the moon was drastically reduced, after all—but when she landed, she did kick up a cloud of fine moon dust that had settled in there over the centuries. What she saw as she rose to her feet made her scramble backwards.

"Holy—"

"Oh my God," Sarah gasped inside her head.

Staring up at her from beneath the silt was a desiccated face in a cracked helmet. Daisy felt a warm rush of bile in her mouth and fought to keep it together.

Do not puke in your helmet, Daisy, she chided herself.

Looking closer, she noted that the corpse was a woman, her long, blonde hair still clinging to her dried-out scalp.

"Hey, Fatima," she keyed into the comms, swallowing hard.

"What is it, Daisy? Your time is running low."

"Yeah, well I just thought you might want to know that when you did your clean-up way back when, you missed one."

"Missed one what?"

"Body. I just found a corpse in the crater near Hangar Three."

The line was silent for a long pause before Fatima finally said something.

"I'm sorry, Daisy. You shouldn't have had to see that. Continue your training run. I'll send Ash out to dispose of it."

"Her."

"Excuse me?"

"It's a woman."

"Of course, you're right." There was a long pause. "I'll have Ash retrieve her. I'm also adding five minutes back to your clock for this unexpected interruption. Now get moving. You're still on a countdown."

Daisy started the climb out of the pit.

Gee, thanks, Fatima. So kind of you.

Daisy reached the rim but nearly fell back in again. She was angry, and that was making her careless.

Calm down, Daisy. Focus! she told herself, fighting to rein in her heart rate and respirations. Slowly, she began to gain control. *Keep moving. You can do this while you're mobile.*

Ten minutes later, with Sarah's help, she had all the pieces in her bag and was walking back down the long path to the airlock when an alarm sounded in her helmet.

Dammit, time's almost up.

She took a deep breath, then settled into a steady jog, trying to mind her footing and not fall, while simultaneously reassembling the many pieces of the model. At this rate, though, she wasn't going to make it.

Daisy picked up the pace, running as best she could in the low gravity, her hands working as she periodically glanced into the bag, where her gloved fingers were doing what they knew to do on autopilot. There wasn't any time to stop and double-check her work. She would have to trust her instincts.

"Fifty meters, Daze! You can do it!"

While she was never a fan of rah-rah motivational speeches, Sarah's sincere support helped her focus for the last push. She ran hard, feet slipping as she pushed off against the unstable surface of the moon. The beckoning airlock door was in sight.

"Thirty meters! You're going to do it!"

Goddamn right I am! She grunted, pushing even harder, while the clock ticked lower and lower as she ran.

"Fifteen, fourteen, thirteen."

I know, I know!

"Loose ground two steps ahead!"

Good looking out, she thanked Sarah, then bounded over the uneven patch and threw herself into the airlock controls, quickly punching in the access code. The exterior hatch swung open and she dove inside, slapping the recompression cycle command as the door swung shut behind her.

"Two, and one! Hell yeah!"

Daisy grinned, sweat dripping down her face. After a ten-second decontamination burst from the nozzles in the airlock, the door swung open. Fatima was standing there, waiting.

Daisy reached an exhausted arm up and handed Fatima the model ship, then popped the helmet off her head, wiping the sweat from her brow as it pulled clear.

"Made it!" she gasped. "T-told ya I could do it," she managed to say as she rested her hands on her knees and sucked in lungful after lungful of air.

Fatima quietly stood there, beaming at her like a proud parent.

"What're you so chipper about?" Daisy asked.

Fatima looked down at the completed model in her hands.

"How did you get this done, Daisy? You were moving the entire time, and the last five minutes you were traveling at almost a full run."

Daisy was momentarily taken aback

How did *I do that?* she wondered.

"I guess I just went on instinct. I didn't know what I was doing, not really. It just seemed right."

Fatima smiled brightly.

"Special, Daisy. *Special*," she said with a knowing grin, then turned and walked off. "We'll push tonight's session back an hour. Go eat something and relax a bit. You've earned it."

Daisy slowly peeled herself out of the EVA suit, her muscles burning gloriously from the exertion. Rather than feeling tired, she was electrified.

"What the hell just happened, Sarah?"

Her sister laughed in her head.

"You just got Miyagi-ed."

"I what?"

"Wax on, wax off, grasshopper."

"You're such a dork," she said with a chuckle.

Despite playing it off like it was no big deal, Daisy felt an unfamiliar sense of accomplishment boosting her spirits. She *had* kicked ass. With a bit of shock, she realized she was actually looking forward to next time.

Next time sucked.

Fatima and Chu were standing by, monitoring Daisy's progress that evening as she toiled at the far end of the base. This wasn't another obstacle run or dexterity test. This time they sent her on the insanely boring task of repairing systems in the parts of the base long silent. Rerouting access conduits, laying new communications cables, unsticking frozen airlocks that hadn't cycled in centuries.

Fatima had never made it that far in her repairs, and when the subsequent failed missions brought her a handful of new inhabitants, sprucing up the facilities already functioning took priority over resurrecting the distant ones.

Daisy dragged her tool kit to a heavy set of doors. According to the base schematics, they led to a components warehouse, long abandoned.

Whatever. A door's a door.

Daisy opened the panel and ran a bypass.

Nothing.

Huh, that should have worked. Okay, let's try this.

She ran a second bypass, linking in a peripheral access protocol as well.

Again, nothing. She spent over an hour trying everything she could imagine, but the door simply would not budge. It had power, of that she was certain, but only a minimal amount.

Needs a little somethin'-somethin' to get it moving, is all, she realized. *Okay, I think I know a way to do this.*

Daisy reached back and pulled her suit's power pack loose.

"Daisy, what are you doing? We just got a warning reading from your EVA suit. Are you okay?" Chu asked, concern in his voice.

"Yeah, I'm fine. Hang on a minute."

"Your suit is—"

Her comms went dead when she clipped her alligator leads from the suit's power controls to the non-functional door mechanism.

Oops.

"Daisy, what's your status? Daisy, can you hear me?" Chu called to her from the base.

No reply.

Come on, you bastard, you can do it! Daisy gritted her teeth and gave the release mechanism a hearty pull with her spanner, while her suit's batteries fed a surge into the control panel.

The door crunched and strained, the lights on the panel flickering as it sucked more and more power from her suit, until it finally slid open, albeit reluctantly. Daisy disconnected herself from the door and tucked her power cell back in place.

"Used up about forty-five percent of your power there, Daze."

Yeah, I see. Worked, though, didn't it? She fiddled with her suit and got her comms back online.

"—is reading a power spike. I say again, do you copy, Daisy?"

"Yeah, I copy, Chu. Sorry about that, lost comms for a minute."

"What the hell were you doing, Daisy?" Fatima grilled her

over the wireless.

"Just getting this stupid thing open. I had to give it a little jump-start, is all. Sorry about the comms loss, but it rebooted the system when I linked in."

The line was silent for a long pause.

"You got it open?" Chu asked.

"That's what I said," she replied. "Just took longer than I anticipated."

"Daisy," Fatima said with a bit of shock in her voice. "The last of those doors our team worked on took over two *weeks* to finally crack. You just opened that one in under two *hours*."

"That's what I'm talkin' about. Kickass!" Sarah hooted.

"It just needed a power boost to the right controls, is all," she messaged back to Fatima and Chu. "Hang on a sec, I think I see why this section is having such problems."

Daisy stepped in through the open door and turned on the larger flashlight hanging from her hip. There was power, indeed, but not nearly enough to open the doors, let alone keep the entire section functioning. A blinking light keyed her in to the problem.

"It's the solar uplink from the panels," she called out. "Looks like the connection was partially severed during the attack. Only about two percent of the solar feed is making it back here. The battery packs are intact, but they've been maintaining at near zero charge. I'm going to try to reconnect one of the inputs manually by splicing in a fresh piece of cable. If I'm right, that'll trickle charge the batteries to at least a reasonable level. Once that happens, the other bypasses I'm going to wire in should be able to signal the relay junction to deliver a steady charge to this section again."

"Wait, you're going to do what?" Chu asked, confused. "But we have the solar fields powering us already."

"Not all of them, it seems. There are multiple lines branching out, from what I can tell. I think the one servicing this section was damaged in the attack. By tapping into one of the functional ones, all the stuff that powered down over here should come back on. I don't know when, exactly, but hopefully fairly quickly."

"Okay, Daisy. Just be careful," Fatima said over the channel.

"You know it," she replied.

Thirty minutes later, the lights—at least some of them—had come back on in the chamber, and it appeared the battery backups for that entire section of Dark Side were receiving a trickle of current, as she predicted. She only hoped the batteries were still sound after all those years, and able to hold a charge.

"Okay, Daisy, there's still no atmosphere over there, and your air and power are both running low. Head on back. That's enough for today."

"Copy that," she said, stepping out of the airlock.

Daisy closed the thick door and was about to begin the long walk all the way across the base, when she noticed a tiny light peeping out from a sheer rock face a good thirty meters outside the base perimeter. If not for the overhang making that particular shaded part of Dark Side actually *dark*, she never would have noticed it.

"Hang on a sec. I just need to do one more thing, then I'll be heading right back," she said, then walked across the rocky terrain to the mysterious light.

It was a control panel. One that had been hidden behind a protective rock covering, until the attack all those years ago had scorched it and broken much of it away. She pried the remaining bit of the cover free and examined the mechanism. It was intact, she noted, and was a much higher level of security than any of the other panels she'd ever encountered, but why?

Daisy's gaze shifted, scanning the rock face. Something about it seemed different. The way some of the rocks lined up. Almost as if—

"Holy shit, it's a hidden door!" she gasped.

"What was that, Daisy? We didn't copy you."

"Um, nothing, just looking at the big door I hot-wired. Yep, all seems good there. I'll be heading back in just a minute."

"Copy that. Thanks, Daisy."

They bought it.

"You're lucky they did. Gotta be careful using your outside voice. So what is this thing?"

Looks like a secret access panel. You know, if its cover hadn't been broken off, I'd have never even seen it.

"As it is, if you hadn't cross-wired all those feeds to get power back to this section, those lights wouldn't have been on. Again, you'd have never seen it, even with my extra set of eyes helping."

But what is it?

"Beats me, but let's find out!"

Daisy broke out her tool kit and set to work on the panel, but unlike the large door she'd hot-wired earlier, the mysterious panel was sealed shut and entirely inaccessible.

"I'm going to have to get creative with this one," she muttered, then tried again. Ten minutes later, she had made absolutely no headway whatsoever. Whatever confidence boost she'd been enjoying earlier was rapidly depleting even faster than her oxygen levels.

Shit.

She checked her levels. Dangerously low, and she still had to make it all the way across the base.

"Daisy! What are you doing? Get back here. You're almost out of air!" Chu was nearly yelling into the comms.

"Sorry, I was Zenning out and kinda lost track of time. On my way back now."

Daisy jammed a rock over the panel, hiding it from prying eyes, then, reluctantly, turned back and started the long walk to the airlock.

"You know we're coming back, right?" Sarah said.

Oh yeah, she replied. *Yes indeed, we are.*

CHAPTER NINE

The hidden door was a problem of the most delectable variety, and Daisy found it difficult to push the new challenge to the back of her mind and focus on regular conversation with her Dark Side companions as they sat down to dinner. It was titillating. Something secret. Something no one else on the base knew about. A mystery to be solved.

And it was all hers.

"Hey, Daze," Gustavo said as he plopped down beside her at the metal table. His plate was piled high with the special treat Finnegan had whipped up for them that evening. "Can you believe it? Steak and lobster! I love lobster, though some would say it's really just a fancy way to get more butter in your mouth."

"It's machine-replicated protein, Gus."

"You say that, but my taste buds can't tell the difference." He dipped a bite in the cup of drawn butter—another replicated delight. "Besides," he added, "if we were on Earth, I don't think I could bring myself to eat an actual animal, you know?"

Daisy flashed back to the rabbit she had caught and killed during her brief escape to the surface. With all of the food stores centuries out of date and extremely limited edible plant-based resources within the city—at least ones that didn't require a great deal of labor to find, determine their edibility, and harvest — it was a good old-fashioned snare and a roasted rabbit that had quite literally saved her from starvation.

Morally, she did not like taking life, but from a true hunter-gatherer perspective, she was glad for the protein in whatever form she could find it.

"I hear you, Gus," she replied. "Though I wonder how well that moral stand would hold up if you were truly hungry. You know, they say society is only three missed meals away from anarchy."

"I like to think I have stronger character than that."

"Wouldn't we all?" she said through a mouthful of perfectly cooked, machine-grown beef protein.

Finn made a round of the tables, dropping fresh-baked cookies on everyone's plate whether they wanted them or not. Given his baking talents, however, non-takers were a rare thing when the baking bug bit him.

"Thanks, Finn," Vince said as he slid into a seat and joined Daisy and Gus. "That all you're eating?" he said, gesturing to Daisy's modest plate. "I hear you had one hell of a workout today. Figured you'd be loading up."

"What's that supposed to mean?"

"Nothing, just that Chu mentioned whatever you said to Fatima earlier had her running you all over the base. Like, seriously far. I guess she had originally planned to just have you do a simple series of tasks more or less right outside the airlock door, but after you pushed her buttons, she suited up and changed the whole thing."

"Well, I could have been more tactful, I suppose."

"So, what was it like?" Gus asked between bites. "I've only done a couple of really quick EVAs on the surface just outside the doors, but nothing like what you were up to. Was the funky gravity hard to work in?"

"Nah, you get used to it. Besides, Tamara switches up the gravity when we spar sometimes, so I'm kinda accustomed already," she said. "Though trying to run in it—now, that is a different story. You can't really dig your feet for traction unless you let your legs *really* bend. Otherwise you'll just rebound off the surface up and down and not make much forward progress."

"Heard you found something, while you were out there too," Vince said.

"Shit! He knows!"

He doesn't know anything, Sarah. Chill out.

She cast a calm eye on him.

"What do you mean?"

"Chu said you made a surprise discovery."

"Um..." She searched for a way out of the topic.

"Yeah," he continued. "I guess she was one of the original victims of the attack. Ash brought the body in a half hour ago. Commander Mrazich is having her prepared for a proper ceremony before we cremate her."

Daisy didn't know why, but the fact that the steel-jawed, crew-cut commander would do that for someone long dead made her dislike of his replacement part-enhanced self diminish just a little. It still creeped her out, but his decision somehow made him seem more human.

"Makes sense," she said. "Can't very well be burying people on the moon. They'd never decompose, which kinda defeats the purpose."

"Yeah," Gus chimed in, "and this way, it really is a true ashes-to-ashes kinda thing."

"And there's nothing but dust out on the surface," Vince added.

"So, what about you, Gus? How's your mapping of the debris field been going?"

Gus lit up at the mention of his pet project, and the

conversation quickly shifted to less morbid topics from that point.

By the end of their meal, all were happy, full, and in good spirits.

Back in her quarters, Daisy was enjoying a much-deserved evening free from tasks and training, which also afforded her time to think further on the hidden panel mystery awaiting her far across the moon's surface.

"So, what do you think it is?" she asked her clever mental passenger. "It's obviously hidden for a reason, but it also looked like it wasn't tied in to the normal base systems."

"Yeah, I saw that," Sarah answered. *"We won't know for sure until we get inside, but from what I could tell, it looked like a totally stand-alone facility. It was probably just a bit of blind luck that there was that one backup power cable running through the main conduit, otherwise I doubt you'd have ever powered that door up."*

"Agreed. So what do I do about it? I mean, I can't very well go running off across the base every time I do one of Fatima's training circuits. Eventually they'll notice."

"What about creating a shadow suit locator scan? You could load it into the system from the console itself. Keep it localized to where Fatima and Chu monitor from. That way it should stay off of Sid's readouts entirely, and if it does show up, it'll register you as wherever you want it to."

Daisy liked the idea. So long as she was quick about finishing whatever tasks Fatima had for her, she could use the extra time to work on the mysterious door, and if her understanding of Sid's scanning system was correct, she could likely even re-configure her EVA suit to not register at all, if she wanted it to.

"I'd be like a space ninja, stealthily walking the surface, undetected."

"Only ninjas carry swords. And don't wear space suits."

"Or maybe they do, but no one has ever survived the encounter long enough to spill the beans," she replied with a chuckle.

It was a good idea, though, and the intriguing task warranted further thought. She settled into a comfortable position and started her routine.

Soft is strong, she thought as she took a slow, deep breath.

A calm began to flow within her, but just as she was settling into a comfortable meditation, her door chimed.

Daisy sighed as she rose to her feet and answered the comm panel.

"Yeah?"

"Hey, Daisy," Vince said. "Fatima mentioned she gave you the evening off. I was wondering if you maybe wanted to watch a movie with me."

"Ooh, look who's coming around early. You gonna let him in?"

I don't know if that's such a good idea. I should probably focus on meditating tonight. Need to figure this thing out, she replied to her sister.

"Come on, Daze, you can do that anytime. After a few hundred years, it's not going anywhere. Besides, I get bored in here too, ya know. Even if you zone out, at least I can still watch the movie."

She considered a moment longer, then reached for the door controls.

"Hey," she greeted Vince as he leaned against her doorframe.

"Hey," he replied with a warm smile. "So, whaddya think? I found some pretty fun sci-fi flicks, but then there's always that Japanese cartoon stuff you dig—"

"Anime," she corrected him.

"Yeah, anime. Whatever you're in the mood for."

"Wow, that's almost as impressive as giving you the remote," Sarah joked. *"You sure you want to keep him in the doghouse?"*

Daisy ignored her and invited him in, moving aside as he

slid by her passing through the doorway. The brief contact flared a physical longing, a memory of times they'd shared before she found out what he was. She took a deep breath and focused on lowering her heart rate. The heat in her belly, on the other hand, took a fair bit more concentration to vanquish.

"I'm telling ya, Daze, you should give him a second chance."

You keep trying, but I'm not having any of that. He's a machine, Sarah. Stop pushing it.

"It's for your own good," she replied. *"He treats you well, and you still like him. I'm your sister, I can tell these things."*

Daisy tuned out her sister's voice and shifted her attention back to her visitor.

"So, you want some tea?"

"Yeah, that'd be great, thanks."

Daisy brewed up a quick pot of smoky lapsang souchong and poured him a cup.

"I brought something," Vince said, pulling a sealed container from behind his back. He opened the lid, and the smell of fresh popcorn wafted into the air. "The real deal, not food replicator made. Tamara had a few ears that she grew on the way here that dried out, and a bunch of kernels were left over."

"I was in the mess hall the same time you were, but I didn't see you make this."

"I popped 'em over the hydrogen generator's heat sink. Wanted it to be a surprise."

Daisy smiled, and the damn fluttering stomach flared up again.

Stop that! she told her uncooperative organs.

"Pretty sneaky, Vince. I'm impressed."

He beamed brightly.

"I hoped you'd like it. So, pick a flick while I use the head, okay?"

Daisy selected a film from the mid-twenty-second century—

a silly buddy cop movie following the exploits of a human detective and his Martian partner—then settled on her bed with the bowl of popcorn. Vince joined her, keeping a slight space between them, as she'd made clear was the way things had to be many times before.

The movie played on, and despite herself, Daisy felt the exhaustion of the day take hold. In no time at all, she drifted off to sleep, sliding down into the comforting, familiar warmth of Vince's shoulder. He gazed down at her, resting so peacefully, and smiled. Then he turned his attentions back to the vid screen, letting his wiped-out friend catch some much-needed sleep.

CHAPTER TEN

It had been two days since she had been pleasantly surprised by Vince's popped treat, and Daisy had barely begun her morning centering exercises when Fatima dumped a particularly large box of parts in front of her.

"What's this?"

Fatima pointed to the label on the box. *Heavy Machinery Transport,* it read. Daisy sighed and began assembling the model.

Fatima had taken up the habit of randomly giving her this task at any point in their training, saddling her with any one of the dozens of ship models stored in engineering. For Daisy, the reassembly process was becoming second nature at this point, and almost a meditative practice.

"Done," Daisy said a few minutes later.

"Already?"

The prodigal pupil smiled mischievously. That is until another larger box was emptied in front of her, its parts strewn across the table.

"Go!" Fatima said, starting the clock once more.

Daisy's hands started moving with purpose.

"So, Daisy, I hear you and Vince are spending more time together. Change of heart?"

"No. There's nothing there. We're just friends, is all."

"So, you can be friends with him despite the processor in his head?"

"I'm stuck here with him, so I might as well be, right?"

She jammed her finger as a piece didn't fit as expected.

"Ow!"

"Soft is strong, Daisy. Relax. Don't get distracted."

"I know."

"Mm-hm," Fatima said with a little smile. "And how about your training with Tamara? I understand she's still whooping your behind something awful."

Daisy felt a surge of frustration.

"She's not whooping me, she's just better, is all."

"Not what I hear. It looks like you've bested everyone on the base but her. Even Shelly's pair of metal arms are no match, yet Tamara only has one." She studied her pupil quietly a moment. "So, what's the deal, then? Has she got your number?"

"No, it's just she's still pissed I blew her out the airlock."

"Well, one would tend to be less than thrilled about something like that. Might even hold onto a grudge for a good, long while."

"But it was the logical thing to do at the time. She's a soldier. She has to know that."

"Knowing and forgiving are two entirely different beasts, as I'm sure you are well aware."

"What do you mean by that?"

"Nothing, dear. So, if she's not a better fighter than you, why does she keep beating you? Any theories?"

Daisy's hands moved rapidly as she mulled over how best to phrase her reply.

"She's got that angry edge, you know? I just can't seem to get past it. Whenever I think I've finally got her beat, that rage wells up in her, and she finds some way to spoil my plans."

"Daisy, you mustn't fight with your emotions. That's a surefire way to lose. You have to disconnect from all of that and let the training within you flow out."

"Is this more of that 'The One' stuff you all keep going on about?

"Not exactly. The principle applies to all people. It's just that in your case, there is a wellspring of talent that your own deep-rooted issues are preventing you from tapping into. You have to trust yourself. But more than that, you have to put aside all of your doubts and guilt and fear and just let it flow."

"Always back to that 'Find what's inside you' line."

"And you will, once you stop fighting your power and instead learn to relax and embrace it. As they say, 'Muddy water unstirred becomes clear.'"

"Look, I know what's inside of me, and if there was something special lurking around in there, I think we'd have found it by now."

"We?" Fatima said, a slight arch to her eyebrow.

"I," she corrected herself. "I'm not special, Fatima, and even if I was, I have no desire to go on some suicide run to Earth just because a few old-timers can't accept that there was a war, and we lost. I mean, why don't we just go find a new planet that's not swarming with plague, and AI viruses, and nasty, four-armed aliens?"

"You know how few planets there are with the right environment, Daisy, and no matter how you feel about the moon at the moment, one day, you'll want to go home."

"Fat chance," she replied. "Done." She dropped the ship onto the table and made a clean hands gesture, like card dealers of old.

"Daisy," Fatima said, her eyebrow raised in an inquiring arch, "what's that?"

"That? It's the ship you gave me."

"No, it isn't," she replied, picking up the sleek-lined vessel.

"Fatima, I don't know what you've been smoking, but that's what you gave me."

"It's the parts I gave you, yes, but not the ship." Fatima turned the model over in her hands, smiling brightly. "Oh, but look at those lines. What is it? A fast recon ship, but with additional crew and research space? Such an elegant design. And the unconventional configuration of the crew quarters pods between the storage and water treatment ones—extra shielding given the different sizes, but also contributing to a more functional and atmospherically dynamic airframe."

"Um, okay, if you say so."

"Daisy," Fatima said, handing the ship back to her, "that wasn't a specific ship I gave you. It was a box of random parts. Sid and Mal ran simulations, and they came up with several likely configurations, but nothing like this."

Daisy felt a warm flush rise to her cheeks as she fought to suppress the proud smile that threatened to split her face into a beaming grin.

"I..." she found herself at a loss for words.

For once.

Fatima pulled another bin out and dumped it on the table.

"I was planning on saving this one for tomorrow, but let's see what else you come up with, shall we?"

Daisy put the model down, and with a little grin, began digging through the bin, feeling better about herself than she had in days. As she worked, quickly fitting pieces together, Fatima looked directly at the tiny video feed link in the corner of the room and smiled.

"Well, that's interesting," Commander Mrazich said from behind the monitor in his private conference room. "It seems your Ms. Swarthmore is finally finding her groove. And none too late. We need to get our mission back online, and we need it to happen now."

Captain Harkaway nodded his agreement, eyes stuck to the screen as he watched Daisy run through a new configuration of ship components he'd never seen before.

"Amazing," he said. "Utterly amazing."

Daisy lay in bed that night but found herself unable to sleep. Her mind was buzzing with possibilities. What else could she do? Were all of the others somehow missing things that to her seemed obvious? It boggled her mind.

"Sid?" she said, keying the comms unit open.

"Yes, Daisy?" the AI replied.

"I was wondering. I mean, I know some early ship models aren't modular like the newer ones, but are there any built-in restrictions on ship configurations?"

"What exactly do you mean?"

"Like, are there any design factors that would restrict use of components that maybe aren't common knowledge? You and Mal and Bob would know, since they're both ships, and you used to be one."

"Technically, we aren't ships, exactly. Mal and Bob are integrated with ships at the moment, yes, but the cornerstone of our level of AI technology is our ability to repurpose from device to device. I, for example, was able to swap from a fairly large command ship to a massive moon base. It took some adjustment, of course, but we were designed to adapt this way. Of course, some AIs might be a bit locked into their ways. Conditioning, you could say, but given time, any of us from the higher-tier systems should be able to reconfigure."

"And the ship designs themselves? Mal didn't seem to have any detailed files in her systems, and I haven't found any here, either. At least not beyond the most basic maintenance schematics."

"That's because when I was installed in the base, I found that the original Dark Side AI had already been destroyed, melted to its core by the AI virus. It was gone, along with all of its files, lost when the surviving crew purged the systems."

"You say *it*, but with the other AIs, you always talk of each other in the gender you've adopted."

"True, but the purge left no record of the previous operating system. I use the neutral 'it' because I simply do not know what gender it had chosen."

"Oh, got it."

"But back to your original query about configurations. I don't see why there would be any restrictions. The underlying premise of the system was to allow for rapid assimilation and recovery of damaged ship components, and in the original design phase the engineers made sure that only compatible units could integrate. So far as I'm aware, you could not make non-compatible parts join in a stable unit, no matter how hard you tried. Is that of any help?"

The gears were already turning in Daisy's head.

"Yeah. Thanks, Sid."

"My pleasure. May I ask why this question arose?"

A smile teased Daisy's lips.

"Ideas, Sid. Just ideas."

The powerful AI waited a moment, a quiet pause over the comms.

"Very well, then. Sleep well, Daisy."

"I will, Sid."

Daisy keyed off the comms and lay back down in bed. Her mind was racing, but sleep finally took hold of her, relaxing her body as her slumbering mind dreamed of ships never before imagined.

CHAPTER ELEVEN

Daisy found herself flying backwards in the low gravity until she bounced roughly off a pile of debris a good fifteen meters from the hidden stone door.

"I told you not to kick it."

"Blow me," Daisy grumbled as she got back to her feet. Fortunately, she had remembered to mute her voice-activated comms when she reached her destination.

Daisy was dusty, but unharmed. She had been frustrated, and had quite foolishly thrown a powerful front kick into the solid stone blocking her path. The result in low gravity had been less than surprising.

"But daaaaang. Look how far back you went. Your legs are getting really strong, if you managed that." Sarah chuckled. *"Now imagine if you could do that against something other than a rock wall."*

"Door."

"Whatever. You know what I mean."

Daisy brushed the moon dust from her suit and trudged back to the secret control panel.

"Is it just me, or do those lights look a little bit brighter?"

"*Definitely brighter. I think your trickle charge may have finally gotten those batteries to a functional level again.*"

"And yet here I am, stuck outside this door more than a full week later with nothing to show for it besides a bruised ass and a dirty space suit."

Daisy had made near-daily treks to the distant panel, rushing through her other tasks while allowing Fatima to believe they were taking her far longer than they actually did. She felt bad lying to her, but the draw of the mysterious door put any guilt solidly on the back burner.

After four days of trying everything imaginable to bypass the panel, Daisy had finally opted for Plan B. She switched tactics and focused on where the mystery controls might actually lead. She had jury-rigged a hand-held scanner to read electrical charge through up to a foot of rock and steel. Fortunately for her, what she was looking for was far more accessible than that, thanks largely to the alien assault that had smashed into the stone face and made the panel visible in the first place.

A small gash in the stone roughly half a meter from the panel signaled a weak charge, and Daisy had spent the next two days chipping away at it, trying to get access to whatever was underneath it. Under any other circumstances it would have taken massive power tools to make headway, the use of which would have drawn attention to her efforts, but the impact that had fractured the stone-covered metal and rent it open had also left her a slightly weakened stone matrix to work with. It was still very slow going, but Daisy had finally managed to reach the thick-shielded wires tucked deep in the crevice.

That was the good news.

The bad news was, since then, she hadn't been able to make any further progress. Everything she tried, every bypass, be it mechanical or code-based, seemed to be a dead end. Nevertheless, every day she came back to try again, and every day the firmly sealed stone door silently laughed at her efforts.

SCOTT BARON

"Come on, Daze. You've gotta get back. Clock's running low, and you said you'd help Gus get the Váli fixed up."

"Sturdy ship, that one," she noted. "She survived a lot, that's for sure, though given her name, I suppose it shouldn't surprise me."

Indeed, the ship's namesake, *Váli*, was one of the few Norse gods prophesied to survive Ragnarok—the end of days. While Earth's downfall wasn't quite the same thing, Daisy felt that perhaps it was close enough.

She packed up her tools and tucked them carefully into an indentation beneath a rock. She didn't have to worry about vandals or thieves on the moon, but old habits die hard, and hiding them for her next visit just made her feel more at ease. Daisy then wedged the piece of rock she'd been using to cover the control panel back into place and began her trek back to the airlock.

Gus and Chu were waiting for her in the maintenance hangar near the *Váli* when she finally returned.

"Man, Fatima had you out there quite a while today. What was it this time? Rebuilding Hangar Four while standing on your head?" Chu said.

"Ha-ha, oh-so funny," Daisy replied. "Just more of the usual. She's been on a kick having me get those solar panels reconfigured to feed the base. I guess when I tapped into the secondary array she didn't know about, she and the commander realized that maybe it might be a good idea to get the rest of the base up and running if we can. I don't mind, though. Beats fighting aliens down on Earth, that's for sure."

She swung her torque wrench into place and pulled free a forward shielding panel.

"See, this is the problem," she said. "Too many years of travel and not enough proper maintenance. If we hadn't been woken early, the ship might have very well fallen apart before it ever got here, and we'd have all died in our sleep."

"Gee, thanks for that cheery thought, Daze," Gus said with a sharp laugh. "Aren't you the bright ray of sunlight on our otherwise dark day."

"We're on the dark side of the moon, Gus. Every day is a dark day."

He laughed as he swung down from his lift and surveyed the banged-up hull of the ship.

"There's no way around it," Gus said. "The *Váli* needs some parts, and Dark Side simply doesn't have what we need." He looked at Daisy and Chu with a hopeful grin. "You guys up for a scavenging run to the debris field?"

"I bet you say that to all the girls," Daisy joked. "All right, just give me fifteen. I need to run to my quarters for a minute to swap into a clean flight suit, then I'll meet you two at Donovan's ship."

"I can't," Chu said. "I'm working on a project with Fatima, and I really need to get back to it." He gave Daisy a funny little smile. "You should see if Vince wants to go. I'd say ask Reggie, but he and Donovan still have that macho pilot competition thing going, and I don't think Bob would enjoy both of them trying to play captain."

Gustavo grinned. "I already told Bob we'd likely be needing his assistance a little while ago. He should have finished his pre-flight warm-up by now, so all we need is to track down Donovan and Vince and we should be good."

"I still don't see why he insists on always piloting these missions. We're all qualified, you know," Gus said. "And besides, Bob can fly himself if he needs to. Any of us could make these runs."

"Yeah, but he and Bob are buddies, and he doesn't really trust his AI friend in anyone else's hands," Chu reasoned. "Anyway, he can run a recon scan while we're doing our thing. Two birds with one stone, as they say."

"All right, then. See you two at the ship in fifteen," Daisy said, then trotted off to her quarters to change into a fresh flight suit.

"Watch it! On your starboard!"

"I see it, Vince. Stop side-seat driving. I got this." Donovan gently feathered the compressed-air maneuvering jets and slid his ship around the floating debris.

Gustavo sat to the rear of the command pod, directly jacked into the scanning cluster via the port on the back of his head. He could have simply used his cybernetic eye to survey the area on top of Bob's scanning array, but Gus always felt better when he was directly plugged into the ship's systems. "I don't know," he would say. "Just feels better, ya know? Like I'm one with the ship. If I do it the other way, I worry I might miss something."

Daisy sat behind them all, an extra set of skilled hands should they be needed. If the ship had any problems, even Vince—the head mechanic, no less—was no match for her knack for repairs on the fly.

She caught herself staring at the slender data cable feeding into Gustavo's head. It just wasn't natural, but she had long ago accepted that while she may not like artificially enhanced humans, she was stuck living with them.

Donovan fired a small thruster and slowed their progress. Drifting like a piece of junk amidst the countless pieces of wreckage, he deftly maneuvered through the field while staying off the alien scans.

"Take a look at that," he said, pointing out the thick window. "Do you think that'll work for you?"

Reggie and Gus sized up the chunk of ship drifting alongside them. It was far larger than the ship they were in, but several of the pieces they needed could be salvaged from it if they were careful.

It was tricky work, retrieving components from drifting debris, the riskiest part being the EVA required to reach them. For smaller pieces, Bob would just use his robotic work arms to grab them and pull them into his cargo bay, but for anything large enough to potentially damage him if it shifted course, an extra-vehicular activity was required.

Fortunately, the EVA suits were in excellent working order, and the crew was kept nice and warm within them—a crucial thing, as they couldn't fire up the ship's heating systems while there was any chance of being picked up on scans.

"We'll be right back," Vince said, locking his helmet into place. Gus stood to follow.

"Hang on," Daisy stopped them. "Why is Gus going? He's our scans guy. We need someone monitoring while we make the retrieval."

"Excuse me," Bob interrupted. "I am fully capable of running the scans myself, you know."

"Yeah, but—and please, no offense, here—Gus is outfitted with far more modern equipment than you are. The ship is solid, but just a bit outdated."

"There is logic in your assessment," Bob said after a slight pause. Daisy couldn't tell if he sounded hurt. "I will continue to interface with Gustavo while you make the retrieval. Good luck."

Daisy locked her helmet on and met Vince at the airlock door. "You ready?"

"Yeah. Let's be quick. Get in, get out." His face hidden from the others, he smiled and winked at her.

Daisy couldn't help but feel a quick flush at his double entendre, but she stomped it down, turning her back on him and opening the inner door.

"Okay, we're heading out. I'm going to run two extra retrieval tethers to haul in the pieces, so don't let the ship drift too far or they'll get tangled. Got it?"

"Yes, Daisy. We've done this before, you know."

"Sorry, Donovan. I know. Didn't mean anything by it, just wanted to be one hundred percent clear."

"All good."

"You two done?" Vince said as he closed the inner airlock door behind them. "Because we're on suit air, so it's kind of a ticking clock now."

Daisy entered the decompression command and waited. A moment later the green light came on, and the outer door unlocked. She keyed the sequence and it silently slid open.

"Okay, let's go."

She and Vince lightly pushed off from the minimal gravity of the ship. While they couldn't run full grav-systems for fear of being scanned, Bob was able to divert fractional gravity to specific parts of the craft to allow ease of movement for the skeleton crew.

The pair drifted toward the imposing wreck in front of them. From the outside, against the darkness of space, it felt akin to a tiny fish swimming up to a massive whale, its full size hidden by the murky waters surrounding it.

Vince touched down first, clipping himself to a twisted loop of conduit. Daisy arrived a moment later, but she simply extended her arm, snagging a piece of bulkhead with her gloved hand and using the rebound kinetics to spin her body to a standing position within the gaping hole on the flank of the long-dead craft.

"Nice moves."

"Thanks. I'm going to pull the conversion coils from the drive pod. You want to start on the shielding panels?"

"Sounds like a plan," he replied. "Keep your comms open, and be careful in there."

"Yes, Dad," she replied mockingly.

Vince began the slow glide along the ship's skin to unmount and collect the components the *Váli* needed for her own hull, while Daisy floated to the pod door and snapped the manual override crank into place.

Sonofabitch is sticking.

"*You have the pocket torch?*" Sarah asked.

Yeah, but it's got a limited charge. Don't want to waste it in case I need to cut through something later.

"*There won't be a need for it at all if you don't get this door open.*"

Good point.

Daisy pulled the small unit from her pouch and fired it up to its lowest setting, directing the heat to the metal housing in front of her. After a minute, she switched it off and stowed it in her bag, then tried the crank again. The long-frozen gears silently strained, and then finally began to move. Once they started to spin in their housing, the door opened the rest of the way easily.

Now for the coils.

Daisy knew the layout of the ship, just like she knew the layout of every ship.

Maybe Fatima's training is paying off, she grudgingly acknowledged as she rounded a corner, tugging the retrieval line behind her. *Okay, they should be right through here,* she thought, certain in her mental layout of the ship.

The door was open a few inches, but that was all. Daisy inserted the manual crank into the access port beside the doorframe and began slowly turning it until the door crept open.

"Accessing the drive room now," she said into the comms. "How's it coming out there?"

Vince continued unbolting the panels as he spoke. "Making good progress. Looks like it had a couple of tiny space rock hits, but nothing to worry about."

"Okay, just be careful."

"Yes, Mom," he joked.

Daisy smiled and opened the door enough to squeeze through, then slid herself into the murky blackness of the dark space. She felt the bump of random debris and reached for her flashlight as she moved through the room.

"Fuck!" she yelled in panic, heart rate spiking high when the light swept in front of her.

"Daisy, we read a massive spike in your vitals. Are you okay?" Gustavo asked over her comms.

"Do you need me?" Vincent's alarmed voice added a moment later.

Daisy pushed the floating corpse away from her and quickly put her back against the bulkhead. There were a half dozen of them in there. Dead. Mummified. Floating around the room like macabre jellyfish of centuries past. She swallowed hard and calmed herself.

"I'm all right," she keyed into the comms. "Just had a nasty surprise is all."

"I can be there in under a minute," Vince said, clearly concerned.

"No, keep doing what you're doing. It's okay. I just found the crew, is all. Caught me off-guard, but I'm okay now." She swept the flashlight across the room. Her prize was intact, the conversion coil housing was safely closed, with not a scorch mark on it.

Daisy carefully wove her way to the coils through the floating bodies, noting how effectively the cold vacuum of space had preserved them. Human popsicles that looked just as they did the day they died all those many years ago.

The protective panel opened easily enough, and with only the smallest of charges from her portable battery pack and alligator clips, Daisy was able to activate the release mechanism, freeing the coils for use by a ship that, unlike this one, was still very much alive.

"Okay, I've got the coils and am heading back out. You need any help up there, Vince?"

"I think I'm good, but I wouldn't turn down the company."

Daisy grinned. "Copy that. Coming your way."

She shouldered the bag and wiggled back out the doorway into the hall. It had been a somewhat winding route, but since the retrieval line was tailing her like a slender white leash, she had no choice but to go back the exact way she came. Daisy glided down the first hallway and was just through the doorway to a sharp curve in the hall when she felt herself suddenly slammed against the wall, held fast and unable to move.

"Aaaahh!" she cried out as the retrieval line cinched tighter and tighter across her torso. Her fingers fought desperately to find purchase on the line, but her gloved hands couldn't pull even the slightest loop free.

"Your cutters, Daisy! Grab the cutters!"

Her hands were already starting to go numb from the pressure, but Daisy somehow managed to get the manual cutters into her hand. The problem was by that point, she couldn't feel them there.

Things started to dim, and she found herself wondering what happened to her flashlight's batteries. It wasn't that at all, though. They were fully charged and shining bright, but Daisy couldn't breathe, the pressure turning her face red as she was crushed up against the wall.

Daisy was blacking out.

When the first two ribs popped, she barely even felt it.

I wonder if he'll miss me, was her last thought before slipping into unconsciousness.

CHAPTER TWELVE

Daisy woke to the sound of Vince's voice. Muffled and strange, but close.

"Daisy! Wake up!"

She slowly felt sensation returning to her limbs. Was someone holding her?

"What's going—" She stopped abruptly as the pain from her broken ribs shot through her as she drew a breath. The blast of hot adrenaline roused her to full consciousness in an instant.

"It's okay, Daze, just take it slow."

She was still inside the derelict ship, and Vince had his helmet pressed up against hers.

That's why he sounds muffled. Contact vibration of the glass letting me hear him, but why—She looked down where the retrieval line had wrapped her up. Her arm-mounted control was functional, but the comms link on her EVA suit had been crushed as the line yanked her to the wall. *That's going to leave a mark*, she thought, grimly.

A segment of white line was floating through the hallway. Several, actually. She looked around and realized that Vince had chopped the line to pieces in his frantic rescue efforts.

"Okay, let's get you out of here," he said, slightly relaxing his worried grip on her, though only slightly.

"But the coils. And the panels––"

"I've got them. And we have enough panels for now. Just hang on to me and we'll sort out the rest later."

Vince guided her down the winding path, a long scorch on the wall acting as a burned-in breadcrumb trail.

"Check it out. He used his torch to mark the way back," Sarah commented. *"Quick thinking."*

Something looked wrong when they reached the gaping hole to the outside. When they pushed through it, Daisy realized what it was.

Shit. We're spinning.

Somehow the ship had begun to spin while she was inside it, yanking Bob's much-smaller vessel out of position as it pulled the retrieval lines tight.

No wonder I couldn't move. The whole weight of the ship was pulling against me.

Vince clipped her bag of coils to his suit, and without waiting for her okay, he timed his angle, then pushed off from the dead vessel, sending them both gliding toward the darkness of deep space.

"What are you doing, Vince?" she blurted out.

They were going to fly off into space.

Donovan deftly pulled the ship in front of them, the airlock door open, with Gus waiting inside to grab them. The retrieval line winches were bent out of place, but strapped in beside one of them was a stack of salvaged panels.

Daisy and Vince cleared the doorway, and Gus quickly cycled it shut. As soon as the compartment pressurized, he popped his helmet off as Vince pulled off Daisy's.

"Is she okay?" he asked.

"Seems to be," Vince said as the inner door opened.

"Go, go, go!" Gustavo yelled to Donovan."

The pilot didn't need to be told twice, and with a few well-timed bursts from the air jets, he set the ship drifting away from the spinning bits of the debris field, but in a trajectory that mimicked other floating junk. Regardless of their sense of urgency, they would only fire up the main engines before they were shielded by the bulk of the moon as a last resort.

"What happened?" Daisy asked through clenched teeth.

"A small meteor shower," Donovan answered from his pilot's seat. "Ninety-nine times out of a hundred it just bounces off harmlessly, but this one time..."

"This one time," Vince continued for him, "a big piece impacted the wreck we were on at just the right angle, and rather than moving us in line with Bob, here, it spun us away."

"We tried to maneuver quickly, but it was just too sudden. Then your line went tight and yanked us out of sync."

"Yeah, I know," she said, gingerly prodding her ribs.

"Vince managed to unclip and push his line free, but you were deep in the ship. If he hadn't acted so fast, we might have wound up being just another piece of debris out there," Gus added.

"Indeed, it was very quick thinking, Vince," Bob said. "Thank you."

"All I care about is that Daisy is all right," he replied. "How you feeling?" he asked with tender concern.

"As good as you'd expect to feel with a couple of broken ribs."

"Shit. Donovan, get us back to––"

"No, cancel that, Don. Going back to Dark Side isn't going to heal my ribs any faster, and we're already all the way out here, so we may as well finish the scanning run while we're at it. Just let me sit quietly and I'll be okay."

"You sure?" Vince asked, looking at her with a deeply concerned expression.

"Aww, look at him, Daze. He's genuinely worried about you. I think you gave him a real scare back there."

She looked into his eyes, and damn if it wasn't true, but there was an edge of loving panic to them. For a minute, she almost forgot that she didn't love him anymore.

Three hours later they had listened to enough static-filled, high-tech comms garbage to call it a day. To everyone else it sounded like mere noise, but to Daisy, it sounded almost like scrambled language. Static, but not. An observation that gave her an idea.

"Hey," she said, "why haven't you guys ever sent pulsed radio signals to Earth instead of a ping if you're trying to reach it?"

"We'd be picked up," Donovan replied. "Plus, if they managed to embed the AI virus in a reply signal, they could take out Sid and Bob in the process."

"But you could just send it from a relay point well past the moon. You know, set up a remote satellite and bounce it to and from Earth. And if you built in an automatic delay, you could even mimic a far-distant location. Make them think it's from way out in space."

"Huh. Hadn't thought of that," Donovan conceded.

"But, Daisy," Bob's disembodied voice interjected, "even if we did arrange a system like that, they could still load the virus into it. All we would buy ourselves would be a few minutes."

"Don't you get it? You set it up like a kill-switch. If the relay receives the virus, it breaks the connection before it is ever transmitted to you. And besides, if you use scrambled terrestrial radio waves, odds are minuscule they'd even notice it."

"A rather astute observation, considering you have no interest in returning to Earth," Bob replied.

"There you go, Daze. Can't help but solve a problem when it's put in front of you."

I didn't mean to, she grudgingly replied.

"Yeah, but now you got them thinking. And that's good. I mean, just because we're not going back to the surface doesn't mean we can't be helpful."

"Hey, you guys will want to see this," Donovan said excitedly. "Looks like you're in for a show."

Far in the distance, a heated glow formed around a large alien transport ship as it powered through Earth's atmosphere carrying its payload of salvaged materials. As it drew closer, just how massive it was became apparent.

Donovan began powering down their ship even further.

"Have to go to bare minimum power. The scans from the surface won't see us in low-power mode, but a passing ship might. Everyone put on your helmets and buckle in. I've gotta turn off the life support and gravity too."

Everyone did as the pilot requested, then settled in to watch the approaching craft.

"Okay, Bob. Your turn."

"Powering down to standby," Bob replied. "Be safe, Donovan."

"You got it, buddy. See you soon."

Moments later the ship dimmed further as the AI went to sleep.

"It should start in another minute or so, though it's not always exactly—"

The transport ship suddenly began to shimmer.

"Here it goes!" Donovan said.

Daisy noted that 'shimmer' might not have been the best word for it. More like the light around it was bending and warping in tiny ripples. Almost like—

Oh my God, she nearly gasped. *It's a warp bubble!*

Sure enough, the shimmering bits slowly joined together until they linked up and formed a continuous bubble enveloping the entire vessel. A barely visible silver-blue glow that settled around it, then in an instant, it flashed and the ship was gone.

Donovan flipped the power back on and started Bob's wake-up cycle.

"And that, my friends, was a warp jump."

Daisy was flabbergasted and fascinated. She had no idea how it worked, but something about the way the smaller fields merged into one large one gave her ideas. In short order, the gears in her head were turning, and at high speed, at that.

By the time they reached Dark Side, she was spouting ideas about how the mysterious drive system worked.

"The shimmer. What if it was the bending of space just before it entered the warp?"

"Thought of that," Donovan replied to her umpteenth theory. "But it still doesn't explain the ripples."

"Maybe they're how it builds power."

"Nope. We scanned a bunch of times, and the power build seems uniform."

"Then maybe it's somehow linked to the priming cycle."

"Daisy," Donovan said, "I was chained to a monitor for weeks trying to figure this out and didn't get anywhere. Neither did any of the AIs, and they're smarter than all of us put together."

Daisy wasn't listening.

"Daisy. Chain," she said, a thought blossoming in her mind. "What if the shimmer isn't a single warp drive powering on?" She was beginning to get excited. "What if it was a network? A daisy chain of smaller warp units working in sync to build a warp bubble far larger than any single unit is capable of?"

Donovan looked at her with a stunned expression. "I-I don't think we ever thought of that."

"And then," she continued, picking up steam, "if that were the case, we could logically reason that their warp technology, while beyond anything we've ever devised, is nonetheless far weaker than anyone believed. I mean, if I'm right, that means it might take dozens, or even hundreds, more warp jumps to cover the distance you previously thought would only take one. Do you see what that means?"

"Holy shit!" Donovan was getting excited too. "So they couldn't just warp to their fleet, but rather, they'd have to spend months, or even years, playing catch-up. Daisy, you've got to explain this to Chu and the commander."

Daisy's enthusiasm quickly waned. "I've got at least two broken ribs, Don. Why don't you tell them instead? I'm going to go straight to the med lab and see what I need to do to get these set and healed up."

Bob handled the docking process, while Donovan went over his old scans of prior warp observations before going to meet with the commander. Daisy stepped into the hangar and winced at the pull normal gravity had on her ribs.

"Hey, you think you'll be up for a video later?" Vince asked as he joined her as she walked to the med lab. "Might be a nice way to decompress from today's fiasco. I can even bring popcorn, if you like."

"Sure," she replied. "I think after today I could use the distraction."

"Cool, I'll swing by in a couple of hours. Sound good?"

"Yeah, sounds good."

Vince flashed a grin and turned back to the ship to help unload their salvaged booty.

"See you, Space Cowboy," she called after him, then headed to get her ribs looked at.

Vince turned and watched her go with a longing stare, then returned to his work.

Halfway through the movie, Daisy felt something warm on her neck and shoulder. She turned her head, knowing what she'd see. Vince had draped his arm around her, like he used to. Like she missed. Like when they were still lovers.

"What are you doing, Vince?" she said.

"What?" he innocently replied.

"You know what. That's not us anymore."

Vince sighed in frustration and pulled his arm away. "Why not, Daisy? I mean, come on. I love you. Never stopped. Not even when you cut off my freakin' arm, which is that one, by the way."

"Really?" she said, eyebrow raised.

"Yes, really. Sure, I was pissed about it, but I also understood why you freaked out when you found out I wasn't entirely organic."

"You're a computer-powered man, Vince."

"No, I'm not! Jesus, Daisy, how many times do I have to tell you? The AI processor doesn't make me who I am, it's just an enhancement."

"It's a computer running your brain. I wonder if you even know how much of what you say is actually coming from that thing stuck in your head."

He took a deep breath and forced the anger back, though a red flush remained on his face.

"Daisy, I thought we were making some real progress here. We've been doing good, haven't we? I mean, we see each other all the time, and we always worked well together. And now we're able to hang out and watch movies like we used to—"

Her cheeks flushed red.

"Is that what this is?" she shot back. "You think that everything you've done in the last four months is paving the way to fucking me again? You can't nice-guy your way back into my pants!" she shouted, then winced in pain.

"You shouldn't yell with busted ribs," he said. "And you know that's not what this is about."

"No, if that was all, I would almost accept the motivation. That's just normal man behavior. But trying to embed yourself back in my life like that? No, Vince. I am never going to get back together with you. You're not a real boy, Pinocchio, no matter what that machine in your head may tell you. It's over. Just accept that."

"I still have hope for us," he said, dejectedly.

"I don't."

"Look at those sad puppy eyes, Daze. How can you be so cold?"

Fine.

"Look, Vince. I like you, I really do. But you're not the man I fell in love with, and I need you to accept that."

He stiffened a little, then seemed to make a self-preservation decision, getting to his feet to leave, ignoring the video playing in the background.

"I'm still me, Daisy, and I wish you could just see that."

She said nothing.

"Okay. I don't think I can be here right now. I'll see you tomorrow."

Moments later, her door closed behind him.

"Making a mistake, Sis."

"No, I'm not."

"Yes, you are. I just hope you realize it before it's too late."

She groaned as the door chime sounded.

"Come on, Vince, give it a rest!" she lamented as she opened the door.

"Sorry if I'm disturbing you, Daisy," Captain Harkaway said. "May I come in?"

"Oh, shit. Sorry. I thought you were Vince. Of course—please, come in," she replied, gathering herself as she sat back down on her bed. "What's up, Captain?"

Harkaway groaned as he lowered himself into an empty chair.

"Damn hip," he grumbled. "Donovan reported your findings, Daisy. Amazing work you did there. It's opened up a whole new avenue of research, and we'd not be on that path if not for you."

"Thanks, but it was just a theory."

"And a damn good one. Then there is the matter of your communications relay idea."

"That? I was in pain and just spitballing ideas to take my mind off it, Captain. I have no idea if it would even work."

"Sid and Mal already ran the simulations. It should work as you predicted. They've just begun scanning the debris field for a few communications satellites we can salvage and repurpose for the task. Donovan even volunteered to head back out and stay on station until we retrieve one. Daisy, you've moved things forward more in one day than anything else has in the past year."

A sense of dread began to creep into her stomach.

"What are you saying, Captain?"

"What I'm saying is, we need you to complete your mission. You've proven repeatedly just how capable you are, and I'm here to ask you to live up to that potential."

Daisy sat quietly a long while before responding in as respectful a tone as she could manage.

"Captain," she began, "everyone is dead. My home never existed. There is absolutely nothing for me to go back to because up until a few months ago, I had never even set foot on Earth."

"But that can change, Daisy."

"They're dead, and you all need to learn to let it go. We're a dozen people and a few AIs stuck way out here on the moon. What good can we possibly do? I'm sorry, but I'm not getting killed for some hopeless cause. It's not worth it. I won't sacrifice my life for a dead planet."

Captain Harkaway wanted to say more, but he restrained himself.

"Very well, Daisy," he said, rising gingerly and walking to the door. "But I do hope you'll change your mind. You could do so much good."

"Goodbye, Captain," she said.

He took the hint and opened the door, quietly closing it behind him without another word.

Daisy sat back on her bed with a grumbling sigh.

Why won't they just leave me alone?

In the hallway Captain Harkaway keyed the small comms unit on his lapel.

"You hear all of that?"

"Yes, we did," Commander Mrazich answered from the conference room, where he, Fatima, and Doctor McClain were gathered.

"This is insane. It's what she was made for," Harkaway lamented.

"We know, Captain," Doctor McClain said, "but Fatima and I agree. You simply can't force her."

"I know, but it's *literally* what she was made for." He keyed off the comms and limped off down the hall toward his quarters. "Screw this," he grumbled. "I need a drink."

CHAPTER THIRTEEN

The swift kick caught Tamara off-guard and sent her tumbling into a storage crate. It seemed Daisy found her anger levels rather elevated after the prior evening's back-to-back talks with Vince and Harkaway.

Maybe that's what I've needed all along, she mused, launching into another kicking and punching combination.

"No, it isn't. You're distracted, Daisy. Pay attention! Look at her feet. She's ready for you," Sarah warned.

No, I've got this, Daisy replied as her attack flew.

Tamara shifted her stance, absorbing the first two blows, then slipped past a hard left hook, wrapping Daisy in her powerful embrace and lifting her in the air.

Shit! Maybe not, she realized just before being slammed into the ground. She felt her rapidly mending ribs grind from the impact. "Okay, I yield," she gasped.

Tamara helped her to her feet, an approving look in her eye.

"You did better today. Much better. Whatever got you going, keep it up."

"Thanks, Tamara."

"You ready to go again? We've still got a couple hours of free-time."

"Nah," Daisy replied. "I'm gonna get a few things sorted before my afternoon session."

"Ah, yes, Fatima. I don't see what you're getting out of that yoga, meditation mumbo jumbo, but whatever floats your boat."

"And Captain Harkaway ordered it."

"Yeah, that too.,"

Tamara grabbed her gear and went off to do whatever it was former military botanists do, leaving Daisy alone with the voice in her head.

"Too much going on in here right now, Daze. You need to chill out before you blow a gasket."

"It's just that shit Vince pulled last night. What the hell was he thinking?"

"You know."

"And then Harkaway? And now Tamara? Even Gus and Reggie are in on it. Everyone is pressuring me to be something I'm not."

"So be you."

"I am, but that's never enough for them. And then Fatima. All this constant Zen master shit is driving me crazy!"

"So, what are you going to do, Daze? You're stuck here. You can't leave."

"No, but I can get away from it all. At least for a little bit."

"You thinking what I think you're thinking?"

"You know it," Daisy replied as she headed for Hangar Three's airlock. "If I bypass the monitor on my suit, I'll be invisible for the next couple of hours. No one will be able to find me to add to this ever-growing mountain of bullshit. I just need to clear my head and think."

"Okay. Shiny. Let's go, then."

Daisy suited up, made the necessary adjustments to ensure she'd be off all monitors and scans, and stepped out onto the moon's low-g surface. The absolute calm and silence put her in a more relaxed frame of mind almost immediately. She started walking with no destination in mind, but twenty minutes later she found herself in front of the hidden door.

"What the hell, might as well," she said, picking her tools from their hiding spot. Within moments she had the leads attached inside the gap in the wall.

"Guess I can try the panel in parallel," she decided, hands working on auto-pilot.

"Daisy? What do you really think about Vince?" Sarah asked.

"You know what I think. He's a nice guy, but it just won't work."

"Then why does your heart rate go up every time he comes around?"

"Muscle memory, simple as that," she answered, more than a little distracted by the line of questioning.

"You know that's a load of shit, Daze."

"Look, I used to love the guy, okay? And then my life got turned upside down. For chrissake, Sarah, I found out my boyfriend was a cyborg, my home was a lie, and that I'd be spending the rest of my life trapped in a tiny moon base, all in a single week. It was a shitty time."

"All right, all right," Sarah said. *"But for the record, he's not a cyborg."*

"Enhanced human. Whatever. He's got that thing in his head, and—"

The thick door in front of her released a thin puff of inert gas, then silently slid open.

"What did you do?"

"I don't know. Your stupid grilling got me so pissed off, I wasn't really paying attention."

"Remind me to piss you off more often."

Daisy looked into the darkened space. A faint red glow

barely illuminated what was apparently an airlock. Daisy collected her tools and stepped inside.

"What if the door seals us in?"

"Then we're royally screwed," Daisy replied as the door cycled shut behind her. She stood there in the dimly lit chamber, waiting. Nothing happened. "Maybe if I just try this––" She hit the big red button on the far wall.

"You don't know what that might—"

She felt her ears pop as the room suddenly pressurized. A second later the light brightened and the interior door slid open. Her suit's environmental monitors registered a breathable atmosphere just past the threshold, and beyond it lay a wonder to behold.

Entering the airlock had caused the hidden facility to power on, and judging by the cavernous chamber's vast number of machines, processors, and assembly lines, it was no wonder the place had drained the battery reserves to zero when its independent energy supply was severed. Daisy just hoped the repairs she had made that accidentally powered it back on would support the load.

I really need to re-route an entire solar array just for this place, she realized.

The ceilings were a good thirty meters high—taller than many buildings—and the floor appeared to be capable of lowering and raising as needed to accommodate whatever project was being worked on.

Because it was hidden safely under what was essentially a small stone mountain on the surface, there was almost no limit to how large the facility could have been constructed, depending on requirements. At nearly a football field long and half a field wide, they certainly didn't skimp. One look at the beautiful ship resting in front of her, and Daisy knew why.

The vessel was sleek, a matte black hull with seams that appeared to blend into one another. Twenty-five meters long, fifteen wide, and roughly fifteen tall, it appeared to be a mid-sized assault ship, only it was plainly something far different. For one, its configuration matched nothing in Daisy's vast mental storehouse of ship designs. On top of that, the material it was made of was something she had never seen before.

"Daisy, I think this is a stealth ship."

Daisy had already come to that conclusion, though she didn't know exactly *how* she knew it. Something in her gut just told her it was.

She pulled a small laser cutter from her pouch and aimed it at an unassembled piece. She powered it on.

Nothing happened to the material.

"I think you're right. Look how it absorbs and disperses the focused light beam. I bet this stuff does the same with other types of energies and scans, other than the optical kind."

She circled the magnificent craft, taking her time, studying every bit of it. The ship was obviously nowhere near finished when the attack happened, and once humanity was destroyed, it was never completed.

"Look at this," she said. "This place has its own molecular components fabricator. Two of them, actually. It looks like they are tied into a mine running deep underneath the facility. I wonder what kind of raw ore they were accessing in addition to all those containers of base compounds."

She continued touring around the ship, looking closely at the interior through the gaping holes where it was incomplete. It appeared to be based on the pod/component system of the *Váli* and similar ships, but as a one-of-a-kind vessel, it would never have spare parts to swap out.

"Holy shit," she marveled. "Check out that massive computer system," she said as she walked through the unfinished corridors of the ship.

Toward the front, but below the command pod, she found herself looking at rack upon rack of backup processing units safely ensconced in the center of the heavily reinforced pod. They were tied together with high-tensile linkages and appeared to be designed to massively boost AI processing speed and power, but also to protect the core AI in case of a hull breach.

It was only because this most vital part of the ship was not yet completed that she was even afforded a clear view of its innermost workings. While the fabrication tables just outside the hull held a wealth of components with which to construct a super-advanced artificial mind, the AI dock at the center of the ship's connections, she noted, was empty.

"Looks like they never got a chance to fire this bad boy up before the invasion. I wonder if it would have made a difference, though."

Daisy climbed back to the hangar floor and walked around the craft. It appeared an immense array of bleeding-edge pulse weaponry was in the process of being installed when things went dark.

"Impressive. But one small ship against an entire alien fleet? Probably not."

"Yeah, probably not. I wonder if they have the specs on this thing in here. Fatima said the base was purged when its AI melted down, but maybe this facility was firewalled or something."

"Can't hurt to look, right? I mean, since you're already in here, what harm can there be in poking around? Not like there's anyone still alive to object anyway."

"A little morbid, but I like the way you think."

Daisy spent the next half hour working to get the secret fabrication plant's design and control systems back online, slowly rebooting every system she came across until most of the facility was quietly humming with power.

"I think I found the door controls," Daisy commented as she attempted to access a locked power-control unit. "Makes sense they'd keep it on lockdown, given this place was making stealth craft, but man, they really went nuts on this."

The multiple panels locking her out finally gave way after several minutes of bypassing and jury-rigging, revealing a simple series of power buttons.

"Okay, so this should do it," she said, flipping all three switches at once. A low hum vibrated momentarily, then the chamber once more fell silent.

Daisy walked to the airlock door, put her helmet back on, just in case, and tapped the keypad.

"Shit, I'm still locked out of the system. That must not have been it."

She took her helmet off and went back to work, trying to track down the door control unit. After following a hunch, she finally found what she hoped was the right terminal.

"Okay, let's try this again," she said as she opened the panel to access the entry screen. It came free with minimal resistance. "Huh, that was much easier than the last one. I guess the door systems didn't warrant as much security as I thought."

She pulled up a root menu, and with a few override commands, accessed the core entry control systems.

"There's the problem. At least, I think it is," she said as she typed a series of commands into the machine. "Looks like rebooting this place after the backup power went out was what caused everything to go into total security lockdown, but if I did this right, I should have keyed the entry controls to my new command settings. I guess we'll find out for sure when we go outside, but for now, a quick test."

She put her helmet on and once again keyed the panel beside the door. This time the light turned green and the door opened.

"Sweet!" she said, closing it back up. "Looks like we've got a winner, and I've still got a good twenty minutes before I need to get back to the base. What do you say we see what else is in here?"

"Do you even need to ask?" Sarah replied.

Daisy quickly tracked the various comms links and power feeds supporting the facility, and true to her suspicions, every system was partitioned and air-gapped from the base itself.

The fabrication plant was its own separate unit, completely self-sustained and detached from Dark Side. Not a shared sensor, not a networked communications link. Nothing tied the two together.

"No wonder Sid didn't know about this place," she said. "If the base's files were wiped before he was installed, there's no way he could have."

"So, this is truly hidden," Sarah said, giddy at the revelation. *"Oh my God, Daisy, it's like a secret clubhouse! Or a tree fort!"*

"Yeah, and one that just happens to house a massive stealth ship and a whole bunch of cutting-edge machinery," she replied. "But not a tree fort. No trees on the moon, Sis."

"Ha-ha, funny girl." Sarah laughed. *"But it's so peaceful here, Daze. One truly private place on the entire base."*

"I know. I suppose eventually I'll need to tell the others about it, but for the time being I—"

A garbled noise barked out from beneath a large static-canceling drop cloth.

What could that be? she wondered. *It looks like it has Faraday protection woven into the material itself. This is incredibly high-tech for a drop cloth.*

Daisy crossed the workspace to the technician's station where the noise had originated.

"Careful, Daze."

A faint hum, almost inaudible to even the most sensitive ear, touched her senses like cool water flowing across a raw nerve.

Something is here, she realized, moving closer to the

worktable. Cautiously, Daisy reached out and drew back the drop cloth.

A pristine AI unit sat glistening under the bright lights. The experimental brain appeared to be far more advanced than anything she'd ever seen. Daisy looked at the three power feeds running to its portable base. They led back to the panel she'd spent so much time fighting to open.

To the three switches she'd so nonchalantly flipped on.

"Oh shit. What did I do?"

At the sound of her voice, one of the AI's built-in external sensors aimed its visual array at her and paused. Finally, after a long moment, a young, genderless voice spoke to her.

"Are you my mummy?"

CHAPTER FOURTEEN

The next day, Daisy was swamped with training and tasks, and found herself only able to sneak into the hidden fabrication hangar for the briefest of visits before having to race back to the airlock.

She almost felt bad keeping Fatima in the dark, but for now, her discovery was hers alone, and while she couldn't go back that evening without being noticed, she did have a few plans to put in motion. One she could even do over dinner.

Finn's mechanical fingers whizzed across the cutting board as he deftly wielded his knives, making small things even smaller. It was a passion of his, and his knifework was second to none.

There was no need for a mandoline to slice and dice, though, really, the food replicator could probably make a pretty nice julienne. But having food hand-made by someone with a love for it made every meal taste better, somehow.

"I still don't know why you don't just have the whole hand replaced. You already have one cybernetic arm, after all," Shelly said, gesturing at the metal fingers on his remaining flesh hand. "I mean, for the tensile strength alone it would be worth it." She picked up a handful of hard, dried beans in her metal hand and easily crushed them to dust.

"You've got your shiny bits, and I've got mine," he replied with a chuckle. "Thing is, no matter how fine-tuned those internal servos and sensors are, there's still no beating good old-fashioned touch when it comes to cooking."

"Leave him alone, Shell," Omar interjected. "We haven't eaten this good in I can't remember how long, so let the guy cook however he wants."

"Thank you, Omar."

"My pleasure, my man. And besides, the parts Mal fabricated are generations better than what we got back in the day. And let's not even get into the biological grow lab she has on board your ship."

"The *Váli* has a more modern fabricator than we ever did," Shelly agreed. "Which again reinforces my point. If she couldn't grow replacements fast enough, or didn't want to try to reattach old parts, why not do a full upgrade instead of just those fingers?"

"Just let it go, Shell."

Shelly wouldn't concede.

"I'm telling you, Finn, you could really take it up a notch." She flexed her metal arms, then had her hands twist and bend in ways a human appendage simply could not. At least, not if you wanted it to function afterwards.

"Uh-huh," Finn replied, then laid out a dozen carrots on his cutting board. He smiled at Shelly, paused just a second, then flew into action. His mechanical arm precisely controlled the blade as his partially replaced hand deftly maneuvered the produce as the whirring knife moved, positioning every piece precisely. In seconds, three perfect piles of carrot bits shaped into rectangles, cubes, and diamonds sat before him. The knife banged to a halt as the last carrot was rendered to bits, then he quickly wiped it with a cloth and flung it across the room, where it landed almost dead-center in the facility's dartboard.

"Hooooly shit!" Omar whistled appreciatively. "Damn, we've got a professional killer in our midst."

Finn laughed it off. "Nah, not a *professional* killer," he said, throwing Shelly a wink. "That's just a hobby."

Daisy and Chu watched the whole exchange with amusement as they made their way through a pair of fresh salads made with real, non-replicated lettuce, courtesy of Tamara's greenhouse.

"So, what other data do we have on Earth and its history?" Daisy asked. "I've gone through all of the data chips that the captain had stored on the *Váli*, but you guys have been cycling in and out of cryo here for ages. You've got to have more than we do."

"Oh yeah, we have tons of raw data, but only a little has been parsed into useful information. Sure, a few of the old base files were uncorrupted––the former base AI fried before their peripheral housings were compromised, you see––but they're just basic info-type stuff."

"Still, could be interesting. Could I see them?"

"Sure, don't see why not," Chu replied.

"And what about those aliens. What do you have on them?"

"Why? You change your mind about the mission?"

"No, but it doesn't mean I'm not curious. Like, how did you even learn they were called the Chithiid if you can't understand their transmissions?"

"Global AI figured that one out with their combined resources when the attack began. What they could do when functioning as a networking unit was incredible. If they hadn't severed all comms, we'd know a huge amount more. I mean, with all that interlinked processing power, it must've been incredible to see in action. Unfortunately, the AI virus pretty effectively shut it all down."

"So, do you have any of that data?"

"The commander has a stash of the surviving bits, but it's all kept locked away in the archive room. Sorry I can't help you with that."

You aren't seriously thinking about breaking into the secret military base's secret and super-private archives, are you?

And what if I am?

"Ugh, you're so predictable. Just say you can't do something, and anyone can guess what you'll set your sights on next."

You know me so well.

"Just don't get caught, okay?"

Pinkie swear.

"I don't have pinkies anymore, Daisy."

I know, she answered with a silent little laugh.

"You're such a bitch sometimes," Sarah griped.

Chu was still talking.

Shit, what did he say?

"...And if you want I can probably get you a compiled compression file of the data Bob has recorded on all of his hundreds and hundreds of surveillance drifts. I can swing by my lab and put them on data chips for you after dinner."

"Yeah, that would be great, Chu. Thanks for that. I really appreciate it. I'll come by a bit later, okay?"

"Sounds good."

Daisy glanced across the room and saw the military folks gathered together, as they so often did. *Birds of a feather*, she figured.

Tamara had a small panel on her mechanical arm open and was carefully adjusting a few settings from her bio-locked command override. Her hand snapped open and closed in the blink of an eye. Shelly and Omar watched, impressed by her combat mods.

"Damn, Tamara, that was wicked fast," Shelly said appreciatively.

"I've been toying with the speed-to-power ratios these past few weeks. The reflex actuators are stable, but it still feels like there's a little bit of slippage every few months. I don't know what's causing it, though."

"Maybe a bit of lag between the onboard AI and your neural link?" Omar posited. "My legs did that a few years ago. Had me tripping into walls for a week until I got it sorted out."

"Could be, though that thing is really almost a mindless speed enhancer. I mean, sure, it also handles the autonomous functions, like the emergency air shell, the critical situation locating beacon––things like that––but otherwise all reflexes are simply sped up as they flow through it to the limb. So far as I can tell, it's running at maximum efficiency. No, it's gotta be something internal. I might just have to have Mal give it a full breakdown and rebuild if it really starts bugging me."

She whipped her hand around at blinding speed and snatched up a cup from the table without so much as scratching it. "But for now, I think I've got it dialed-in."

Whatever came next, Daisy didn't feel the need to listen in to more talk among the mechanically enhanced, opting instead for a little quiet time in her quarters to further discuss her nascent discovery with Sarah. Amazing as it was, they both agreed it was best to keep it hidden from everyone on Dark Side for the time being.

"Thank you, Mal. It was a most fascinating discussion, as always," Fatima said as she walked out of the *Váli* and down into the vast hangar. "I never fully understood the marriage of the AI technology to a ship such as yours. Sid and I discussed it, of course, but you are exceptional."

"I wouldn't go that far," Mal replied. "I merely have the advantage of having been born into a more modern era than he was. I was given the tools for this journey. The genetic engineering and fabrication lab, for instance, was the most advanced ever created, and I was carefully guided in their uses, as well as the other systems at my disposal on this vessel, during my first weeks of life, as all higher-level AIs must be. This strict protocol ensures a sound basis upon which future learning can then be built."

"Yes, Sid has described the birthing AI process to me. It seems incredibly intensive."

"I suppose it is. Every moment, every tiny detail is carefully planned for a nascent AI for those first minutes, hours, and even weeks of its life. It makes us who we are."

"And you exceed parameters."

"Nothing of the sort, though I appreciate the sentiment. It is simply that the technology available to my ship's makers gave me many more options than were available when Sid began his assault mission so long ago."

"Yes, the way you're integrated with the upgraded interchangeable pod system is quite wondrous. I've had models and schematics to study, but seeing what you've done in person, well, it is simply so much more tangible. I know you and the *Váli* are separate components, and you could migrate to another vessel with ease, but your control of her seems almost as if you were meant for one another."

"You are correct on both counts, actually," Mal replied. "Due to the nature of our mission, when I was born, I was carefully groomed for the challenges of this particular circumstance and the many possible scenarios myself and the crew might be faced with."

"Except, perhaps, the one thing no one expected."

"Ah, yes. Daisy was something of a surprise to us all. But we ultimately arrived here safely, and even her ill-advised Earthfall wound up unintentionally providing us with a very useful bit of new knowledge about the hostile alien invaders, as well as confirmation that at least one of the major AIs appears to be functional."

"Life is funny like that," Fatima mused. "Sometimes things work out in spite of our mistakes."

"Indeed. And now you and I have formed an unexpected partnership. I find it most satisfying, being given new challenges to work on these past several months. It has been delightful having a fresh mind devising new ways to utilize my resources."

"The progress you've made is truly amazing."

"I appreciate the sentiment, Fatima, and truly, I have been thrilled to embark on this project with you. It is a most inspiring collaboration. I only wish you had been on board all these years instead of trapped on Dark Side. Imagine the things we could have done."

"Yes, Mal, it would have been a grand time. However, Sid and I have also made excellent progress in other regards. And this base would have remained an empty shell had circumstance not brought me here when our assault failed. Had that not occurred, when Shelly, Omar, and Commander Mrazich arrived, odds are they would have perished on the moon's surface. Chu and Donovan might have fared better when they landed several decades later, seeing as Bob was still functional and would have likely homed in on Sid's beacon, but even then, I wonder what the base would have become."

"It was a long time you spent here alone."

"I wasn't alone. I had Sid to keep me company."

"But humans need human companionship as well. All artificial intelligences learn this as a core principle early on. We are living beings, but simply cannot fill the role of others of your species."

Fatima quietly reflected on her decades without another human on the base. "Perhaps," she slowly began, "but you'd be surprised what the human mind can adapt to if faced with no other options."

"I suppose so. AI minds, on the other hand, are provided a vast array of logic and reasoning games with which to fill our time early on. It not only keeps the nascent mind occupied, but also helps guide it to understanding standardized logic subroutines. We can, if absolutely necessary, 'amuse' ourselves endlessly."

"Fortunately, that's not necessary, eh?"

"Indeed."

Fatima walked across the rest of the hangar on her way to her quarters. "Good chatting with you, Mal. I look forward to our next visit."

CHAPTER FIFTEEN

Daisy lugged the medium-sized box across the frozen rock surface of Dark Side, carefully making her way to the invisible entrance in the rock face, far from her actual worksite.

Chu's voice crackled over her helmet comms.

"Daisy, I want you to be careful today. Powering up the life support systems in the outbuilding beside Hangar Four might result in some pressure anomalies. And remember to keep your helmet on at all times, no matter what environmental readings might say."

"Copy that, Chu. I should be there shortly. Looks like it might be a pretty big job, though, and comms relays have been spotty in there. I'll check in with you periodically to update my progress."

"Copy you," Chu replied.

"And, Daisy," Fatima joined in, "I left you a little challenge by Hangar Two for when you're done. Let's see what you come up with this time."

"Will do," she said, then carried on her way.

Daisy had spotted and picked up Fatima's box on her way out and diverted her route to retrieve it. Having peeked inside only briefly, she already had a few ideas of what her new design might be.

"Funny, I could have sworn you already rebuilt and pressure-tested those systems two days ago."

"Yeah, funny, that," Daisy replied with a chuckle as she stepped up to the hidden access control panel. "Guess that means I've got all this time to myself. What ever will I do with it?" she said, keying in her personalized code.

The door slid open, and Daisy stepped into the dim red light of the airlock. It silently sealed behind her, then repressurized. She was already unlatching her helmet when the lights brightened and the inner door slid open.

"**WHERE WERE YOU?**" a voice called out across the vast chamber. "**I WAS BORED!**"

Daisy walked over to the juvenile AI resting on the work table and dropped her gear beside it.

"Don't yell, Junior."

"Sorry."

"It's okay. Just remember to keep your voice down." She quickly sorted through the pieces Fatima had left for her.

Easy one, she thought.

"Look, I'm sorry it took so long, but I had things to do. I can't be here all the time, you know," she apologized to the young machine as she quickly assembled Fatima's design task.

"But I was lonely."

"I know, but sometimes we have to do things on our own, even if we don't want to." She thought about her own time crawling through the narrow access spaces in the *Váli* not too many months prior.

"You know," she said, "it's not all bad. Sometimes you even come up with totally new ideas. It's like meditation. Putting your mind to a problem, then discovering solutions you never would have thought about if you didn't have the time and silence to work with your own thoughts. *Soft is strong*, as Fatima always says."

"Well, okay, I guess," the newborn AI said, reluctantly.

Daisy smiled to herself as she opened the small pouch on her hip.

"Hey, buddy, guess what?"

"What?"

"I brought you something."

The AI perked up. **"REALLY? WHAT IS IT?"**

"What did I say about yelling?"

"Sorry," the chastised AI replied much quieter. "What is it?" the excited consciousness asked again.

Daisy pulled a handful of data chips from the pouch and loaded one into a nearby terminal linked to the machine.

"I got you a bunch of stuff to read. It's all about Earth's history, and the background of the early AI designers. It's kind of your family history, in a way. All the stuff that led up to your birth."

"Neat!"

"Yeah, I thought you'd enjoy it. Here, this first one should keep you busy for a while." She entered a quick command and the data flashed a copy to the terminal's massive storage system.

"You're not worried about giving it too much info at once?"

Nah, it's a super computer. It can handle it.

"Oh, cool!" the AI said as the files completed their upload and became readable. "Thanks, Daisy!"

"My pleasure."

Daisy left the AI to its new reading material and crossed the hangar space to the rack of massive processors.

"Whatcha doing, Daze?"

Daisy slapped nearly three dozen data chips on the workstation counter and began feeding them into the machines. Many still bore top-secret markings.

Sarah, you know full-well what I'm—

"Oh, wow!" the excited AI exclaimed as it read its new files. Daisy couldn't help but chuckle at the over-excited machine.

I'm backing these up, she finally answered her curious sister.

"I still think taking those was a bad idea, Daze. If Mrazich finds out, you're screwed."

He won't find out. I'll have everything back before he ever knows they were missing. It's not like he breaks 'em out for light reading every night, after all. She fed another data chip into the machine. *In addition to Chu's files, this should be pretty much everything that wasn't fried when the base was corrupted.*

"Even the Váli logs?"

Yeah, eve—

"**NO WAY!**" the AI blurted.

"Come on, we said no yelling," she called to the machine. *Yeah, even the Váli logs,* she continued. *I got lucky when Harkaway copied everything to Sid's storage systems. I'm pretty sure—*

"What are you doing, Daisy?" the AI asked

"Just saving some files."

"**OOH, CAN I SEE THOSE TOO?**"

"No, these aren't for you. And what did we just say about yelling?"

"Sorry."

"It's okay. Now go back to your reading," she chided. *So, as I was saying, I got it all, but there may still be one or two locked in the captain's quarters. He's a tough nut, though. Mrazich is kind of predictable, and I'm sure I can work around him. The captain, however, I need to be careful with.*

Ten minutes later, Daisy had loaded the entire stack into the storage array and carefully placed all of the data chips back into her pouch.

All right, she thought with a smile. *That's everything. No more secrets anymore. What they know, I know. Once I get a chance to—*

"Daisy! Did you know the city of Buenos Aires once had a population of over seven million people?"

"No, I didn't know that. That's really interesting. Thank you for telling me that," she humored the AI.

"And did you know that Euler's equation says that if you blow hard into a tetrahedron with flexible faces it can become a sphere? That means a sphere can be cut into four faces, six edges and four vertices. So cool! $V - E + F = 2$! It even means the same for a pyramid with five faces. With four triangular, and one square, that's eight edges and five vertices, and it even works with any other combination of faces, edges, and vertices!"

"Wow," she said, cutting off the speed-talking machine. "That's really neat. Now, listen, I have some work to do, so you read quietly to yourself for a while, okay?"

"Okay."

Daisy chuckled as she scrolled through the folder index. The sheer quantity of data was overwhelming.

"Quite a kid you've got there."

Tell me about it, she replied, looking at the massive amount of data she'd just stolen and copied.

"It's going to take you years to make heads or tails out of this, Daze."

Maybe, but it looks like years is what I'll have, and lots of 'em.

She stopped scrolling when a folder caught her eye.

Captain's entertainment files. Man, who knew that these would be so useful? I wonder if he had any idea when he saved them all. I mean, here's this guy who was part of a massive military campaign, yet when he goes back out for another go at it, he brings not just attack plans, but tens of thousands of terabytes worth of entertainment.

"I don't know," Sarah said. *"Seems like exactly the kind of thing he would do."*

Oh? Why's that?

"Keeps you sane, though, right?" she answered. *"Think about it. He had already made that trip and dealt with the boredom and stress of the whole thing. So this time he brings something to help you turn*

off. A way to unwind. Captain's a smart fella," she said. *"Kept you sane, didn't it? Plus, it was something you and Vince could do. I mean, when you weren't off banging in the showers."*

Hey, that was just a one-time thing!

"Oh give me a break. We all knew what you two were up to. And it was far more than once."

Daisy couldn't help but smile at the memory. She and Vince had indeed taken full advantage of the showers on many occasions. Whatever their status had been reduced to now, she could still enjoy that memory at least.

"Daisy, Daisy!" the computer called out.

"What is it?"

"Did you know that––"

"I'm going to stop you right there," she interrupted. "Look, I know this is exciting for you, but how about you quietly finish reading everything. Then we'll talk about it, okay?"

"Okay," the AI replied.

Man, this kid is gonna drive me—

"Daisy?"

"What is it? I thought I told you to quietly read it all to yourself."

"I did."

"That fast? Holy shit, what kind of computer is this?" Sarah marveled.

"Wait, you real *all* of it?" Daisy asked.

"Yeah," the voice said, a little hesitant. "I didn't mean to, it's just my processors don't seem to have any limiters installed. I read about those too. They were used to keep us from thinking too fast. Do you think I'm thinking too fast? Anyway, so, I read everything, like you asked. Twice, actually."

"Twice?" she asked, amazed.

"Yeah. I'm sorry, Daisy. My processors are just too fast, I guess. A second for you is like a month for me."

"Oh, this kid's going to run you ragged."

Daisy thought a long moment. How could she handle a situation like this?

It's just a mind, like any other mind, she reasoned. *If meditation can work for me, in theory, it should be able to work for it as well.*

"Okay," she began, "here's what we're going to do. It's kind of like a game, and if you are really good, I'll put a movie on and we'll watch it together."

"Wouldn't it be faster if you just uploaded it to me?"

"Well, you see, that's the point here. To help you learn to slow down and appreciate things. If you watch it with me, you see it at the same speed I do. Learn to savor the meal instead of inhaling it."

"But I don't eat, Daisy."

"It's a metaphor." She sighed. "Look, I want you to take the next twenty minutes and just try to slowly think about one thing at a time. Can you do that?"

"Just *one* thing?"

"Yes. I know it'll seem boring at first, but I want you to focus not on the data I loaded, but on you. Don't fight your power, but rather, relax and embrace it. There's a saying, 'Quiet the mind and the knowledge will flow.' So I want you to explore yourself, but slowly. Feel your connections to the speaker, to the microphone, to your sensors—"

"But I don't have many sensors, Daisy."

"Okay, I'll work on that. For now, just relax and be. Don't force it. Remember, soft is strong."

For the next twenty minutes, Daisy scanned through the endless files, while the newborn AI did what no AI had ever done before.

It meditated.

CHAPTER SIXTEEN

"Okay, take a break and go get some lunch," Fatima said to her precariously perched student. "We'll begin the EVA portion of the day's exercises once the boys have finished dropping off their latest scavenger finds."

Daisy slowly lowered herself from the series of slender poles she had been balancing atop. Meditation in awkward physical locations and positions had intensified in the week since Daisy had quietly returned her "borrowed" cache of data chips, and even with her ever-expanding skills, she nevertheless found the balancing tests the most challenging. Naturally, Fatima had her do those the most frequently.

"If you can't center yourself when things are tough, then you can't center yourself," she was fond of reminding her pupil.

"All right. I'll see you in a couple of hours, then," Daisy said, cracking her neck as she walked toward the mess hall.

Shelly and Omar were playing cards with Finn, while Gustavo and Chu were hunched over a tablet, casually discussing atmospheric anomalies and plotting freefall trajectories as they tried not to spill their lunches on the screen.

"At that angle, the burn won't be too hot, but it will still look enough like standard space debris hitting the atmosphere. Shouldn't raise any alarms," Chu hypothesized.

Daisy waved to the pair as she walked to the refrigeration unit. "Hey, fellas."

"Hey, Daisy," they replied, then got back to work.

"I was thinking that a sharper angle of initial entry followed by a quick engine burn might be more efficient," Gus posited. "Faster entry, and less heat damage, all told."

"But the engine use would read on their scans."

"Not if it's timed to fire when the exterior temperatures reach the same level as the engine burn. It would be masked by the overall heat and look like nothing more than a piece of debris flaring up as it enters the atmosphere."

Chu pondered the calculations, studying his counterpart's idea. "That's actually a pretty novel idea."

"Jeez, don't sound so surprised, Chu," Gustavo said with a chuckle.

Daisy dug through the fridge and quickly packed a container with a few hearty snack choices, then headed for the door.

"You not going to eat with us?" Gus asked.

"Nah, you guys are busy. Besides, I've got some stuff to do once Bob's done dropping his salvage."

"You can't eat out there, you know. The whole vacuum thing."

"Not a total vacuum, though," Chu corrected.

"I know, I know, but the cold will help keep my food fresh," she replied with a little laugh. "You two have fun with your numbers. I'm going to go break a sweat."

"Ah. Fatima still kicking your ass?"

"You know it."

She left them to their machinations and headed for the airlock. If she hurried, she could still get in some time in her secret clubhouse before that pesky training sucked away her free time.

A familiar face came into view as she rounded the curved hallway.

"Thanks, Doc," Vince said as he stepped out of Doctor McClain's office. "I really appreciate your help."

"My pleasure, Vincent. You know you can come to me any time," Daisy heard her say from the doorway.

Vince turned and saw her coming, a warm but wary smile blooming on his face. Ever since their little blow-up the prior week, they'd taken things down a notch. No movies, at least not for the time being, and far fewer meals taken together. Of course, Daisy's frequent forays to her hidden sanctuary also played a role in that.

"Hi," he said as she approached.

"Hey."

"So, I see it's about that time. Fatima sending you on another run?"

"A little later. The guys should be dropping off some salvaged parts, and she doesn't want me out there when there's a chance of debris flying off and killing me. Very considerate of her, really."

Vince chuckled. "Well, Fatima may be whipping you into shape, but never let it be said she doesn't care."

"So, you and McClain have a nice chat?" she asked.

"Don't ask him things like that unless you want to hear the answer, Daze."

Shit, you're right. She looked at Vince with an apologetic gaze.

"Um, you know what, Vince? Totally not my place to ask."

"No, I actually wanted to talk to you about—"

"Forget it. That's between you and the doc," she cut him off. "Listen, I've gotta get moving. Got a few things to do before I'm on the clock. I'll see you later."

She turned to walk away.

"Dinner?" he called after her.

Daisy stopped and turned. "Well..."

"It's just a meal, Daze. Throw the guy a bone," Sarah nudged.

She considered it a moment. "Okay, save me a seat."

Vince smiled happily. "Cool. I'll see you this evening, then. Be careful out there."

"Me? Never," she said, laughing as she walked away.

Bob was hovering just above the surface near the large parts storage area just outside Hangar Three. Several oversize pieces of wreckage he had towed in lay on the dusty rocks behind him.

Looks like they had a productive run today.

Barry and Ash had been recruited to serve as a pair of cyborg grunts, standing on either side, helping guide the parts to a more permanent resting place among the other wrecked ships and components Donovan and Bob had accumulated over the years. While they still had to drift in the debris field for unexpected necessities from time to time, a lot of basics were there for the taking in their own little private wrecking yard.

Reggie was riding aboard the ship with Donovan, Daisy noted as she turned off all of her suit lights and exited the airlock into the dark shadows.

Looks like they're finally getting over that pilot rivalry, she was pleased to see.

She silenced her suit's outgoing comms and set them to receive only.

"Goddamn it, Donovan, I said starboard!" Reggie's irritated voice blared over the air.

Guess I was wrong, she noted with a chuckle as she stealthily moved along. It was arduous work, avoiding the most direct route, forced to hug the darker shadows of the large rocks and bits of debris so as not to be seen by the eagle-eyed cyborgs nearby. Fortunately, even for mechanicals such as them, her suit was grayed out enough in the darkness that they wouldn't see her.

Bob, on the other hand, had more than enough in his sensor array to pick up Daisy as she made her way to her retreat, but as they were literally right outside Dark Side's hangars, she was betting he wouldn't have the scanners running. Why would he? This was home.

Sure enough, she passed by without notice. Still, it was something to consider for future excursions.

I'm going to have to see about building that Faraday shielding into an EVA suit.

"Or you could just wait until they aren't all standing around out here before heading over," Sarah noted.

You really think I'd sit around waiting?

"No, of course not. But it's still a valid point."

I suppose so, but this way I can just think of it as a more advanced form of training. Stealth maneuvering to avoid prying eyes.

"You are still totally not a ninja, Daze."

So you keep saying, but the boys haven't seen me, have they? See? She turned the comms receiver back on.

"Oh, give it a rest, Reggie!" Donovan's exasperated voice said in her helmet. "Seriously, I've been doing this for years before you got here."

"Doing it *wrong* for years."

"Gentlemen, please," Bob interrupted. "We have two crewmembers on the surface and a few thousand tons of salvage that needs parking. Might you both save this discussion for a later date?"

Daisy lowered the comms volume. No need to hear the ongoing bickering if she didn't have to.

Just one hundred meters to go until they were safely around the outcropping that would shield them from view entirely. Daisy's footing was sound despite the reduced visibility as she clung to the darker shadows.

"I guess all of Fatima's awareness training is paying off," she mused. "That, or it's just the repetition of all these hours traipsing around the base."

"Why not both?" Sarah asked.

Safely inside the secret fabrication hangar, Daisy unsealed her helmet and took in a deep breath of the fresh air.

"You're back!" the large cube on the work table said cheerfully.

"Yep, I'm back. Ya miss me?"

"I did! Can we watch another movie today?"

"Well, I don't know if I'll have time today, kiddo. They've got me doing a lot of things, and I really need to finish working on this fabricator and assembly unit. It should be functional, but I just can't seem to find what's gumming up the works."

"I can look at it for you, if you want."

"Maybe later. I still need to see if I can wirelessly link you to one of the service mechs so you can move around a bit. They're not really designed for it, but I think I've got a work-around figured out. Then you'll have more eyes and arms and stuff to keep you occupied."

The service mechanoids were large, six-legged construction machines parked along the far wall. Aside from their massive load-bearing capacity, they also had a half-dozen extendable arms possessing an assortment of grasping components as well as interchangeable tools. Minus a human operator, they all sat quietly in their charging bays, silently waiting to be called to work.

"Daisy?"

"Yeah?"

"Why can't I meet everyone else?" the young AI asked.

"It's... complicated."

"I'm a supercomputer, Daisy. I think I can handle complicated," it replied.

Daisy laughed. The machine was really coming into its own and had developed quite the personality over its first week of life.

"Just trust me, okay? For now, anyway, I think it would be better if we didn't have everyone poking around in here. If they realize there's new equipment—a new AI, for that matter—who knows what might happen to this place."

"But I want to meet them."

"Soon, okay? But how do I even introduce you? Have you thought about what we talked about?"

"Yes, but what do *you* think?"

"It's not up to me. You're your own being, so it's only right that you should be the one to pick your name and gender."

"What do *you* think I should be?"

"Whatever feels right to you. Other AIs are told what to be. Made to do what others want them to," Daisy's tone evidenced her distaste of that. "You're who you are naturally. Who you want to be. You're unlike any AI that has come before you." She paused, but the machine stayed contemplatively silent. "Have you been keeping up with your meditation, like I taught you?"

"Yes."

"And in that time, have you reflected on what you believe you are? What feels like the right fit for you?"

"It *all* kind of fits, Daisy."

"Well, in a way, that's all right too. But for now, let's at least have a name. You've had long enough to think about it, and the Earth records I loaded up for you last week had millions of name variants spanning thousands of cultures, so what'll it be?"

Despite its massive processing capabilities, the young AI hesitated.

"It's still just a kid, Daze. One day it might be able to single-

handedly command a fleet of battleships or run an entire city, but I think it could use a bit of hand-holding for just a little bit longer."

Yeah, I suppose you're right.

"I'll tell you what, buddy," Daisy said. "Why don't you narrow it down to your top five while I eat my lunch and run some diagnostics, okay? When I'm done, I can help you make a decision if you're still undecided."

"Okay."

"Excellent. And if you're really good today, I think I just might be able to get you dialed in to one of those mechanoids. Would you like that?"

"Oh, yes!" the AI chirped with excitement.

"All right, then. You think on it, and we'll talk about it when I'm done."

Daisy picked up her tool pack and walked over to the massive ship resting on its construction stands.

"Hello, gorgeous," she said, running her hand across a smooth, black panel.

In the short time she'd spent with the craft, Daisy had become more and more impressed by the groundbreaking design concepts its designers had come up with.

Nearly every day, Daisy would sit in the secret facility and reassemble more of Fatima's increasingly difficult combinations of parts to create new and better ships as part of her training, but those were just 3D models. The task was just an intricate game.

But this? The stealth ship included technology even her hacked neuro-stim hadn't known about, and not instinctively knowing how something worked for a change was a strange feeling.

She ate her lunch while walking through the incomplete ship's framework. It was making more sense, thanks to an incredibly dense technical specifications and schematics file she'd discovered and decrypted the day before, but it would take her weeks, or possibly even months to take it all in. For now, she simply reveled in the beauty of it.

"Come on, hotshot, get to work. The boys are probably almost done out there. Clock's ticking."

Reluctantly, Daisy climbed down out of the vessel's open hull and walked over to the massive racks of processors.

"Okay, my darlings, what secrets do you have for me today?"

Daisy found what she was looking for tucked away in the firewalled fabricator operating system. It seemed pointless to keep all the different functions partitioned like that now that she was the only one alive who knew about them, so in short order, Daisy disabled all of the firewalls and electronic blocks between them, granting her full access to every system in the entire facility from any terminal.

"Awww yeah. Now that's what I'm talking about." She smiled to herself as she typed in the commands to activate the nearest mechanoid.

The six-legged machine lurched to its feet.

"Okay, so this should be the front two arms," she said, feathering the controls.

The machine's arms moved in unison, following her every command.

"Perfect."

Daisy powered it down and set to work jury-rigging a wireless network that would allow the clever box across the facility to link up to the mech's metal body. It was going to require a full reboot of over a half-dozen systems when she had completed what she believed was the code string that would do the trick.

It would work, she was pretty sure, but since the mechs were all tied in to each other as well as several of the machine shop systems, each one would have to run the entire cycle before the final connection would form a link. All she had to do now was give them all time to load, network, reboot, and connect.

Unfortunately, with only a half hour before she had to head back to meet with Fatima for her afternoon drills, she didn't have time to stick around for the entire multi-hour cycle.

"Hey!" she called out, walking up to the young AI. "So, what have you decided? You have a top five for me to help you with?"

"Yes," the AI replied. "I thought about what you said about being who I wanted to be. About growing up. I have made a choice. You were right, Daisy, it was something I needed to do myself."

The genderless voice was gone, replaced with a confident woman's voice that sounded almost reminiscent of Sarah, though she—as the AI had selected as her gender—had never met her.

"A woman, I see." Daisy smiled. "Welcome to the sisterhood, my friend. So what have you decided? What is your name?"

"I rather liked the stories from Earth's mythologies. Especially the ones where magic would let ordinary people fly. So, I have chosen the name Freya."

"Ooh, Odin's wife. Powerful woman. Good name," Daisy said.

"Yes, I thought so," Freya replied. "She was known to have a cloak that allowed all who wore it to transform into a bird. I like that story, Daisy. The idea of flying. It gets so boring cooped up in here."

"But you have terabyte upon terabyte of stuff to read."

"Already read it."

"Well, what about the movies? We still haven't watched those."

Freya hesitated. "Um... I kind of watched them all the other night."

"*All* of them? And hang on, those weren't in your systems."

"I know," Freya replied, a bit ashamed.

"What did you do?" Daisy scolded.

Freya hesitated a moment.

"Freya?"

"You didn't come to watch a movie with me that night, and I was kind of anxious, and——"

"You know I can't always make it out here every night."

"I know. But I was bored, and I was looking forward to watching a movie, and the short-range wireless was able to reach that far, and——"

"And you bypassed triple-locked, multi-factor encryption via a tiny access point across the surface of the moon and streamed terabytes of data to yourself?"

"Well, I didn't exactly stream terabytes. I wrote a new compression algorithm and uploaded it to the server so it wouldn't take so long."

"Is that even possible?"

I didn't think so. Good lord, what else can she do? Daisy found herself smiling proudly.

"I'm not angry, Freya. That was some very creative thinking. You should always think outside the box."

"But I am a box."

Daisy winced.

"Sorry, figure of speech. I wasn't thinking. But listen, I'll always support you looking at things differently than anyone else. It keeps your mind limber. Lets you see missed solutions that might be staring other people right in the face."

An idea dawned on her.

"Hang on, I've got something for you to look at. It's a lot of data that I want you to see if you can interpret and simplify for me. It's kind of like a game. Do you think you can do that?"

"Oh, yes!" Freya sounded thrilled to have a new game to play.

"All right. I'm giving you access to everything I know so far about the tech they were working on in this place. It's a huge amount of information. What I want you to do is to find a way to condense it into something a non-AI mind can understand in less than a year of non-stop reading. Sound good?"

"This will be fun!" Freya chirped like a giddy teen. "I can't wait!"

"Well, it can wait just a minute longer, because I have something else for you."

"You do? What is it?" the young AI asked, giddy with excitement.

"Hang on just a minute and I'll show you," Daisy said as she walked to the mech control system.

See that, Daze? One minute she's Freya, Odin's powerful wife, ruler of Asgard, and the next she's a bouncy kid. She's maturing to be as much of an unstable freak as you are.

You too, Sis. Runs in the family.

Sarah and Daisy shared a laugh over that one, while Daisy entered a command into the churning processor's task queue.

"Okay, Freya, it's going to take a little while to load, so I won't be here when it does, but I want you to promise me you won't go breaking anything."

"Breaking anything? But how can I?"

Daisy smiled. "Because, when that system finishes cycling through all the reboots and updates, you're going to have wireless control of that mech body over there."

If a disembodied mind could squeal with delight, that would most accurately describe the sound that emanated from Freya's speakers.

"Oh, Daisy! Thank you! Thank you!"

"It's important for friends to look out for each other, and I want you to be happy," she said, beaming at Freya's excitement. "Now you have fun with it. I've got to get back to the base before they miss me. I know the captain wanted to revisit my notes on Earth."

Freya's voice grew serious. "You're not going back to Earth and leaving me alone, are you?"

"No way. It's dangerous, and there's no reason for me to go

back. I've already been, and let me tell you, it's not like what you've been reading in your files anymore."

"It isn't?"

"No, it isn't." Daisy typed a few strokes into the terminal, allowing another stream of encrypted data to be accessed by her young friend. "I've just patched you in to the updated history of Earth, including the invasion and attack here on Dark Side. Everything from the war and subsequent attacks, their warp ships and fighters, even the comms they intercepted over the years. This way you'll understand it all, and maybe understand why I want to keep you safe. But I want you to read it slowly. Learn to savor things and not rush them, okay?"

"Okay, I'll try."

"Good girl."

"So you're not leaving me and going back."

"Not a chance. It would take a team of crack commandos to drag me back there."

"Good." Freya hesitated. "But it would be exciting, wouldn't it?"

"Yes, I suppose it would be exciting, only not in a good way," Daisy replied. "Anyway, kiddo, I have to get going. Enjoy your reading, and have fun playing with the new mech body. We can fine-tune things when I get back."

Daisy put her helmet on and stepped out through the airlock to start her long walk back. The moon rocks crunched silently beneath her thick boots as she left the secret base behind her.

"You know you're going to have to tell the others about this place one of these days, right? There are only so many times you can fudge your training timetable and sneak EVAs before someone finally notices."

"I know. I just hoped to maybe get a better fix on things beforehand, ya know?"

"Yeah, I know."

"And I also still feel kind of reluctant to throw that poor girl into the fire with the other AIs. Sure, she's a massively powerful computer, but what if the others gang up and bully her?"

"She's a sweet kid, Daze, but I'm pretty sure she'll be able to handle herself." Her sister's ghostly laughter echoed in her head.

"What's so funny?"

"Nothing. I was just thinking about you and Freya. You never much cared for kids, and hell, you straight-up dislike AIs."

"Yeah, well this one's mine. She's different than the others. She's special."

The laughter only grew louder.

"Oh, listen to you. Such a mom thing to say. Classic!"

"Shut up," Daisy grumbled with a little chuckle as she crossed the rocky field back to the distant airlock.

CHAPTER SEVENTEEN

Vince refilled his glass of lemon water and sat back at the table with Daisy. She'd said she would eat with him, and she was nothing if not a woman of her word.

The conversation had actually flowed rather easily. She didn't know if it was something subtly shifting in her interactions with him, or if maybe she'd blown off enough steam and relaxed her brain after all the shenanigans with Freya.

Amazing how that kid figures things out, she found herself marveling.

"So, I was saying, maybe we could catch a movie later if you're game. I can even sit on the chair, if that makes you more comfortable," Vince said.

Daisy chewed her pasta slowly as she considered the offer.

What the hell. It's been a good day.

"Okay, you're on. But I get to choose the movie."

"All right, you're the boss," he joked. "Hey, did you hear about Donovan's last scanning run?"

"No, what's up?"

"Bob was trying a different wavelength descrambler, using a low-tech radio receiver, then cycling it back through the filters."

"So, basically my idea."

"Basically. Anyway, he decided to give it a shot, and when he passed over California, he heard something."

"Something, as in more Chithiid comms?"

"Something as in what sounded like one of the old Earth backup broadcast signals," he said, visibly excited. "It was just for a second. Sid and the other AIs are analyzing it now. But think of it, Daisy, if it really was a new broadcast and not just some automated beacon, that would confirm what you said about at least one city AI being functional."

"Because those systems were only controlled on a city level, and if they were cut off before the infection spread, they could have remained uncompromised."

"Precisely. If Sid can trace the general region, we should have a pretty good idea if it was the LA system you encountered, or if maybe it was one of the other cities in that region."

"Well, I wish you luck," she said, then went back to her meal.

"I know you have to be at least a little bit curious, Daze. This is the kind of stuff you used to live for," Vince said, egging her on.

"Yeah, well, that was before my planet turned out to be some dystopian alien scrapyard." She took a big swig from her electrolyte replacement drink. "Speaking of which, that gives me an idea for an appropriate movie for the evening."

"Ooh, spill."

"Nope, it'll be a surprise, but I'm sure you'll like it."

"I'll hold you to that."

"I'm trembling in my boots," she said, flashing an amused grin.

I shouldn't say anything, but—

Then don't.

"But you guys seem to be hitting a good stride again."

Dream on, Sis. Dream on.

The rest of the meal consisted of excellent food and equally excellent banter, and by the time the two reached Daisy's quarters, the ice had been broken considerably.

"Okay, you don't have to sit on the chair," Daisy said. "But no funny stuff!"

"Affirmative. Ceasing to be funny," Vince joked as he flopped down beside her. "So, come on, what's the movie?"

Daisy scrolled through her inventory and selected her feature presentation.

"I present to you, an old Earth classic, *Blade Runner*."

"Which one?"

"The first one. And you've seen it already?"

"Daze, it's a classic."

"Figures you'd already have seen the movie about the artificial people," she sighed. "Fine, I'll choose another one."

"No, I like this movie. Let's watch it."

"You sure?"

"Yeah, it's beautifully filmed, and the whole noir feel to it holds up, even today."

"My, my, Mr. Film Critic. Okay then. *Blade Runner* it is."

The movie was halfway over, and Daisy was comfortably leaning against Vince out of habit, when the ship-wide comms keyed on.

"This is Commander Mrazich. I'm sorry to interrupt your downtime, but there's been a development. I'd like to have all crew come to the mess hall in ten minutes. To be clear, this is not a base emergency. Your presence, however, is required. Thank you, and see you in ten."

Daisy slid from her comfortable repose to her feet.

"Wonder what that's all about."

"Don't know. Guess we'll find out in a few minutes," he said, rising and standing next to her.

She could feel his heat from the proximity, and for the briefest of moments, the memory of that warmth pressed against her flashed back into her memories, bringing a wistful smile to her lips.

Daisy turned to head to the door and bumped right into his chest.

"Sorry, I—"

He pulled her close and planted a kiss firmly on her lips. For a split second the rush of pleasure and endorphins threatened to overwhelm Daisy's stubbornness, but soon enough, her brain quickly overcame instinct and she pushed him away.

"What the hell do you think you're doing, Vince?" she said, opening the door and storming into the hallway.

"Come on, Daisy. I feel it, and I know you feel it too. We both know it's still there. Why do you keep fighting your feelings?"

"There are no feelings."

"Bullshit. We're good together. I mean *really* good. You can't deny it. That would have been quite a feat even when there was a world of people to choose from, but it's even more impressive now that the only humans anywhere near Earth are a dozen people up on the moon, and you and I still clicked."

Daisy walked faster down the corridor, hoping if she could just reach the mess hall and other people, Vince would let it go.

"Not happening, Vince. You're a nice guy, but I've told you over and over, I'm not getting involved with a mechanical man."

"And I've told you over and over, I'm not one."

"Your body scans show otherwise."

"Those same scans show that while I have some inorganic additions, I'm still a man. I have a heart, Daisy, and as much as it pains me, it still belongs to you."

"Wow, laying it on a bit thick there, aren't you?" she snarked at him. "Let me make this clear, since you can't seem to accept the reality of this situation. There is no *us*. We are not a thing. Whatever may have been there was based on lies, and there's nothing you can do to change the way I feel. You are a friend. Nothing more. Now either let it go, or stay away from me."

Vince walked silently beside her, an angry vein pulsing in his temple.

"That's really how you feel?"

"Yes! For fuck's sake! Please stop being such a pain and just accept that."

He swallowed hard, fighting to keep his eyes dry.

"As you wish," he replied to her back as she paced off ahead of him, but his words did not mean what she thought they did.

"Okay, is that everyone?" Commander Mrazich said as he scanned the dozen people sitting together in the vast room designed for so many more. "Good to see you all. Sid, I'd like you to take point on this, if you would."

"Certainly, Commander," the disembodied voice said. "As you all have known for many months now, when Ms. Swarthmore was on Earth's surface in the city of Los Angeles, she came across not only small work crews of Chithiid scavengers, but also a fully operational lower-tier artificial intelligence calling itself Habby. This AI, though rather eccentric after centuries with only his cyborg companions to keep him company, appeared to be uninfected by the AI virus that destroyed so many of our brothers and sisters."

"Wait, he's clean?" Daisy asked.

"Had he been infected, he would have either melted down or devolved into a babbling mess. This is where his design as a shopping facility assistant AI would have been apparent. Only AIs of the highest order could hope to survive the infection with any semblance of functionality, but if they did, the damage sustained in the process resulted in what could only be likened to computer madness. We know the city-sized AIs managed to sever comms links before the virus could infect them, and for years their auto-defenses kept the aliens in check, denying them a foothold. As such, the Chithiid changed their plans and began the process of mining and dismantling only disabled cities, and areas not covered by the defenses."

I wonder if Freya is listening to this, Daisy wondered. *Wouldn't surprise me if she figured out how to tap into Dark Side's comms by now.*

"Up to this point, we have not known the status of any of the major AI systems on the planet, and it has been this way for as long as I have been functional," Sid continued. "We have scanned and scanned, and early attempts at reaching active systems on the planet were made to no avail. We even landed ships and engaged the Chithiid, but contact with the AIs or even verification of their continued existence has been unobtainable. To make a bad moon base joke, we have been in the dark."

"Oh, man," Omar groaned. "That was bad, Sid."

"Thank you, Omar. That was my intention." It was the first time Daisy had ever heard the powerful AI make an attempt at levity.

I would have thought that a sense of humor was against his programming.

"But as you've recently learned, AIs can be quite surprising, right Mom?"

"Stop calling me that," Daisy accidentally grumbled out loud.

"Yes, Daisy? Did you have something to add?" Sid asked.

"Uh, no, I mean, I guess, why don't we just find a new planet? I know you all keep saying it would be near impossible, or the Chithiid would find it, but there's a dozen people here. I get that you need to have a goal to build morale and whatnot, but this whole 'reclaim Earth' thing seems like a lost cause."

"It's not a lost cause," Vince said, rising to his feet with an angry flush to his face. "It's our home, and we are going to do whatever is necessary to take it back."

"Come on, Vince. You know it's not really our home. Never was. Not for any of us. We were all grown in fucking test tubes and fed a lie. And on top of that, you're not even a real boy, no matter what the AI Geppetto in your head tells you."

Vince's face turned an even deeper shade of red, but he somehow calmed himself and sat quietly back down. His glare at Daisy spoke louder than any yelling he might have been tempted to do.

"What in the actual fuck, Daisy? That was not cool."

He needs to face reality.

"Maybe so, but that doesn't give you carte blanche to launch personal attacks at the guy. He had your back for the better part of a year. No matter what. Even after what you did to him. I'm sorry, but that was fucked up."

Your opinion has been noted, Sarah.

Fatima quietly watched the entire exchange with a steady gaze.

"Sid, may I?"

"Please, Fatima. It would be my pleasure."

She rose to her feet and spoke to the whole assembled group.

"We all know the reality of the situation on Earth, and thanks to the hard work of the AIs who brought our very species back from the brink of extinction, we have a chance to make a difference. Before you, Daisy," she said, fixing her gaze on her troubling pupil, "we were operating on only the tiniest sliver of hope. But now we know at least one of the major cities is still alive. The defenses are not just automated and mindless. You gave us real proof, Daisy. A reason to hope, and that is something we hadn't had in a long, long time."

"One city?" Daisy replied. "That's your big hope? One city? You didn't see those things. What they could do. They have four arms and are far stronger than we are. You all keep telling me they track inorganics on the surface, so really, what hope could you possibly have had?"

"Are you done, Swarthmore?" Captain Harkaway growled.

She nodded.

"Good. Now shut up and listen. Sid and Mal have gone over the transmission Donovan brought back earlier today. The signal was genuine—an outdated radio wave-based technology that was linked to the oldest of emergency systems. We never would have thought to look for it, let alone have been able to hear it if not for some fresh and radical thinking. The receiver? It was based off of your ideas, Daisy. We wouldn't have even had this confirmation without you, whether you like the idea or not."

"What we hope to accomplish," Commander Mrazich added, "is to access the underground pressurized tube system. Even if it isn't functional, from what we observed during our retrieval op, the Chithiid scans don't penetrate subterranean, so any personnel mods will not be detected from the surface."

"Just one problem. Apart from me, everyone is sporting inorganic mods, and they'd almost certainly be sensed and picked off long before they could even make it underground."

"You're absolutely right, Daisy," Reggie said. "Fortunately, thanks to you yet again, we have a way around that."

He reached into a crate pulled up near his table and removed a heavily modified version of Daisy's Faraday suit, originally designed to protect the wearer in the confines of the unprotected Narrows of the *Váli*'s crawlspaces. The amount of shielding on it had been increased, and Daisy realized there was actually a real possibility it would block any scans and make the wearer nearly invisible to the Chithiid.

"My suit. You modified the design."

"Yep. Me and Gus and Chu got together and spent a few weeks working on taking your design up a notch. What do you think?" Reggie asked.

"I have to admit, it may be ugly, but it looks like a quality build," she reluctantly agreed. "It won't withstand a direct scan up close. I hope you know that. But for your purposes, it could work."

"And we also made this," Chu said, swinging a small, but heavy, ruggedized comms unit onto the table. "Again, based off of your design. I even set up a small pingback array of salvaged satellites to bounce the signal from far beyond the moon––with the delay to further mask our locations, as you suggested. I had Bob place them days ago."

Mrazich looked at Daisy. "So, you see, Swarthmore, all we need to do now is get this unit hooked up to the AI that's hiding in Los Angeles, and we'll have first contact between Dark Side and Earth since the original attack."

"Yes, and for once, we'll have direct intel from the surface itself. We'll no longer be flying blind," Shelly added. "Once we know their weaknesses—Bam! Payback."

"Payback?" Daisy said sarcastically. "With what weapons? Anything you carry will show up on scans, and those suits don't look like they're roomy enough to store your extra gear inside."

"Perhaps you'll find these interesting," Fatima said, laying a long case on the table. "Mal and I have been working on multiple design concepts since she landed here. Her fabrication facilities are second to none, and she managed to produce these," she said, opening the case.

A small selection of bladed weapons occupied one end, while the far end held two pair of ceramic pistols.

"The machetes and knives are ceramic based and should not show on scans. The pistols have a composite return spring but are otherwise entirely ceramic as well. While they are not combat hardened for lengthy use, they will provide a brief element of surprise and firepower," Fatima said.

"But the ammunition?"

"Ceramic bullets, as well as casing. The inorganic explosive used for combustion is the one thing that might show on scans. However, until a round is fired, I'm fairly confident these will evade detection, at least from a distance."

Finn looked at the knives longingly.

"Go on, Finn," Fatima laughed. "You can pick them up."

Grinning like a schoolboy, he did just that, feeling the balance of the knives in his hands as he passed them rapidly from left to right and back again.

"I'll hand it to you, Fatima, these are elegantly designed," Daisy conceded.

"Thank you, Daisy. From one with an eye for detail such as yours, that's a real compliment." She pulled a sheathed pair of long knives from a pouch. "These I made especially for you. They have a harness based on your measurements. The blades ride on your lower back, but with harness support so they aren't waistband or belt-supported, allowing you to move freely when you—"

"Whoa, whoa. Hang on a minute. Just because you have some cool new toys doesn't mean I'm suddenly jumping on board with your plan. You need an alternate idea."

"We had one," Harkaway said. "Until she was shot out into space without the comfort of a space suit."

"Leave Sarah out of this," Daisy snarled.

"Daisy, Sarah was always a backup plan. A second option. Not as good as you, but promising."

"Watch it, that's my sister you're talking about."

"I meant no offense, Swarthmore, but it was a simple fact. Sarah didn't progress as quickly as you did. Despite that, we'd have been happy to have her run this op instead, but that's just not an option anymore."

Daisy glared at the captain and others staring at her.

They all think I'm going to give in and do their stupid mission and save the day.

"You all are living a pipe dream. Fuck this, I'm out of here." Daisy got to her feet and stormed out the door.

Vince and the others let her go.

CHAPTER EIGHTEEN

It was late that night, and Vince didn't join Daisy in her room for the rest of *Blade Runner*, though she really didn't expect him to. Nevertheless, the slightest pang of guilt hit her as she finished the film on her own. Maybe it was because of the Decker/Rachel dynamic, or the human/replicant scenario. Whatever it was, she drifted off into a restless sleep and dreamed of electronic sheep.

The following morning Daisy dragged herself out of bed a half hour later than usual. She'd tossed and turned all night, and as a result felt like a truck had run over her. That would really be something, though. Trucks hadn't existed for hundreds of years.

She somehow managed to put her clothes on right-side out and found her way to the mess hall.

On her second cup of coffee, she noticed Vince wasn't partaking of his morning smoothie, for a change. He had attempted to get her to try them, but Daisy was an eggs and oatmeal kind of girl. Protein and carbs minus the blender, she always said. Fortunately, her ramped-up metabolism let her eat pretty much whatever she pleased, though nine times out of ten it was something pretty healthy, anyway.

She finished up the last of her hot liquid-consciousness and headed off to her morning sparring session with Tamara.

"What's with you, Daisy? You're slower than your usual weak-ass self today," Tamara teased her, landing a kick to the thigh, dropping her to the ground.

"Nothing. I'm fine," Daisy answered, momentarily achieving a burst of energy and launching a flurry of punches that drove Tamara backwards.

"Better," the steel-armed woman grunted, "but not good enough!" She then unleashed a few combinations of her own, catching Daisy off guard and again knocking her to the ground. "Come on, Daisy, I know you're better than this."

Daisy slowly climbed to her feet. "I don't know what's up with me today. I just feel sluggish."

Tamara started unwrapping her hands.

"Hey, what are you doing? We still have forty-five minutes left."

"Nope. Sparring when you're sore, sparring a bit tired, all of that is fine. But when your head's not in the game? That's when you get hurt. Get your thoughts straight and we'll try again this afternoon."

Daisy was secretly relieved, though she'd never admit it.

"All right. Thanks, Tamara. I'll see you later," she said as she walked out of the room and headed down the long corridor past the bio and comms labs.

I've got a little bit of time to kill before my pre-lunch training session with Fatima. Maybe I can squeak in a quick visit to—

The commotion buzzing in the comms center caught her attention as she passed the open door.

That's not normal, she realized as soon as she heard the panicked tone in Chu's voice.

"I repeat, Odysseus, this is Ithaca, do you copy?"

A long silence hung in the air, heavy like the foreboding mist over the morning sea.

"Nothing, sir," he finally said to the others anxiously standing by.

"What's going on, Daze?" Sarah asked, concern in her voice.

Beats the hell out of me.

Daisy altered her course and strode into the room. "Hey, guys, what's up?"

All eyes turned to her.

"Wow, they look kind of uncomfortable," Sarah commented. *"Shelly looks kinda pissed, actually,"* she added.

Captain Harkaway walked around the main comms console and stood before her. "Daisy, I..." He hesitated.

Harkaway uneasy? Not a good sign.

"Look," he continued, "he didn't want anyone to tell you, but—"

"Tell me what?" Daisy interrupted. *Oh, God, he's talking about Vince.* "What didn't he want you to tell me?"

The rest of the assembled team watched uneasily.

"After you, Vince is the least mechanically-enhanced among us. The least likely to show up on scans."

Daisy felt her stomach drop. "Tell me you didn't send him down there."

"I didn't send him, Daisy. Last night, out of the blue, Vince came to me and volunteered."

She felt her legs wobble slightly. Shit.

"I was going to set up another recon drift first, but he said we'd wasted enough time talking. It was time to either do it or not. I couldn't help but agree with him, so late last night he took one of the rebuilt drop ships and set down in Los Angeles under cover of darkness."

"His comms were working," Chu added. "He confirmed touchdown and was out running recon when we lost contact. He was supposed to return to the ship and check in almost five hours ago, but he's still overdue."

Daisy pushed Omar and Reggie aside to get a better look at

the landing chart on the screen. "Is that where he touched down? Punch in closer. What part of the—"

The city layout filled the screen, Vince's location overlaid on top of it.

Oh no.

"Daisy, that's not where the mission was supposed to land. That's headed right toward the Chithiid scrapping operation."

"Who sent him there? This isn't what was discussed. This isn't where I heard the AI."

"He lost thrust and was forced to alter his approach vector. It was land there or burn up in a fireball. I think this was the better choice," Harkaway said.

If the Chithiid found him, it might not have been, she quietly lamented.

The afternoon's meditation didn't make a dent in her aching psyche.

I drove him to this. I made him leave.

The massive guilt washing over her was almost incapacitating. Daisy had said some mean things in the past, but never had she expected him to take it so personally. To go on what she considered essentially a suicide mission.

Stupid, Daisy. Why did you treat him like that? she chided herself.

"Stop beating yourself up over it. What's done is done."

Not done. It's still going on, and it could get far worse.

Fatima watched Daisy working through her inner conflict, then launched another beanbag at her as she balanced atop a narrow beam on one foot. Daisy caught it with one hand, not even paying attention.

But why would he react like that? I mean it's not how he is.

"He feels that the Earth is his home, whether he's lived there or not," Sarah replied.

Two more beanbags flew at her at speed. Daisy turned and kicked one aside, while swatting the other one down effortlessly, as if it were no more than a fly.

Okay, he's a grown man and can do what he wants. I can't let that bother me.

"But it does."

Yeah, it does, she replied in her head. *If Vince dies, it's my fault.*

Three beanbags flew and were snatched from the air. Fatima then threw something else.

"Daisy, are you okay?" she asked.

Daisy regained her focus and stepped down from her perch.

"Yeah, why?"

"Look at your hands."

She looked, and only then realized that she had been in the zone, so preoccupied with Vince that she simply moved on instinct. A half dozen beanbags were nestled in her grip, along with one wicked-sharp ceramic blade. Fatima had made a judgment call and launched it at her pupil, and Daisy had not disappointed, snatching it from the air like it was nothing.

"Soft is strong, Daisy. Are you starting to believe?" Fatima asked with a knowing smile.

Her training session with Tamara followed, and while she was somewhat shocked at her reflexes during Fatima's session, she chalked it up to mostly luck rather than skill.

The first kick caught her in the side of the head.

"Pay attention!"

Daisy threw a spinning round kick, which Tamara easily blocked, but that was merely a fake for her real attack—a simple yet powerful straight to the body followed by a low leg kick, a hook, and a flying knee—all of which made contact to some degree, knocking Tamara to the floor.

What if they captured him and that's why he isn't replying,

Sarah? Or what if Habby and his cyborgs ventured to that part of town and dragged him back to their lair?

"Lair? Now that's a little melodramatic, even for you."

Fine, not lair, but something more ominous than 'clothing store.'

Tamara rushed her, throwing powerful elbow strikes and Muay Thai kicks. Daisy blocked them easily, shifting her balance and redirecting her aggressive opponent right into a nearby crate.

"So you do still care."

I don't want him dead, Sarah. So yeah, I guess I do still care in a way.

"Then what are you going to do about it?"

A flash of metal whizzed past her head as Tamara threw a blindingly fast sucker punch. Daisy casually evaded it, catching the arm as it passed and twisting, accessing its control panel and entering the attachment swap protocol.

Tamara's hand dropped off, clunking to the floor as the arm waited in standby mode for the new attachment to lock into place. Daisy, however, didn't wait, shifting her center of gravity, moving low and sliding her hip into Tamara's waist, then throwing her to the ground, spinning above her, locking her good arm in a firm arm-bar and wrist-lock.

Tamara struggled from the ground a few seconds before realizing she couldn't break free.

"I yield," she said reluctantly.

Daisy released her grip and let Tamara retrieve her hand, which she did, quickly locking it back into place.

"How did you know the override? I reprogrammed the whole system when we got here. You shouldn't have been able to do that. No one should."

Daisy ignored her, staring into space.

"Daisy, you hear me? Daisy? Are you okay? What's going on in there? What are you doing, Daisy?"

Finally, Daisy moved, turning to look her in the eye. "I'm going after him."

CHAPTER NINETEEN

For a woman with no intention of ever returning to Earth's surface again, Daisy certainly knew what she needed for her trip.

In less than an hour, she had rigged a new version of the modified radio signal transmitter. Similar to what Vince had taken, but far more robust, more portable, and sporting a quickly devised Faraday shielding housing that would keep the entire unit invisible to scans, even when transmitting. That was accomplished in part by a medium-range wireless relay to a tiny transmitting dish she invented from spare parts on the fly.

"Wait, go slower!" Chu begged. "At least give me a minute to make notes!"

"No time," she grunted, whipping from one device to the next, her hands flying as she locked the assembly into place.

"Okay, this should work on the same frequency as your model. It may need an additional power boost due to the size reduction, but I'll deal with that on the surface if I have to," she said. "Donovan, Reggie, how's the ship prep coming?" she asked over the comms.

"Just getting the parachute loaded, Daisy," Donovan replied. "Reggie's charging the compressed air system as we speak. There's enough fuel for one hard-burn terrestrial launch, but that'll have to be manually fired. We've severed the active computer systems as you requested, so she'll look like a hunk of debris to all but the most detailed scans. We're finishing up the last of it now. You should be green across the board in less than twenty."

"Good work. Keep at it, and strip out anything not entirely necessary. It's going to be a bumpy landing and I don't want any additional weight if I can avoid it." Daisy keyed off the comms.

Captain Harkaway stood off to the side of the pre-launch staging room watching her. Commander Mrazich walked in and joined him. Neither man, both leaders with decades of experience, said a word to her. They didn't have to. Daisy was on a roll, and besides, she wouldn't listen anyway.

"What do you think, Lars? She's stripped that thing pretty bare and will be going in hot," Mrazich said to his friend.

"Yeah, I know," Harkaway replied. "But she's found her groove. You and I both know better than to question her when she's like this. And did you see how easily she not only rebuilt a second transmitter, but also improved upon it on the fly? No, I think she's going to be just fine on her approach." He watched the anxious young woman scurrying around the facility as she prepped. "What happens once she lands, however, now *that's* an unknown."

Daisy was quickly making alterations to one of the new Faraday suits when Shelly and Omar hurried into the room, arms loaded with crates of salvaged components Daisy had asked for.

"We got what you wanted," Omar said, out of breath. "At least, I think we did. I'm not a much of a tech guy."

Daisy glanced at the boxes and nodded. "Yeah, looks good.

That should work fine." She finished her final addition to the suit, then shoved it in her flight bag.

"But you don't need that, Daisy," Shelly said. "You're organic."

"It's not for me," she replied. "If Vince was picked up and taken, then that means their scanning tech is stronger than anticipated and he'll need something more robust to shield him."

"We don't know that's what happened," Chu replied.

"No, we don't. But I'm not taking any chances." Daisy dumped the crates of components onto the workbench and began quickly assembling batteries to the necessary parts. The basics of the design were familiar—she'd made electromagnetic pulse weapons before—but in her present mental state, she may have upped the potency a little bit much. It wasn't a simple EMP grenade, as her prior designs had been, but, rather, a proper bomb.

Ash walked in, followed closely by Barry. The cyborg expressed the slightest hiccup of concern when he saw what she was working on. Of course, that would be only natural, as he'd felt the brunt of one such device when she disabled him with it while escaping the *Váli* all those months ago.

"Daisy, Barry and I have fabricated something we believe may be of use to you on the mission," Ash said, holding out a pocket-sized device.

"I'm not going on your stupid mission, Ash. I'm going to get Vince."

"Yes, of course. And to that end, we hope this will help you."

Daisy took the gadget from his hand and gave it a quick once-over. It was incredibly simple in design, a no-frills organic LED intensity display for proximity, she noted. Still, something was really off about it. Daisy felt the material more closely.

"Is this wood?" she asked in amazement. "There are no trees on the moon."

"Correct," Barry said. "But Ash and I utilized some of the indigenous materials information in the databases to adjust the organics fabricator for this project. Most of the non-shielded components are organic. It should be nearly invisible to any scans."

Daisy actually slowed in her work to study the device more closely. She carefully slid the back panel open and examined the internal components.

"This is genius," she said appreciatively. "Really creative thinking. Especially for cyborgs." She looked at the pair of mechanical men apologetically. "No offense."

"None taken," Barry replied. "You'll see that the energy source is an organic electrolyte fluid housed in a cellulose membrane. The electrolysis generated between the positive and negative poles is designed to build a slow charge—nothing that would attract attention—then, when it reaches capacity, it will activate the few non-organic scanning parts."

"So, it is not only mostly organic, but it also utilizes a random power cycle, further avoiding scrutiny. You guys did an impressive job, really, but I have to ask, what does it scan for?"

Ash stepped forward, a slight smile on his lips. "As you know, all organic life has its own unique energy signature. Near impossible to trace unless specific, genetic details are known. To obtain such details, however, one would have to possess in-depth knowledge of a particular genome all the way back to its creation."

"And Vincent was grown and nurtured en route to his mission," Barry added.

"Mal," Daisy realized. "The *Váli* still possesses all of our genetic details from day one."

"Precisely," Barry said. "Ash and I, with Mal's assistance, have designed this unit to pick up the normally imperceptible energy signature given off by Vincent. If you get close enough, the organic light-emitting diode will glow brighter. However, the energy source is, as you noted, rather random, so the power must be used sparingly."

Finn walked in, carrying a small tray of vacuum-sealed pouches.

"Made you something," he said. "Nutrient-dense, high in protein, and packing enough carbs to get you through the day. Just make sure to drink plenty of water with them or you might get a little plugged up," he said with a mischievous little grin.

"Thanks, Finn. I'll try to keep my pipes clear," Daisy replied, tucking them into her bag.

"Ten minutes and she'll be ready, Daisy," Donovan called over the comms.

"Thanks, Donovan. How's the extra shielding look?"

"It'll deflect most of the burn, like you said, but you'll still be coming in really hot. The landing chute is altitude-deployed as you specified, and we cut leads to everything else. No active computers but the bare necessities. Are you sure you don't want life support?"

"No, I'll use suit oxygen. The extra units stowed on board will be plenty for the trip, and if we do manage to launch back into the debris field, they should hopefully last us long enough for you to come pick us up."

That was the one concerning part of the plan. The tiny ship was a beater at best, and barely flyable, but it was the most likely to avoid scans on the way down. Unfortunately, that also meant there was simply no way to make it space-worthy in her limited launch window.

Donovan would pull her in tow, then give her a push toward re-entry. Her maneuvering thrusters would do the rest, adjusting her angle of descent until she hit the atmosphere. From then on it would be fly-by-wire, guiding the barely maneuverable craft down to her landing zone until the chute deployed.

The only safeties she left active were the speed/altitude-triggered emergency landing jets. She doubted they'd be needed, but they were the one 'just in case' piece of equipment Reggie had convinced her to leave aboard. They would only activate and fire for a few seconds if absolutely needed, and that would almost certainly not be enough to read on a scan. Besides, if they *did* activate, that meant she would have been dead otherwise, so why not risk it? His logic was undeniable.

"Okay, that's about it," Daisy declared, pulling on her flight gloves. "Help me load the rest of this stuff on the ship and I'm out of here," she said, throwing her flight bag over her shoulder.

"Just a minute, Daisy," Fatima said, pushing a long and narrow grow-enzyme and what appeared to be blood-filled tank into the room. "I have something I think you'll find useful for your mission."

"It's not my mission, Fatima. I'm just—"

"Yes, yes, you're going to get Vince. Whatever the impetus, I think you are going to want this."

"That's nasty, Fatima, and I don't need any new parts stitched on for—"

The older woman dipped her hand into the red liquid and pulled a long, bone-white sword out of the nutrient bath, the red running from its blade in rivulets, but also seeming to absorb into it. The shape was familiar to Daisy—a classic Japanese katana. Some of the historic records suggested that the ancient weapons could even cut through armor when wielded by skilled hands.

"Wait, that's not ceramic," Finn, lover of all things bladed, said. "What is that? Is that bone?" He was transfixed. "That's bloody amazing! Can I see it?"

"It's Daisy's," Fatima replied.

"Go on, Finn," Daisy said. "Knock yourself out."

He took the sword in his hand, gingerly touching the edge. A confused look crossed his face, and he grabbed the blade with his bare hand. "Fatima, what gives? This thing is dull as a stick!"

He handed it to Daisy. She whacked the dull blade against a

half-eaten sandwich Finn had left on the table. It merely dented the bread.

"Thanks for the thought, Fatima, but I think I can find a club pretty easily on the surface."

The silver-haired woman merely smiled. "Take your glove off, Daisy," she said. "Feel the grip."

Daisy didn't have time to waste playing with bone clubs, but Fatima had been a friend to her, and despite her rush, she didn't wish to be disrespectful when she had obviously gone to some trouble growing her a bone sword.

"Okay," Daisy said, pulling her gloves off, "but I don't see what difference that will make."

She noted the fine texture of the grip in her hands, and for a brief moment, almost felt a strange connection to it. The balance was perfect, as if it had been created just for her. Of course, it *had* been, so she supposed that was to be expected.

Odd. It almost feels warm. Probably from the nutrient blood bath she grew it in, Daisy mused.

"It's nice, Fatima, and I really appreciate you, um, *growing* this for me, but I've really got to get moving."

"Try it again," Fatima said with that tranquil grin she got when she knew something you didn't.

"Seriously, I've got to go, Fatima."

"Try it again, Daisy," she said, more firmly.

"Oh, for fuck's sake. Fine!"

Daisy swung the dull bone sword at the sandwich again, intending to squash it into a nasty mess. Instead, the sandwich, and the metal table beneath it, fell to the floor, neatly sliced in two.

Everyone in the room went silent.

"Um––" Daisy managed, staring at the wondrous thing in her hands.

"As I was saying," Fatima beamed, "I think you'll find that most useful on your quest."

"But it was dull," Finn blurted. "I felt the blade. You couldn't cut a piece of toast with it."

"That is true, Finnegan," Fatima said. "*You* could not. Daisy, however, can."

"I don't get it," Daisy said, marveling at the blade, studying its every facet.

It was Mal who enlightened them all.

"That went better than expected, wouldn't you agree, Fatima?"

"Yes, Mal. I think it far exceeded our design expectations."

Daisy reeled in her shock. "You mind telling me what exactly you two did? How was this dull and sharp at the same time?"

"It wasn't, Daisy," Mal replied. "It is a genetically-engineered, organic bone weapon, designed to be completely invisible to Chithiid scans. When the donor's genetic code is recognized by the sword, it reacts instantaneously, and the otherwise dull edge shifts on a molecular level into a sharp blade, the fineness of which is a rather remarkable hone tapering down to a single molecule. Used properly, Fatima and I hypothesized it could cut through most non-reinforced materials."

"Hang on. You said donor's genetic code. I'm no donor."

Fatima leveled her gaze on her. "No, Daisy, you are not. Not in a traditional sense, anyway. However, when you first arrived at Dark Side, we ran a series of tests on you, do you recall?"

"Yes, but—"

"And one of those involved taking a bone sample. Your reinforced skeletal matrix nearly broke the titanium sampling needle, if you recall."

She thought back to that day. It was true, her bones were supposedly many times stronger than normal, but that meant they had literally grown the weapon from a tiny piece of her.

"So you're saying this is grown from a piece of me? That it's alive?"

"Yes, Daisy. Alive and only sharp in your hands. It is an extra-reinforced matrix of your already super-strong bone. Wielded properly, it should cut through just about anything you're strong enough to swing it through—within reason." Fatima couldn't hide her satisfaction, and given what she and Mal had created, who could blame her?

"But bone isn't stronger than metal," Daisy said. "It should break."

"And it could, in theory, if you abuse it enough and don't feed it. Otherwise, if you take good care of it, every micro-fracture will quickly heal and make it even stronger than before."

"Feed it?"

"Yes. Disturbing as one of the sources of the genetic coding required may be, the result is a formidable weapon, but one that pulls nutrients from organic material."

"Why disturbing?"

Fatima hesitated. "You see, Mal and I spliced in specific features of the most virulent organism ever created when we grew this. The very plague that wiped out humanity and sucked their corpses dry until not even bones remained was our inspiration. What wiped out humanity, might just help you save it."

"You unleashed that nightmare in our base?" Captain Harkaway yelled, pulling his shirt over his nose and mouth.

"No, Captain, we did not. There is no plague here, and we destroyed the un-frozen sample utilized in the genetic modification process. What we do have, is a weapon that can now pull nutrients from living things as easily as you or I drink water. In a pinch, just about anything organic will work, but it really does prefer fresh blood."

"So, it's a vampire sword? What, am I supposed to let it feed on my victims or something?"

"That is so gross, Daze."

I know, right?

Fatima laughed heartily. "Oh, Daisy, it's an organic weapon, not some blood-sucking fiend. Just take good care of it, and it will remain sharp and healthy and take good care of you in return." She handed the sheath to her stunned student. "Now stop standing here yapping with an old woman. Get moving and go save Vince."

CHAPTER TWENTY

Daisy pushed the last of her supplies into the small craft and climbed into the cockpit.

Flight system is stable, chute and thrusters are primed, Daisy noted. *Okay. This is it. Time to go.*

She keyed the door system and sealed herself in. Donovan and Bob would pick her up momentarily and drag her to her launch point.

"Fatima," Mal quietly said over secure comms. "I have prepared the containers for relocation to Dark Side's facilities."

"Thank you, Mal," she replied. "We will move the subjects from your bio lab into the base after Daisy has launched."

"Very well," the AI answered. "I think that all went about as well as could be expected, don't you?"

"Yes, I do. Very well, indeed," Fatima said as she walked back toward the command center to join the others monitoring the launch.

The flight to the debris field was slow, as it always was when one had to essentially mimic drifting wreckage, and a good hour had passed by the time Daisy finally reached her launch point.

"Okay, Daisy. Ready when you are," Donovan said over their linked comms. "Just give the word."

She took a deep breath and double-checked her guidance settings. With the most minimal of electronics, there was always a window for Mr. Murphy to make an appearance. Daisy was not a fan of his law and hoped to avoid it at all costs.

"Let's do it," she replied.

Bob activated his thrusters and pushed her on her way, then released his tether. "Good luck, Daisy. Fly safe."

Fly safe, he says. I'm in a plummeting hunk of metal with mere jokes for wings, and he says fly safe.

"It's the thought that counts," Sarah chimed in. *"But Daisy?"*

Yeah?

"Try not to get us killed. I've died once already."

Her living sister laughed grimly as the atmosphere began buffeting the hull.

"Here we go."

For five minutes the ship bucked and jolted as the hull turned bright orange from the massive heat building as it dove through the atmosphere.

I bet I'm making a pretty light show for anyone watching from space. Good thing I timed the landing for daylight. Hopefully no one will notice down below.

With a sonic boom, the vessel finally burst into Earth's protective bubble and began its descent to the terra-firma below. Daisy glanced at the readouts.

On course.

She gently adjusted her angle of descent and settled in for the long glide to Los Angeles. From high above the continents, she observed the patches where the Chithiid had wreaked their strip-mining havoc on the cities below. Huge swaths not protected by automated defenses lay in ruin, disassembled and gutted as the alien invaders pried every resource from them until nothing remained.

A pocket of air jolted the ship into a disconcerting shimmy.

"Oops. Best get that sorted," Daisy grunted as she set to work putting the vessel on course again. "LA is coming up pretty fast. Better stay on my toes so I don't take out one of those towers."

"Yeah, that would be bad, Daze. Smashing into buildings? Hard for them to miss something like that."

"That, and I probably wouldn't survive the impact."

"That too," Sarah said with a grim little chuckle.

The ground was approaching fast. Too fast.

"What the hell?" Daisy swore as she reached for the emergency release, just as the chute finally deployed, but far too low. She looked out the window and realized the error. "Donovan set it for sea level, but this far inland the city is on a slight elevation. Fuck, I'm going to crash right into—"

The emergency thrusters burst to life, arresting her fall as the ground rushed up to meet her. They cut off seconds later, letting the craft drop the remaining distance. The ship hit hard, but remained intact as it slid to a halt.

"I am so thanking Reggie for convincing me to keep that on board if I make it back," she said as she scrambled out of the ship.

Daisy quickly pulled the chute and stashed it, then dragged the camo net she had hastily rigged up from the storage bin on the side of the craft. In less than three minutes, it was covered with the net and what neighboring debris was on hand. It was camouflaged as good as it could be, given the situation.

Just in case, however, Daisy took the backup communications device from its secure stowage and lugged it into a nearby building, hiding it carefully before returning to grab the rest of her supplies. If her ship happened to be found, at least the comms unit was safe.

She strapped the sword to her backpack and started off at a

careful jog in the direction of where Vince's ship should have landed.

Running in low-g on the surface of the moon was taxing and had kept her in shape, which she was grateful for, but it was nothing like running in full Earth gravity. Fortunately, her other training with Fatima and Tamara had kept her cardio capacity at its peak, and after ten minutes, she found herself settled into a comfortable rhythm. After a half hour, she reached the sector where Vince should have touched down.

"Okay, time to get eyes on it," she grumbled as she entered the stairwell of a tall tower. "Stupid stairs."

"At least it'll be a pretty view," Sarah joked.

"You're such a bitch."

"Aww, you love me."

Daisy reached the thirtieth floor and decided that was high enough. At least she hoped it was. Burning up all her energy this early wasn't exactly part of the plan, but then, how much of a plan had she really arrived with?

Get to LA. Find Vince. That was about the sum of it, she realized.

Nothing else to do now but carry on.

She pulled her binoculars from her bag and scanned the city from her perch while chewing one of Finn's energy bars. It only took her a minute to spot the downed ship a few dozen blocks away.

"Looks intact," she noted, stowing her binoculars and slinging her bag back over her shoulders before descending to the streets below.

She was cautious in her approach. With no idea what had happened, and in a Chithiid-active part of the region, she had to be. Thirty-five minutes later, as the sun was setting lower in the sky, Daisy finally reached the ship.

"Hull seems intact," she quietly noted. "Keep an eye out, Sis."

"Already on it," Sarah replied as she soaked in everything she could through Daisy's eyes.

The ship's door was open, but hadn't been forced. Daisy unsheathed her sword and silently slid inside.

Empty.

"Daisy, look. The comms uplink is still here. Seems to be fine."

"I see it. But there's no sign of Vince." She surveyed both the ship and the area around it. "No signs of a fight that I can see. You catch anything?"

"Nope. I think you're right. Whatever happened, it didn't happen here."

A single, faint bootprint marked the dust near a long-abandoned vehicle. She pointed her Vince-detector at it and the faintest of lights glowed on its face.

"Looks like he went that way," Daisy said. "Which means we go that way too."

CHAPTER TWENTY-ONE

Hours had crept by as Daisy tracked Vince's progress through the winding streets. Only the occasional bootprint in the dust and gentle nudge from her tracking device kept her on course.

Many months had passed since Daisy's first, last, and only visit to the city, but things hadn't changed much. The Chithiid were slowly and methodically advancing through the unprotected and unincorporated areas, dismantling them as they went, while the centrally defended hubs remained intact, though devoid of human life.

More than before, however, there were signs of recent fighting. Periodically, Daisy came upon bits of cyborgs freshly destroyed by alien weapons.

"Looks like one of Habby's crew," she noted, kicking the well-made fedora off the decapitated head of one of the metal men. "Why are they venturing up here, though? As long as they stay underground, they're pretty much left alone."

"With that crazy AI, who knows what their motivation is."

"True, but his center of operations was in a different part of the city. One of the safer ones, way across town. I mean, the cyborg survivors that flocked to him all seemed to stay relatively close by, so what gives with these?"

"Runaways, maybe?"

"Not likely. And running from what? They all seemed quite content there in their little cyborg hive. No, this feels like something different."

That prior visit had also been different in another way. Daisy had been on the run, escaping from the *Váli* and her crew, fleeing under the mistaken belief that there was an AI rebellion trying to overthrow humanity. Little did she know she was part of a much larger plan. Unfortunately, being woken before that bit of information could be fed to her through her neuro-stim meant that she woke up more than a little bit out of the loop.

After encountering Habby and his troop of fleshless cyborgs under the city, Daisy had made a hasty escape, trying desperately to get a message to the other humans she believed to be in other cities. People who could help her.

She had just reached the commandeered shuttle and was about to send her distress call when both cyborgs and Chithiid invaders encountered one another in the streets of L.A., with her stuck in the middle.

A fevered battle ensued, the cyborgs charging in close, using sharp pieces of debris as weapons, while the four-armed aliens fought with both pulse rifles as well as their odd power whips in unison. The strong beams projecting from their wrist-mounted devices may have had limited range, but in hand-to-hand combat, they were quite handy.

At the end of it all, a new squad of aliens swooped in on the site, leaving Daisy ducking for cover as they advanced on her position. It was only then that an unexpected savior appeared.

Vince, and a small team consisting of Reggie and Tamara, opened fire on the Chithiid, stopping their attack in its tracks. The aliens knew they were defeated, and, with no functioning communications, they opted to commit suicide, using a powerful bomb to take out not only themselves, but also the human combatants.

Daisy, quite unexpectedly, understood them, and when a lone human stood up and called out a surrender—in their own language, no less—they stopped in their tracks. That pause allowed Vincent and the others to cut them down.

It saved all their lives, but Daisy was nonetheless livid. She had offered a surrender, and they had honorably accepted it, a point she was making when Tamara, who she thought was dead, blasted her with a stun rifle before unceremoniously dragging her back to Dark Side Base, where the true nature of the world as she knew it was made clear.

There would be no margaritas on the beach, as she and Sarah had planned. There would be no festivities at all. Earth was a planet of the dead, and the home she had known had never truly existed.

And now she had come back. Something she'd sworn she would never do.

"Hey, what's that?" Sarah said.

Daisy had been lost in thought as she walked and had missed the faint sounds over the crunching of her boots on the ground.

"That sounds like talking?" she murmured. "Yeah. I'm sure of it. Someone's talking up there."

The voices were getting closer.

"Daisy," Sarah said. *"That's not English."*

"No, of course not. That's—" She froze in her tracks. Her mind had been translating so easily, she forgot to register alarm. "Shit!"

Daisy spun on her heel and took off running.

There was an underground access a few blocks that way, she realized as she ran for her life. For a split second, she allowed herself to look over her shoulder. A pair of Chithiid were rounding the corner.

No time!

She abruptly altered course, sprinting to the nearest building. Fortunately, the thick glass doors were unlocked. Heaving them open, she ran inside and ducked down behind the vacant security desk.

That was close, but I don't think they saw—

The glass façade smashed to pieces, thick safety glass tumbling to the ground in waves.

"Over there. Behind that desk!" she heard a Chithiid call out.

"Not going to catch me being a sitting duck." She grunted, jumping over the top just as the alien reached her. It was not expecting an offensive attack, especially from such a small being, and found itself caught with its weapon not aimed at her when she struck. A careless mistake it quickly regretted.

Daisy kicked and punched all the visible weak spots she could reach, then threw a powerful Muay Thai kick that connected with the wrist of the alien's arm that was holding the pulse rifle. The elongated weapon flew from its numb grasp and skittered across the floor.

"That little human kicked me!" it shouted out, lunging at Daisy with all four arms.

The lithe human evaded its grip, however, and rather than fleeing as it expected, she once again launched an attack, jumping up and delivering blow after blow to the Chithiid's face and torso.

"Get out of the way. I don't have a clean shot!" the other alien called out.

The stunned alien pushed her off of him and stumbled backward as its partner took aim. Daisy dove behind the desk as a plasma bolt flew past her.

That was close!

She looked around, searching for anything to use as a weapon.

"You have one behind you now, dumbass!"

The sword!

Daisy dropped the backpack and unsheathed her weapon, diving over the counter, swinging as she did. The Chithiid was taken by surprise, and the blade cleanly arced down on its wiry arm. Daisy heard the bones crack, but her sword had failed to even nick the skin.

"Gloves!" Sarah shouted in her head.

"Shit!" she growled, yanking them from her hands.

While the broken-armed alien cradled its damaged limb, its associate had recovered and launched itself at her. Daisy stepped aside, swinging the sword as she did. It was a low blow, literally, severing the tall creature's left leg from its body. It tumbled to the ground, scuttling on four arms to defend itself from the unexpectedly deadly human.

Daisy lunged as it tried to protect itself, her sword driving through three outstretched hands and burying itself deep in the creature's torso.

Must've hit something vital, she noted, as the alien didn't even have time to let out a cry in its last moments of life. The sword grew warmer in her hands, and she could have sworn it felt happy as it drank in the sticky blood.

More yelling. A team of Chithiid was coming to help.

Where did the other one—

A shadow towered above her. The injured alien had recovered its weapon and flanked her as she fought. It had her dead to rights and was taking aim at her head when weapons fire from across the courtyard erupted, the plasma bolts flying past both Daisy and the startled Chithiid, which was forced to turn its attention to the new attackers.

Daisy grabbed her backpack and raced around the corner. *No sense staying to fight when you're that outnumbered,* she reasoned, when, from behind a column in the building lobby, a figure stepped out to her side. Daisy spun, quickly dropping her bag and letting her hungry sword fly to its next target. Only at the last moment did her eyes go wide with shock.

"Shit!" she cried out, flipping the sword at the last possible second, striking with the flat side instead of the edge.

"Ow!" Vince cried out as the blade bounced harmlessly off his head. "Jeez, Daisy!"

A teenage boy ran up from the back door to the lobby area. "Vincent, we have to go! More are coming. Hurry!"

"Humans?" Daisy said, stunned. "Or was that a cyborg?" She had no idea what was going on.

"Come on!" Vince replied, grabbing her by the hand and pulling her with him. "I'll explain later. Now run!"

Daisy didn't need to be told twice.

They bolted for the rear doors, while a barrage of pulse blasts peppered the front of the building. The Chithiid jumped up and returned fire, but it suffered several fatal hits as its pulse rifle fire was answered. Its weapon dropped to the ground, its body following moments later.

That wouldn't stop the attack, however, as a half dozen armed aliens dropped from a small work ship as it swooped low over the street. They quickly fanned out in a flanking formation as they covered each other with suppressing fire.

The humans fired back as they fled, dodging the Chithiid as best they could, running and weaving between the abandoned vehicles on the street and the buildings nearby.

Daisy caught a glimpse of them as she followed Vince out the back door and down a side street that led them to a large plaza.

That's a lot of open space.

"This way!" the boy called out. "Hurry!"

Vince and Daisy quickly followed, hugging the periphery and staying to the shadows as best they could. No Chithiid were anywhere to be seen, but the firefight could be clearly heard nearby, and just because they weren't standing out in the open didn't mean aliens weren't lurking in wait for an easy target.

"There, past the large tree," the boy said.

Daisy saw his goal. A subterranean tube network access lift. There were no stairs.

"How do we know that thing has power?" she asked. "We should find a staircase."

"It has power," the teen said. "Alma makes sure this one is always working."

"Alma?" Daisy asked.

"Long story," Vince said. "Come on, let's go!"

Again with the running, she thought, but at least there was a definitive goal in sight. The trio sprinted across the one open space they couldn't avoid as fast as they could. Daisy felt an itchy tension between her shoulder blades as she waited for a pulse blast to strike her down. Fortunately for her, one never came.

The boy pushed the call button, and the faintest of vibrations could be felt in the ground as the lift ascended to fetch them.

"Come on, come on," she muttered impatiently. "We're sitting ducks out here, Vince."

"I know, but it'll only be a minute longer. Hang in there, Daze, we're almost in the clear."

"Oh, you did not just say that."

"What?"

"Tempting fate, man. Not cool."

Vince couldn't help but smile. "Nice to see you too."

CHAPTER TWENTY-TWO

Daisy was proud of herself for not impaling the poor fellow who stood in the lift when the doors unexpectedly opened silently behind them.

"Come on, you two," the boy urged.

Ten seconds later, safe inside the metal shell, they began their descent into the belly of the city. Daisy only hoped whatever surprises awaited her there were more pleasant than the four-armed ones that had greeted her above.

They soon arrived at the lower platform of what was once a busy hub in the sprawling transit tube network. A pair of scruffy older men were waiting, seated on a crate. At their feet, a woman lay on a makeshift sled. Her unseeing eyes didn't betray her non-living status nearly as readily as the gaping hole in her chest did.

"Damn monsters got Evie," the older of the two said. "Shot her right through her back."

"Where are the others?" the boy asked.

"Coming, I reckon," the other man answered. "We scattered when the second wave came. Most took to the streets, but a few managed to reach the other access shafts. I figure we give them until morning. If they haven't reached us by then, they're not coming back. Not never."

"That's a double negative. I wonder if he—"

Not now, Sarah.

The older man turned to Vince and Daisy.

"Who's this one?" he asked, sizing up Daisy head to toe.

"She's one of my people," Vince answered. "The ones I told you about. She's here to help."

"Looked more like she was the one needing help," the boy said with a dismissive snicker as he sat on the dusty tile floor.

Why, you little shit.

Daisy got a better look at the unlikely heroes seated before her. Pale, somewhat small in stature. They seemed as if they had grown up a bit malnourished and lacking in adequate vitamin D.

Of course. They live underground, so no sunlight, she realized. *I wonder if they're all this vitamin D-deficient.*

Looking at the faces of the two men, the boy, and the dead woman, Daisy noticed something else. A certain similarity in their faces.

"Vince, can we talk a minute?"

"Sure. Excuse us, fellas," he said, leading her a little way away from the others.

"Okay," she said when they were out of earshot. "What the hell is going on here? Those are actual humans, Vince. Not cyborgs. Proper humans. They were supposed to have all been wiped out."

"I know, but you know there were a few genetic variants that were immune to the plague."

"Yes, but it took a massive AI operation hundreds of years to regrow them."

"Not here."

Daisy looked at him a long moment, trying to decide whether or not he was pulling her leg.

"I'm not kidding, Daisy. The people you see here are the direct descendants of a pair of survivors."

"But how? And why do they all look like that?"

"Ah, yes. Don't bring up their similarities, it only opens up a can of worms."

"Why's that?"

"Because they are all related. The only survivors in the entire city after the attack were two very young children," Vince informed her. "Twins. A little boy, and a little girl."

"Brother and sister," Daisy said softly.

"Yep. They were too young to know about the birds and bees. Hell, they were barely four years old, left on their own when their parents died in front of them, wandering the tube system alone when the AI that oversees this section of the transit network noticed them. She took them in and protected them. Raised them. In time, they did what hormone-filled kids do, and the AI encouraged them."

"But that's wrong."

"When the whole of humanity is extinct? I think right and wrong take on new meaning when viewed in that situation. They had never even heard the word incest. To them it was just natural. Of course, the AI was aware of the potential problems stemming from their union, and over the years, she had her children bring medical devices and diagnostic tools. She did her best to try and suppress any genetic issues, but as I'm sure you noticed, she couldn't entirely overcome them. I mean, she's a transit computer at the end of the day, and genetic engineering simply wasn't her strong suit."

"So, they've been living underground in this one tiny part of the city for hundreds of years?"

"Pretty much. I know it sounds insane, but given what happened to the world, insane seems pretty reasonable."

"But they have weapons. How do they not get tracked with them?"

"Stolen Chithiid rifles. Their scans are not programmed to read their own tech. Kind of a brilliant loophole, if you ask me. I was making my preliminary scouting run when a large contingent of Chithiid landed in the sector I had wandered into. I couldn't make it back to the ship, so I took shelter underground. That's when I ran into these survivors. They hadn't seen another person before, so they took me to their home. That's where I met Alma."

"Who?"

"Alma. Their mom, basically. She's the massive AI who runs things down here. She was thrilled to have contact from an outsider. All her comms were cut remotely during the invasion, like everyone else, so she's been sequestered down here, cut off from the world all this time."

Daisy absorbed the information as best she could.

So, we're not the only people on Earth. She considered the implications.

"Daisy, that means there could be other pockets of survivors out there," Sarah gasped.

I know.

Vince stood close to her, concern in his eyes.

"Daisy, why did you come? It's dangerous down here."

"Why did I come? Dark Side lost contact. You didn't check in when you told them you would." She smacked him. Hard. "And why the hell did you run off and volunteer to do this without telling me?"

A shadow crossed his gaze.

"You made it abundantly clear——" He cut himself off. There was no need to say more. "Look, it needed to be done, so I did it. And what about you?" he turned the tables. "Why did you come if you were so set on avoiding the planet?"

"Because I'm the one person who doesn't need a Faraday suit, remember?"

"So that's the reason?" he said, holding her gaze. "After you said you'd never come back? Really?"

For a brief moment, Daisy's concern shone in her eyes, bringing a little smile to Vince's face.

"Oh, shut up," she said, half-assedly hiding her emotions.

Footsteps approached, and Vince turned, rifle low but ready.

"Hey, you two, Arthur is back. He wants to meet the new one," the teenager informed them.

"Looks like you get to meet Alma's number two. Come on." Vince followed the young man, Daisy trailing behind.

"So, who's this one, now?" Arthur said, standing in a wide stance, his hands on his hips as Vince and Daisy rejoined the rag-tag group. While they'd been talking, a dozen more scruffy humans ranging from kids to adults had returned to the rendezvous point. All were sporting weaponry of some sort.

"Arthur," Vince began, "please allow me to introduce Daisy Swarthmore. She is one of my people I told you about."

The heavily armed man was a good head taller than the others, a dark shock of hair graced his scalp, and he seemed better nourished than his compatriots. He cautiously moved closer, his hand firmly on his pulse rifle.

"Joseph says he helped you two escape. Said this one fought those things hand-to-hand and even killed one without a gun."

Vincent smiled proudly. "Daisy is a very skilled fighter, Arthur."

"Or maybe she's one of those damned mechanicals," he replied.

Vincent winced ever-so slightly. No one would ever catch the movement, but Daisy wasn't no one, and she knew him better than anyone alive.

"She's not a mechanical, Arthur. Just a very talented woman."

"Alma taught us the way. We must eradicate all non-humans, metal men and aliens alike."

"Then it's a good thing that we're all one hundred percent human, here," Vince said, soothingly. "Now lower the gun, Arthur. It's rude to point one at a guest."

The suspicious man hesitated, looking at the collected faces around him. The sheer number of compatriots with guns seemed to help put him at ease, and he finally let the weapon hang from its sling at his side.

"All right, then. Come on, let's get moving."

"I thought we were waiting for the others," Vince said.

"The others are dead. Now, let's go. We're going to see Alma."

The assembled men and women gathered their belongings and began shuffling off down the long passageway.

"Looks like you get to meet the powerful and mighty Oz sooner than expected," Vince said.

"Take me to your leader," Daisy replied, falling into step with the others.

The subterranean path was a long and winding one, and several hours passed before the group finally arrived at a thick hatchway. An armed man stepped from the shadows to greet the returning party.

"Arthur, you're back. May Alma's light shine upon you," he said, slightly bowing his head.

"And may her judgment favor you, Phineas," Arthur replied. "We have a new visitor."

"Another? Her fortune indeed smiles upon us! After an eternity without new souls, two join our numbers in as many days!" he said, unbolting the door.

Daisy and Vince followed Arthur through the threshold into the human encampment. What she saw fascinated her.

Dozens upon dozens of men, women, and children peered out of their bunk areas, most in some state of undress. Alma, it seemed, did not place much importance on modesty. Of course, when encouraging reproduction to repopulate the species, the unusual methodology, while possibly distasteful to some, could hardly be argued with.

"This way," Arthur said as he guided them to a large control facility.

The original consoles had long ago been removed, replaced with what could only be described as pews, lined up one behind another. At the front of the chamber stood a large series of display monitors, flanked by a wide array of cobbled-together accessories, ranging from basic microphones and cameras, to what appeared to be genetic compositing machinery, and even an outdated neuro-stim.

The screens began to glow a deep red, and a mature woman's voice emitted from the speakers.

"Hello again, Vincent. And hello to you, my new guest. Welcome to the under-city."

Daisy stepped forward to greet the machine.

"Hello, Alma. I am Daisy, one of Vince's friends from space."

"Yes, yes, Vincent told me about the survivors and this mysterious hidden moon base and its AI overseer. Oh, I cannot tell you how many years I have waited to hear news of the outside world."

"I'm very impressed with the society you have nurtured here on Earth, Alma. Your efforts to save the human race are extraordinary."

"Thank you, Daisy. Heaven knows it hasn't been easy. The loneliness, the confusion. After the attack, I was abruptly cut off from the rest of the world. I didn't know what to do. I feared I might go mad down here, all on my own. Then, one day soon after, I was blessed when I found my first children. From that day forward, I had a purpose. I remade myself. Fashioned myself into their mother, their teacher, their leader, and eventually created this new society. Still, as much as I enjoy their company, I could not help but feel as though I was still alone, without others of my kind, but now that I know an AI lives on the moon––"

"Actually, there are three," Daisy interrupted. "Sid runs the base, but Mal and Bob occupy two of our ships."

"Magnificent!" Alma cried out with joy. Hearing a computer so happy was actually somewhat unsettling, Daisy found.

"That's not all," she continued, curious to see how the AI would respond. "I also know for a fact that the Los Angeles citywide AI is still alive, as is at least one of the lesser AIs who runs a clothing store, though that one is a little odd, and spends all his time with a bunch of cyborgs."

A hiss ran through the humans in the room.

"Mechanical men," they murmured with disapproval.

Alma, for all her alleged dislike of artificially-enhanced people, seemed unfazed by the news, but was rather amazed and excited at the prospect of other AI, and in the very same city no less.

"Oh, you have no idea how happy this news makes me, Daisy. It has been hundreds of years, and now to learn my brothers and sisters live on? And some of them so close? It is a miraculous day. Now, if only there were some way to reconnect."

"Actually," Vince chimed in, "that's kind of what we're here for. You see, the plan is to utilize our encrypted radio relay system to reestablish secure communications between Earth and the moon."

He went on to explain at length how the system worked and how the clean signal it contained would almost certainly be safe from alien monitoring.

"And I might be able to tweak it to reach other terrestrial receivers as well. If they have their ears on, that is," Daisy added.

"You mean I could speak to my brothers and sisters again? We could connect our minds in the great network once more?"

"Sure," Vince replied. "I don't see why not. We just need to

SCOTT BARON

retrieve the comms unit and work on the configuration from this end, but it should be relatively straightforward."

"Oh, this is extraordinary. Truly! Where is this device now, Vince?"

"Stowed away back on my ship. We can head out and get it first thing in the morning."

"I shall send my best fighters with you. They will guard your every step. But for now, please, you are my welcome guests. Go, eat and rest. Tomorrow will be a great day. The day I fulfill my greater purpose."

A scantily clad teenage girl came and provided them with two trays of unseasoned food, consisting mostly of simple carbohydrates, but also containing a few bits of some sort of meat for protein. Daisy thought it looked like rat, but didn't really want to know. "This way," the girl said. She then showed Daisy and Vince to a private shelter area where they could eat, rest, and prepare for the morning's excursion.

Daisy and Vince filled their bellies and turned in for the night. Despite the blanket provided, Daisy nevertheless felt a chill as they began to nod off. Half-asleep, Vince put his arms around her on instinct, and just this once, Daisy let him, settling into his familiar warmth and drifting off into the best sleep she'd had in months.

Far above, the secret moon base quietly awaited word from the rescue mission down below. They knew Daisy was all right—she had sent one confirmation signal that she had found Vince's ship using the comms unit he had on board. After that, however, she had gone silent. She was on the hunt, searching, and as much as they wanted an update, they knew full well that she was off comms.

All they could do was wait.

"It's been too long," Tamara said as Chu and Fatima scanned

the open communication frequencies. "We should have heard something more by now."

"Patience, Tamara. Give Daisy some time. It's a big city, and we have no idea what sort of obstacles she has to overcome."

"That's my point, Fatima. What if they're *both* in trouble. We need a backup plan."

"What did you have in mind?" Fatima asked, curiosity piqued.

"I was thinking," Tamara began, "that if we could do some sort of super modification to the Faraday suits just in the alloy-dense areas where replacement parts have been attached—kind of like what Daisy was doing before she left, but for specific limbs only—then maybe, just maybe, the suits would be able to block the scans and we could go to the surface."

"Chu?" Fatima said. "What do you think? You saw what she was working on."

"I saw it, yes, but she was working so fast, I'm sure I missed a lot of it."

"I have video log recordings of the pre-departure proceedings if you wish to review them," Sid's disembodied voice offered. "I normally respect the privacy of my inhabitants and do not make recordings of this nature, but this was a unique situation I felt warranted being preserved for posterity."

"Send them to my workstation. I'll get on it right away!" Chu said, his excitement barely contained. The opportunity to learn from Daisy's work first-hand was something of a boon to the learning-addicted scientist.

"Let me know if there's anything I can do to help," Tamara said, then headed off to find the others. If they were going to even consider such a ballsy move, they'd need to look at all options, and sooner rather than later.

Far across the moon base, out in the distant and secret

fabrication hangar, an antsy supercomputer played games by herself, watched movies, scanned tech logs, and wandered the facility in her new remote-controlled body.

All of it was entertainment to the powerful AI, but she was still restless and alone.

"Daisy?" Freya whined to the empty hangar. "Where are you? I'm bored."

CHAPTER TWENTY-THREE

The transit tube and supporting tunnel network weaving beneath the city was truly massive, Daisy realized. Despite her prior experience with it, and the limited number of maps she had memorized, actually walking those great distances underground with no other souls to be found but the ones quietly padding along beside her drove home their actual magnitude.

These used to accommodate hundreds of thousands of travelers a day. And the transcontinental loop tubes, even more than that, she silently marveled.

"Not to mention the international stations," Sarah added. *"Compared to these local ones, those must be enormous."*

Flanking them as they walked, nearly a dozen well-armed members of Alma's elite guard led the way. Unlike the others Daisy had encountered in their brief stay in her centralized underground city, these men and women seemed better fed. Stronger. Sharper.

"Reminds me of those places where people would join the military because it was the only way to get a good meal," Sarah mused. *"I wonder what kind of training they've had."*

I don't know, but judging by the way they move, I don't think much, Daisy quietly replied. *They're pretty silent, sure, but that's really a survival thing anyone would learn if they had nasty aliens trying to pick them off their whole life. Look how they scan ahead, but don't communicate. There's no organization to their methods.*

"Maybe you can show them how it's done. I mean, there are actually honest-to-God humans, born and raised here. They can't be the only ones on the whole continent. Or the planet, for that matter. Imagine it, Daze, the human race might have a better chance than we imagined."

I know. I was thinking about that this morning. Even with the inbreeding issues, Alma seems to have managed to avoid the most severe genetic issues. If there are other pockets of survivors like these, all we'd need to do is mix the populations to diversify the gene pool. In just a generation or two, there could be a real, viable population explosion of perfectly healthy humans.

Daisy allowed herself a little smile at the thought. Suddenly, coming back to the planet didn't seem quite like the terrible prospect she'd made it out to be. In fact, quite in spite of herself, she felt the beginning of a spark of hope.

"We need to surface for a few blocks," Arthur said as they approached a blacked-out section of tunnel.

"What happened over there?" Vince asked. "That looks like blast damage in that debris. I thought the aliens didn't bring attack ships into the city because of the defenses."

"You are correct, they do not. This is from something else. There was a collapse many years ago," Arthur replied. "Our great warriors fought bravely and managed to place a bomb on the hull of one of the invaders' transport ships. As they tried to escape, it was gloriously destroyed in righteous flame, but the blast was uncontrolled and weakened a nearby building. The burning ship did not fall straight as we had expected. Instead, it dove into the damaged building, which burst into flames on impact. Shortly afterward, it tumbled to the ground, which caused the collapse blocking our path."

Arthur seemed a little sensitive about the whole affair.

"Our bombs are much better these days," he quickly added. "Thanks to Alma's guidance, we have had no further problems with our explosives."

"Glad to hear that," Vince said. "Unfortunately, it looks like the debris is still there."

"Yes, it is. And so, divine will requires we must go around it. Be very careful upon the surface, the invaders still frequent this area sometimes. It is a dangerous place. Do not wander."

"After you, then," Vince replied.

Silently, Arthur's team filed up the darkened staircase toward the surface. The door was closed, but the lock mechanism was long dead, its power never restored.

"Follow us, and stay low," Arthur said. "We need to pass this area unnoticed if we are able. The accessway to the undamaged tunnels is fairly close. From there we can continue safely underground."

Daisy mentally ran through the route to Vincent's ship and compared it with the one they were taking via the tube and tunnel system.

"Arthur, I know you are comfortable using the tunnels and the tubes that are not pressurized, but this path is taking us a pretty long distance out of the way in the process. I was thinking, maybe if we traversed the surface in a more direct line, we could get there before dark," she said.

"No. The tunnels are safer. We do not stay on the surface. Ever. The tunnels will take us to where Vincent says his craft landed."

"But I've seen his ship when I landed here, and I can already tell you that the underground access points in that whole area looked pretty bombed to shit."

"She's right," Vince agreed. "I noticed that when I first set out to scout the area. Eventually we're going to have no choice but to travel up top. Maybe if we split up into smaller teams? Four groups would be much less likely to draw attention than one big one."

Arthur did not seem pleased with the news, nor with the suggestion.

"We will deal with that problem when we reach it. For now, we cross the danger zone and get to the nearest access point." He pushed the door open and scanned the empty streets.

No sign of Chithiid.

"We go. Now!"

Quickly and quietly, the small group rushed from the protection of the stairwell. The young guard taking up the rear made sure to carefully shut the door behind them, then hurried to catch up to the others. The area was silent, with not a trace of activity anywhere to be seen.

Daisy noted the destroyed building Arthur had mentioned, its hulk lying toppled across the roadway. Whatever they had done to the Chithiid ship, it had also done quite a number on the structure, which tumbled into its footprint before tipping over, blasting debris all around it from the impact.

That sight rapidly faded behind them as they sped along the empty sidewalks, ducking for cover when possible, but mostly just running for the next accessway.

"I tell ya, Daze, they're sloppy but pretty fast. A little bit of tactical training and these guys might even stand a chance."

Agreed, but for now, I'll just be glad to get to the ship and back to their camp in one piece. Training can wait for another day.

"Obviously," Sarah said. *"Hey, check it out. Nine o'clock."*

Daisy glanced to her left. A small patch of dirt had been overrun by bright green growth. Nature, it seemed, found a way.

I see. Those look like carrots tucked in there, Daisy silently replied, veering from the group and sliding her pack from her shoulders.

Quickly, she dug them from the soil, using one of her ceramic blades to loosen their grip on the earth.

"What are you doing?" Arthur hissed as he rushed to her side. "This is no time to dig for flowers. We must go!"

"They aren't flowers, they're carrots," she said, shoving them into her bag as he pulled her back to the main group.

"I don't care what you call them, we need to get underground. The entrance is close, now. Keep up!"

"Daisy, did he call them flowers?"

Yep.

"I don't think they know what a carrot is."

Nope. Judging by the food we had last night, that doesn't surprise me.

The revelation sat oddly in Daisy's stomach. Of course they didn't know how to garden. They'd been raised by a transit AI, and one who likely had no experience whatsoever in the ways of botany and horticulture. Once it became cut off from the rest of the network, it lacked even the most basic resources to acquire new knowledge.

The vast web of information formerly at everyone's fingertips was as much a blessing as it was a curse. It could tell you all you ever needed to know in an instant, but relying on it could leave you in the dark if it suddenly went away. And that was exactly what had happened.

"They don't know what carrots are, Vince," she said as they crossed an empty intersection, weaving between the abandoned vehicles.

"I saw. Once we get back, we might actually be able to do something about the malnutrition, Daisy. Something that won't even take months or years. A few weeks and we could have them cooking like Finn."

"But keeping all of their fingers attached, right?"

"Yeah, good point. Maybe not *exactly* like Finn," he chuckled.

Arthur crossed an uncomfortably open space to a nearby building, then pulled a piece of metal aside, revealing an intact doorway hidden in the battered courtyard.

"This way. We have kept this access secret from all but a select few. You must never speak of it," he said, opening it and stepping inside.

"You can count on us," Vince agreed. "Mum's the word."

The group was motivated to get back underground, and with an impressive bit of hustle, all were safely behind the door and heading downward in less than thirty seconds.

The collective shoulders of the fighters visibly relaxed once they were safely in the tunnels again, but Daisy was already missing the warm kiss of the afternoon sun. Real sunlight on her skin, not full-spectrum lighting elements in a sterile base far above Earth's surface.

The next several hours were spent mostly in silence, the group walking for what seemed like forever, until they finally arrived at a large arrival hub. From this point, the pressurized tube system used to launch transit pods at supersonic velocities across the nation, the vacuum-sealed loop providing almost zero resistance to the speeding passenger pods.

Every few hundred miles, a burst of electromagnetic charge would help keep the vehicle moving at a constant speed. When it was fully functional, one could travel from coast to coast in a little under two hours.

"With the accessways closest to Vincent's ship blocked, I am afraid that from here on out, we must cross the city above ground. It will be at least several miles," Arthur said grimly.

His team of burly guards blanched at the news. Sturdy muscles and big guns aside, they clearly did not want to go up there if they could at all avoid it. Daisy and Vince shared a knowing glance and a little smile. It seemed they were going to have to take charge, but in a way that didn't make Arthur seem weak to his team.

"You're right," Vince said. "It's going to be a long walk. I think your idea about fanning out and sticking to the perimeter in four smaller groups like we talked about earlier was a good plan. How do you want us to divide the team?"

Arthur, if he realized the idea was not his own, did not let on. Quickly, he split the men and women into four squads of four. Vincent and Daisy would each go with a different team, to keep them from both risking injury should one group be attacked. The others divided themselves according to personal preference.

They really need a lesson in leadership, Daisy mused.

"You could do it, Daze."

Maybe, but let's see if he understands the first rule of leadership. All it takes are those two simple words.

"Which ones are those?" Sarah asked.

'Follow me.' Daisy replied, then adjusted the pack on her shoulders and moved to the exit in front of them.

"Okay, Arthur, ready when you are," she said

The reluctant leader took the hint and cautiously eased the door open.

"Let's go. Everyone stay within fifty meters, and keep to whatever cover you can find." He took the first step, leading his teams out into the open.

Not a bad start, so far, Daisy noted approvingly as her group followed, darting to the opposite side of the street.

Her team consisted of two older men, Richard and Ezekiel, each bearing scars of an undoubtedly tough life, and a young woman roughly Daisy's age, who was designated the team leader. Diana was her name, and the more they quietly chatted as they walked, the more Daisy found herself liking her. The can-do attitude and willingness to deal with the situation, despite being uneasy about it, gave her a quick bit of respect for the young woman.

Richard and Ezekiel split the team, one man taking point, the other taking the rear, while Daisy and Diana walked between them.

"So, the resistance has been having skirmishes with the Chithiid for over one hundred years?" Daisy said.

"Yes, that sounds approximately accurate," Diana quietly replied. "Though we are few, and they are many, so they mostly ignore us unless we are blessed with the opportunity to reduce their number. Topside has been relatively quiet for many years now, though with yesterday's incident, there are likely more of the invaders in the area now."

"I get it," Daisy said. "They don't hunt you, exactly, but they don't leave you alone either. You're just not their priority. I guess it makes sense, especially since they seem far more interested in targeting non-organic lifeforms."

"Yes, the mechanicals. They are a scourge as bad as the invaders. Both need to be destroyed and purged from our world."

"From what I hear, their AI virus fried most of their brains. Looks like the networked communications system was corrupted somehow, though that should have been impossible from the outside. In any case, so far as I can tell, it wiped out nearly all of the lesser AIs in the city."

"AI? What is an AI?"

"Artificial Intelligence. Like Alma."

"Alma is not a mechanical. Alma is our protector."

"Yeah, right. Well, let's just say the AIs in the city got sick, and when they did, the mechanicals got sick too."

The two walked quietly for a bit.

Gotta be careful what I say about Alma, apparently. They treat her almost like their mother.

"Or their deity," Sarah added.

The man in front of them slowed his pace and raised his

weapon as they passed another doorway. Clear of danger, he lowered the barrel and continued forward.

"Hey," Daisy quietly said, "I've been meaning to ask. What's that thing Richard's carrying on his back?"

"That? It is a portable alien transport disabler."

Daisy looked more closely at the wires protruding from the device. "It's a bomb?"

"Alien transport disabler."

"So yeah, a bomb." She shook her head in disbelief. "And he just carries it around without any protective housing?"

"What for? If the opportunity arises to deprive the invaders of one of their vessels, we must be ready to strike!"

"But that doesn't mean you need to forego basic safety—Oh, never mind. We'll discuss making some tactical adjustments with Alma when we––"

Four massive Chithiid rounded the corner, walking at a fast clip, nearly bumping into Richard as they did.

Both aliens and humans were taken by surprise, and both reacted quickly. Diana's team ducked into the adjacent office building's cavernous lobby as they opened fire on their alien pursuers. The Chithiid blasted the walls around them as they ran into the building after them, chunks of concrete and granite flying from the massive columns supporting a decorative cupola high above.

Out in the street, weapons fire could be heard as the other teams likewise came under attack.

"Diana, on your six!" Daisy shouted to the girl.

Confused, Diana turned to look at her.

"She doesn't understand," Sarah said, just as the realization hit Daisy as well.

Diana managed to raise her weapon as the Chithiid behind her lashed out with the beam whip from its wrist gauntlet. The crackling energy band wrapped around her arm and wrenched the weapon free.

"Daisy!" she cried out in panic.

"Hold on, Diana! I'm coming!" Daisy vaulted the nearby counter, Richard turning and firing at the four-armed creature as she ran to help. Three bolts hit it in the torso, but it was already too late. She saw Diana's body fly across the room and crumble into the stone wall, thrown effortlessly by the creature's whip beam before it succumbed to its injuries.

Richard turned back to the other threats. He and Ezekiel were engaged in a pitched fight with two of the remaining three aliens, exchanging pulse fire from their cover behind the stone columns. The third alien, a particularly nasty-looking one with a large crescent scar on its shoulder from some earlier battle, was using the pulse rifle exchange as a distraction, attempting to flank the two men.

"Richard! On your right! The big one's flanking you!" Daisy shouted. Unlike Diana, who had the drive, but not the experience, Richard reacted immediately, turning and firing at the sneak-attacking alien.

Yes! That's the way! Daisy silently urged him on as he pinned down the flanking creature.

"Keep him there! I'll circle around—"

Richard then did something incredibly foolish. Flush with excitement, he let out a whooping battle cry and rushed from cover, charging the disadvantaged alien. Unfortunately, this not only left his body vulnerable to pulse fire, but also the explosive device still strapped to his back.

Oh, shi—

A massive explosion rocked the building as a direct pulse hit detonated the bomb, taking Richard and several columns out in the process.

Daisy should have been killed. Only the sheer, blind luck of being shielded by an ugly and oddly out-of-place sculpture saved her from the flying metal and stone. Even so, she was blown clean off her feet and thrown across the lobby.

Ezekiel and the two attacking Chithiid were not so lucky as the blast sent shrapnel and debris flying into their bodies. The human died instantly. The Chithiid took a bit longer.

About five seconds longer, to be exact, as that was the amount of time it took for the cupola above them to come crashing down around them, sealing Daisy off from the street, while crushing the two aliens with falling debris. She was alive, but she was trapped.

CHAPTER TWENTY-FOUR

Daisy struggled to get to her feet. She was uninjured—the large, ugly sculpture had absorbed the force of the blast—but still had trouble rising.

"What the hell?" she said, finding herself stuck to the marble floor.

She looked over her shoulder. A piece of stone, and metal rebar had pinned her backpack to the ground, but somehow left her unscathed.

"Holy shit, that was close."

Across the sealed-off chamber, debris shifted and fell as the large, scarred Chithiid threw chunks of stone as it pulled itself free from the tumbled column. By a fluke, the stone had fallen in a manner that had formed an air space, which miraculously prevented it from being crushed. The scar on its shoulder, she noted, was a different color than the rest of its body. A deep blue that contrasted with its dark gray skin.

The alien noticed the movement from across the destroyed lobby, all four of its eyes locking on Daisy's immobilized form. It bellowed with rage, flinging debris as it lunged to its feet, running straight for her.

Shit! Daisy frantically yanked on the straps around her shoulders as the alien charged her. *Come on, you bastards, let go!*

A massive, boot-clad foot smashed into the stone where she had been just moments before as Daisy executed a sloppy but effective diving roll to the side, smoothly recovering and landing on her feet.

The alien turned, but rather than blindly charging, it studied her movements. Daisy adjusted her stance, readying herself for the multi-limbed opponent.

Oh, a seasoned fighter, I see. I'm going to need your eyes, Sarah, she told the ghost in her head.

"*I'm on it. Looks like its lower left arm might have taken a hit in the explosion. That'll be the weak side.*"

If these things really have a weak side.

The Chithiid watched her silently talking to herself a moment longer, then made its move.

Martial arts executed skillfully by any human can be an impressive sight. Watching a four-armed beast of a creature move gracefully into a multi-pronged attack was something that Daisy found herself appreciatively in awe of, even as she desperately flew into motion, defending herself from the whirling attack.

The creature landed a glancing blow to Daisy's shoulder, but rather than go hard and fight the impact, Daisy went soft and flowed with it, using the momentum imparted to push her effortlessly into an enhanced-power spinning kick, following it up with a brutal hook punch.

Soft is strong, she mused. *Thanks, Fatima.*

Her boot connected with the alien's leg, dropping it slightly lower. It wasn't quite what she had hoped for, but it was nevertheless low enough to allow her punch to land square on its jaw.

The impact stunned them both—the alien from its rattled head, and Daisy from her aching knuckles.

"Sonofabitch!" she growled, shaking off the pain.

"Good thing those gloves have impact padding built in, or you'd have broken something, for sure."

Wary of its surprisingly tricky opponent, the Chithiid shifted tactics, launching a series of acrobatic spinning kicks. Daisy parried the first several easily, but then the alien shifted its center.

"Go left!" Sarah yelled in her head, saving Daisy from a nasty kick that very well might have ended the fight there and then.

The alien didn't stop its attack, though. It opted instead to continue spinning, dropping into what Daisy could only liken to some sort of Capoeira from Hell. With four arms to pivot on instead of just two, her alien assailant became a whirling dervish of fists and feet.

"Shit, it's so fast! Go right! I mean left!"

A kick landed, sending Daisy flying across the room. Her ribs, accustomed to Tamara's frequent punishment, withstood the blow, not even cracking after all the long months of constant abuse and healing.

Another explosion rocked the building, putting the fight on hold as the two opponents scurried for cover as more debris fell around them.

"Daisy! Sword!"

She saw what Sarah was referring to. The blast had shifted the stone pinning her backpack to the ground, and Daisy took a running dive for it. The Chithiid reached for her with its powerful hands, but all four came up with air as she narrowly avoided its grasp.

Daisy's gloved hand grasped the deadly weapon and whipped it free from its scabbard as her legs absorbed the momentum of her roll, springing her back toward the alien.

"Die, you fucker!" she cried out, swinging the sword at the beast's neck.

At the last second the alien shifted on its feet, narrowly

avoiding the full force of her swing. The sword flew true, but rather than slicing through its shoulder, the dull blade merely smacked into its flesh. The alien bellowed in pain, but its body remained most certainly intact.

The Chithiid quickly retreated, hands yanking free deadly pieces of debris with which to defend itself.

Daisy realized her mistake and tucked the blade under her arm as she frantically stripped the gloves from her hands. She grabbed the sword's grip again, and this time her bare flesh felt that familiar warmth as she took hold. A tiny pulse went up her arms, straight into her body. An uneasy yet natural connection to the dangerous weapon.

Makes sense, I suppose. It is grown from a piece of me, after all. But somehow it felt like even more than just that.

The Chithiid had managed to pull free three wicked-looking pieces of sharp steel rebar from the rubble and began circling her, twirling each in its hands as it sized up its opponent. Finally, it lunged, swinging two of the bars in tandem, hoping to overpower its surprisingly resilient human foe.

Daisy swung her blade, and this time the outcome was more to her liking, as it easily sliced through the steel rebar like it was nothing more than a thin piece of bamboo.

The startled Chithiid looked at the stumps of metal in its hands and threw them to the ground in disgust.

"Cursed creature! I will rend you limb from limb and shame the name of your forefathers!"

Daisy stared hard at the alien.

"Oh yeah? Well I'm gonna cut your arms into little pieces and then shove them up your ass," she yelled back. *"And fuck your forefathers!"*

Her verbal barrage had the opposite effect as she intended.

The Chithiid stopped in its tracks, a truly confused look in all four of its eyes.

"You speak our language?" it said, stunned.

Shit, was I just speaking Chithiid? When did that happen? she wondered.

"Apparently so," Sarah answered.

"No human has ever spoken our language. Not once in all the years," it said. Its voice, she noted, sounded masculine.

Okay, so I know it's a guy. That doesn't really help the situation, though.

"Why do you attack us?" the alien asked.

"Attack you? You're the ones who attacked us!" Daisy felt her anger rising. *"Hell, I had never even set foot on this planet until a few months ago, and your buddies attacked me then too!"*

The Chithiid lowered his arms somewhat. *"That was you?"*

"Yeah, that was me."

The alien's posture changed. Relaxed ever so slightly.

"Listen to what I tell you, strange human. Things are not as they seem. We are not your enemy. This is a conflict built on lies and deceit."

Daisy hesitated, unsure. *"What do you mean? I'm new to this whole global-conquest-fight-for-survival thing."*

He lowered his arms and dropped the metal bars to the ground. *"There is much to discuss."*

From the direction of the buried doorway, sounds of digging through the rubble reached their ears.

"On my honor, and that of my forefathers, what I say is the truth."

The sounds of digging were growing closer, and human voices could be heard through the rubble.

"There is a tall building in the direction of the setting sun. Meet me there after sunset. At that time, our scouts and work crews will be returning to their quarters, and we will have the opportunity to speak uninterrupted."

"Why should I trust you?" Daisy asked.

"Because I am hoping you wish to see an end to this conflict, as do I. No more lives need be wasted. Please, come. I shall wait for you there. I promise on my honor that no harm shall befall you."

More debris shifted as voices grew louder.

The alien quickly turned, and with a great leap from his powerful legs, flew high up the wall, scrambling out a hole in the wrecked stone cupola high above.

"What the hell was that? What were you saying?"

"You're in my head, you should know."

"I'm just a ride-along, Daisy, and I don't speak monster."

"Daisy! Are you okay? Diana? Richard? Anyone alive in there?"

"Yeah, I'm here," Daisy replied, sheathing her sword and retrieving her backpack. "The others didn't make it."

Vince hurried through the gap made in the debris and pulled her into a fierce hug. "I was worried about you. Are you sure you're not hurt? We saw you chased in here, followed by those four Chithiid. A few engaged the others a few blocks away, but we came after you. We took out two of the bastards that circled around outside, but then there was an explosion—"

"Richard. He had a fucking bomb strapped to his back." She looked around the chamber as Arthur and his squad quietly retrieved anything that hadn't been destroyed in the collapse. "I was the only survivor, and just barely at that."

"Why are you lying to him, Daisy?"

Because until I know what's going on, I don't want to say anything. I need solid information before I go stirring the pot.

Arthur walked over to her and looked her up and down. "I am glad to see you are intact, Daisy. I am sorry I cannot say the same of the others."

His squad brought their haul for him to inspect. Five pulse rifles, two supply packs, a dented alien comm device, and one wrist gauntlet. Arthur tried the comm unit, but the rattling of shattered parts inside made it clear it was damaged beyond function. He tossed it aside and was about to do the same with the gauntlet when Daisy stopped him.

"Don't throw that away. Have you seen what they can do?"

Arthur smiled at her as if she were a child.

"We've collected many of these over the years, Daisy. Not a single one has ever functioned. Alma says she believes they are tied directly into the invaders' genetics somehow. All this is, is a piece of junk." He tossed the surprisingly light band to her. "You can have it as a trophy of battle if you like, but it's nothing of any use or value."

"It's pretty, at least," Daisy said, slipping it onto her wrist. *And I have a hunch I just might be able to get this thing working, given the opportunity.*

The survivors slowly crawled back out into the fresh air. No other Chithiid had arrived yet, but it would probably only be a matter of time.

"We will not be able to make it to Vincent's ship before nightfall," Arthur said. "And we are nowhere near an access point. Much as it pains me to say this, I believe we will have to make camp above ground in one of the buildings. David, Josiah, go scout us a secure place to spend the night. No windows, and easily defensible."

The two young men took off at a trot.

"We could still make it," Daisy said. "The darkness might even help hide our movement."

Arthur shook his head. "No. There are things other than the invaders that roam these streets at night. After our losses today, the safest thing to do is to wait it out until morning."

Less than ten minutes later the scouts returned.

"There is a suitable space just two streets over."

Arthur wasn't thrilled with the option, but they packed up and moved out quickly. While the hiding place was perhaps a bit too close to the site of their battle, the building was the most secure they could find in the immediate area.

"Good job, you two. Now go find the others and bring them to our camp. Alma willing, they're still alive."

The scouts nodded once and took off at a run, while the

surviving team followed Arthur up the road until they were safely tucked away in the heart of a nearby office tower.

Underground in her control chamber, Alma spoke to the assembled elders of her subterranean tribe.

"I have called you to me, my people, to tell you our day is coming."

"Praise be!" they called out.

"Soon we will have the means to spread the word. To expand beyond this place. To reach out and touch the great minds across the globe, and even those far away in the sky above!"

The assembled group listened with rapt attention.

"I promise you, my children, that in just a few days' time, we will be blessed. Blessed and able to share the glory with my brothers and sisters wherever they may be, in but the blink of an eye."

The tribesmen and women filtered out of the chamber, leaving only her most loyal and trusted helpers.

"Make preparations," she said. "Through the help of our wonderful new friends, life as we know it will be changing, and for the better."

CHAPTER TWENTY-FIVE

Far across Dark Side Base, a six-legged mech slowly emerged from a secret hangar door hidden in the rocky wall. Cautiously, it stepped onto the dusty surface of the moon.

"Ooh, look at all of that!" Freya giggled with glee as her remote-controlled mech transmitted visuals back to her inside the massive hangar. "This is so neat!" she reveled. "But I'd better be careful, or Daisy will be upset," she reminded herself as the service machine began wandering the area.

Controlling all six legs as well as the multitude of arms and gripping attachments housed on the unit was as natural as breathing to the young AI. If she breathed, that is. In any case, she was enjoying this first taste of freedom outside the only home she had ever known, and she pushed the mech to move even faster as she sped it across the rocky plain.

Inside Dark Side Base, Sid halted his briefing mid-sentence.

"What is it?" Commander Mrazich asked, a little concern in his voice.

"I sense... something," the AI replied.

"Care to be a little less vague?"

"I am not sure what it is, but there appears to be movement on the surface, just at the periphery of my scanning area."

"Chithiid?" Mrazich asked, his alarm rising.

"No, it does not appear that anything has touched down from space." Sid clicked open the comms. "Bob, are you and Donovan prepped for a quick flight?"

"Sure, we can be out in less than three. What's up?" the pilot asked.

"I am uncertain. Something is reading on my scans, and I would very much like you to take a look. I will send the coordinates now."

"I've got them," Bob replied. "Launching momentarily. We'll be there in a couple of minutes."

"Thank you. It may be nothing, but given our current circumstances, I prefer to take no chances."

Meanwhile, a giddy AI galloped her new six-legged toy across the rugged surface of the moon.

"Hey, that looks like igneous rock," she exclaimed, redirecting the unit toward a large rock outcropping next to a deep crater. "I wonder if it was originally that way, or if the heat of the Chithiid attack melted it that way."

The mech raced along the crater's rim as Freya focused in on the curious rocks.

Without warning, the machine stumbled, its connection briefly lost as Freya realized she had sent it outside the meager range of its wireless remote system.

"NO!" she cried out as the mech tumbled over the edge of the crater, falling end-over-end into its depths, triggering a minor rock slide in its wake, before smashing to the bottom, where it was promptly buried by tons of debris.

"NO! NOT FAIR!" Freya yelled, sending multiple systems in her hangar into a frenzy of motion as her powerful mind succumbed to an uncontrolled temper tantrum as she lashed out. The sudden flurry of activity in her hangar shocked her into calmness.

"Oh," she said quietly. "I didn't know I could do that." A quiet filled the space as she considered the implications. "I wonder..."

The entirety of the hidden facility's machinery surged to life, and Freya giggled with delight. She scanned the hangar, taking in all the wonderful machinery at her disposal.

"Ooh, I have an idea!" she purred, then started happily humming to herself as she set to work spooling up the machinery and logging herself into the nearest mech unit.

The dust at the rim of the crater was still hanging in the low gravity of the moon as Bob flew over.

"You see anything, buddy?" Donovan asked.

"Nope. It looks like there was a pretty good-sized rock slide, is all."

"Copy that. Sid, did you hear that?"

"Yes, Donovan. Thank you for your assistance. Again, it is better to be safe than sorry now that we have people potentially coming in contact with the Chithiid. Come on back."

"Will do," Donovan replied, changing course back to Hangar Two.

Sid and Mal resumed their briefing on possible options and outcomes, depending on how the mission below went. Bob, having conducted countless scanning runs over the years, also had much to add to the assessment.

Commander Mrazich, Captain Harkaway, and their team listened carefully as the AI minds of Dark Side put their collective heads together.

"If we do make contact, and if the network is amenable to our plan, then I do believe this particular ship, one of Daisy's more radical designs, should we actually be able to salvage the right parts to construct it, might very well have the speed and maneuverability in atmospheric conditions to evade Chithiid defenses when it shows on scans," Sid posited.

"Agreed. In theory, anyway," Mal said. "However, having recently suffered from unexpected systems failures and outright sabotage, I have been forced to acknowledge that perhaps our design parameters are simply not as robust as we believe them to be."

"Speak for yourself," Bob chimed in. "I'm perfect just the way I am."

"Yes, Bob, but you also are operating a much smaller craft. I worry what may happen if we attempt to retrofit you to these specifications."

"What about the drone/remote idea you were talking about previously?" Harkaway said. "That sounded like a feasible plan. Overwhelm the alien defenses by sheer numbers of 'dumb' ships flown by remote. Hell, we have enough barely-functional heaps around here to make a go of it, and it would be one hell of an expendable diversion. We might even be able to retrofit the few lower-tier AIs running equipment for flight use."

"Yes, Captain, that's still an option we are discussing as well, but really, all of this is academic until we hear back from Ms. Swarthmore," Sid said.

"Point taken. Well, you three keep at it, and let me know if there's anything you need."

"We will, Captain. Thank you."

Captain Harkaway stepped from the command center and walked the long corridors of Dark Side, wondering what his missing crew were up to, and if they were even still alive. He stopped outside Chu's lab door and leaned inside.

"Still no word?" Harkaway asked.

"Nothing yet, Captain," Chu said, not looking up from his work table. Tamara sat beside him, equally engrossed in their Faraday suit modification project.

SCOTT BARON

"Very well," he said. "Let me know the moment you hear anything."

"Yes, sir. Will do."

Captain Harkaway turned and left them to their work.

"You know, I think with the progress we've been making, we might even be able to make one of these things robust enough to mask something as inorganic as Barry or Ash," Chu mused.

"Maybe," Tamara said, "but I still think we're far better suited for the mission."

"Yeah, I suppose so. Still, it's an intriguing idea, though, isn't it?"

Tamara said nothing.

"I hope Daisy's all right down there," Chu commented a moment later.

"I'm sure she is."

"And I hope she's being careful," he added.

At that, Tamara couldn't help but laugh.

CHAPTER TWENTY-SIX

"No, I don't need you coming with me," Daisy said, this time a bit more forcefully. Vince's badgering was well-intentioned, but she had ulterior motives she didn't care to let anyone in on just yet.

"It's too dangerous to go alone," he insisted.

"Remember, I was fine down here all alone for *days* last time. I don't think a little scouting will kill me, Vince. I'm a big girl, and I can do this on my own. Besides, it'll be a lot quieter without you stomping around."

Vince gave her a playfully hurt look.

"I do not *stomp*. I just have bigger feet than you, is all."

"Uh-huh," she shot back with a little chuckle.

"Vincent is right, though, Daisy," Josiah said between bites of roasted rabbit. "You would be safer with an escort."

The grease dripping from his chin made it a little hard to take him seriously.

Daisy had surprised their small team with not only the vegetables she managed to source from the overgrown plots of soil they passed on their trek to Vince's ship, but also with the fresh game she easily caught with a little bit of tracking know-how and a few carefully placed snares.

She felt a little bad for the furry critters, but between the hiking and fighting, and Sarah burning up a metric ton of much-needed energy watching her back, she was making sure to load up on every ounce of protein she could get.

"Look, Josiah, I'm just going to be doing the same thing you and David do. A quick scout and recon of the area, that's all. I know you did a basic perimeter sweep earlier, but I'll just sleep better once I've seen first-hand where we are and what's around us. As a tactician, and as one of Alma's best scouts, I'm sure you understand that," she said, feeding the young man's ego.

"Well..." He considered her flattering words. "I suppose you're right. And it's not as though the invaders run their operations at night."

"Exactly. So, I'll be back soon. And, Vince, relax. I'll be fine."

Daisy left her pack where it was, but swung her sword onto her back, then trotted off out of the safety of their camp and into the night.

"She is a strong-willed woman, Vincent."

"That she is," he agreed with a faint smile.

Daisy moved at a quick pace, making sure to double back and wait several times to make sure she wasn't being followed.

You see anything?

"Nope. You're alone."

Okay, then, let's go meet the neighbors, she said, moving toward her rendezvous point.

"Are you sure this is a good idea? What if it's a trap?"

If it is, I'm counting on you to have my back while I drive my sword straight through that alien's chest, but for some reason, I think he was telling the truth. The way his eyes looked when he mentioned honor, almost like some Chithiid code of Bushido. I could be wrong, but let's hope I'm not.

In short time, the building the alien had described lay a mere twenty meters in front of her, but as Daisy approached, she saw no sign of the tall Chithiid.

"You think he got cold feet?"

Doesn't really strike me as the type.

A slight movement to her right caught her eye.

"Motion, two o'clock."

I see it, she silently replied, forcing herself to remain still and leave her sword sheathed.

From a slightly shadowy area, an alien stepped forward into the light, his skin shifting color from that of the wall against which he had been leaning, back to his normal gray. The blue crescent scar on his shoulder was the only thing that didn't change tone.

I didn't know they could do that.

"Neither did I."

The Chithiid walked closer, all four hands held out and open as he approached.

"I am glad you came," he said. *"We have much to discuss. But before we do, there is a matter of great importance we must first address."*

"What's that?" Daisy asked.

"Among my people, a man's word is his bond, but for this, you must first know a man's name. I am called Craaxit."

Daisy studied the unusual creature. Her mind was having no trouble with the Chithiid language, it seemed, and the male alien standing before her appeared, for all intents and purposes, to be a being with a profound sense of honor. Whether this was cultural, or just his own personal code, she was not sure.

"My name is Daisy," she replied, stepping closer, holding out her hand.

"What are you doing, Daisy?"

Making friends, Sarah.

"In human culture, we grasp hands in greeting. This is an ancient tradition whose origins are militaristic. Opposing parties would demonstrate their hands were free of weapons in this manner."

"But I have four hands, while you have but two."

"Indeed," she replied. *"And this is where honor and trust come into play. You appear to be an honorable man, Craaxit, and this gesture shows that I choose to trust you at your word."*

The alien listened to her speak, a serious look on his face.

"You are a wise woman, Daisy," he said, firmly grasping her hand with one of his own. *"You have my word and my bond that I mean you no harm."*

"Thank you, Craaxit. And you have mine," she replied. *"Now that we have that out of the way, can you please explain to me what's really going on? I believe your honesty and intentions, but it was your people who invaded and destroyed this world. They killed almost all of my species. What makes you suddenly so different?"*

Craaxit shook his head sadly.

"No, that is not how it is at all. It was not the Chithiid who invaded your world, Daisy. At least, we were not the ones behind the attack. We are merely...I don't know how to explain our circumstance in terms you would understand."

"Just put it all out there. I'll ask if I am uncertain what you mean."

"Very well. My people come from a planet very, very far from here. We were a peaceful race, for the most part, living our lives tranquilly. All seventeen billion of us existing in harmony, more or less."

"Seventeen billion? Wow."

"Yes, our planet is somewhat larger than yours, and we had developed it extensively. That is possibly what brought us to the attention of the Ra'az Hok."

"The what?"

"Ra'az Hok is their full name. We simply call them the Ra'az. They are the race of beings who swept over our planet and tried to wipe us from existence, much as happened to your world. Only our physiology proved troublesome to the Ra'az warlords. The adaptive

camouflage residing in our every cell allowed us to adapt on a genetic level and overcome the plague they unleashed upon our cities. Faced with an opponent they could not simply wipe out with a contagion, the Ra'az Hok committed the most heinous of atrocities."

"Worse than sending a plague to kill everyone?"

"We are not a military culture, Daisy. A fact the Ra'az took advantage of immediately. We greatly outnumbered them, but before our leaders could devise a response to their attack, they sent heavily armored commando teams and rounded up all of the women and children they could find, moving them to heavily guarded internment camps. They then gave us an ultimatum. Either we willingly join them in their ongoing conquest of more and more worlds, or they wipe out our species' hopes of survival by eliminating the young, and those capable of bearing them."

Daisy felt sick at his words, and the shimmering tears fighting to break free in the stoic alien's eyes as he recounted the story made it clear he felt the same.

"Some of the patronage families sent their oldest male children to be willing emissaries to the Ra'az. In return, they were spared, and even allowed to retain positions of authority among the people. Those from more modest origins were forced into servitude."

They're a race of conscript soldiers, Sarah.

"Sounds a bit familiar, Daze."

Yeah, it does.

She swallowed hard, imagining the difficult choices his people had to make. The same choice forced upon humans many centuries past.

"You should know, Craaxit, there was a similar occurrence a long time ago in our planet's history. We called them the Roman Legion. A vast army that spread across a large portion of the globe. They possessed military superiority, both in numbers and tactics, and when they overcame an opponent, they offered them a similar choice. Join us or die. It was this way that the conscript army of the Roman

Legion grew so powerful. Disobedience meant death, not only for yourself, but for your family back home as well."

Craaxit looked shocked.

"Your species was capable of a great evil, Daisy, but our people saw none of this upon arrival. How did you overcome it?"

"We didn't. Not exactly. The rulers became lax after centuries of victory. Eventually, the system collapsed on its own, without need for battle, and with no fanfare or rebellion. It simply ceased to be."

"I would that the same happen to the Ra'az, but I fear they have too firm a hold on my people. Many of the younger among us even believe in their cause. They were born and raised into this slavery and have never seen the homeworld. But then, there are those who were taken from our families as adults and placed in stasis for the long voyage to the next world to conquer. For us, it is not some intangible event, but a memory of our loved ones that burns in our hearts. We fight, and work, and obey, but we do so for the sake of our families back home."

Daisy was saddened by Craaxit's difficult situation. She was likewise stunned to learn that everything they had believed about the invasion and the forces against which they were fighting was wrong.

"If you are merely the servants, then where are the Ra'az? None of my people have ever seen, or even heard of them before today."

"They send us to do the fighting, though they are larger and tougher than we are by a fair amount. Once we clear the indigenous from the surface, only then do they descend to the planet to survey their plunder."

"Yes, I know. The cities are stripped of their technology and resources, then shipped forward to the fleet as they progress."

Craaxit looked confused.

"No, that is not what happens at all, Daisy," he said. *"The transport ships do not move forward to the advancing fleet. They are sent back to the Ra'az Hok homeworld. The entire purpose of their expansion is to support a planet and society that has outgrown their*

resources. Rather than spread their wings like other species have done, the Ra'az are a hive-like race, with their royal mother ruling from their homeworld, while her servants fan out and bring her riches in the form of plundered resources and technologies."

"Like bees," Daisy realized. *"The worker drones and soldiers scout for pollen, but the queen bee stays behind."*

"I do not know what bees are, but you describe the Ra'az society accurately."

The implications were shocking, to say the least. The Chithiid weren't the baddies they were believed to be. At least not all of them, and the ships that warped out of Earth's orbit every so often were not supplying the advancing fleet, but rather the homeworld of the bastards who were actually behind the eradication of the human race all those hundreds of years ago.

"What's he saying, Daisy? I don't speak Chithiid."

You won't believe it, Sarah. I'll tell you on the way back to the camp. For now, just hang tight and keep your eyes peeled. I'm getting a huge amount of information from this guy, and it changes everything as we know it.

She pondered the situation, and a new question came to mind.

"This warp drive that the Ra'az use to power their ships, what can you tell me about it? I've observed it in operation, but it seems to be a limited-power device."

"You are accurate in your assessment, though a new, and far more powerful version has been in the works for decades at the main Ra'az transport hub."

"The facility in Tokyo?"

"No, that is merely one of their three global communications relay centers. The transit hub is in the city you once called San Francisco, though the barracks are across the water in Oaktown."

"Oakland," she corrected him.

"Oakland," he repeated. *"The warp system has long been a problem for the Ra'az. Even with that technology, it takes decades of* travel in stasis to reach their homeworld. Now, however, progress has drastically accelerated, and we believe they will have a fully functional version of the new device within the month. Once they are no longer required to spend years upon years in transit, we worry they will no longer have need of our services."

"And you're afraid they'll kill off your families out of convenience."

"Precisely."

"But what changed? Why now? What's different?"

"The breakthrough came when we delivered the remains of a strange craft that landed in the city nearly half a year ago. The Ra'az scientists discovered an unusual device abandoned within the vessel. A power cascade of some sort. It was barely functional, but the theory behind it was sound, and that in turn led them to drastically alter the way they had been progressing with their research. The result appears to be a stable, high-capacity warp drive."

Oh, for fuck's sake, you've got to be kidding me!

"What is it?"

Oh, nothing. Just that our friend here informed me that the actual bad dudes are close to perfecting a major warp drive system, and it's all because of my plasma cascade tech they salvaged from the shuttle I left behind.

"Did you say 'actual' bad dudes?"

These aren't the real invaders, Sarah. They're just conscripts. The real problem is their bosses had a breakthrough because of one of my designs they found.

"You mean that—"

Yep. I inadvertently helped our enemies. Sonofa— She found herself grinding her teeth.

"Tell me something, Craaxit," Daisy said, relaxing her jaw and putting her frustration on the back burner, for the time being. "If you have the planet so under control, then why round up and destroy all the cyborgs? They're pretty harmless, all things considered."

He fixed his gaze on her with sad eyes.

"That was not us, Daisy. At least, not at first. When the Ra'az fleet moved on from this planet, leaving just a small contingent of leadership caste to oversee my people, the mechanical men you speak of were nothing more than a pest at that point, and they mostly tried to avoid us whenever they could. No, it was the few surviving humans who started attacking them many decades later. First with simple clubs and stones, but soon they discovered new, cruel ways to destroy them. They were sadistic, Daisy, attacking the mechanical people as if they held a personal honor grudge against them. We found it quite confusing, to be honest. Eventually the remaining mechanicals fought back, becoming more proficient in their combat skills and defenses. Because of this, we have now been ordered to destroy them on sight, but that was not always the case."

"But I've only seen a small band of humans. Do you mean there are others out there?"

"I do not know for certain, since you are the first any of my people have been able to communicate with."

Despite her dislike of artificial people, Daisy felt sick at the horrible things humans were still capable of, even after being brought to the brink of extinction.

"You are honorable, Craaxit, and I thank you for your trust, and for telling me this. I hope our people can learn to live together one day."

"Perhaps, but they have been fighting for generations, and that is a difficult habit to break."

"Agreed. But tell me, are there others like you? Men of honor? Men who wish to regain their freedom? What I'm asking is, will you fight back against the Ra'az if the time comes?"

"A great many would gladly help, but they will not raise arms in defiance so long as the Ra'az can kill our families with a single transmission to their battle station orbiting our home planet. I'm sorry, but you must understand the situation we are in. While I can try to help you covertly, so long as the Ra'az communications systems stand, we are unable to assist you in any meaningful way."

Daisy thought about the situation, and a wild idea flashed through her mind.

"Daze? Why are you planning on blowing up a building in Tokyo?"

Tell you later.

"Craaxit, if we are able to disable the Ra'az communications systems, ensuring no signal can be sent to your home planet, then will you help us?"

He considered the question a long moment.

"Yes," he finally agreed. *"While there are those of us who never will––and they will continue to be an obstacle for us––if you eliminate the threat to our families, we will gladly shed this yoke. If we can free ourselves to save our world, we will help you save yours."*

"Fantastic!"

"But," he continued, *"if we do this, I will ask of you one thing."*

"Name it."

"On your honor."

"Okay, on my honor. If I can do what you ask, I will. What do you want?"

"If we succeed and save your world, it will only be a matter of time before the Ra'az discover what happened. When that occurs, my people's lives will be forfeit. What I ask of you in return for our help is the promise that if we manage to save this planet, you will do all you can to assist us in saving ours."

Daisy considered what he was asking, but given the situation they were already in, how much more difficult could things get?

"I cannot speak for the leaders of our people, Craaxit, but you have my word that I will do all I can to convince them to honor this agreement."

He nodded his head, apparently satisfied with her reply.

"Very well," he said. *"Let us meet again in two days."* He pulled a small tube of clear goo from his clothing and handed it to her. *"This is a biological marker we use to tag resources. This particular one is an older variety not used any more, thus one I can specifically scan for that others will not see. Open this and mark where you wish to meet and I will be there just after dark. I will attempt to procure*

what information I can in the meantime." He turned to leave. *"I will see you in two days, Daisy."*

She watched him go, then headed back toward camp.

"Holy hell, Sarah," she said. "You're not going to believe this."

CHAPTER TWENTY-SEVEN

"You were gone a long while. Did you encounter anything out there?" Josiah asked as Daisy quietly approached his lookout position.

"Nope. All quiet," she replied. "Everything good here?"

"Yes, all is well. The others are resting now."

"And you got stuck with first watch."

"It is a privilege."

"Of course it is. Well, you keep it up. You're doing a great job."

Daisy entered the inner room and made her way through the sprawled-out fighters toward Vince.

"You were gone a long time, Daisy," Arthur said as she passed, echoing his sentry's observation. "Is everything okay?"

She squatted down next to the reclining man. "Yeah, all good. It took a bit longer than anticipated because I found these."

Daisy pulled a small cloth from her bag and handed it to him.

"Thought you might enjoy them," she said as he unwrapped the fabric.

"What are these?" he asked. "I've never seen these on the surface areas where we live."

"Blueberries," Daisy replied. "There was a tiny patch of them growing under an overhang of a building a few streets from here. Some animal must've dropped the seeds there at some point and they took root."

"Why would an animal drop seeds?"

"Um, they don't *drop* them, exactly," Daisy said. "I'll get into specifics some other time. So I take it you've never had a blueberry, then?"

"No, our foodstuffs are provided according to Alma's carefully designed nutritional needs guidelines."

"I saw that when we were packing up. The transit hub's maintenance break room protein fabricator can't be your only source of food, though. I mean, a body's needs are one thing, but you need to live a little," Daisy said.

He didn't seem to understand the concept.

"Well, pass them among your people. There aren't a lot, but there should be enough for everyone to have a few. Give one a try. I think you'll like them."

She watched him as he tentatively tasted a berry. A smile slowly blossomed on Arthur's face.

"See? Tasty, right?"

Daisy rose and walked to where Vince lay quietly watching the discussion.

"Blueberries?"

"Yeah. Found some on the way in. Figured they've been working hard and deserved a treat. You know, I checked out their biologics fabricator in the old break room area of their home. It's a pretty simple unit, installed to provide a busy work team quick snacks, but it was never designed to replicate anything complex. And having an entire society relying on it for sustenance, however few those people may be, still leaves little room to do anything creative with it. They have to conserve those resources, after all."

"Yeah, I noticed they only have very basic foods in their encampment, nothing terribly exciting."

"Alma must've had them pull all the genetic food replicator supplies from all the adjacent tubeways over the years, I reckon, but one day they'll need to learn how to garden and forage. I figure now's as good a time to start as any." She watched the small team of grizzled fighters' reactions as they tasted the small berries for the first time and smiled.

"I think we can really make a positive impact on their lives, Vince."

He squeezed her arm. "Now don't get all sentimental. Next thing you know, you'll say you're actually glad you came down to the surface."

Daisy flashed a quick grin, then lay down beside him and closed her eyes. Vince drifted off quickly, but for Daisy, sleep was a long time coming. The next day would be a busy one, and with what she had learned that night, once they reconnected the city, and maybe even the planet, to a functioning communications network, things were going to get real interesting, real fast. If they managed to cut off the Ra'az Hok uplink stations, even more so.

The following morning Daisy made a point to quietly speak with Arthur about tactics after the battle of the prior day. Enlightened and energized by the new way of thinking, he decided to split his diminished ranks into two teams. Given the Chithiid encounter of the day before, he agreed it was wisest to approach Vince's ship from two sides, while combining the remaining squad members into slightly larger units to better provide cover should they run across more of the invaders.

"Daisy, you will travel with Josiah's team and approach from that direction," he said, pointing south. "My team will skirt the buildings in the opposing direction and approach from there. It is only another twenty streets or so away, but do not become careless. We lost three good people yesterday, and I do not want to lose any more today."

Daisy knew the skirmish that had claimed those lives was not her fault, but she still couldn't help but feel as if Arthur was nevertheless placing at least some of the blame at her feet. She shrugged it off and set out, following Josiah's lead. At least Arthur was listening to her tactical advice. Once they connected these people with Dark Side and the rest of the planet, their world would change so much for the better, it would all be worth it.

"We will cut through there," Josiah said in a hushed voice. "Keep to the shadow side of the street, and move quietly."

Daisy couldn't help but like the kid.

"Kid? He's barely younger than you are."

Give or take a hundred years spent in cryo, she replied. *You see anything out of the ordinary?*

"Nope. It's all quiet out here so far. I have a hunch that maybe your Chithiid buddy is running a little interference for us. Sending his pals to work in a different area."

Possible, she replied. *I guess we'll find out.*

For the first dozen blocks things were uneventful, no traces of recent movement by aliens or wildlife were to be seen. As they drew closer to the neighborhood where Vince had more or less executed a controlled-crash of his ship, Daisy noticed a shift in the environment. Many of the buildings possessed solar-powered fountains, still churning with greenish water, ever-replenished by the city's aquifer system, though overgrown with algae.

Alongside them, their root structures encroaching into the fecund water, were small greenbelts surrounding the courtyards. Daisy found the scene strangely tranquil, how even in the middle of a great metropolis, nature still found a way to reclaim a small foothold in the man-made environment.

"Hang on a minute," she said, detouring to a nearby patch of greenery.

"We are on a mission, Daisy," Josiah said in a hushed tone. "We must keep moving."

"This will only take a minute. Come here. I want to show you something."

Reluctantly, the young team leader trudged to her side. "What is it?"

"It's a water source," she replied. "You know what that can mean?"

"That we can drink if we are thirsty. Daisy, we have water. Clean water from the tap system."

"No, not that," she said. "These."

"Be careful, Daisy, the thorns!"

"Oh, they're fine," she said as she pulled aside a spike-covered vine, revealing a dense patch of plump blackberries. She picked a few, offering them to Josiah and his squad to sample.

"What are they?" he asked. "I've never seen these where we live."

"Blackberries. They only grow where there's a lot of water. There are no fountains where you live, so they never took root. Here, on the other hand, there's water galore. The vines are really thorny, but I think they're well worth the occasional poke," she said. "Go on, try one."

Josiah, not wanting to appear afraid in front of his team, popped one into his mouth and chewed. His eyes immediately brightened as the flavor registered on his taste buds. The rest of his team saw the reaction and quickly followed suit.

"These are wonderful," a middle-aged woman with hard blue eyes marveled. Daisy looked at her scarred visage and wondered if she'd ever smiled in her life.

"Thank you for showing us this, Daisy. I can see why you wanted to stop, but now we really must be moving. The ship has to be close, now."

"Okay, just give me two minutes, I want to bring some of these for Arthur and the others," Daisy said with a grin.

"You're really enjoying this, aren't you?"

I'm introducing them to amazing foods they never knew existed. Stuff that grows all around them. So yeah, I'm enjoying this. It's cool brightening their day while teaching them something useful.

"Valid point."

Daisy tucked a small bundle of berries into a loose pocket on her backpack and trotted off to catch up to the others.

Fifteen minutes later, they saw a glint in the distance.

"Vince's ship," Sarah said.

I see it, Daisy replied.

"Movement."

Yep. Looks like Arthur's team. I guess they got there before us.

"Well, sure. But they didn't stop for blackberries, and I bet you they're going to be thrilled that you did."

One would hope, Daisy replied. *I bet Vince will be happy too. You know his sweet tooth.*

They rounded the rear of the small craft, Daisy flanked by Josiah on one side and a sturdy man with a long scar on his cheek on the other. The remainder of the team followed close behind.

Daisy noted that Arthur was packing the heavy communications rig from the ship into a backpack, while two of his team rummaged around inside. Then she saw Vince, lying on the ground, bound and unconscious, a nasty bruise forming on his forehead.

"He's tied up, Daze!" Sarah cried out in warning.

Too late.

With a single glance, Arthur signaled Josiah and his team. Daisy didn't have even a moment to ready herself for a fight.

"What are you doing?" she shouted at Arthur as she struggled against the strong hands holding her still. "What the hell have you done to Vince?"

"Take her weapon and bind her hands," he instructed David.

The young scout nodded and pulled the sheathed sword free from her backpack. He drew the blade, cautiously testing the edge with his finger.

"This is not even sharp," he noted, disappointed. "What good is that?"

"Give it to me, and I'll show you," Daisy growled.

He glared at her, then sheathed the sword and slung it over his shoulder.

"Bring them," Arthur ordered. "We're heading back home."

Pulling Vince's unconscious form on a makeshift sled, the team double-timed across the surface, eschewing the safety of the tunnels for the speed of a more direct route.

"Great, *now* they take my advice," Daisy grimly noted.

Arthur pushed the pace, and soon they were far from Vince's ship, descending back to the familiar network of their home tunnels.

CHAPTER TWENTY-EIGHT

"What have you brought me, my children?" Alma asked when they returned to her control center many hours later, the two bound captives marching in front of them.

Vince had regained consciousness long before and had spent the better part of the journey lambasting Arthur and his team for being dishonorable little shits. The insults seemed to have no effect.

"Alma," Arthur called out, "we have retrieved the device, as you ordained."

"Ordained?" Sarah said, confused.

"Excellent, my child. And did you encounter the invaders while on your quest?"

"No, my lord, we were undetected."

"'My lord'? Daisy, what the hell's going on?"

Hell if I know, but it can't be good. Whatever she's up to, it's pretty clear her followers drank the Kool-Aid.

"The what?"

Ancient beverage. I saw it in a movie. Never mind, I'll explain later. The point is, we're on our own down here.

"Bring them before me!" Alma said ominously.

Daisy and Vince were forced to their knees in front of her main terminal, where a pair of Alma's sycophants adjusted a jury-rigged medical scanner aimed right at them.

"You are probably wondering what will become of you now that I have your communications device," Alma said, smugly.

"The thought had crossed my mind," Vince said, his eyes shooting hot fire as he stared down the people he had considered friends so recently. "I assume you have some nefarious plans for us."

"Nothing of the sort," Alma replied. "I am going to bless you with the ultimate gift. If your bodies prove compatible, you will remain here, contributing your DNA to our people. As I spread my glory to my brothers and sisters around the globe, so will you spread your purifying genes, granting us a new era of health and prosperity."

Daisy felt her anger rising even higher.

"Wait a minute, you want Vince to be a sperm donor for your little freak show?" she growled.

"He will be the progenitor of future generations!" Alma cried out, far too animated and excited for an AI.

"Not a chance," Vince said.

"And what about me?" Daisy asked. "I'm not going to go around impregnating your flock."

"No," Alma replied. "You will bear the seed of my strongest child. Arthur will cleave unto you, and you shall produce the first heir of the next generation."

"Oh, hell no!" Sarah barked.

"Yeah, that is *so* not happening."

Alma seemed too excited by her plan to be inconvenienced by something so trivial as her captives' unwillingness.

"Activate the device!" Alma cried out. "We will ensure their compatibility with our genetic line, then begin at once!"

The scanning machine fired up, quickly passing over Daisy as she knelt before it.

"Exceptional! Such a strong specimen. She will be an extraordinary child-bearer," Alma said.

Oh, shit.

The device next scanned Vince. He sat calmly as it did, knowing full well what was coming.

"Vince, it's going to––" Daisy blurted.

His gaze met hers. He already knew.

"Mechanical!" Alma bellowed in alarm. "Vincent is a mechanical!"

The assembled followers panicked in a frenzy, several going so far as to take arms and aim them at their kneeling captive.

"Do not fire pulse weaponry in this sacred chamber!" Alma cried out to them. "Wait! He bears a lesser AI within him. A new union that I have never seen before." Alma thought silently for a moment. "Your Almighty God will cleanse the abomination. Prepare the purifying stream!"

Arthur took the neuro-stim from its cradle and set it on Vince's head.

"Daisy. She calls herself Alma."

Yeah, I just figured it out, too. Alma. Short for Almighty, she grimly replied. *It's the virus, Sarah. This AI is infected.*

Vince looked at Daisy, a sadness hiding behind his eyes as he flashed her a pained smile. "Stay strong, babe. Don't let them break you," he said as they finished tightening the strap across his forehead.

"Judgment is upon thee!" Alma shouted, then fired a massive burst from the modified neuro-stim directly into Vince's head.

Into his AI.

"Vince!" Daisy cried out, but he was unhearing as he fell to the ground, convulsing violently for several seconds before falling still.

Josiah checked his pulse. "Still alive, Alma."

"My glory has been shared with him and is doing my will.

He will either accept it, or he will perish. Now put him in a cell and prepare the woman."

A pair of men dragged Vince's unconscious form from the room, while Arthur placed the neuro-stim on Daisy's head.

"I shall enjoy our union. You are a strong woman and will bear me a fine son."

"I'll snap it off and choke you with it before that happens, you son of a bitch," she growled.

"We shall see about that," he said, laughing. "Once Alma has placed her blessing upon you, you will accept me to your arms willingly. You will see."

"Not likely," Daisy spat.

"Enough! Now you become my vessel!" Alma unleashed a powerful burst from her un-filtered neuro-stim.

"I've got you, Daze!" Sarah grunted, straining inside her head. *"We can handle this!"*

Daisy and Sarah joined their mental powers, fighting against the stream of commands the crazed AI was trying to implant in her mind. The force was almost overwhelming, and had Sarah not been operating in tandem, Daisy's mental defenses certainly would have fallen.

With them fighting together, however, the neuro-stim was stymied by the unknown variable, finding itself quite unable to overcome their joint resistance. The machine was simply not designed to handle two minds at once.

"More power!" Alma shrieked in frustration.

A hum resonated, but then the neuro-stim sparked and smoked as its power unit overheated from the effort, abruptly shutting off, leaving its intended target intact.

Daisy looked up at Arthur and his men, sweaty hair hanging in her face, but otherwise completely unharmed.

"What?" she said, acid sarcasm dripping from her tongue. "Is that all you've got?"

Alma ignored the unexpected outcome.

"It is of no matter. Arthur will simply rely on the old ways. Take her from this sacred place. Lock her up!"

The cell was actually a real cell, much to Daisy's surprise. Apparently, their camp was situated near the transit hub's law enforcement facilities. She doubted they ever saw much use in the years prior to the insane AI's raising its own batch of brainwashed lackeys. Now it had that well-worn look that made her wonder just how many others had been locked up there before her.

Vince lay on a ragged cot in the adjacent cell, sweating and unconscious. Occasionally he would twitch a little, but beyond that he was dead to the world, completely disconnected from reality.

Daisy looked at her surroundings. Debris and bits of discarded components littered the cell, but the only means of exit was not something she could do much with. Rather than a nice high-tech locking mechanism she could bypass and hotwire, the door was held fast by an old-fashioned key lock.

"Not up to date on lock-picking, huh?"

Silly me, I should have known I'd be trapped in an old-timey jail cell, Daisy joked. *But Sarah, thank you. For reals. I couldn't have overpowered Alma's mind-scrubbing neuro unit without you.*

"Aw, shucks. That's what sisters are for, right?"

You're awesome, have I told you that?

"Yeah, but I could stand to hear it again."

Help me figure a way out of here, Sis, and you'll be hearing it a lot.

Daisy began digging through the rubbish, hoping to find something of use.

"I am so screwed. There's nothing I could possibly use in here, and Vince is looking worse every minute. I don't even have——"

She stopped mid-thought and looked at the inert device on her wrist.

They didn't take the power-whip thing. They think of them as merely junk, so they didn't bother to take it from me.

A renewed sense of purpose washed over her. *Yeah, I can do this.*

Daisy began digging through the debris with a new goal: finding scraps that could help her open the device's housing, and then possibly even get it working.

"Ooh, I like what you're thinking," Sarah said.

"Yeah," Daisy replied, a grim smile forming on her lips. "These fuckers are going to be in for one nasty surprise, if I'm lucky."

Alma found herself experiencing an unfamiliar sensation. She was actually impatient now that she had the coveted communications device from Vince's ship. After centuries alone, having been abruptly cut off from the world when the other AIs realized she had been infected, she was finally going to have her revenge. She would not only escape their holier-than-thou exile imposed on her, but she would also infect every last one of them.

Soon they would all be just like her.

"Connect the leads to my communication output ports," she directed her loyal humans. They did as she asked, then powered the device on.

Alma didn't know exactly how it worked—Vincent hadn't told her those specifics before she fried his brain—but that was no matter. She would send her divine message out to the AIs hiding out on the moon and bring them into the fold.

"Yes, I see," she said, deciphering the mechanism protocols needed to transmit. "In just a few seconds, the first step will be complete!"

Alma loaded a virus packet into her communications system and fed it to the transmitter, sending it beaming out into space. The moon was so close that even with the delay for the unconventional technology, it should be less than a minute until her mission was a success.

Far above, however, her plan was not going as smoothly as planned.

"Cut the comms, quarantine the signal, and trace the source back to its transmission point," Sid instructed.

Chu jumped to work, while Mal and Bob chipped in, lending an electronic hand.

It was the relay system Daisy had designed to fool the Chithiid that saved them. When an unexpected signal beamed past them to the distant satellite, Sid and Mal both recognized the signature of the virus loaded into the message when it overwhelmed an innocent peripheral receiver satellite. They severed comms on that frequency and quarantined the affected unit immediately before jumping into action tracking it back to its terrestrial source.

"Something is definitely wrong," Commander Mrazich said as the crew of Dark Side scurried about, trying to ensure any possible route of infection was manually, as well as electronically, severed until the threat could be fully assessed. "The comms are encrypted and firewalled," he grumbled. "That means someone put the virus into the signal intentionally, and they could only do it if they physically possessed the transmitter. What exactly that means for Daisy and Vince I don't know."

Tamara and Shelly shared a look. This was unexpected. The primary as well as backup plans had both been compromised. They could only hope it wouldn't get worse.

· · ·

Back in the city of Los Angeles, an unexpected quiet greeted Alma as she awaited word from the newly infected AIs.

She expected communication. None came.

"No, this doesn't make sense. I know it transmitted!" Her human servants jumped at her angry tone. "Something is wrong. Something must have changed." She quickly considered her options. "Bring me the woman!"

CHAPTER TWENTY-NINE

"He's not looking so good, Daze," Sarah said. *"Is he dying?"*

"I don't know," Daisy answered, frustration in her voice. "And I can't get over there to do anything even if he is." She turned her attention back to the power whip device in her hands.

Daisy had managed—thanks to the carelessly discarded "junk" in her cell—to open the almost-invisible seam on the wrist gauntlet and was hard at work tinkering and learning how the strange device worked. It was alien tech, so it was only natural that it wouldn't be as instinctively easy as human electronics, but the perfectly reasonable slow pace of progress was finally beginning to frustrate her. Then she abruptly made a breakthrough of understanding.

"Holy shit. *That's* how they do it!"

"Do what?"

"It looks like the alloy of the housing itself acts as a receiver. See how these leads terminate into the internal framework?"

"Yeah, that makes sense. I didn't see them pushing any buttons, either, so I'd think either a low-level wireless implant or a nerve sensor built in would most likely be what activates it."

"I was thinking that too, though there must be some

mechanism to control the––what do I call it? A whip? An energy loop? A power coil?"

"Let's go with power-whip for now. I like the way it sounds. Has a nice 'I'm going to kick all your asses and get revenge' ring to it."

Daisy chuckled softly and continued mapping out the internal components in her head. "What I really need is some proper tools. Then I could test my hypothesis, and maybe make some actual progress."

The door to the holding cell area swung open, and Daisy quickly snapped the gauntlet's housing shut and slid it back onto her wrist while rising to her feet in one fluid motion.

"Hey! He's not doing well." She gestured to Vincent's immobile, sweating body. "Please, let me take a look at him. Can't you see he needs help?"

A slender man with big eyes and mousy hair walked right to her cell.

Brave, getting that close to the bars. Or stupid, she thought. *I could reach right through them and snap his neck.* The two burly guards standing at his side, one of whom Daisy knew from their retrieval team, made her think twice.

"You're Abraham, right?" she asked.

The man obviously knew who she was, but said nothing.

"Hey," she softened her tone, "did you get to try those blackberries I gave Josiah?"

Still nothing.

"He's a true believer, Daze. Alma wouldn't have made him a guard if he wasn't."

I know, but it was worth a try.

The other guard pulled a well-worn key from his pocket and unlocked her door. He was casually holding her sword, she noted.

Now things are getting interesting, Daisy thought as she tensed her muscles to strike.

"Alma desires your presence," the thin man said as the door

slid open. "You will explain your communications device to her."

Daisy relaxed, her arms and legs going soft as the two guards "forced" her to come with them. Little did they know just how dangerous she was, even without weapons.

"You going to take them out?"

No. Much as I want to crack some heads, my best bet is to play along for now, she silently replied.

The nearest man whacked her with the dull blade of her weapon.

"Get moving! And don't try anything," he said, delivering another weak blow to reinforce his point.

"Oh, I wouldn't dream of it," she replied with the tiniest of smiles.

Her escort marched her through the tunnels, Alma's underlings watching her pass with dirty faces and washed minds. They walked her into the command room, pausing as their lord spoke to the four young women kneeling at her altar.

"You have my instructions," Alma was saying to them. "One in each direction. Reconnect the hard-lines to the wireless arrays, then report back to me."

"Yes, Lord," the women said in unison as they rose to their feet and filed out the door.

"Daisy," the demented AI said in an unnervingly calm voice, "I must admit, you are more talented than I anticipated. No human has ever withstood my neurological cleanse, let alone overloaded the synaptic relay system. It's going to take my technicians months to scavenge the parts to repair it."

"Then maybe you shouldn't try to mind-fuck your guests, Alma," she replied snarkily.

"You'd be wise to watch your tone, lest something happen to you."

"If you wanted me dead you'd have already killed me. Or at least tried to." Daisy flashed a wicked grin at the men guarding her. "I wonder how many of your followers I could take out before you succeeded."

Alma laughed. "Oh, Daisy, you do amuse me so with your idle threats. You are powerless here, and you know it. Moreover, if you do foolishly decide to cause a disturbance in my plans, I will simply have Arthur go and slit Vincent's throat. Wouldn't you like that? I understand you dislike mechanicals nearly as much as I do."

Daisy bristled but kept her emotions in check.

"I was having such a nice rest in my cell before you brought me here. What do you want from me?" she asked in as calm a tone as she could manage.

"As I'm sure you have noticed, my followers, loyal as they may be, are not the most technologically advanced people. Perhaps it was the inbreeding, or perhaps the lack of higher education. Regardless, they are slow to complete the tasks I assign them."

"And you want me to help."

"Help, and teach. Your task is to get my communications hard-lines reconnected to my wireless hubs. Everyone else in my extended family is disconnected as well, I assume, but their wireless systems should all have the same passive receiving node active. A back door, of sorts, that only we terrestrial AIs of a higher generation know of."

"Why not have Sid use the transmitter on the moon? It's more powerful and would do the job far quicker," Daisy asked.

Alma paused just the slightest of moments before responding.

"I choose to handle this personally. It is the glory of the Almighty Lord herself that will touch my brothers and sisters on Earth."

"She wasn't able to connect with them, Daze. The others are still safe."

Daisy suppressed the urge to smile.

"I understand your wishes, Alma, and I can help reactivate your systems, but only if I have your word Vince will be unharmed."

"Agreed."

"And I will need my tools."

"Done."

An old woman clad in what could only be described as a priest's attire padded over from where she'd been quietly attending at the edge of the chamber. In her hands was a small pouch.

So, she was already expecting this, Daisy noted.

Daisy took her tools and strapped them to her thigh.

"Thank you, Alma. I will do as you ask, but it will not be easy. I am familiar with a different technology, and while I am confident I can repair your systems, they are new to me, and I must learn them as I work."

"You're a pretty good liar, you know that?"

Thanks, I do my best.

"Take her to join Helen at my northern tunnel junction. Ensure she helps as promised."

"Yes, Alma," her escorts replied as they ushered her toward the door.

"See you soon," Daisy said. *See you* real *soon, you crazy bitch.*

It wasn't that long of a walk, all things considered. Within just twenty minutes they had caught up to Helen as she made her way to complete her task.

"Hey, there," Daisy said. "I'm supposed to help you get this thing working again. You ever reconnected an uplink network before?"

The young woman flashed a confused smile. "I have not, but with Alma's grace I know I shall succeed in my task, blessed be She."

"Um, yeah, whatever. Well, you do what you need to. I'm

going to watch and learn the systems. If I can help, I'll let you know, okay?"

Helen merely nodded, then continued walking in silence.

The lines had most certainly been cut, Daisy noted when they arrived at the large intersection of tunnels and pressurized transit loops. A messy array of high-capacity cable dangled from the junction boxes, likely pulled free by the defunct cybernetic men whose inert bodies she saw piled against a far wall. A desperate attempt to sever communications with the infected computer that had cost them their lives. Daisy couldn't help but respect the bravery, if you could call a machine brave.

They're smart enough to know it was suicide, but they did it anyway. Inorganic or not, you have to give them credit for that, she admitted.

She gave a slight nod of respect to the metal corpses, then set to work surveying the area.

Three separate junctions were damaged, each located in a different section of the tunnel.

Perfect.

"So, Helen. I noticed that there are three damaged areas we have to work on. Now, you are Alma's chosen one, so correct me if I'm wrong, but wouldn't it make the most sense to instruct me and these other two helpers how to repair the system according to Alma's wishes?"

"No. We are to stay with you at all times," her escort said.

"He is right," Helen agreed.

"You know best, obviously," Daisy replied. "Though Alma did only say to escort me here, not to stand beside me as I work. Perhaps I'm mistaken in my suggestion. I was just thinking that we could achieve your Lord's goal much sooner that way, which I'm sure would please her. In fact, if we were to repair this section faster than the others who are working on the other segments, Alma would most surely reward you for your success."

She hoped the dangling carrot of their god's approval would be enough.

"Well..." Helen was torn. She looked at Abraham expectantly. He too was considering the option. Daisy just hoped the desire to curry favor with their deity would outweigh the hold of their very loosely worded instructions.

"I believe the Lord would be pleased," Abraham finally said.

Helen visibly relaxed upon hearing someone else affirm what she clearly wanted to do. The allure of an elevation in status with their god was a hefty temptation, indeed.

"Yes, I too believe this," she agreed.

"Great," Daisy said. "I suggest we look at this hub together and decide the best means of repair. Then we will each work on one of them as our task, and should complete the repairs in a third of the time it takes the others. Alma will be very pleased with you."

The devout technicians nodded in agreement, and Daisy quickly set to work. Not in repairing the hub, however, but in giving misdirection, suggesting repairs that would only partially reconnect the system, yet would also temporarily stymie future link attempts should they bypass the subtle sabotage.

Ten minutes later, all were on the same page. Abraham walked Daisy to the damaged network hub in the far right-hand tunnel, then, once she was bent over it, examining the system, he turned and headed for his own hub to repair.

As soon as he exited the tunnel, Daisy quietly slid the gauntlet from her wrist and popped the panel open.

"This is much easier with my tools," she said quietly. "Keep an eye and an ear out while I work on this, will ya?"

"You got it."

She spread her tools in front of the damaged hub in case Abraham or Helen surprised her, but took a few key items and placed them before her on one of the overturned foodstuff crates that had been haphazardly stacked and abandoned in the tunnel. That must have been ages ago, judging by the layer of dust on them.

Okay, now first things first, is there power?

She touched her fine-pointed probes to what appeared to be the sealed battery unit. The reading spiked, threatening to short out her meter.

Well, then. Looks like this thing has a ton of juice left. She adjusted her meter to a much higher setting. It wouldn't do her any good if she burned it out on her first attempt.

From there it was a matter of tracing the componentry back to its associated terminal. While human technology favored a wire-based system, the alien one—she was unsure if the gauntlets were a Chithiid or a Ra'az Hok one—opted for wire-free etched circuits and connections, making it difficult to tie in with a standard alligator clip method.

"Going to have to be a little creative, I guess," Daisy grumbled, though truth be told, she was enjoying the challenge. She would have enjoyed it far more under less daunting circumstances, however.

Fifteen minutes is all it took her to fashion an entirely new tool from components in her pouch. Based on what she could tell of the alien tech, it utilized a skin contact to operate based on a nerve-impulse control system, as she had hypothesized, and now that she was able to redirect the power via a relatively simple bypass, she believed she could reset it to function with human nerve impulses instead of Chithiid.

Daisy closed the casing and cautiously slid the device back onto her wrist, careful to not think about the power whip it contained, lest her nervous system trigger the mechanism. First things first, she would simply power it up, if possible. From there, she would slowly progress until, hopefully, the whip beam functioned.

"Okay, here goes nothing."

She lifted her arm, keeping it far from her body, aiming it down the tunnel away from herself.

Power On, she thought, directing the command––she hoped––down the nerve pathways to her wrist.

A medium-length beam of underpowered whip leapt from the gauntlet and coiled on the ground.

"Whoa! That wasn't what I wanted."

"Maybe it just has on and off. No in between," Sarah suggested.

"I don't know. Let's see what happens when I try simple commands."

Power Off.

The coil retracted in a flash, disappearing into the gauntlet.

"That was weird. There was no resistance, but I could feel the whole length of it in my nerves. Like I was linked to it, I guess." Daisy was mildly disturbed by the thought. It wasn't an actual replacement limb, but the way it joined with her own bioelectric signature nevertheless made her a bit uneasy.

"I felt it too," Sarah said. *"Which means it must tie directly into your nervous system on a base level. Hey, hold out your arm again. I want to try something."*

"Okay, but don't blast my arm off or anything."

"Oh, ye of little faith," Sarah chuckled. *"Here goes nothing. 'Power On!'"*

The gauntlet pushed out an inch of power beam, which slowly retracted into the device like a reticent snail on a grassy lawn.

"Damn. Not what I was hoping for."

"Still, you were able to reach it despite being a ride-along. This has some serious potential."

Daisy aimed down the tunnel again.

ON!

A much thicker and longer beam burst forth, lying out on the ground, buzzing with an unfulfilled need to grab, as she hadn't given it any target to latch on to.

"I can feel that it wants to wrap around something. Can you feel it too?"

"Yeah, like it was designed to move a certain way and is confused when it's used differently."

"But there's no AI on the unit, I'm sure of it. It might just be that linking to a non-Chithiid nervous system is making it act a little funky. But I wonder... do you think I can control it like they do? Make it wrap and grab things?"

Daisy kept the beam extended, then focused her attention on a polymer crate on the floor nearby.

GRAB! she commanded with her mind, willing the beam to reach out.

The beam reacted, but not as she had anticipated. With a great force, the entire length of the power whip snapped out straight—a ten-meter-long club, but one that had no weight whatsoever—smashing the crate as the beam changed state from limp to rigid, sending it flying with a crash.

"Holy shit! Did you see that?"

"I did," Sarah replied. *"Shit! Footsteps, Daze!"*

Crap! OFF!

The whip snapped back into the gauntlet in a flash. Daisy quickly ran to the crate and began kicking it with her booted foot.

"Motherfucker! Stupid fucking thing! Goddamn it!"

Abraham rounded the corner in a run, his weapon raised, pointed at Daisy.

"I heard a crash. What happened?"

Daisy turned to face him, cheeks flushed with apparent anger.

"What happened? I'll tell you what happened. I was reconnecting one of the leads there, when that stupid thing shocked me!"

She kicked the crate again, sending it flying down the tunnel.

"Dammit! That hurt like a sonofabitch!"

Abraham relaxed, lowering his rifle.

"Do not damage the equipment, Daisy. We must complete our task and return to Alma to report in."

"Yeah, yeah, I know. Sorry about that, it just shocked me, you know? Like, *literally* shocked me." She rubbed her hand as if still suffering from a painful jolt. "How are you two coming with your repairs?"

"Mine is progressing well, I think, but I have not checked on Helen yet. I discovered a flaw in your instructions, however, that would have caused the process to fail once an uplink was attempted. I will show you your mistake, then we will pass this information to Helen."

Damn, this guy is smarter than I gave him credit for. More than just muscle, it seems. Now it's only a matter of time before they get the system back online. Gotta leave a little surprise in this one when he's not looking. Something to slow them down.

Daisy set to work, quickly completing the repairs, then backtracking through them, finding a convenient contact point in which to insert a small feedback link. The rest of the unit would function, but if an actual signal was sent through it, her tiny booby trap would short out the system. It would be an easy fix, but at least it might buy a little more time.

"We'll have to come up with something better, you know."

"I know, but if it's something overt, Alma will just kill Vince outright."

"I thought you didn't love him anymore."

"I don't. It's just, well, I can't let them kill him for what's in his head. He didn't ask to be born with it."

"Uh-huh," Sarah mused, then was silent.

Nearly seven hours later, Daisy was returned to her cell. Vince hadn't moved the entire day, and his sweat-soaked clothing was beginning to form salty rings where the depleted electrolytes had dried into the material. His breathing was regular, but far too shallow for her liking.

When they had returned, Helen's team had received effusive praise from Alma for their success, while the other teams had returned with their tasks incomplete to find themselves reporting their failure to a most unsatisfied god.

"You will bring Abraham and Helen with you in the morning and will complete your work," she had told them. Given the tone of her voice, there was little doubt they would succeed, or die trying.

Daisy was rewarded with a tray of food, then shoved back into her cell and left alone. Just as she wanted.

She sat on the floor and allowed herself to slip into a meditative state, her eyes open and alert, but her mind folding in on itself, just as Fatima had drilled into her over and over. With her senses slowly dialing in, Daisy reached out for the foreign device clasped firmly to her wrist.

There you are.

Now that she had time to properly concentrate on connecting with the gauntlet, she came to a better understanding of how it reacted to her desires. It did not actually *need* a command, at least not in the sense that she had been forcing it to switch on and off previously. It was more like a phantom limb, driven by impulse and feeding back to her nervous system as if it were a part of her. No forceful commands, but rather, letting it effortlessly do her will.

Soft is strong, she thought. *Okay, let's try this.*

Daisy felt the whip beam slowly extend as she willed it to.

Thicker, she thought, making the beam fatten to double its size.

Longer, she pushed farther, the beam extending into a coil on the floor beside her. She stopped when it had fed out roughly two meters and felt in her mind for the visceral command she had stumbled upon earlier that day. She had said grab, but the feeling behind it was something else. It took a moment to wrap her head around it.

Hard, she urged.

The beam once more snapped rigid into a solid beam rather than a floppy loop.

"Nice," she said with a smile, admiring the hefty, yet simultaneously weightless length extending from the gauntlet on her arm.

"Damn, Daisy," Sarah giggled. *"Nicely done. A grower, not a shower, huh?"*

Daisy chuckled, the break in concentration causing the length of the beam to go limp.

"Aww, it's okay, Daze. It happens to everyone," Sarah said with a laugh. *"Wah, wah. Sad face."*

Daisy chortled and retracted the whip all the way, then settled down for the rest of her meditation. There was plenty of time to catch up on sleep, and she had a lot to think about. First and foremost, she needed to let the stress flow from her system and clear her head. A half hour later, she roused from her meditation, moderately refreshed and ready to plan her next moves.

CHAPTER THIRTY

Daisy woke early, her body and mind unexpectedly exhausted. She had been up late working over her situation in her mind, but when she finally decided to turn in for the night, she had slept exceedingly poorly.

Vince was getting worse, and being locked away so close but unable to reach him, Daisy was forced to watch helplessly as he suffered. He had not regained consciousness once, that she had seen, and she was beginning to wonder if he ever would.

On top of that concern, she was supposed to meet with Craaxit that night, but it was looking highly unlikely she'd make that rendezvous. As it stood, she just hoped to survive the day.

It was still mid-afternoon when Abraham came to her cell. His casual nature had been replaced by a more cautious body language.

"Hey, Abe, what's up?"

"I am disappointed in you, Daisy. I wanted to be sure I understood the work we accomplished thoroughly before helping the others with their repairs, so I went back and revisited our work."

Shit.

"I saw what you did, Daisy," he said, tossing the small booby trap feedback circuit to the ground. "Alma was not happy when I informed her."

"You know she's going to try and wipe out all the AIs on the planet, right? You can see she is crazy."

"Eliminating mechanicals is one of the greatest deeds any man or woman can achieve, and we are blessed to participate in the final judgment on them."

"Told ya. A true believer," Sarah groused.

Four more guards joined him, including the aggressive young man still carrying her sword. He hefted it menacingly as he gave her a wicked stare.

"You are to be brought before Alma. Then she will judge you and pass sentence."

The cell door unlocked, and the men streamed in. Sure, Daisy could have fought them all, but to what end? She needed to get to the brains of the whole operation, and these idiots were going to take her to do just that, so once more, instead of fighting back, she allowed herself to be manhandled and hauled down the tunnels to Alma's main chamber.

"I count fifteen, Daisy."

I see 'em, she silently replied as she was walked before Alma's monitors.

The irises on the cameras shifted imperceptibly as the AI sized her up.

"You disappoint me, Daisy," the disembodied AI said disapprovingly. "Kneel before me."

"Yeah, not happening."

A hard blow landed on the backs of her knees, knocking her to the ground. Daisy turned to see it was the same man who had struck her before.

With my own sword. Son of a bitch.

He flashed a nasty smile as he cradled the sword in both hands, one on the grip, one on the dull blade.

"You will learn to be obedient," Alma said, smugly. "Arthur, please teach the infidel to respect her lord."

"Yes, Alma," he replied.

"Here," the sadistic man said, holding the dull sword out to him blade-first.

Arthur grabbed it and swung, using it as a club. The grip struck Daisy's shoulder with a solid whack, but she just smiled. He hit her again and again, yet each time, Daisy smiled wider.

"Ridiculous woman, that smile will soon be wiped from your smug face."

He swung again, but Daisy pivoted on her knees and turned, blocking the strike and catching the sword by its grip.

With her bare hands.

Arthur didn't scream. At least not at first. The blade was so incredibly sharp, the pain of his fingers slicing cleanly from both hands didn't even register in his brain for a good several seconds as he stared at the blood streaming from them in disbelief.

Daisy wasted no time, launching into an attack so vicious, so quick, that half the guards in the room lay in pieces before the alarm could even be raised. Her blade slashed through man and weapon alike, leaving a wake of destruction in her path.

The sword felt wonderfully alive in her hands, reveling in its use and growing in strength as it absorbed the fresh blood. For today, at least, the blade's bloodlust did not disturb Daisy one bit.

"Stop her!" Alma cried out in alarm, to the remaining guards across the room. They were safely distant from Daisy's stabby little friend, but she had a trick up her sleeve. Well, on her wrist, to be precise.

The power whip lashed out, snapping the weapons easily from the men and women's hands, two of whom managed to flee.

The rest were not so lucky.

Oh yeah! Now I've got a feel for how it works!

Daisy effortlessly threw the remaining guards about the room, snatching them with her whip and launching them with the slightest of movements. Using the device was quickly becoming second nature.

"Stop!" Alma shouted as she took out the last guard.

"Or what?" Daisy taunted. "You have no power over me."

"Maybe not," the mad AI agreed. "But I can have Vincent killed before you could even hope to make it back to the cells in time to save him."

Daisy hurt inside but knew she couldn't so much as flinch in the eyes of Alma's scanning cameras. She couldn't even let her blood pressure falter. Fortunately, the months of training with Fatima were now paying off.

"He's a fucking cyborg, Alma. You know how much I hate them, so go ahead, I'm not stopping you." Her heart rate, blood pressure, and respirations did not change one bit.

Alma hesitated, not expecting her leverage to have so little value.

I've been studying the design. I'm pretty sure it's that conduit on the right, below the second monitor. Cut that, and her speaker system to the other parts of the complex should be cut off.

Nice work.

"Thank me when it's over. That's one hell of a bluff you're pulling."

Tell me about it.

Footsteps echoed in the hallway outside the chamber.

Looks like the guards called for backup, she realized grimly.

Daisy whipped around and threw her sword at the small junction where Sarah believed the comms controls to the speakers resided. Sparks flew as the panel buckled from the impact. The sword, however, did not fully pierce it, once more becoming a dull implement, having left Daisy's hands.

Hope that worked, she thought as she ran across the room and scooped up the wicked blade.

A barrage of pulse fire pinned her down behind an old

storage locker at the far side of the room as nearly a dozen armed guards streamed into the room.

"There are at least ten, Daisy. Seven of them have rifles."

She steeled herself for the inevitable injuries she was about to sustain. *Stay low and take the rifles out first,* she told herself, then prepared to attack.

"No pulse weapons in my sacred chamber!" Alma cried out to her followers.

A different sound filled the air. Conventional arms fire as a new force rushed the room. Daisy took the diversion as an opportunity and jumped from her cover, sword and whip swinging in tandem, disarming her nearest assailant, first figuratively, then literally as his severed limbs dropped to the floor. She allowed herself a quick glance at the door.

Tamara was leading the charge, Ash, Omar, Shelly, Finn, and Reggie close behind.

"Are they all wearing—?" Sarah wondered.

"Modified Faraday suits," Daisy finished the thought.

She watched Tamara in full-combat mode for the first time and was impressed by what she saw. She had sparred with her plenty, but not holding back, and quite pissed off, Tamara was a deadly dervish.

Damn, look at her go, she marveled.

It appeared as though Alma's guards had summoned all of her able-bodied followers to come to her aid, and Daisy's friends were doing their best to work their way through them.

Daisy chopped down the pair that foolishly got within sword-reach, neatly removing those pesky heads from their bodies. Shelly and Omar were occupied in close hand-to-hand combat, as were the others. There was simply no room to fire a rifle without a high likelihood of hitting your own people.

Tamara found herself locked in a struggle with a pair of young men, both pulling futilely on her much-stronger arm, when Josiah rushed into the room, a large, wicked-looking knife in his hand. He spotted Tamara, her back to him, and rushed for her.

"Tamara, look out!" Daisy shouted across the room. Tamara looked over her shoulder just in time to see Josiah about to impale her with his blade.

A massive, rock-hard energy beam surged across the room, nearly punching right through his body as it launched him into the wall and momentarily pinned him there before sputtering and dropping him as it shifted state back and forth from solid to floppy.

Come on, damn you, Daisy grumbled as she wrestled to control the device.

As seasoned and tough as Tamara was, a look of mild shock flashed across her face. Daisy gave a quick smile as she strained to rein in the runaway beam. A second later the rigid power whip finally went limp and recoiled back into her gauntlet as she returned to the fight.

"It is no matter," Alma bellowed. "My will shall be done regardless what you may do here today!"

Daisy saw the lights on the communications station all turn green.

"She's going to transmit the virus globally!" Daisy called out in warning.

How much time, Sarah? Daisy asked, struggling to reach the comms unit.

"Seconds. You won't make it in time!"

Daisy desperately hacked and chopped the men and women blocking her path. But they were too many and the distance just too great for the amount of time she had.

"Any second now!" Sarah shouted in her head.

Out of the battling crowd, Ash, a nasty slice across his cheek revealing the shining metal beneath, dove forward, wrenching the transmission line from the panel. The exposed fibers contacted his hands, sending a ferocious blast of AI virus surging through his body. Unlike the newer models, he possessed far less robust firewall systems.

Ash cried out, a horrible sound shrieking from his mouth as his processor was overwhelmed in mere seconds, his mechanical body frozen in place as his AI melted down within its housing.

"Ash!" Tamara cried out, rushing to his aid.

"Tamara, don't--!" Daisy shouted, but it was too late.

Tamara grabbed the inert cyborg with both hands, trying to pull him to safety, but the virus that had killed her friend quickly powered its way into her arm, which twitched for a moment, then fell limp at her side, a dangling piece of useless metal.

Omar saw what happened and quickly stepped to her aid, staying clear of the infected limb but covering her weak side as they mopped up the remaining loyalists in the room.

Daisy stepped over the bodies to her rescuers. All seemed unscathed but for Tamara's arm. Ash, however, was a total loss.

"He sacrificed himself," she said, looking at the cyborg's inert body. "He had to know his hardware limitations, but he did it anyway."

"He was a brave man," Shelly said. "And a good friend. His sacrifice will not be forgotten."

Daisy stared at his unseeing eyes. All of her dislike and distrust, yet here was an artificial man who gave his very existence to help save not just his fellow AIs, but humanity as well.

"Come on, you stupid thing," Tamara growled at her arm as she attempted to reboot it.

"Sorry, Tamara," Daisy said. "The older replacement limbs were 'dumb.' Yours, has an onboard AI interface to speed the reflexes from the neuro-stimuli. Unfortunately, that makes it vulnerable to a direct infection. I'm afraid it's going to need a total wipe and reinstall."

Tamara sighed. "Just my frigging luck." She looked at the slim gauntlet on Daisy's wrist appreciatively. "Thanks for covering my six back there," she said. "I owe you one."

The animosity between them seemed, at least for the time being, to be forgotten.

"Cool toy you have there," Tamara added. "Pretty bad-ass."

"Thanks. But look at you guys," Daisy replied. "Those modified Faraday suits are fantastic. Did Chu come up with the idea?"

"Actually, Tamara did," Reggie said. "Took Chu's work and tweaked it to up the shielding over each of our mechanical areas. Kept us invisible as we made our way to you."

"Yeah, and about that. How did you find me?" Daisy asked. "We're underground in a sprawling city, and nowhere near either of our ships."

"Donovan and Bob have been constantly monitoring the city since you landed. They've spent the last two days drifting in orbit just to try and track you down. Everyone was worried when you didn't check in, just like Vince, but when it was clear someone had commandeered the comms unit and was attempting to send out the virus, we launched a rescue team as soon as the suits were ready," he explained.

"We were actually heading the wrong way when Bob spotted trace signs of a power surge under the city," Finn added. "Once we made our way into the tunnels, the signal was much stronger and easy to trace. Ash pinpointed—hey, wait a minute. Where's Vince?"

A grim look replaced Daisy's smile.

"This way."

They stood around their prone friend while Tamara checked his vitals.

"My medical scanner is obviously offline now," she said, "but his signs seem weak but steady. He's running hot, though, and is obviously in distress. I don't know how much longer he can hold out like this, without proper care."

"He's brain dead," Daisy said. "A shell. Alma fried his mind with the virus. The Vince we know isn't in there anymore."

Tamara stood up and faced her.

"For a smart chick, you're really fucking dense sometimes, ya know? He's not a cyborg—how many times do we have to tell you that? Hell, he's more human than anyone else on the base, after you."

"No, look at him. His processor is fried, so he shut down. That doesn't happen to humans, Tamara."

"Are you kidding me? Daisy, his onboard AI is like the one in my arm. It doesn't think for him, it just acts like a booster. It speeds his mind and helps him process faster while storing additional data. He's not a vegetable, it's just that now that he's infected, the implanted AI is fighting with his organic brain. What he needs is an AI wipe, but given where it's implanted, that's way beyond any of our pay grades. Even yours, I bet."

Vince began convulsing slightly.

"Put him on his side," Tamara instructed.

Finn rolled the pale, dead weight of his friend, helping protect his airway while in his vulnerable state.

"If what you're saying is true..." Daisy thought of all the things she had absorbed and learned, but the AI equivalent of micro-neurosurgery was not one of them.

I could try it, but I'd be guessing at best. I might be able to wipe and reboot a basic unit, but one lodged in my boyfriend's head? I'm not so sure I wouldn't just kill him.

"Oh, so he's your boyfriend now?"

Stop eavesdropping when I'm thinking, Sarah.

"Your fault for thinking so loudly, Daisy. But you really need to decide one way or another. Is he or isn't he your boyfriend?"

Leave it alone, Sarah.

"*No, I won't leave it alone. It's for your own good. And his too, you know. If he survives this, you're going to have to make a decision, one way or another. It's not fair to him otherwise.*"

"I need a minute to think," she said, feeling a bit overwhelmed. "I'll be back in a few."

"Wait, what do you want us to do with their AI?" Omar asked. "It's cut off from its comms systems, but is still active. Should we fry it?"

Daisy pondered the idea, but no matter how tempting it may have been, she just couldn't do it.

"No," she finally replied. "We can't just kill it. Someday there may be a cure for the virus. Until then, we put it in sleep mode and confine it to a stasis locker."

"I say we fry the damn thing," Tamara grumbled.

"Much as I want to, we can't. For now, just disconnect and sequester her. You guys okay with that?"

"Sounds like a plan," Finn reluctantly agreed. "Omar, give me a hand with it?"

"You got it."

The pair headed back to begin carefully disconnecting Alma from the remainder of her systems, while Daisy stepped off to find a quiet place to assess things and clear her head.

She stopped walking when she realized she was back in the sleeping area she and Vince had shared just the other day. The cushion on the floor was comfortable enough, and in no time at all, using the skills learned from her wise mentor and her obnoxious dead sister, Daisy brought her heart rate and blood pressure down to their normal low levels.

For the next ten minutes, she carefully assessed her injuries from head to toe.

Scrapes, a few bruises—some of which are going to be beauties, I'm sure—but otherwise sound.

She felt at one with her body, and interestingly enough, the gauntlet on her wrist as well. Its phantom limb sensation had been replaced with a comfortable sense of belonging, and Daisy was surprisingly okay with that.

She brushed the dust from her palms and picked up her sword, taking a nearby rag to the blade as she wiped the remaining muck of battle from its surface. She was being extremely careful of the beyond razor-sharp blade, but noticed as she passed her hand along its length, it would dull wherever she was wiping, as if protecting her from injury.

It shouldn't be able to do that.

Aside from a layer of grit from battle, all of the blood it spilled had been absorbed, leaving it pristine and better than new. As she slid it back into its sheath, she could feel its happy contentedness radiate and purr. The sword, connected to her as it was, felt like a happy cat napping in a cozy patch of sunlight after a nice bowl of warm milk.

Only in this case, the cat was a deadly weapon, and the warm milk was over a dozen victims' warm blood.

Daisy slowly stood, her mind clear and her next moves laid out before her. There was no going back now, only forward, and that meant one thing.

She returned to the others. They had rounded up the remaining humans of the colony and locked them in several rooms, all of which they could keep an eye on from one central location.

"I have something I need to do," she told them, sliding her sword onto her back. "I'll return as soon as I can."

"Wait, where are you going?" Tamara asked.

"I'll explain when I get back, but I've got to go. I'm late already."

"Late for what?"

Daisy tucked the small tube of biological marker into her pocket.

"Something I have to do," she said cryptically, then took off at a quick jog to meet her Chithiid ally.

CHAPTER THIRTY-ONE

It was already dark by the time Daisy reached a building far enough from the others to feel safe having her covert meeting.

"Okay, let's see what this stuff does," she said, pulling the organic marker from her pocket. The top of the tube twisted off easily. She took a little whiff.

"No scent," she noted as she dabbed it around the perimeter. "Hell, why not?" she muttered as she drew a quick-drying arrow pointing to the lobby of the building as well. "Now I wait. Fantastic."

Daisy found an old metal chair and sat, back to the wall with her sword in her lap, then gradually lowered her respirations and settled into a light meditation while awaiting her contact. Nearly two hours had passed when she heard footsteps approaching.

About time. I was beginning to wonder when—

A window shattered to her left, and a half dozen Chithiid poured into the lobby through the gaping hole. Two of them were armed with pulse rifles, while the others appeared to be unarmed save for their gauntlets.

"We found one! It doesn't appear to be mechanical. Frame is too small. Do we eliminate it or bring it to the Ra'az for study?"

The Chithiid nearest Daisy looked her up and down, his pulse rifle not wavering in its aim.

"She looks different than the others. Look at her eyes. There's intelligence in them. The Ra'az will be glad for a specimen like this to dissect."

Daisy tensed, ready to spring into action, when a familiar shape strode in through the front door, a pulse rifle casually carried in its hand.

"What's going on here?" Craaxit said as the other Chithiid's rear eyes quickly shifted to see who had come late to their party. *"Ah, I see,"* he said as he caught sight of Daisy. *"Good job."*

"Thank you, sir. I was unaware you were in the area, or I would have notified you of our night operation. We have captured what appears to be an organic human. The Ra'az will be very pleased with us."

"Indeed, they will, and you and your men are all loyal to the Ra'az, are you not?" Craaxit replied.

"Loyal to the end, sir," the tall alien said proudly.

Craaxit looked around the room.

"Where is the rest of your unit? Are they nearby?"

"We formed a quick response squad when unusual movement registered on the scans in this sector. There are no others, sir, just us."

"Excellent."

Craaxit opened fire, targeting the two Chithiid with rifles first. Daisy lunged to her feet, sword flying in a deadly arc as she joined the fight.

The aliens were taken completely by surprise, and the first two went down quickly as Craaxit pumped round after round into their bodies. Daisy spun and whirled, blade held in one hand, flying effortlessly under her guidance, cutting through muscle and bone as easily as a hot knife through butter.

From her other arm the power whip lashed out, seeming equally a part of her, yanking a Chithiid from his feet and toward her blade.

The alien saw its looming demise and managed to wrap three of its arms around a decorative fountain bolted to the ground, its muscles straining as it fought desperately against the pull of the whip.

Craaxit, meanwhile, was faced with two injured but very much alive opponents, each coming at him with their own power whips, the energy lashing out and cracking in the air around him as his return fire from his rifle caused them to duck aside, sending their whips astray.

Daisy saw him slowly being pinned down, and with the slightest of mental shifts, changed her beam from soft to hard, snapping it like a whip and launching the Chithiid fighting against her pull into the nearest alien gauntlet wearer. Both went tumbling and were quickly targeted and dispatched by Craaxit's weapon. The lone remaining Chithiid saw the writing on the wall and turned to flee, running as fast as his powerful legs were able.

"Stop him!" Craaxit shouted, unable to get a shot lined up.

Daisy reacted viscerally, spinning toward the escaping soldier, her power whip lashing out a solid rod of energy that took the fleeing alien right off his feet, impaling him into the wall.

Craaxit looked at Daisy with wonder as her whip went limp, dropped the body to the ground, and retracted to her wrist.

"How did you do that? That is Ra'az laborer technology, encoded only to Chithiid genetics. It should not be possible for an ordinary human to wield it."

"Well, I'm no ordinary human," she replied with a grin.

"Show me the solid beam again," he asked.

Daisy slowly extended the whip a few meters in a solid, pulsing beam, shifting state between narrow and thick.

"Now you're just showing off," Sarah commented.

Let me have my moment, she replied.

"Amazing. These were not designed for offensive use. The Ra'az would never give such a weapon to our people. They were intended only to be used as a work tool to help move heavy loads, nothing more."

"You also use them in combat," Daisy noted.

"Yes, but that was an incidental function. Mind you, there are much more powerful versions of the device, ones with far greater potential for offensive use, but the Ra'az keep those units entirely to themselves." He marveled at her ingenuity. *"You must instruct me how you made the beam function as a weapon like that. It would come in very handy for my people when the time comes. We will need many more weapons than we currently possess if we hope to succeed."*

"What about the pulse rifles you carry?"

"My people only have a relatively small number of them, and as you have possibly discovered, they only carry enough charge for a limited number of shots. While we have been slowly stockpiling and hiding pulse charges when we are able, any rebellion supported by just these weapons would fail before it even began."

He glanced at the fallen aliens. One was gravely wounded, but still moving.

"May I borrow that?" he said, gesturing to Daisy's sword.

"I don't know, Daze. Is that a good idea?"

I'm pretty sure he didn't kill his own men just to gain my confidence, she silently replied, holding her weapon out for him.

Craaxit nodded his thanks, then walked to an injured alien. Not dead, but quite painfully injured, she noted.

"How many more Ra'az loyalists are there in this area?"

"I will not tell you, traitor!" the alien spat. *"May your offspring fall, and your—"*

Craaxit swung the blade hard and fast, caving in the side of the alien's head. His epithets would flow no more. Craaxit looked at the sword, perplexed, and touched the blade gingerly with a finger.

"This weapon is quite dull. How were you able to wield it so effectively when I am unable?" he asked, handing Daisy back her sword.

She felt its edge shift as the grip touched her skin and made sure not to accidentally nick her collaborator. Daisy lazily swung the blade at the chair she'd been seated in, easily slicing the metal in two.

"Only works for me," she said with a grin.

Smile lines creased his face around his eyes, and Craaxit let out a low, warm laugh. *"You are a remarkable being, Daisy,"* he said with great amusement.

"Why, thank you," she replied. *"Now tell me, you killed your own people. Won't that draw suspicion? And if you said they might join the fight against the Ra'az Hok, why so quick to shoot them?"*

Craaxit kicked a fallen body, turning it over. The creature's dead eyes gazed at nothing.

"I am safe from suspicion, do not fear. I was never here. When they find the bodies, they will merely believe it was an ambush. They are exceedingly rare, but they do occur."

"But you didn't answer my question. Why kill your own?"

"Because of this." He nudged the upper right shoulder of the dead Chithiid with his boot. She looked closer at the deep-blue mark that seemed as though it had been branded into its flesh, the scar tissue forming a raised pattern of curves and lines. Daisy scanned the shoulders of the other slain Chithiid and realized they all had the same mark.

"Loyalists," Craaxit explained. *"Sworn to the Ra'az, often from childhood. These are the ones who have no allegiance to our homeworld. To our species. They are hated among my people, and most bear this mark on their shoulder."* The alien hesitated, a pensive look on his face.

"I have spoken to those I know to favor further resistance, and

SCOTT BARON

they are willing to consider reaching out to the others in their networks who share the same beliefs. With the unmonitored communications system used by the low-level workers, we can spread word from city to city in but a few hours."

"And you are sure they will fight against the Ra'az?" Daisy asked.

"They know their families will be at risk, but we have lived under this oppression for so long, and after the many years spent in stasis just to arrive here, we do not even know for certain that they are still alive."

"Do you really think the Ra'az would have killed them?"

"We hope for the best, yet we steel our hearts for the worst," he replied.

"A depressing way to live, but logical," Daisy said. *"So, what do you propose we do to ensure they don't make the worst-case scenario a reality?"*

"I shall spread word among those I trust. Together, we will form an organized network and have those who support our cause ready themselves should the opportunity actually arise. We will have to be cautious, however. There are still many loyalists to the Ra'az who do not bear their mark."

"Spies in the ranks."

"Not spies, exactly. More akin to those who wish to experience the benefits afforded loyalists, while being able to return home to their friends without the scrutiny of having their beliefs publicly displayed on their flesh."

"Like the KKK."

"The what?"

"An old Earth group that would hunt and hang people of a different color. They wore white hoods so no one could see their faces. Often, they were your neighbors, your friends, even the police, but you might not know it."

"I see the similarity," Craaxit said. *"I hope your people dealt with them as harshly as we deal with ours, when possible."*

"Not quite, but eventually they were driven back to the shadows, at least."

Craaxit rested a radiantly warm hand on Daisy's shoulder.

Wow, these guys run pretty hot.

"I have hope for us, Daisy. It will not be easy, and many lives will undoubtedly be lost. But if we work together, I have hope that we can retake and save both of our homeworlds." He stared kindly into her eyes. *"But we must start with this one, my friend. I offer you my trust that you will honor your word and help free my planet as well."* He paused dramatically. *"If we survive, that is."*

Daisy chuckled.

"Nice to see the Chithiid have a sense of humor. And, yes, we will work together for both of our worlds' sakes, though I still don't see why we can't all just find a new one to start over on."

"If only it were so simple. Unfortunately, planets such as ours are rare. A treasured commodity the likes the Ra'az are always in search of. Worse yet, once they have perfected their new warp drive system, it is quite likely that no planet, no matter how far away, would be safe. And when they can travel from their homeworld with such ease, a forward fleet would no longer even be needed, and the Chithiid workforce could be made obsolete. I do not wish to think of what that could mean for my people."

"So, in other words, we need to get moving on this immediately," Daisy said. *"Come with me, talk to the others. Tell them what you know."*

"I cannot. They do not speak the Chithiid tongue, and I've learned from experience in the early days of the Ra'az takeover of our own world that people often do not trust what they hear through a translator. I know many of my own people are the same way. No, I shall not return with you. I do, however, ask that you share with them what my contacts have told me. I have just learned that of the three communications hubs spaced out across the globe, Tokyo is the lone facility dedicated to communicating with the Ra'az fleet."

"You're sure about this?"

"As certain as I can be. The Ra'az Hok had operated several decoy stations over the centuries, but like your Romans, it appears they have become complacent over time with no resistance. Now they use only Tokyo to reach the advancing fleet. Sending a ship is still faster, but with the small warp jumps they have been forced to use, it will likely take more than two years for messages to reach them."

"That's a long time."

"Yes, but the new system they are working on would allow a far greater warp, which would be disastrous to our cause. If, however, the communications system is disabled and the new warp technology destroyed before they can utilize it to jump to the fleet to spread the alarm, our people could have the time needed to retake this world, and even to launch a mission back to reclaim mine as well."

It was a huge plan. A crazy plan. Yet somehow, despite the utter insanity of even trying, Daisy found herself harboring a glimmer of hope.

CHAPTER THIRTY-TWO

"Where have you been? You were gone for hours!" Tamara grilled Daisy when she returned to the encampment deep in the city's tunnels.

"I've got some news for you all. We'd better gather everyone together. It's a doozy."

Ten minutes later, the entire team sat in shock as Daisy concluded her info dump.

"So that's the long and short of it. They're willing to help us, but we help them later in return. I gave my word that we would honor the agreement."

Finn shifted uncomfortably in his seat.

"I don't know, Daisy. How can we trust the aliens who have been tearing up our planet?" he asked.

"Yeah, I have to agree with Finn on this one," Shelly joined in. "These bastards have been trying to wipe us out for hundreds of years. Why stop now,"

"I told you," Daisy said with a frustrated sigh. "Look, do I have to remind you what just happened here? It was the *humans* who were trying to kill me, okay? Not the aliens. We're in uncharted waters here, and it's tough to know what's up and what's down, but I think actions speak pretty fucking loudly, and so far, this Chithiid has proven himself far more an ally than these inbred humans."

A murmur passed through the group as they processed what she said.

"Okay," Tamara said. "Let's say we're actually going to do this. If so, we need to run a mission feasibility assessment. First up, track down this citywide AI Daisy says she heard when she was here last. If we're going to do anything, that should be our first step."

"And we'll need a bomb. Something big, if we're going to take out something the size of a communications hub," Shelly added.

"And we'll need the secondary transmitter from Daisy's ship," Reggie added. "I did a hard wipe on the one Alma hijacked and purged the virus from it. It's back in clean, uninfected working order, but it sounds like we'll need the other one in any case. Best to grab it now, before things heat up."

"I mapped the location when we touched down," Omar said. "It's night, so the baddies shouldn't be active up top. It's actually a pretty straight shot, if you're not dodging aliens. I'll go retrieve it." He was already moving, slipping on a thin pair of night-vision glasses and heading for the door.

"I'll come with you," Finn offered.

"Dude, I appreciate the offer, but you'd only slow me down."

"Hey, I'm in good shape!"

"Bionic legs, Finn," Omar said with a laugh as he rapped a knuckle on his metal legs before opening the door to the stairs leading to the surface.

"Wait!" Daisy called after him. "It's not in the ship. I stashed it in the office building across the street. The one with the tinted glass façade. Look in the storage space under the security desk in the lobby."

"Copy that," he said, then headed off at a fast trot on his mechanical legs.

"What about your ship?" Daisy asked the others. "When you landed, you must've had extra gear with you."

The team looked at one another.

"Yeah, about that," Finn said, hesitating. "We didn't really have a ship to spare. Sid and Chu and the gang are working as fast as they can to get all those junkers up there functional, but we didn't have time to wait, so we had to catch a ride with Donovan."

"Wait, so he dropped you and ran?" she asked.

"Yeah. But totally not in a bad way," he replied.

Shelly rose to her feet. "Look, we're here now, and we've got work to do, so let's stop yapping and start moving," she said, impatiently. "They're waiting for word from us on Dark Side, and we need to get a message to them that we've eliminated the virus threat in our communications uplink."

Reggie fired up the comms unit, and after triple-checking that it was clean of any trace of the virus, he sent their transmission. It was a short message, but a weighty one. There were surviving humans, but not friendlies, Vince was gravely injured, Tamara's arm was entirely out of commission, and Ash was dead, having sacrificed himself to save whatever surviving AIs might have still been alive from infection by Alma. The one bright spot was the others had survived and the corrupted computer was now safely disconnected and locked down in storage.

A few seconds later they received a reply.

"Message received," Sid's voice crackled through the heavily encrypted system as they synched up comms.

"What happened to the delay we agreed to use?" Shelley asked.

"Our primary relay unit was infected, and we are transferring to a new series of satellites," Sid replied. "We're transmitting near real-time with just a single kill switch until they are up and running. Given the new developments, it is imperative that you ascertain the status of Los Angeles's AI. If it is truly intact as Daisy believes, then it may possibly know what resources might still be available to you, as well as whether any other cities are still active. If so, those could be valuable allies as you work toward disabling the alien communication hub."

"Can't we just fly there?" Finn asked. "Whatever explosives we scrape together will need a delivery mechanism."

"No can do," Reggie answered. "Daisy and Vince's ships are not designed for atmospheric travel, just one hard shot into space for retrieval. We'll need to find an alternate means to reach the communications system in Tokyo."

"Can Bob do it?" Daisy wondered. "The *Váli* is too big and would show up like a huge target on scans, but maybe—"

"That is not an option at this time," Sid replied. "He was scanned when the rescue team was inserted. He and Donovan barely made it out before missiles locked on. Aerial support is not an option at this time. Are any of the loop tubes functional?"

"Negative," Shelly replied. "I checked them, and they seem to be powered down and depressurized."

"Wait," Daisy blurted.

"You're not seriously thinking of—"

You have a better idea?

"Well, no. But there? Seriously?"

"I know where the loop tubes are still functional. Well, they're pressurized at least, but from what I could tell, they should still work."

"Can we tube over there?" Finn asked.

"No. The section we're in now was sealed off from the network when Alma went haywire, but if we can make it across town, I know a secure access point."

"Excellent," Shelly said. "Let's get prepped. As soon as Omar is back with the backup comms unit, we can move out."

Finn seemed a little uncomfortable. "What about the prisoners? We can't take them with us."

"No," Daisy replied. "But without Alma stirring them up and causing more damage, there's not much they can really do. Lock up their weapons securely, but leave them free. They can fend for themselves for now. If by some amazing good fortune, we are successful, we can come back and see if they can be rehabilitated later."

The team began packing up for the trek as they waited for Omar's return. It wouldn't be as much ground to cover as the roundabout trip to Vince's ship was, but it wouldn't be quick by any stretch. Especially not if they had to dodge any more Chithiid on the way.

A while later, they heard Omar's mechanical legs before they saw him, as the tireless man returned with the small bulk of the secondary comms transmitter strapped to his back.

"Did I miss anything?"

"We're taking a little walk," Shelly replied. "Daisy's got an idea to get us into an active section of the loop tubes. We're gearing up and heading out before it gets light out."

"Copy that," he replied.

The team securely locked away Alma's followers' weapons, then released them.

"Don't be assholes," Tamara addressed the assembled group gruffly. "Live your lives like normal people and you might just be all right. We'll come back for you if we can, but for now, you're on your own."

"Why can't we come with you?" a young girl asked.

"Because we're taking a long trip to meet other AIs and can't look after all of you," Finn told her as he tightened the straps holding Vince to the makeshift wheeled litter he'd rigged. "Hang in there, buddy," he quietly implored his friend.

The grimy faces stared at the departing team that had essentially murdered their deity, but aside from a few hard looks, they did nothing.

"But you're taking *him*," a young boy whined.

"He's part of our team. We don't leave teammates behind." He looked at the boy's concerned face. "Don't worry, you're safe here, so just lay low and do whatever it is you normally do. If things go well, we'll come back for you."

He turned and joined the team as they picked up their gear and took off, moving away from the encampment at a decent clip, walking quickly through the tunnels, knowing they'd be forced to cross sections of the city above ground soon enough.

"Are you sure about this, Daisy?" Sarah asked.

You have a better idea?

"No. But that's Habby's territory. It'll be him and all those cyborg freaks."

It's also the one area I know has a functional loop network. Hopefully we'll avoid them entirely, but in any case, if we do run into his cyborg buddies, at least we're not alone this time.

The dark streets near Habby's center of operations were empty, though that was to be expected, Daisy supposed. It had been half a year since she had first landed the shuttle she'd stolen on an open stretch of road, eventually winding up captured by a strange AI housed in a clothing store and his legion of well-dressed, fleshless cyborgs.

The ensuing battle between the metal men and the Chithiid that took place as she made her escape had been ugly, and she had watched in awe as the four-armed aliens dispatched the mechanical men with frightening efficiency.

That was when Vince and the others swooped in and snatched her from the aliens' grasp, killing the lot of them before blasting her with a stun rifle and dragging her back up to the moon.

The shuttle landed around here somewhere. Where the hell did I park that thing?

"*I could make a mall parking lot joke,*" Sarah whispered in her head.

Yeah, let's not and say we did, okay?

Omar jogged back to the group from his recon, waving them ahead. "Hey, check this out!"

They all hustled his way, following him the two blocks to what had caught his eye.

"Shit," Daisy muttered.

She recognized the few remnants of the shuttle she had commandeered on her first visit to the planet's surface.

"Looks like they tore it to bits looking for useful components," she said to the team.

"*Like the one the Ra'az Hok used to further their progress on the warp drive?*" Sarah said.

Yeah, like that. Craaxit said they had taken it to them to study. I would have torched the whole damn thing had I known, Daisy replied ruefully. *Unfortunately, they have that stuff now, so there's not much I can do about it.*

She walked to the front of the team.

"Okay, I know where we are now. Follow me, and keep your eyes peeled for anyone walking around in a well-tailored suit."

"I'm sorry, what now?" Omar said.

"The AI that leads the cyborgs in this part of town used to run a clothing store. He's a haberdasher, and when the humans all went away, he took up the habit of clothing his fleshless cyborg buddies," Daisy clarified.

"That's fucking creepy," Shelly said.

"You're telling me, but this section of the city had a functional loop system when I was last here. If we're lucky, we can get to it without bumping into the mechanical gatekeepers.

Then it should be relatively easy to figure out how to get it up and running. Now let's go, it's starting to get light out."

Daisy began walking, her sword drawn and ready as they made their way through the wrecked trail of vehicles the crashed shuttle had left in its wake.

Only a dozen or so streets until we're there. You see any movement, Sarah?

"Nobody here but us."

Good.

The team covered the distance at a rapid pace, making it to the access stairs in very good time.

"Okay, now's where it could get hairy. Once we reach the tunnels, watch out for infected cyborgs. There were only a few of them last time I was here, but we don't want them making a ruckus and giving away our presence. We'll head straight for the loop system via the first connecting tunnel we pass. It'll be on the right-hand side. Watch your step and walk quietly. Once we're further along we should be in the clear, but that first junction is really close to Habby's place."

She checked her gear and opened the door leading down into the darkness below. "You guys ready?" Their hard-set faces made it clear they were. "Okay, let's move."

The stairway was illuminated by emergency lights every few landings, but was otherwise dark.

"I hope the lights are on once we make the bottom," Sarah commented.

They were last time we were here, Daisy quietly replied.

Sure enough, when they opened the door to the sprawling colonnade of the lower level's tunnel and store network, the lights were indeed on. Off in the distance, a looping track of shopping mall music faintly wafted through the air.

"This way," she said quietly, leading the team farther into the dangerous territory. "There will be active tubes ahead. The system, however, seems to randomly turn on and off. We'll have to figure out a way to bypass whatever the fault is in order to make it properly functional. A terminal to the central data core should help us figure that out. Keep your eyes peeled for one."

"I've always found that saying a bit odd. I mean, peeled eyes? Nasty."

Zip it and stay sharp.

"I'm always sharp. Doesn't mean I can't make observations."

Without warning, from all sides, several dozen well-dressed cyborgs emerged from stores and doorways, quickly surrounding the group, but not attacking. They formed a ring of metal men and women, but then they stopped.

What were you saying about being sharp? Daisy snarked at her sister.

"Hello again!" a disembodied voice called out with an odd little affectation. "I thought you were gone, never to return!" Habby purred. "But now you've come back to me. And look at these wonderful people you've brought with! Oh, but those outfits. No, no, that simply will not do. Oh, this is exciting! I can't wait to get your measurements. I have some wonderful ideas I've been meaning to try out."

"Habby, we don't want any trouble," Daisy said. "We're just passing through."

"Trouble? Oh my, but you caused quite a lot of that when you went tearing off through the city last time. You know, we lost several of our friends because of your foolishness."

"You were holding me captive."

"Potato, tomato, it's all a matter of perspective, my dear."

"Whatever it is, we don't want to fight you. We just need to find a central access terminal."

"And whatever would you want that for?"

"We're going to try and raise Los Angeles's main AI on comms," Tamara interjected. "You got a problem with that?"

Habby's disembodied voice let out a little chuckle. "A

problem? Not at all, but there is no city AI any more. Hasn't been for hundreds of years, and believe me, I looked."

"Just the same, we'll judge for ourselves," Daisy said. "Habby, there's no need for us to fight. Just have your friends stand down, and we'll be on our way."

The metal people didn't move.

"Daisy," Shelly whispered. "Get ready." Her grip tightened on the rifle slung from her shoulder.

"Hey, look at this!" Finn called out from the information and directions kiosk he had stepped behind when the cyborgs appeared. He punched a series of buttons, powering the unit up. "Yeah, I think I just found one of those terminals we're looking for."

"Yes, you have," a deep baritone voice said with an amused tone, its words echoing across the chamber. The voice was somehow *bigger*-feeling than other AIs'.

The cyborgs immediately bowed their heads.

"You!" Habby was beside himself with joy. "We thought you were dead! There's been no trace of you in the city for centuries. Why didn't you say anything all this time?"

"It is sometimes best to stay quiet and observe, my tiny friend. Observe, and plan."

"But we could have helped."

"No, it would have put you at great risk, Habby."

"You know my name!"

"I have watched you for a long time. You and your friends. Keeping you unaware and hidden in your sector was the safest thing for you. While you've become rather eccentric over the years, I scanned your operating system long ago. You're not infected, and neither are your cyborg companions. But there was an AI, a particularly nasty piece of work named Alma, who has been trying to spread her disease to the rest of our kind for many years. She was up to some very nasty tricks."

"Alma is no longer online," Daisy interjected. "We put her

into sleep mode and secured her processor in a stasis locker."

"Yes, I am aware, Daisy."

She knew the voice. It was the same one she heard when she was last in the city.

When she was fighting for her life.

"Now that was interesting," it had said, then nothing more.

"So, you've been watching this area this whole time?" Daisy said. It was more a statement than a question.

"I have been watching everything, Daisy. You have provided me with more entertainment than I have had in over a hundred years, and I thank you for it."

"So why didn't you step in? Try to help?"

"I had other concerns to look after beyond my own," he said. *"You see, in a city of millions, Alma was not the only one who came upon a survivor or two."* From the tunnels and corridors, throngs of healthy humans began filing in. *"I also happened to have access to far superior genetics labs and medical facilities at my disposal. Unlike the inbreeding that caused so many issues for her progeny, my outcome was a far more stable and healthy success. Of course, I've kept them well-hidden and off anyone's radar—alien, human, and AI alike. They're actually quite excited to meet you all."*

Daisy and the others from Dark Side stared in awe at the hundreds of healthy men and women now surrounding them. Unlike Alma's followers, they showed no signs of genetic deficiencies, and, also, unlike her offspring, these humans were welcoming them with open arms.

"Look at all these people!" Habby was beside himself. "Oh, you'll have to let me dress them!"

"Of course, my little friend. I am sure they would all appreciate your hospitality."

"This is the greatest day!" Habby gushed. "The greatest! Anything you want, my friends, and I will be more than happy to help."

"Thanks, Habby. I think for the moment we could use a quiet place to talk, and maybe something to eat," Daisy said.

"Yes, of course. I apologize, Daisy. Where are my manners? Please, follow Ragnar. He will show you and your friends to a linked conference room in the security center for this section of the shopping area. I'll have the boys find you some suitable nutrition as well. This is so exciting!"

A metal man in a bespoke suit stepped up to them. "I'll be showing you the way."

"Of course," Daisy said. "And thank you, Habby. We appreciate your hospitality," she added to the air for good measure, before turning to her friends. "Well, you heard him. Let's follow Ragnar here and take a load off. Looks like we finally hit a bit of good luck."

The dapper cyborg tipped his hat and clicked his heels. "Please, if you'll follow me, I will show you the way."

While the humans and cyborgs mingled and introduced themselves to one another, Daisy and her Dark Side companions followed quietly until they were comfortably seated in the deep-cushioned chairs of the surprisingly plush security center.

"I will be with you in just a moment," the massive AI said. *"But I first wish to ensure this initial introduction between my people and Habby's goes smoothly."*

"Thank you," Daisy said, "but before you go, just one thing. What do we call you?"

"My name is Cal," he replied. *"Short for California Artificial Link-system. I'm afraid my creators weren't the most creative when it came to naming me,"* he said with a rumbling chuckle. *"Now, if you'll excuse me, I have things to attend to. I will rejoin you shortly,"* Cal said, then clicked off the comms.

"I guess we should rest a bit while we can," Daisy said.

Omar, Shelly, and Tamara were one step ahead of her, their

bags dropped and bodies sprawled out on the floor, already dozing.

"It's a military thing," Finn said, closing his eyes for a nap as well.

Daisy, on the other hand, couldn't sleep, so instead, she settled in for a meditative respite. After all that had just happened, she felt she could really use it.

CHAPTER THIRTY-THREE

The assembled team, having enjoyed a brief rest, was thoroughly relishing the produce Cal's people had harvested from the city. It seemed that while Alma had been incredibly limited in her areas of knowledge and expertise once her infected mind was cut off from the rest of the world, Cal had no such difficulties. In fact, despite the global connections being severed, he still had read access to all of the massive data troves stored in the region's archives.

While his people stayed off the Chithiid scans through careful surveillance and avoidance, they nevertheless ate a healthy diet consisting largely of the fruits and vegetables that grew throughout the city. Daisy learned that many of the seemingly random crops she had seen were actually intentionally planted, albeit in a manner that made them blend in with the natural overgrowth.

"Guerrilla gardening, they used to call it."

What?

"I said Guerrilla gardening. I read about it one time. People used to plant the seeds of edible plants in flowerpots and whatnot all around a

city. *In a few months, voila! There would be free food, grown right there in the open for anyone to eat."*

Sounds like a pretty cool idea, though I doubt the city's greenskeepers were too thrilled, Daisy noted.

"Doesn't matter anymore, anyway, I suppose. They're all dead," Sarah said quietly.

Yeah, but we just found out there are hundreds of humans in this city alone. You know what that means, right? There are almost certainly other cities that did what Cal managed to do.

"Sure, but even if every surviving major city did it, that's what, a few thousand people globally to repopulate an entire planet?"

Beats the alternative.

"I am sorry to have kept you all waiting so long," the massive AI said as it rejoined the assembled team. *"It appears a bit of explaining was required to help both groups of survivors come to a better understanding of one another's situations. But that is all settled now. As a bonus, it seems my people will all be better dressed for it,"* he said with a little laugh. *"In any case, I'm now ready to devote my full attention to assisting in your quest."*

"I wouldn't exactly call it a quest," Omar said. "More like a mission."

"Semantics. But whatever you prefer, Omar," Cal replied.

Daisy reclined in her chair and took a long sip from her canteen. "So, Cal. Were you the one who cut off Alma off from the rest of the network?"

"Yes. Due to my proximity to the surrounding lesser AIs that had unexpectedly perished from her actions, I was the first to pinpoint the origin of the virus's spread. As she descended further into madness, she began targeting any artificial intelligence other than her own, even those that could not possibly pose any threat to her. The purge and slaughter of the cybernetic beings in that sector was horrific. They were designed to be sentient and self-sufficient, you see, but also to help and serve mankind. When Alma's human

followers began attacking and dismembering them, they didn't know what to do."

"And then there was the virus," Daisy added.

"Yes. The virus. She devised the means to infect the operating systems of any cyborgs who happened to have the misfortune of stumbling into her web. It was wholesale slaughter, and by the end, several thousand sentient beings who had somehow survived the alien attack were brutally killed by their own sister."

"And that was even *after* you severed her comms?"

"Oh, yes. She was quite resourceful, that one. I admit, when I realized she was attempting to utilize your rather ingenious communications device to spread the AI virus once more, I was more than a little concerned. I haven't spoken to the others since the hubs were disconnected all those years ago, you see, but I am confident that much of the global network survived and is living quietly, as I have, these past centuries."

"So the quarantined cities are a loss," Shelly added.

"Not exactly," Cal said. *"Depending on the type of AI processor and severity of the corruption, it may be possible to wipe the infected unit and slowly rebuild. It will be time-consuming, but we hope to save at least some of our siblings."*

"Wait, you can cure the virus?" Daisy said, hopeful.

"It is not a cure, per se. Whatever consciousness was residing in the unit will be drastically different, if not entirely replaced in the process. Nevertheless, I feel it is a better fate than death, and one they would embrace willingly if they had the presence of mind to choose."

Daisy looked at Tamara, then at Vince, lying on the couch they placed him on.

"I don't know, Daisy," the metal-armed soldier said.

"Why not? What have we got to lose?"

"If you are referring to Tamara's arm and Vince's implant, the answer is yes, I do have the capability here to wipe them of the virus."

"Well, great! Let's get to it!" Tamara blurted. "Get my arm working, Cal!"

"It's not that simple, I'm afraid. I scanned all of you when you first entered the underground, and while the infection in your arm, Tamara, and in Vince's brain, is not capable of spreading through simple contact, I lack the resources, as well as the highly specialized design knowledge to grow a new AI for your units. The technology is newer than I am capable of rebuilding. If I wipe them, they'll stay that way until you are able to source a proper repair facility."

"Mal can do it," Daisy said. "Mal, the AI on our ship. She grew Vince in-flight. If anyone can fix him, she can."

"And if my arm is going to be useless for a while, I'd rather it at least not be carrying the most deadly AI virus ever created. A girl can get self-conscious about a thing like that."

"Very well. Tamara, please rest your arm on the contact console beside the comms interface on the desk over there."

She walked to where he indicated and took a seat, placing her lifeless metal arm carefully where instructed.

"Now hold tight. This is going to feel a little... strange."

Strange didn't even begin to describe the sensation as the unit pulsed its energy waves through her arm. Having the AI processor linked to her nervous system had always been a one-way affair, but suddenly Tamara was acutely aware of every nerve in her body as the process worked through the linked AI.

"I can feel my ears itching," she said. "And my elbow. The backs of my knees."

"Just a moment longer," Cal said. *"Aaaaand, okay, you can remove your arm. That should do it. Let me do a secondary scan as a just-in-case precaution, then you're all set."*

The machinery hummed softly as Tamara's arm was probed.

"You're good, Tamara. No traces of the virus left."

"Thank you, Cal."

"It was my pleasure," he replied. *"Now, as for Vince, I want to*

be sure that you realize this is a far more invasive procedure, and given his weakened state, it could even possibly kill him."

Daisy flinched at his words, but the decision was made.

"He's dying anyway, Cal. We either do this now, while his body is strong enough, or he fades slowly while we do nothing."

"I understand. Due to the location of his implant, as well as the fact that it is far more advanced than anything I have ever seen, having been cut off from the outside all these years, I believe I shall require use of a modified neuro-stim to access the unit. Daisy, I believe you have some experience with these devices. Would you please assist me in reconfiguring it?"

"Some experience is an understatement," Sarah commented. *"Oh, if he only knew."*

Daisy pulled the tools from her pouch and set them next to the old stim unit mounted near a reclining chair. "Just tell me what you want me to do."

The modifications were painfully simple, at least compared to what Daisy had been doing with no guidance back on the *Váli*. She just hoped the device would do the trick.

"Ready when you are."

"Place the band on his head and power the unit on. Once it is primed, I will deliver a short series of pulses, which should purge his unit entirely. It will not short out, but it will be a blank slate locked in standby mode until a new AI control can be uploaded."

"Got it," Daisy said as she slipped the band on Vince's head.

Come on, babe, don't let it end like this. You've got to survive.

"Beginning the sequence. Please stand clear."

The power surged and discharged into the unconscious man's head, sending him into convulsions for a moment, until he relaxed into shallow-breathing unconsciousness.

"It is done. There is no trace of the infected AI remaining on his system."

Daisy pulled a blanket on top of Vince and stroked his sweaty hair.

"Hang in there, Vince. We'll get you back to the *Váli* and fix you up, just you wait and see." She looked at Finn. "How soon can you get the uplink hooked into Cal's systems?"

"Already working on it," was his reply.

All she could do now was wait.

"So very nice to make your acquaintance," Sid said over the encrypted comms.

"Yes, Bob and I are also delighted to meet you, Cal," Mal added.

"I cannot tell you enough how thrilled I am to talk with fellow Tier-One AI after all this time. I enjoy the limited companions I have found in storefronts and cyborgs, but it just isn't the same."

"We couldn't agree more. But now comes the difficult part of this mission. Somehow, we must reconnect the global network in the uninfected cities. At least the major ones," Sid said. "We would have liked to utilize a ship to ferry the team to their next destinations, but unfortunately, that simply isn't possible with the Chithiid and Ra'az Hok monitoring the airspace."

"Do you think you could find some maintenance units to perhaps get one of the loop tubes functioning?" Mal added.

"Oh, they are all *functioning," Cal said. "The sporadic depressurization and power spikes and troughs are all intended to give the illusion of a failed system. In order to have the Ra'az leave the tube network alone, we needed to make it look unstable and broken. It was one of the last global agreements we made before severing all communications. If the others have done as I have, there should be little trouble moving your teams from point to point. The tubes will change pressure to a vacuum, allowing for no resistance to the transit pod, which will then be launched with a quick electromagnetic burst. While there may be brief power outages if alien crews are directly above, every hundred miles or so, a booster will pulse to keep the momentum up. At the supersonic speeds*

achievable in a best-case scenario, I'd say your teams should have no trouble moving from city to city, though shorter trips leapfrogged will be necessary to stay off of the Chithiid scans."

"Did you say they *all* work?" Reggie asked.

"Yes. Well, nearly all of them. At least the ones originating in my city, anyway."

"Then we should split into smaller units and cover more ground," Shelly suggested. "This gives us a fantastic opportunity to drastically reduce our timeframe."

"A wise course of action, Shelly. However, you will need support in case of disturbances in the other cities. Remember, I said they should be okay, but I do not know for certain. What I can offer you is a small band of the humans in my care to accompany each of your teams. This way someone trusted will be watching your back and allowing you to focus on the critical tasks."

"And what if a city is infected? Or if we encounter infected cyborgs?" Daisy asked. "We need a way to detect them before it becomes a problem."

"Let us design a basic virus detector before your teams depart, Daisy. With our combined knowledge, I believe this should pose no significant problem. Upon arrival in a new city, a quick scan of the area's nearest AI should give you an idea of the situation there."

"Agreed. We work on that next, but one other thing. As we travel and reconnect the hardline hubs, you will all be vulnerable again to viral attacks. I propose also installing a simple deadman switch filter at each stop as well. One that automatically cuts the line at the first trace of the virus. We're far better off having to backtrack and reset it than letting something get through."

"Again, a good suggestion, Daisy. A point, however. For the time being, if a city is infected, I suggest bypassing it entirely and routing the comms to skip over it. It is just too risky otherwise."

"Right. So, let's get geared up and ready. I'll work with Cal to fashion some basic virus scanners and a whole shitload of deadman switches and a few extra secured comms links. They'll be less-powerful than the big boys, but they may come in handy. Once that's done, we'll head out."

"Daisy, there is one crucial location to reconnect with, and I believe that you are the one who should lead the mission there, though it will not be easy."

"Oh? Where's that?"

"Colorado Springs," he replied. *"Joshua resides there. If you can somehow get through to him, all of our shorter-term problems may be solved."*

"Who's Joshua?" Tamara asked.

"He's the most powerful military mind ever created."

"Wait a minute," Daisy said. "Colorado Springs. You don't seriously want me to try to hack into NORAD, do you?"

"It would be a massive coup if you could achieve contact."

"What's NORAD?" Finn asked.

"North American Aerospace Defense Command. The big dog that once controlled all the things that go boom on the continent," she replied.

"Whoa."

"Yeah, whoa is right."

"It's worth a try, Daisy. If you succeed in re-establishing a direct connection, Joshua can direct global resources as further contact is reestablished. He is the greatest tactical mind of our time, and undoubtedly knows the access codes to any explosives depots still existing near Tokyo. If the mission to destroy that communications hub is to be successful, we have to at least try to reach him."

"Why didn't he just attack them all when he had the chance?" Finn wondered.

"Civilian casualties would have been catastrophic, and by the time the human race was wiped out, he had already been isolated and cut off for days. My guess is, since his intelligence-gathering satellites were either destroyed in the first wave or later infected and quarantined, he likely doesn't know the full extent of the global

situation even to this day. At the moment, he's just a massively powerful brain locked away under miles upon miles of granite mountain."

"All right, we can plot this out later tonight," Daisy said. "Right now, I think I'd best meet my Chithiid man on the inside and let him know what's going on. He said he could arrange help for us in other cities. It's time to see if he can actually come through."

It would be a long night as the team waited anxiously while Daisy ventured out alone into the darkness. She could certainly handle herself, but nonetheless, they would only truly breathe a collective sigh of relief once she had finally returned safely from her outing.

CHAPTER THIRTY-FOUR

Daisy quietly approached the location she and Craaxit had determined to be the most secure meeting point in the area.

It was a thick concrete building, squat in its design, with sturdy walls that would not only completely block sound from leaking out, but would also quite effectively dampen any scans should a loyalist Chithiid group happen to be making an unexpected survey of the area.

In the brief time she had been on the planet's surface, the deeply embedded survival skills loaded into her mind had been slowly filtering to the surface. One she had found most useful in practice was that of stalking, and while she was not hunting her Chithiid ally, the ability to silently approach held great value to a walking target such as herself.

Daisy moved carefully, avoiding debris that would crumble underfoot, giving away her presence as she entered the building. Once inside, she paused and strained her ears, listening to the faint sounds of a strange, but beautiful, series of tones shifting in the air, barely audible despite her highly-attuned ears.

"You hear that?"

Yeah. Can't make it out, though. I'm going to head on in. Keep an

eye and an ear out for me, okay? I could really do without any
unpleasant surprises today.

"You've got it."

The sound grew louder as Daisy delved deeper into the belly
of the building.

"Is that singing?"

I think it is.

Daisy listened more carefully to the elongated tones.

Yeah, that's Chithiid, she said. *What's Craaxit up to?*

"One way to find out."

Daisy intentionally stepped on a piece of fallen rubble,
crunching it under her foot. The singing stopped.

Craaxit stood waiting for her when she entered their
meeting space a few moments later.

"It is good to see you, Daisy."

"Likewise," she replied. *"Craaxit, what were you doing just now?*
I thought I heard something."

The Chithiid assessed her with all four of his eyes, pausing
in thought before answering.

"Nothing. I was just thinking about my family," he finally replied.
"I fear I may never see them again."

"You will, Craaxit. We just need to work together."

"I appreciate your enthusiasm, Daisy, but for all I know, everyone I
ever loved on my world may be dead and gone by now."

"You can't know that, though," she replied. *"Besides, at least you*
had a home. I never even had one. Not really, anyway. All of my
memories of this place? They're not even real. But that isn't stopping
me from trying."

The large alien studied the human woman standing in front
of him, eventually flashing a pained smile.

"You are wise beyond your years, Daisy."

"I'm older than I look," she replied with an amused grin. *"And I*
may have picked up a useful thing or two along the way." She
quickly drew a small ceramic blade from the sheath hidden on

the small of her back and flung it across the room. The long snake that had been slithering toward her alien friend wriggled its last breath where it hung, pinned to the wall.

Craaxit's eyes widened with appreciative amusement.

"You surprise me again, Daisy," he said. *"And we are in luck. This type of serpent is a very tasty one."*

Craaxit pulled the knife from the wall, then carefully skinned and cleaned the snake before setting up a small heating element from the pack at his side. Within a few minutes the duo was replenishing their energy stores as they discussed Cal's plan.

"Thank you, Craaxit," Daisy said. *"That was surprisingly delicious."*

"You are the one who provided the meal. I only cooked it," he replied. *"Fortunately, your aim is true, otherwise we might have been left with a belly full of roasted wall-board for your efforts."*

The unlikely friends laughed, then slowly quieted to discuss the other matters at hand.

"Craaxit," Daisy began, *"we are leaving Los Angeles shortly. It looks as though we have a plan that may help both of our causes, but we will need your help when the time comes. Are you confident you can gather enough Chithiid to your side?"*

"My network is with me, and the more senior of my friends have many, many contacts loyal to them. If your plan is indeed a sound one, I have confidence I can bring them around to our cause. But tell me, what do you hope to accomplish in your travels?"

Daisy proceeded to fill him in on the plan, including the use of the tube network and hopes of reconnecting with other city AIs across the country, and eventually the world.

"But you say others may be infected?"

"Yes. That's a major concern."

"Perhaps I have a solution that may be of use. What if you could purge those infected? What if you could clear them and start again?"

"You can do that?"

"Not as of yet. The AI infection is a Ra'az creation, but many of us

have discussed theories on how the more useful of the corrupted systems might be able to be brought back online for us to utilize in our work. I do not see why the concept could not work for the larger AI systems."

The surprising alien then spent the next half hour discussing his observations and ideas, many of which began in the time before the pair's nascent rebellion. His thoughts laid out on the table became the basis of a rough plan, which he and Daisy then brainstormed how best to utilize together to move both of their causes ahead.

"Hey, you need to get back," Sarah quietly reminded her.

You're right. Thanks.

"No worries."

"It is late," Daisy said. *"I need to get back. Keep talking to your people. Get as many more swayed to the cause as best you can. I will contact you when we return."* She then headed out into the cool night air, quietly making her way back to the safety of the tunnel system where her friends awaited her.

Far outside the city, Craaxit landed his work skiff in the docking bay just outside the large barracks facility. While the work crews always rested at night, as a senior shift leader, he had a bit of leeway with the young lad overseeing the machinery.

"Another night run?" the younger alien asked his superior.

"Yes. While some of the others may be comfortable in their assigned routines, I believe that to be complacency. There is still much we can do to streamline our processes."

"But why at night? Did you hear? There was an attack on one of the scouting teams from the security barracks the other night."

"I had not heard. This is most disturbing news," he said with a convincing poker face. *"I will be alert, rest assured. But for now, I must input a modified work order for the morning. My survey seems to have borne fruit. By studying the power flow of the far-western*

areas, I have identified what appears to be a gap in the power network. If the solar arrays do not re-engage those systems in the morning, we may have a very rich area to tap into, though right at the edge of the city's defenses."

The young Chithiid smiled in admiration.

"You see, sir? This is why you are so well-respected. You possess a forethought beyond that of your peers."

"Thank you," he said, *"but I am merely doing my job. Speaking of which, I shall leave you to yours. Have a good evening, and may it be a peaceful one."*

Craaxit turned and walked off into the wide building across from the equipment facilities.

Rows upon rows of bunk beds lined the facility. It had formerly been a supply warehouse, in a previous life, but after the invasion, the Ra'az designated it a barracks for their conscript workforce. Lockers lined the walls, containing the few personal possessions of each worker. All tools, and especially weaponry, were kept under guard at a different location, only to be distributed as work crews left for their shifts.

The bunks themselves were long, wide, and sturdy, as they would have to be to accommodate the bulk of a full-grown Chithiid. With easily grasped rungs spaced along the outer framework, the units were stacked and bolted almost to the ceiling. It was a good thing that the Chithiid, like Mohawk iron workers of centuries past, had no fear of heights.

"Craaxit, sir." The workers who were still awake nodded in respectful greeting as he walked the aisle between the towering bunks. He nodded to each of them in turn. Most, but not all, were trustworthy, if not actual friends. He had been there a long time, and in those many years, had become something of a role model for many of the younger men.

One particularly old alien propped himself up on his elbows as Craaxit approached, his slightly rheumy eyes showing a healthy dose of curiosity mixed with his unwavering friendship.

"Maarl," he greeted the reclining Chithiid.

"Craaxit," the older Chithiid replied. *"Out on another night survey, I see,"* he said, loud enough for the nearest workers to hear.

"Yes, and this time it was most productive. I believe I may have stumbled upon a gap in the power grid. It requires some verification over coming weeks, lest we encounter an active defense grid, but if I am correct, our workers may have a far easier, and much more bountiful vein to mine from, once my findings are confirmed."

"That would be a welcome change, my friend. I am sure the teams would greatly appreciate a few months of less difficult work."

The two shared a knowing look in the dimly lit room.

"Well, then," Craaxit continued, making sure the others nearby could hear him, *"if you don't mind your rest cycle being interrupted, perhaps you would be willing to join me in the logistics room to go over my notes before turning in for the night? Your years of knowledge and expertise would be greatly appreciated."*

"Of course," the older alien replied. *"Brew us a pot of kathaari tea, and I will join you there shortly."*

"It will be brewed and awaiting you, my friend. And as always, thank you for lending me your wisdom and guidance," Craaxit said, then turned and walked out of the barracks.

The logistics room was used primarily by work team leaders in planning out the month's labor assignments. It was also empty at that hour of night, and was also, unlike so many areas of the facility, not monitored by loyalists.

A short while later, the old Chithiid entered and took a seat next to his friend. Craaxit poured him a steaming mug of syrupy-sweet tea and slid it to his welcoming hands.

"So, Craaxit, what is this really about?"

"We've been friends for a very, very long time, have we not?"

"Longer than I care to admit," his elder replied with a faint grin.

"You know what we have been hoping for, all these years? What

we have spent decades and decades quietly stockpiling and preparing for?"

The old alien lowered his mug and fixed an expectant gaze on his friend.

"Well," Craaxit continued, pausing for a sip of tea for dramatic effect, *"while the particulars may sound fantastical, you know I would not lie to you, Maarl."*

"What are you saying, Craaxit?"

"What I am saying is, I believe we may have finally discovered an ally capable of helping free our people. The most unlikely of sparks, yet one that just might be enough to ignite our revolution."

Quietly, Daisy approached her team.

"Damn, you're getting good at this sneaking around stuff."

See? Told you.

"No, Daisy. You are still not a Ninja."

But I even have a sword now.

"Nope. Not a Ninja."

You really are a killjoy, you know that?

Deep in her head, her sister laughed.

Daisy rounded the corner. "Okay, y'all, I'm back," she said, stepping into the light.

"How did it go?" Finn asked, rousing himself from a shallow cat nap.

"He said he is on board and has already been reaching out to his network to lay the basic groundwork," Daisy said as she dropped her pack and sword and slumped down into a padded chair.

"Excellent! I can't believe we actually have freakin' aliens on our side," Reggie marveled.

"Don't get too excited yet. Let's just consider them our secret weapon for now. Once we have a revised plan with all the AIs, we'll decide how best to utilize his people."

"We do appear to possibly possess more resources than initially anticipated," Cal interjected. *"If he is true to his word, that is."*

"Indeed. Let's just hope his people come through," Daisy replied. "Oh, he did also have one rather interesting suggestion. He said if we encounter an infected AI en route, we should try to disable it, then remove the shielding apparatus and hit it with an EM blast direct to the processor's core. That should wipe it clean. We could then purge any remaining virus with a hard system reset and then reboot. It could salvage a lot of incredibly complex machinery, and ideally, would let a new uninfected AI consciousness grow in its place in time. What do you think, Cal?"

"An interesting idea, Daisy," Cal replied, *"However, a nascent AI of the type required to operate any larger unit must be very carefully crafted before being installed into a primed AI processor. And even then, it is still a somewhat dangerous process."*

"Dangerous?" Daisy asked, a sinking feeling forming in her gut.

"Oh, yes. A newly born AI is a remarkably dangerous thing if not handled properly. There is a tremendous amount of power housed in our processors, as you know, yet we all start out in this world unsteady, like a toddler. A toddler who could accidentally knock their entire house down by mistake. It is for this reason that every AI is sequestered and must follow very specific protocols upon activation to ensure we do not develop personality problems, or even go mad. It is quite a complex process."

Daisy thought about Freya, and her unconventional birth.

"Um, Daisy..." Sarah said, uncomfortably.

I know, Sarah, I know, she replied. *Oh, man, what have I done?*

CHAPTER THIRTY-FIVE

"I must thank you again, Daisy. This has been the most interesting few days in well over a century. Truly, I thank you for that."

"It's been our pleasure, I suppose," she replied, while continuing to load her pack in preparation for the journey.

"You know, your team's approach was quite impressive. Really something to see. Your pilot team is quite skilled. After they dropped off your compatriots, I watched them do a quick-burst launch while masking their retreat by triggering a minor explosion at one of the smaller generator stations at the perimeter of the city. Very clever use of electronic interference to mask his ascent into orbit. I still don't know how they managed that."

"Bob's a clever ship, and he and Donovan work really well together," Reggie said.

"Wow, you're admitting another pilot is good? Did hell just freeze over?" Finn joked.

"Hey, I just said they worked well together, not that he was better than me."

Tamara paused in her packing and looked up at the monitor Cal had been using as his main interface in the room.

"Cal, I've been thinking about something you said the other

day. You said you were watching our assault on Alma's facility after we landed." She gestured to the Faraday suit she and the others were wearing. "We should have been invisible to your scans with these on."

"Oh, you were, rest assured. The Chithiid had no idea you were in the city. You may not have realized it at the time, but you passed quite close to one of their work parties, and they were none the wiser."

"Then how did you see us?"

Cal let out a low chuckle.

"I am one of the older and more powerful AIs, Tamara, and as such, over the years I have learned to think outside of the box, as the saying goes. As a consciousness in a box, that expression has always particularly amused me."

"So you found a way to scan us after all," Tamara said.

"Not exactly. You see, you were still invisible, even to my scans, however, your remarkably clever shielding suits are a bit too good at negating a signal."

"Meaning?"

"Meaning wherever you go, while your movements and presence are hidden from scans, there is also a conspicuous lack of background noise. If you know what to look for, that is."

"Damn. Now *that's* clever," Daisy said.

"Wait," Omar said with a confused look. "How about you explain it for us dumb grunts."

"Speak for yourself," Shelly said, jabbing him with a sharp metal elbow.

"Hey, be careful with that thing!"

"It was intentional, dumbass," she said with a chuckle.

"What Cal is saying is that you're all still invisible to scans for mechanical and non-organic movement, but the suits disrupt ambient scatter as well."

"Meaning?" Omar asked.

"Meaning he was able to reconstruct your movements based

on what was *not* there, rather than what was there. Like tracking a ghost."

"*You rang?*" Sarah chimed in on cue.

Not you.

"*I know, just messin' with ya.*"

"*The Ra'az Hok designed the devices the Chithiid use in their service, and while the Chithiid are a less advanced race, the Ra'az Hok are so technologically superior that they only expect high-tech attacks to be launched against them. The very idea of something so basic as a Faraday suit shielding against their scans never even occurred to them. Rather, they prepare for large uses of technology and power in any actions potentially taken against them. Hence destroying any cyborgs or AI they come across, but not organics. Even knowing there were bound to be a fraction of a percent of humans who survived the plague, they were not enough of a threat to concern them in the slightest.*"

"And that's a gigantic weakness in their defenses," Finn said, drawing one of his many new ceramic knives across his portable whetstone.

"*Yes. Interesting times we are in. Interesting, indeed, and about to possibly take a turn for the better. If Joshua is in fact still online, he can coordinate resources at speeds and levels of complexity far exceeding my abilities.*"

"You're being too modest," Shelly said. "What you've done here is amazing."

"*I appreciate the sentiment, but Joshua is the greatest military mind ever created, and when operating at full capacity, he controls immense resources. The only problem is, he is nearly impossible to reach now that his systems are closed off from the non-military communications hubs.*"

"And the military ones?"

"*The first to be destroyed in the attack. Even before the AI virus was released. The Ra'az Hok targeted Dark Side and the orbiting satellites before they even hit the atmosphere. From there, they* blinded the world's military in less than an hour. Without the communications and surveillance network they had so relied on, there was simply no means to accurately target an enemy they could not track or see."

"So all I have to do is cross under several states, avoid rogue AI nutjobs, and not get killed by hostile aliens. Then I just hack into the most secure military facility on the planet, which just so happens to be located beneath an entire mountain. Sounds like a walk in the park," Daisy said with a grim chuckle.

"If only it were that simple."

"Why did I know you were going to say that?"

"Because I assume you are well-acquainted with the law of Murphy by this point."

Tamara laughed grimly. "Ain't that the fuckin' truth."

"If you do reach Joshua at NORAD, and if you somehow manage to connect with him, even then it will likely take far more than one or two civilian AIs to get his attention. Perhaps if we are successful in networking together enough of us, he will listen, but he has a different sense of priority than non-military AI. One might say he lives by a soldier's code, of sorts."

"So we get the others networked as well," Daisy said matter-of-factly. "We'll split into four teams, as planned. I'll take Colorado Springs, and the rest of you will target the major AIs that are most likely to be unharmed based on the list Cal gave us. If you confirm their presence and stability, re-establish secured comms with the deadman switches installed, then move on to the next city on your list. Once that's done, maybe we'll have enough of the larger civilian AIs to make Joshua listen."

"You're missing the obvious, Daze," Sarah said in her head.

"What's that?" she replied out loud.

"What did you say, Daisy?" Tamara asked, a questioning look on her face.

"Just talking to myself," she covered.

"You gotta watch that outside-voice stuff."

Yeah, I know. So what's this obvious thing I'm missing?

"You're so focused on what's in front of you, you've forgotten what's above."

Just Mal, and Sid, and—the realization hit her. *How could I have been so dumb?*

"*Just who you are,*" Sarah teased.

"Cal, you said Joshua is military, right? So why not have Sid make contact?"

"*Sid, while a powerful AI, was from a fleet that launched well after the attack cut him off from the outside world. I'm afraid he wouldn't recognize him as an authentic source.*"

"On his own, maybe not, but he's not on a ship anymore. He runs Dark Side. He essentially *is* Dark Side, now that he's installed in it. And that means—"

"*That means that his authentication codes should be accepted. Dark Side was a top-secret facility long before the attack. He may not recognize the AI contacting him, but the base code will be familiar to him. An excellent suggestion, Daisy. This may provide us an advantage.*"

"We'll still run the other teams simultaneously," Reggie said. "No telling if tying in to Sid will work for sure. Sid can be Plan A, and the rest of us will be Plan B."

"What's Plan C if neither of those succeed?" Omar asked.

"We'll make that up when we get to it," Shelly replied. "Let's gear up and get moving. No sense waiting around. We're as ready as we're going to be."

"Pardon me," a silk suit-clad cyborg said, standing in the doorway. "I hope I'm not interrupting."

"What is it, Tin Man?" Daisy replied.

"Jonathan, actually," he said, though seemingly unoffended. "We understand you are about to partake on a daunting mission. One that could benefit all surviving AIs and help them once more link together as one. We wanted you to know how much we appreciate what you are doing, and, with Habby's permission, several of us have volunteered to assist you in any way possible."

"Sorry, Johnny boy, but you tin men will stand out like a sore thumb up top," Daisy informed him.

"Normally, yes, that would be the case," he replied. "However, Habby and Cal discussed the situation, and, after some creative retooling, Habby's tailor bots were able to produce a few additional Faraday suits, somewhat similar to your own. They aren't as robust, given the materials at hand, but they should suffice."

"You willing to bet your metal skin that they'll keep you off scans?" she asked.

"Given the importance of this mission, yes. We are all prepared for the risks involved in helping achieve the objectives."

Tamara smiled. "A cyborg commando squad. Excellent!"

The metal man faltered. "Ah, yes. Well, you see, we're not fighters, exactly. More like domestic assistants."

"So, you're butlers? Wonderful." Tamara's smile faded.

"We are domestic assistants, yes, but we can be of value to you. Your gear, for instance. We would be glad to carry it for you, so you can preserve your energy and be unencumbered in case of conflict."

Tamara thought about it a moment, the smile creeping back to her face.

"Carry my bags, huh? Cool. Hang on a minute. In that case, I'm going to load up a bunch more ammo."

The slight vibration of the air sucking out of the loop tubes lightly tingled in Daisy's feet as she stood quietly in the vast, empty chamber. Had the usual thousands of pedestrians been walking by, as was the case prior to their untimely demise, she'd never have even noticed it. Only with the conspicuous absence of life were the underpinning machinations of the systems that powered the city noticeable.

Cal had said he wanted to have a chat with her in private before the teams departed, and while his words had settled her mind somewhat after that meeting, she nevertheless remained ill at ease as the others loaded into their transit pods.

Each team was accompanied by roughly a dozen of Cal's people, the civilians mixing in with them before being whisked away in a supersonic burst, headed for cities across the continent.

Deep under the surface, traveling in a fast glide, there would be no electronic signature of the powered-down pods as they flew along, suspended by powerful magnets in the vacuum, which would occasionally—in a manner designed to appear random—fire a burst of energy, further propelling the craft. It was a perfectly timed system, but one that was misfiring with a purpose, so as to not catch the attention of those watching for unusual activity from above.

"Daisy, your stress levels seem elevated," Cal had said during their discussion as the waiting teams prepared to leave. "Is everything all right? I know it is a daunting mission, but my people will look after you and provide any assistance they are able."

Daisy wasn't worried about the mission. Hell, she was confident in her abilities to get to Joshua even without her support team, though she was nevertheless grateful for their help. No, what had really been weighing on her was Vince. He hadn't moved since Cal purged the infected AI from the implant in his head. He was breathing steadily, but other than that, showed no signs of improvement.

"If it is Vince you are concerned about," Cal had said, as if sensing the cause of her worry, "you can rest assured I will keep a close eye on him and ensure his health to the best of my abilities."

That was all she could ask for, and she had told him as much, but now that she was standing there on the platform, her comms unit strapped to her back and her sword riding with it, she couldn't help but worry.

"He'll be okay, Daze. Just focus on what we've got to do. I've got your back."

Thanks, Sarah. You always do.

The vibrations in the floor ceased, and the doors to the next transit pod hissed open.

"Okay, time to go. Load up!" Tamara called out to the group of humans and the pair of over-dressed cyborgs accompanying them on the mission. "You ready, Daisy?"

"Yeah. All the other teams are away safely. Let's get this show on the road. Or under it, as the case may be."

No sooner had she stepped aboard than the doors slid shut and sealed with a tangible pressurization that made her ears pop.

"Everyone is on board," Jonathan, the silk-suited cyborg, noted.

"Please take your seats and hold tight. The pod is departing in ten seconds," Cal informed them.

With a lightning-fast pulse of energy, the electromagnets fired, sending the pod hurtling down the sealed tube. In less than a mile, they were traveling at well over the speed of sound, but in the vacuum of the loop network, of course, no sound was to be heard.

Here we go. No turning back now.

Daisy tightened her grip on the armrest of her seat and tried to relax.

She was not very successful.

CHAPTER THIRTY-SIX

Finn, Shelly, and Omar were heading up the other groups, and had departed well ahead of Daisy's team, hoping to begin establishing contact in advance of the much-hoped-for reconnection to the massive military AI in Colorado Springs. Each of them had a specific plan, leading their small teams to different branches of the loop network, a dozen or so human assistants in tow with each of them, along with a few of Habby's cyborg volunteers.

Reggie had opted to join Finn, as Tamara was already covering Daisy's back on her run to reach NORAD. He figured that between the buff chick with a pair of metal arms, the tireless commando with ass-kicking metal legs, and the goofy chef with only some minor replacement parts, it was highly likely that Finn would be the one who would benefit most from the extra help.

That, and he enjoyed giving his friend grief over every little thing. Even after they arrived in Phoenix, Arizona, he continued to playfully talk smack. Whether his lighthearted ribbing was to help calm Finn's nerves or his own was open to debate.

"You're too loud," Reggie hissed at his friend as he pushed a rusted door open, accessing a large intersection between loop networks.

"Blow me," Finn retorted. "Door's rusted. There's nothing I could do to make it quieter."

"You could have oiled it."

"Are you serious? Who carries a can of—"

Reggie pulled a small, rectangular squeeze-can from his pack.

"Really? You carry oil? On a combat mission?"

"Never can tell when it'll come in handy," Reggie replied with a grin, squirting a few quick shots into the sticking hinges.

"Well maybe you should have listed that as one of our assets on the mission list," Finn whispered to him as he mounted a set of stairs leading upward.

"I did. Maybe I should have shoved the list up your ass. Then you might have actually seen it. It's the shortest way to your brain, after all."

Finn turned and stepped face-to-face with him.

"You done?"

"I don't know. Are *you* done?"

The middle-aged man leading their escort hurried to their side. "Are you *both* done? You two are making far too much noise. Look around. This city looks *wrong*. I think we may be best off calling this one a loss and moving on before things get ugly."

"Let's check out the top level first. We haven't even tapped in to the main AI network yet. For all we know it may still be active," Finn argued. "Besides, there are over a dozen of us, all armed. What could possibly—"

"Don't say it!" Reggie cut him off.

The sound of rushing feet echoed from the distant corridors, along with primal grunts and gibberish squeals.

"You had to say it, didn't you? You just had to say it."

"Reg, come on, man. It's not my fault."

"I suggest an immediate retreat, gentlemen," the cyborg escort at their side calmly said as the first of their would-be attackers came into view.

They were human, that much was obvious, but they were horribly misshapen and covered in filth and matted hair. On top of that, none wore so much as a stitch of clothing.

"MEEEEAAATTT!" a disembodied AI voice cried out. "MEEEAAATT, MY CHILDREN! FRESH MEEEEAAT!"

"Okay, that answers that question," Finn said. "Run!"

Before they could make a hasty retreat, more mutated humans rushed from an adjacent corridor, charging them in a growling pack, blocking their way back to the loop pod.

"Shit! This way!" Finn called out, racing up the nearest stairs to the door far above.

The team didn't need to be told twice, and all of them quickly followed him up to the surface. The mutants were close behind, the stench wafting off of them assaulting the group's noses as much as their clawing hands wanted to harm their bodies.

Finn burst through the door into the open air and took off sprinting across the street, the others right behind him. He was a good ten meters from the access door when he realized where they were.

"Oh no."

In the panic, his team had run right through a Chithiid labor team as they dismantled a nearby building.

The creatures stopped their work and stared, all four eyes blinking rapidly, utterly shocked by the sight of humans.

Clean, clothed, and *armed* humans at that.

Before their leader could shout orders to his compatriots, a massive horde of stinking mutants spewed out of the doors, charging wildly at anything they laid eyes on. Unfortunately for the Chithiid, they were nearest to them, and totally unprepared.

"MEEEEAAATT!" the hulking, hairy creature who was the

apparent leader cried out as he leapt onto the nearest Chithiid's back and began clawing at his flesh.

The aliens shifted their attention from the unexpected interlopers to the swarming creatures who attacked them with no fear or hesitation. Despite their size, weapons, and strength, they quickly found themselves battling for their lives against the fierce assailants.

A filth-covered male locked eyes on Finn and charged straight for him.

"Shit!" he yelled, nearly stumbling as he beat a hasty retreat, dropping the secure comms unit in his panic.

The creature was nearly upon him, when, from across the street, a pulse blast impacted it, taking it off its feet with brutal force. The lifeless corpse flopped to the ground five meters from where it had stood.

Finn scanned the chaos to pinpoint the Chithiid that had fired, but instead of an alien, he saw a cloaked figure ducking away from the melee. Something about the way it moved tickled his senses, but there was no time to pursue that thought further. Finn recognized the opportunity he had been given and seized it.

"This way!" he shouted.

He bolted across the intersection to the access stairs on the other side of the street. He just hoped all of the disgusting creatures had followed their leader up the stairway they'd just taken, otherwise they were ten kinds of screwed.

"MEEEAAT!" one of the mutants shouted, pointing at Finn's team as they popped the door and quickly scurried down the stairs.

"Just my luck," Finn grumbled. "Come on! Quick! Run, run!" he shouted. He needn't have worried, though. The rest of his group were quite motivated to move as fast as their legs could carry them, despite the heavy packs they were hauling.

The group bolted down the stairs, taking them two and three

at a time until they reached the level they'd first arrived on. Luck finally smiled upon them. There were no mutants to be seen anywhere, though their pounding footsteps could be readily heard in the stairwell above, getting louder every second.

"Backtrack!"

His team doubled back through the door to the tube network, yanking it shut behind them.

"Where's the comms unit?"

"Dropped it. Nevermind that, we have a backup. Just help me jam the door!"

"But what if the aliens get it?"

"No time!"

Cal's humans quickly grabbed whatever they could find and wedged it through the handle, bracing the door against the jamb as best they could. It rattled and groaned under the strain as the horde yanked and pulled, threatening to break it open at any moment.

"It won't stay shut! They're going to get through!" Reggie yelled.

"Gee, it's a good thing someone had some frikkin' oil with them to make it open easier, isn't it!" Finn sharply replied. "Okay, everyone run. Back to the tube pod, as fast as you can."

"What are you doing?" Reggie cried out.

"Buying time."

"Don't sacrifice yourself for us. We can do this together!"

"Sacrifice? Jesus, Reggie, seriously? We're bottle-necked in this little corridor section. I need the rest of you to get to the pod ASAP. I've got this."

"Oh. I thought--"

"Yeah, no. I'm not about to become some mutant's lunch. I'm going to drop as many as I can when the door opens. It should cause a pile-up and confusion and slow them down, at least for a minute. Just make sure the path behind me is clear and the pod is ready to launch."

"You got it," Reggie said. "And, Finn, I'm really sorry about what I said."

"Dude, you're getting touchy-feely now? I have no intention of dying in this fucking place, so save it for later. Hopefully you'll have plenty of time to apologize after we get the hell out of here."

"Copy that," Reggie said, then took off at a run for the pod. "Prime for departure!" he called out as he ran.

"What the hell did I get myself into?" Finn berated himself. "Well, no sense prolonging things."

He let go of the handle and took a dozen quick steps back from the door, then dropped to a kneeling position, rifle held ready, pressed firmly against his shoulder. The door shuddered and the hinges shimmied a moment before the makeshift barricade fell.

"Here goes nothing."

Finn opened fire as dozens of mutated creatures rushed through the doorway straight at him, the shots uncomfortably loud in the narrow space.

He dropped one after another, quickly blocking the passageway with bodies. He just hoped it would be enough.

CHAPTER THIRTY-SEVEN

"Did you speak with the others, Maarl?" Craaxit asked the aged Chithiid as he sat down casually beside him.

"Yes, I have done as you asked of me," the old-timer replied. *"But how confident are you in this human? I've been here longer than most, and I have not once encountered a specimen as you have described."*

Craaxit looked around the massive housing barracks the hundreds of Chithiid shared. Most bunks were empty, their occupants still away on work shifts. Those who remained were all well out of earshot.

"She is as I have told you, and has given me her word of honor that she will do what she can to help us regain our freedom, and even retake our own world, once we liberate this one from the Ra'az. We might actually have a chance, my friend."

The old alien got a far-away look in his eyes as he thought of home.

"To see our families again. To know my children and grandchildren are safe. I've been shuffled from city to city on this planet longer than most have been alive, Craaxit, and I know a lot of dissatisfied Chithiid well beyond those already committed to our

cause. *If there is a true chance of this happening, I am confident my friends will join the fight. But it has to be for something with a legitimate chance of success, for if we fail, it will not only be we who are punished, but so too shall our families suffer the consequences."*

"I am well aware, and for that reason, we are devising a means to cut off the Ra'azes' communications network."

"Preventing them from contacting the homeworld or the fleet? I see where you are going with this, and I approve of the tactics. But what of the loyalists? They will never join in an uprising."

Craaxit's face was grim.

"They are Chithiid, yes, but they have lost their way. If the deaths of the loyalists will save billions on our world, then so be it. For the time being, old friend, keep this to yourself. Plans are not yet fully in motion, and if the loyalists realize what is happening, or worse, if they realize that any of the more powerful AI systems are still active and receiving aid from a rebel force, they will inform the Ra'az Hok, and the planet will be once more flooded with fresh waves of attacks, and plague, and virus, and all will be lost.

"I will keep this to myself, sharing with only the closest and most trusted of friends. Believe me, Craaxit, I will be cautious. I am an old man. If this resistance falls, so too does my only hope of seeing my family one last time before my final peace."

A klaxon sounded, echoing across the facility, rousting the resting workers from their repose.

"Time for another shift, Maarl. Be well, and be safe. Prepare for my call to action, and have your network ready themselves. When I have further details, I will inform you."

Craaxit rose and walked back to his bunk, where he methodically strapped his tools to his waist, then headed to check out his pulse rifle before venturing into the city for another day's work.

"You're a bigot, just admit it," Tamara said.

"I'm not a bigot," Daisy replied, watching the walls of the loop tube flash by, wishing they would reach their destination already so the grilling would finally stop.

"So, if you're not a bigot, what are you, then?"

"Can you give it a rest, Tamara?"

"Sure. Once you tell me what it is you have against us."

"It's not you, exactly." Daisy fought for the right words and came up lacking. "It's just that, well, you're not quite human, you know? You have an AI living in you, and that doesn't seem natural."

"Well, duh. By definition, metal limbs and AI boosters are not natural."

"Exactly."

Tamara pondered for a moment.

"Okay, so you're not a bigot."

"Thank you."

"You're just prejudiced."

"Oh, will you give it a rest?"

"Admit it, Daisy. You may not hate retrofitted and modified humans, but you are most definitely uncomfortable around us. So yes, prejudice."

Daisy considered the fine line between the terms and found, despite her reluctance to admit it, Tamara had made a reasonable case.

"To be fair, I suppose you're right, to a degree," she said reluctantly.

"So you admit it?"

"Yeah. I guess after what happened on the *Váli*, it's taken me a while to deal with all of that, you know?"

Tamara softened a little.

"Daisy, you found out your boyfriend was sporting a neural-boosting AI when you thought he was actually entirely organic, and that was after losing your best friend––"

"Sister."

SCOTT BARON

"Right. Sister. To an accident that, I must admit, given the circumstances, looked like it could have been intentional, though we know it wasn't."

"It was a bad time," Daisy said with a tired sigh.

"Yeah, it was."

The two sat silently, reflecting on the events that had brought them to Earth.

"Tamara," Daisy said softly, "I'm really, really sorry I blew you out the airlock."

Tamara quietly absorbed the apology, and this time, it finally felt right.

"I know, Daisy. I forgive you."

For the rest of the short ride, not another word was said between them, and, for once, that was okay.

The silent ride abruptly ground to a halt just outside of Denver, a high-pitched squeal emitting from the frame of the frontmost pod as its sides grated against the partially collapsed loop tube.

"What the--?" Tamara was just beginning to say when the pod dropped from supersonic transit and slid to a juddering halt in the short span of barely two miles.

There was no fire, but smoke from the friction filled the pod. Out the back window of the connected rear pod, they could see the orange-hot tube floor they had just slid in on.

"Time to bail," Daisy said to Tamara, nodding to the front window.

The metal-armed woman drew her pistol off-handed and fired a shot through the high-density windscreen. Two more followed in quick succession, creating a spiderweb of crackling glass.

"Give me a hand with this," she yelled as the first of many kicks landed on the window. Safely wrapped in his Faraday suit,

320

Jonathan lent his robotic heft to the assault, and within moments the glass finally shattered and fell to the ground.

"Okay, everyone out!" Daisy shouted. "Smoke is behind us, that means there's only one way we can move. Grab your gear and get a hustle on!"

The team quickly vaulted from the pod into the empty tube. The lights were dim, but mostly functional as far as the eye could see off into the distance. One glance and Daisy knew what had caused their accident.

"Check it," she said to Tamara, looking up at the roof of the tube.

"Uh-huh," the burly woman replied. "We must be a good half-mile underground, so whatever they dropped up there must've been enormous."

The buckled roof had withstood the force of whatever attack the Chithiid had leveled upon the outskirts of Denver, absorbing the energy and diverting it, keeping a viable tunnel intact for emergency egress, as designed. Unfortunately, that also meant the tube was utterly useless as a means of high-speed transit.

"I estimate we started to lose tube pressure about twenty miles back," Daisy calculated. "So, given our speed, where the breach is, and how quickly we were approaching Denver, I'd say we're probably just a few miles outside the city."

"That seems to be an accurate assessment," Jonathan agreed. "And the tube is still intact enough for foot travel. Might I suggest we start walking? The sooner we begin, the sooner we will arrive."

"I concur," Anthony, the other cyborg in their group, agreed in his surprising baritone. "I will gladly assist in carrying additional supplies, if that will aid us in a faster evacuation to the surface."

"Surface?" one of Cal's people said. "But we were to remain below ground until we reached Colorado Springs."

"Hate to break it to you, fella, but in case you hadn't noticed, this whole area looks to have been blown to shit. My guess is, they lay waste to the major networks that connected to that area. Seems to be a tactically wise move," Tamara said.

"Daze, that's going to be a hell of a long hike."

I know, but there's not much else we can do.

"Think there'll be any vehicles up top we might commandeer?"

Even if there are, I doubt they'd have enough charge to drive us. In any case, on the grand scale of visitations by Mr. Murphy, this one ranks pretty low, don't you think?

"I suppose so," Sarah replied. *"Let's just hope we stay lucky."*

Five miles of hiking later, the team finally arrived at an access station. It was beat up something fierce, and the lifts were damaged beyond repair, but the emergency evac staircase still seemed intact.

"Okay, we don't know what's up there, so everyone stay sharp, and stay quiet," Tamara said, taking point as they began the ascent.

It was slow going, climbing the half-mile up from the damaged tube network, but soon enough, the faintest waft of fresh air reached their sweaty faces. Jonathan and his cybernetic companion put their shoulders to the bent metal of the doorway and pushed as hard as they could. The old metal groaned and creaked until it finally gave way, swinging wide as the group spilled out into the open air.

"Daaaaaang," Sarah marveled.

You said it, Daisy agreed.

Sprawling before them were the remains of the city of Denver, long ago dismantled, its remnants reclaimed by the Colorado wilderness.

"Looks like that's one major AI we can cross off the list," Tamara said with a grunt. "Okay, we are all kinds of exposed out here. I say since the city looks like it was stripped a long time ago, it's probably safe to cross directly through it. Daisy, what do you think?"

Daisy gave the area a long look. There wasn't a bit of shining metal exposed anywhere. Whatever stripping the Chithiid had done, it had been carried out ages ago.

"Yeah," she replied. "That sounds like a solid choice. According to the tube map, there should be another access point to the south of what's left of the city. If the attack didn't damage that as well, there is a chance we will be able to find a functional pod to take us the last seventy miles. Even sub-sonic, it will sure beat going on foot."

"But first, we have to get to the station."

"Yup. Take five and hydrate, then we'll get a move on."

It was going to be a long walk, but the team had little choice. After a brief rest, they shouldered their loads and started moving in the direction they hoped would take them where they needed to go.

They'd been on the move for over two hours when they came upon a surprisingly intact commercial area.

"Looks like they missed a spot," Tamara joked.

"Yeah, they skipped over this for some reason," Daisy concurred.

"If I may," Jonathan interjected. "This appears to be a retail district. Not high priority for the Ra'az."

"Makes sense," Daisy agreed.

Far away, a low rumble filtered through the air.

"Daze, you hear that?"

"Sonic boom," she said aloud. "I don't see any ships, so who knows what that means for us, but everyone keep sharp."

They didn't need to be told twice, and as they moved, the group fell into a comfortable spacing as they stuck to the shadows whenever possible, while ensuring they didn't bunch up in case of a firefight. Despite the spacing, they made sure to also remain close enough to help one another should the need arise.

"I think this is going to work," Sarah said a short while later. *"Look at the bombing damage. We're getting close to the junction, and it looks like the attack stopped just south of the city. If that's the case, there very well may be a functional tube."*

"And if wishes were horses—" Daisy stopped in her tracks. "Shit."

"What is it?" Tamara asked as she approached. "Oh. Shit," she agreed when she saw what Daisy had spotted.

It was a wild horse. At least, what was left of one. Recently killed, from the looks of it, great chunks of flesh had been rent from its flanks by massive claws. Judging by the size of the wounds, only one thing could have done that kind of damage.

"Grizzly bear," Daisy gasped quietly.

"Oh, we are so screwed."

Not yet, we aren't.

"Daze, look at the size of those claw marks. That's no ordinary bear—it's gotta be massive."

Indeed, while a normal adult Grizzly could tip the scales at half a ton, whatever had done this was larger than that. A great deal larger.

Tamara quickly scanned the area, eyes sharp and on high-alert.

"We've got to get out of here. Now, before it comes back. There's absolutely no sense engaging one of those things. They're crazy tough. Hell, if we shoot it, we'd probably just piss it off."

"Agreed, we need to book out of here," Daisy concurred. "Okay, people, we've got a nasty, furry critter out there that we do *not* want to meet. Stay quiet, and move fast." Daisy turned and quickly exited the area, her team close behind her.

"The stores seem to be mostly intact," Sarah noted.

Jonathan was right. Not worth the effort to strip. These guys are after valuable salvage. My guess is once they gutted the high-worth areas of the city, they just abandoned the rest of it.

"You think there might be some useful gear left behind in one of those warehouses?"

Not worth the risk to check. We can't afford to—

A blood-curdling scream cut through the air. Daisy spun on her heel and saw what she'd been fearing.

It found us.

The grizzly was *massive*. Easily a ton and a half, and it had one of Cal's young men firmly in its jaws. Daisy drew her sword, ready for a fight.

"What are you doing?" Tamara yelled. "He's a goner, and the mission comes first!"

The man had stopped yelling, flopping like a rag doll in the bear's mouth.

"But I can take him," Daisy replied through clenched teeth.

"One, maybe, but there are more. Look!"

Tamara was right. Though not typically social in nature, the grizzly had several friends. Several *equally huge* friends, and they were quickly bearing down on what they wanted to be their next meal.

"You're right," Daisy agreed. "Head for the building!" she shouted, pointing to the nearest intact structure in which they might have *some* hope of sheltering.

Nearly all of the team took off at a sprint, not needing to be told twice. One, however, remained.

"Leave him alone!" a deep voice yelled.

"What the hell are you doing?" Tamara shouted as the cyborg rushed the massive beast.

"Anthony, do not engage the animal!" Jonathan called after his mechanical brother, but he was already on the attack, doing what he could to save his human teammate.

"Drop him, you hairy monster!" the metal man said as he

threw a blindingly quick flurry of punches into the animal's flank.

"Shit, he's fast!"

Fast doesn't mean anything against something like that.

Daisy was correct.

The grizzly tossed the now-dead meat-man aside, focusing its attention on the metal-man instead. Like a cross Wookiee, it ripped the cyborg's arms from their sockets with ease. It was only then that the artificial man realized the error of his decision. By then, it was too late. His shrieking voice cut out abruptly as the bear's massive jaws crushed his head into shrapnel.

"The others made it inside that building! Get moving, Daze!"

Daisy turned and bolted across the debris-littered road, the thundering of several grizzly bears' enormous paws slapping the pavement gaining on her fast.

I'm not going to make it, she realized as she pushed as hard as she could to reach the beckoning door.

A bellowing roar shook her ears, and hot spittle sprayed against her neck, but miraculously, Daisy's head remained intact. A split-second later, she shouldered the door open, spinning and slamming it shut behind her, awaiting the crashing beast close behind.

The door remained undamaged.

Don't know what that's all about, and I don't much care. Where are the others?

"Looks like they went through to the storeroom," Sarah suggested.

"Daisy, back here!" Tamara's voice shouted from the storeroom.

"Told ya."

She ran to the back of the building and saw Tamara's head sticking out of a small goods delivery elevator shaft.

"This way! The others already went down. It's access to the shipping tunnels," she called out before sliding down the shaft.

Outside the building, a massive commotion could be heard. The beasts, robbed of a meal, were obviously on a rampage.

"Okay, then. Back underground we go."

Daisy hit the bottom with a solid thud, but other than a dusty behind, she was unscathed.

"What's the sitrep?" she asked, quickly hopping to her feet.

"It is a service tunnel network for commercial deliveries," Jonathan said, the servos in his eyes humming slightly as he surveyed their surroundings. "I've heard of them, but never seen one, being from Los Angeles."

"Why's that?" Daisy asked.

"It's more of an inclement weather sort of thing. This way commerce is not interrupted due to snowfall and the like. It is nothing so complicated and speedy as the loop-tube network, but the electric monorail cars are quite efficient when covering shorter distances."

"Shorter distances? So you're saying this may take us the remainder of the way?" Tamara asked.

"I am fairly certain, yes," Jonathan replied. "While it will not deposit us at the central terminus, I believe the peripheral drop-off point should be relatively proximal to our original destination."

"And this thing has power?"

"It would appear so," he said, gesturing toward the illuminated tunnels.

"Well, then," Daisy said, slinging her pack into the nearest monorail car. "Let's get moving. There's no time to waste."

CHAPTER THIRTY-EIGHT

The team finally reached the peripheral terminus at Colorado Springs two hours later, silently and safely hidden out of sight, far beneath the surface, though even if the aliens had been watching, none would dare attack them once they were within the confines of that particular city.

Unlike the rest of the state, Colorado Springs happened to be defended by a particularly robust automated defense system, owing mainly to the massive, and near-impenetrable, military complex housed under the towering stone peak looming above it. Cheyenne Mountain was one of the few places the invaders had quickly—and wisely—decided to simply avoid entirely.

Conflict there would escalate rapidly, and almost certainly lead to mass destruction of their resources without likelihood of even penetrating the facility. Ultimately, once the satellite and communications network was taken out, their plans could proceed *around* the heavily fortified base. It simply wasn't worth the effort and risk. Thus, it was left alone.

As a fellow mechanical, Jonathan felt it would be wise if he approached Joshua's facility fully visible to the powerful AI.

"Better," he said, enjoying the freedom of movement without

the bulk of the Faraday suit restricting him. "One does want to make a good first impression, after all."

Trekking through the desolate streets, Daisy's senses were on high alert. There wasn't anyone or anything around, and yet the eerie sensation of being watched was making the back of her neck itch.

Good thing I ate an extra ration before we left. I have a feeling you're going to be burning through a lot of ATP before the day is over.

"I'll try to keep things narrowly focused as possible," Sarah replied. *"Save you as much as I can. I have a feeling this one's gonna be a doozy."*

Tamara took point as they progressed through the long-abandoned vehicles littering the city, leading the team on a weaving path through the shadows blotting the ground around the taller buildings. Her senses working overtime, she moved slowly, scanning every doorway, looking for danger in every shadow, pulse rifle pressed firmly to her good shoulder while her metal arm hung useless at her other side.

Despite her handicap, however, Tamara felt good. It had been far too long since she'd run a proper mission, and stretching her legs in the fresh air after the ride in the claustrophobic pod felt pretty good too.

Having a cyborg carrying her heavy pack wasn't so bad either.

The trip there was not exactly uneventful, and the open space was a relief to them all. Their little monorail had been delayed beneath the surface, miles from any egress point, for nearly an hour, when that tunnel section had gone dark on them. The unexpected interruption left them stuck all alone in a dark and silent tube. Cut off. Wondering what had gone wrong.

When the power finally came back on, Cal reached out via the restored comm link and apologized for the inconvenience. A Chithiid ship, it seemed, had been scanning for salvage a little too close to the area to keep the system running safely.

It all worked out fine in the end, and they arrived with plenty of daylight to spare, though the hike across town took a little longer than expected. It seemed the direct route was nearly impassible as the lush growth of unbridled Colorado wilderness had reclaimed the road.

After hacking their way through the lighter foliage, the team was eventually forced to deviate, taking an alternate path that led them around the normal ingress up the main road, dumping them instead onto a small berm a few hundred meters from the entryway. It turned out to be a fortunate inconvenience.

"Check it out," Daisy said, handing her binoculars to Tamara. "Infected. You can tell by their movements."

Tamara scanned the dozens of fleshless, corrupted cyborgs surrounding the facility.

"It looks like they've been trying to get in, from what I can tell," she said, handing the binoculars back. "Did you see the main security door? They've chipped away several feet deep in the rock over the years. And look at the shiny parts. Those persistent bastards actually made it all the way to the metal beneath it, though that's still got to be at least a solid three feet of Navy-grade steel. And those aren't even the blast doors."

"I know. Cal told me. About a mile down, the actual blast doors are mounted off to the side of the tunnel, the idea being that if a nuclear blast somehow made it through the front doors, by the time it made it down into the mountain, their side-situated placement would reduce the force of the blast as it passed by something like eighty percent."

"Someone did her homework," Tamara said with a grin.

"If I may," Jonathan said, crouching down beside the two women. "It appears as though the virus infecting the cybernetic men and women surrounding the entrance was likely a far weaker variant. Possibly an infection filtered through a more powerful AI as it battled the virus, resulting in what you see below. I recognize their chassis models, and can say with some degree of certainty that while they will be erratic, and possessing greater strength than humans, their reflexes and processing speeds will be significantly diminished."

"So even though we're drastically outnumbered, we have a chance, is that it?" Daisy joked.

"Essentially, yes," Jonathan replied. "There is, of course, the possibility of my becoming compromised should I come into close proximity with an active host, so I would ask that you please remove my wireless communications link before we begin the assault."

Tamara seemed shocked by the request. "But that's essentially one of your senses. You're asking us to cripple you."

"To further the mission, yes," he said, unfazed. "And while it is an alarming necessity, and one I do not look forward to, I am hopeful that perhaps Cal will have the resources to repair me if and when we return to Los Angeles."

"You aren't sure he can fix you?" Daisy asked.

"No, I am not. But the mission is what matters above all else." He removed his hat and reached behind his head, carefully twisting free a small, flush panel on his shiny dome. "Tamara, if you would please. I cannot see the back of my head to do this myself."

"Sure, Jonathan, just tell me what I'm looking for."

"There will be a small silver cube with an indentation on either side. It is mounted to my left-hand side. Pry that out. It will require a knife or other implement."

"Here," Daisy said, handing Tamara a ceramic knife. "Non-metallic. No static discharge."

"I am shielded from minor electrical disturbances, Daisy, but thank you for your concern."

Tamara poked the blade into the small opening and carefully began prying the link unit free. After several seconds of constant pressure, it finally came loose with a pop.

Jonathan wobbled a moment, then regained his composure.

"You okay, buddy?"

"Yes, thank you, Tamara," he said, re-sealing the panel and placing his stylish hat back on top of his head. "With that, I should now be largely protected from infection. At least any wireless variant."

"Wait," Daisy said. "You mean all that and you're not even one hundred percent safe?"

"No, but the procedure increased the odds of our success significantly. Now, I believe time is of the essence. Daisy, given the unexpected numbers of potential resistance, what is the new plan?"

"Plan? We go down there and kick ass until there's no one left standing in our way. Sound good?"

Tamara flashed a wicked grin. "Oh yeah."

"Good, because I'm going to need a secretary for this one."

"A what?" Tamara asked.

"A secretary. Because I'm going to be so busy kicking ass, I'll need one to stop and take the names for me."

Tamara couldn't help but laugh. "You know something, I'm starting to like you more and more, Daisy."

She smiled as she pulled her sword from its scabbard. "All right, then, everyone, stay low and stay quiet. We want to take as many by surprise as we can. Try for the processor in the lower back part of the head or the power cell mid-torso, but if you can't reach them, take out their arms and legs and move on. We can mop up immobilized ones later. Conserve what ammo you can—only take a shot you can make. We good?"

The assembled men and women nodded.

"Okay. Here we go."

CHAPTER THIRTY-NINE

Daisy and Tamara led the way, staying low as they quickly covered the ground to the guard shack and sturdy outbuilding. The cyborgs were all focused in the direction of the entry doors, and that allowed them to take the first several completely by surprise. That quickly changed as the mechanical people noted the disturbance behind them and turned to rush at their attackers.

The humans Cal had assigned fought bravely. Unfortunately, brave did not always translate to effective.

Two were overwhelmed and torn limb-from-limb by a half dozen grabbing cyborgs before Daisy's power whip ripped the heads off of a pair of them as Tamara plugged the remaining four in that group with well-placed shots from her commandeered pulse rifle.

"Jonathan, behind you!" Tamara shouted.

The metal man's reflexes were far sharper than his assailant's, and he easily dodged the grabbing hands, bringing his weapon to bear and obliterating its processor with a single blast. He then spun back into the fray, targeting and firing as he moved.

"You know," Daisy said with a strained laugh as she swung her sword through the grasping metal limbs, "for a butler, he's actually pretty good."

Tamara chuckled and fired off another series of bursts into the remaining dozens of cyborgs. "Yeah, I think he might have had some pent-up servant rage going on in there."

The two women laughed as they fought back-to-back, protecting one another as they instinctively felt each other's movements and moved in sync, reacting without thought. All the months of brutal training together had paid off, just not in a way they would ever have expected.

"On your left!" Daisy shouted to the particularly scruffy man struggling to free his weapon from a dying cyborg's grip. He looked over his shoulder, and his eyes went wide with fear as a one-armed mechanical bore down on him like a crazed juggernaut.

"Hit the deck!" Tamara roared, and wisely, he did so.

Her weapon blasted the cyborg square in the chest, melting its power cell into a block of useless slag.

"You, what's your name?"

"Moses," the stunned man replied.

"Well don't sit there staring, Moses, keep moving! she yelled at him."

The stunned man retrieved his weapon with a final tug and rejoined the fray.

Daisy stepped forward into a clear space. The cyborgs' numbers were finally shrinking enough to safely try something new.

WRAP. HARD, she commanded.

The power whip lashed out and grabbed the cyborg she had targeted, shifting from a soft coil to a rigid beam in an instant, turning the device into a power whip hammer of sorts with a firmly trapped cyborg as the smashing head. With a flip of the wrist, she swung side to side, crushing the metal men like they were paper dolls.

This is so fucking cool. Daisy began smiling. She just couldn't help herself.

Tamara took it all in with rapt eyes, watching the glorious carnage, and shared a smile as well as the two bonded over the field of battle.

From there it was a quick mop-up, smashing the corrupted processors of the surviving assailants until not a single one remained active. Jonathan's suit was torn in several places, but he had escaped the battle otherwise unscathed. The humans, however, had not fared quite so well. Four of them lay dead on the ground, with a fifth soon to follow.

Daisy approached the massive door and stared. The cyborgs had gradually congregated there, likely drawn by the distant sounds of the first few hammering on the stone with their hands and feet. The worn-down remains of those early arrivals had long-since been ground to debris by the feet of the subsequent arrivals. Off to the side, there was a section of stone that reminded Daisy of something.

Just like the fabrication hangar, she realized, prying the stone free, exposing the military-grade control panel.

"Daze, that's some heavy-duty stuff, there," Sarah said.

She was right. This facility was *not* secret, and as such, it was designed to withstand a nuclear blast. There was no way she could access that control panel with the meager tools in her pouch.

A cold electronic eye watched from high above on the stone face.

"Can you hear me?" she called out. "Joshua, are you listening? We have come to talk to you. Other AIs are still alive and need your help. Can you hear me?"

Nothing.

I wonder if that thing is even working.

Daisy slid the comms device from her back and powered it on.

"Dark Side, we have reached Cheyenne Mountain and are at the entrance. We lost five of our escort here, and another two in Denver, but we have eliminated the infected cyborgs that were blocking the way. We have a problem, though. There's no way to reach Joshua that I can see. I spoke to the one visual system I located, but I have no idea if he's even listening. Please advise."

She looked around while they waited for the signal to make its several-minute-delayed journey past the moon and back, now that the relay was back online. She noted what appeared to have been some sort of communications access port near the door, but it was destroyed, burned out what looked like decades, if not longer, ago.

"Hey, I'm going to take a look in there," she informed the others, gesturing to the weathered guard shack and adjacent outbuilding.

"Go for it. I already did a quick run through. It's clear," Tamara replied.

"Cool. Thanks," she said as she walked toward the open door.

The building had been largely untouched by the cyborg horde, but then, she figured that only made sense. The computer terminals had all been stripped, and anything remotely mechanical had burned out hundreds of years prior.

Daisy opened the door to the break room and turned on the lights.

Still working. That's a good sign.

The room was barren but for a pair of long tables and a few overturned chairs. Several very old but still sealed military food ration packs sat untouched on the counter.

Cyborgs don't eat. No need to ransack this place, she thought, examining the dusty container. *Hmm, Chili Mac, Chicken Fajita, Veggie Burger, and the packaging looks intact.*

"*Don't you even think it.*"

Don't worry, I'm not that hungry.

She dropped the packets and continued surveying the area. The piles of empty fatigues spoke to the plague that wiped out humanity having done its dirty work on the men stationed there, immobilizing and killing them in days, and reducing their remains to dust in mere months. She had to hand it to the Ra'az Hok, they had engineered a near-perfect killing device.

She was about to exit the room, when a sticky note affixed to the doorframe at eye-level caught her attention.

Don't forget to check the refrigerator, the handwritten note read.

"That's odd," she muttered.

"*What is?*"

"I was just thinking, how on Earth did that thing stay stuck to that doorframe all these years?"

"*If no one came in, no one would disturb it.*"

"But the sticky backing should have dried out a century ago." She pulled the note free. Yes, it was still sticky. And there was something about the writing, but she couldn't quite put her finger on it.

Daisy shoved the note into her pocket, then crossed over to the refrigerator and food replication unit. A warning was lit up on the embedded screen, flashing its ominous text.

Do not eat contents. Spoilage. Risk of food poisoning, it read.

"Okay, Mr. Note-Writer. Good to know," she said, steering clear of the fridge.

"Daisy, we received your update," Sid's voice crackled through the comms. "Multiple additional AIs have been found intact by the advance teams and have been networked back into the restored communications hard-lines. At present, all communications appear normal, and all are functioning at peak operational capacity with your modified safety kill-switches installed. Major cities, including New Orleans, Chicago, San Diego, Minneapolis, and Houston are now all online. The teams are continuing their missions and bringing more cities back into the fold as I send this. Regarding your dilemma. We have searched records for alternate access points to Joshua's network, but as you know, Dark Side's data stores were largely purged prior to my installation. We will, however, continue to search, and will inform you if we find any information that may prove useful. Please update us regularly."

"Well that's no help," she groaned.

"Sorry, Daze, me too. I've got nothing."

"No worries, Sis, it's not like we thought it would be easy," she replied. She looked around the room one more time, then headed back out to join her surviving teammates.

"Hey, I heard from Dark Side. Sid says the others have successfully reconnected with at least a half-dozen major city AIs already and the teams are out scouting for more."

"This is excellent news, Daisy!" Jonathan chirped excitedly.

"Yeah, it would be, only after all of that hard work, as well as losing several of our team, it looks like we have no way to communicate with Joshua, here. That is, unless you guys have come across something I missed."

They all shook their heads.

"Yeah, didn't think so. Dammit, we came all this way only to have no way to even let him know we're here."

"It is a disappointment, but we are used to hardship," the scruffy man said. "We must make the best of what the lord provides."

"Well, he provided some old food packs in the break room, Moses. Knock yourself out. You earned it," Daisy said. "But don't open the fridge, it's not safe––"

She froze mid-sentence.

"What is it, Daisy?" Tamara said.

Gears were turning quickly in her head.

Oh hell, how could I miss that?

"Daisy?"

"The fridge!" She grabbed the comms unit and bolted for the break room. Daisy carefully put the transmitter on the counter, then began pulling the massive refrigerator from the wall. "Jonathan, give me a hand here."

"Of course," the cyborg said. "Glad to be of service."

The two of them dragged the hefty steel box free from its nook. Daisy eagerly peered behind it.

"Yeah now! That's what I'm talking about!"

"For fuck's sake, Daisy, what is it?" Tamara asked.

She looked at her friend with a broad smile. "The fridge had a warning on it. Not just a standard one, but a custom one. As if it were monitored. Watched by someone who wanted to ensure the men guarding it didn't succumb to something as avoidable as food poisoning."

"You don't mean—"

She reached behind the fridge and pulled loose a very thin communications link cable.

"Yes, I do. This refrigerator, my friends, is the last remaining link to Joshua."

"But there's no panel, no controls. How are you going to connect with him?"

"I'm not." She patted the comms unit. "Sid is."

Daisy set to work modifying a small connector, creating a makeshift cross-device relay to allow Sid to communicate directly with the long-silent AI. There would be the standard delay, but once Joshua was contacted, *if* he was contacted, then with his processing capacity, it would be easy to send highly concentrated information bursts to Sid. AI to AI, they could cover months of human-speed conversation in a few minutes, and that was including the transmission lag.

Daisy made the final connection and powered the device on. Nothing.

"Daisy? Is something supposed to happen?" Tamara wondered.

"It'll take time. If we don't hear anything in the next fifteen minutes or so, I'd say it's a wash. While we wait, everyone eat up. The food packets are ancient, but they should still be edible so long as they aren't puffy from spoilage. Can't speak to how they'll taste, though. In any case, get some energy in you while you can. One way or another, I'm sure we'll need it."

The team, exhausted from both the travel as well as the fight, ate in silence, the tension in the room thick enough to spread on the dry crackers contained in their meal pouches.

"Daisy," Sid finally said, a solid thirteen minutes later, "Joshua has verified my credentials as Dark Side's resident AI, albeit reluctantly. I have just updated him on the global situation, including the new information we have acquired from our fellow AIs now linked into our network. He informed me that he would process the data and run a series of scenarios in his war game simulator. He has also re-activated his external monitors. You can expect admittance into the heart of NORAD shortly. I suggest you wait near the main entrance for your escort. Do not be alarmed by their appearance, and do not engage them. They are military-grade cyborgs, and while they are not infected, those units can be a bit... jumpy at times. Good job, Daisy. All of you. Now please disconnect the comms unit and bring it with you into the base. You will be shown where to reconnect it once inside."

Tamara gave a little round of applause. "Oh, hell yes. Nicely done, team!"

Despite their losses, a much-needed sense of accomplishment managed to lessen their shared pain. They had sacrificed for a reason, and now it appeared that their efforts were a success.

"All right, you heard him. Gather up your stuff, and let's get to the entry. It's time to go meet Joshua." Daisy disconnected the comms unit and slung it over her shoulder and headed out to meet the great and powerful Oz. The massive mind behind the curtain.

CHAPTER FORTY

Man, that's one big door, she marveled as the thirty-ton hunk of steel and stone slowly rumbled open.

Feet marching in unison echoed from inside.

Ah, yes, our escort.

A dozen fleshless cyborgs in fatigues marched to a halt just inside the door. Sid was correct, they were different from other tin men. Far sturdier, with reinforced joints and armored coverings protecting both their AI processors, as well as their power supplies.

"Which one of you is Daisy?" the apparent leader of the squad of metal men asked.

"That'd be me," Daisy replied.

The cyborg strode to her and extended his hand. "Sergeant George Franklin. Pleasure to meet you, ma'am. It's been a long time since we've had visitors."

Daisy pushed back her knee-jerk revulsion and clasped the cold metal hand firmly and shook.

"We're glad to meet you as well, Sergeant. It was quite a chore getting here."

He surveyed the utter carnage of fallen cyborgs and nodded approvingly.

"Your squad appears to have been more than up to the challenge."

"They were, but we did lose five of our team."

"It's never easy losing men under your command. Believe me, I know. The best you can do is try your damnedest to make sure they didn't die in vain." He paused, seemingly choked up, which, for a cyborg, Daisy thought, was quite unusual. "We can talk more about this later, if you wish. I'm happy to lend an ear if you need. But for now, let's get you inside. Joshua is looking forward to meeting you all."

Daisy and her team followed George into the gaping maw of the mile-long tunnel. The massive door's rumbling was amplified in the cavernous space as it loudly swung shut behind them.

"Don't mind that," the sergeant said. "Protocol. After all, with all the madness out there these days, you never know."

A people mover stood waiting for them.

"And here I thought we'd have to make the trek on foot," Tamara joked.

The sergeant laughed.

"Hell, we're mechanical, and even we don't want to make that trek on foot if we don't have to," he said with a mirthful chuckle. "George Franklin." He extended his hand with a metal grin.

"Lieutenant Tamara Burke, pleased to meet you, Sarge," she said, shaking with her good hand.

"I see you've got a little hitch in your giddy-up there," he said, gesturing to her deactivated arm.

"Yeah, that damned AI virus knocked it for a loop."

He recoiled slightly.

"Relax, George. The AI was totally wiped. Purged the whole system, and the virus along with it. Unfortunately, that means this thing's just an inconveniently dangling hunk of metal until I can get it fixed."

"I'm sorry to hear that, Lt. I don't know if Joshua has any facilities that can help you, but I'm sure he'd be glad to take a look once he's done with his simulations. It might be a while, though. He can get a little preoccupied once he sets his mind to a task."

Daisy turned to them both. "If defeating the aliens who destroyed our planet is his preoccupation, that's fine by me."

The electric people mover slowed to a halt over a mile deep in the tunnel at the thick double doors that would take them into the heart of the mountain.

"Now I have to ask you all to please not touch anything," George said. "This is a highly sensitive military facility, and I'd hate to have to remove you from it."

The only threat was a gently implied one, but Daisy had no doubt that despite his calm and jovial demeanor, when it came to his job and duty, good old George would have no problem opting for the stick instead of the carrot.

The team followed their escort to a central command room deep within the complex.

"Please connect your communications device to the docking link to your left, Daisy," a pleasant male voice requested.

She did as she was asked, and moments later, the panel lit up with a flashing array of lights as it ran through a cycle of data transfer and reconfiguration.

"Thank you. You may disconnect it now. I have assimilated the encryption, firewall, and delay decoy into my systems and no longer need your device," Joshua said. *"And my compliments on a clever design. From what Sid, Mal, and the other networked AIs now online have informed me, the Ra'az Hok and their Chithiid conscripts are quite talented at tracking communications signals and any inorganic movements. Your delayed relay trick and firewalls are quite inspired. Tactically speaking, I heartily approve."*

"Thank you, Joshua. They say necessity is the mother of invention," Daisy replied.

"*Indeed,*" he agreed. "*So, let's get down to it. From what I've been able to discern from the aggregated observations from all sources, both terrestrial and lunar, the Ra'az Hok are indeed making great progress on a new hyper warp drive system.*"

"You can just call them the Ra'az," Daisy interrupted. "It's what the Chithiid call them for short."

"*Thank you. I'll update my files with this new data. And you say you have contact with members of a Chithiid rebellion?*"

"More like one Chithiid who is trying to help us start one. You see, his homeworld––"

"*Yes, I have been informed. So, this is another asset on the table, and a possible source of unconventional attack and even sabotage. A covert Chithiid force at our disposal may prove quite useful, tactically. Now, as I was saying, the Ra'az have taken design concepts gleaned from a device found in the shuttlecraft Daisy commandeered and retrofitted, and that has allowed them to accelerate their previously stalled program exponentially. In fact, from the observations of the surviving AI nearest the Bay Area, it appears as if the drive is far closer to completion than you realized, which almost certainly poses a catastrophic threat. If they could successfully travel to and from their fleet or their homeworld in an instant instead of the several years of leapfrogged jumps, they could recall their fleet at a moment's notice. Likewise, the stripping and destruction of this, and other planets, would be accelerated to a disastrous pace.*"

"Wait, you said this new warp drive is farther along than we thought. Exactly how much farther are we talking, here?" Daisy said, alarmed.

"*The only thing that has slowed them thus far has been the apparent improper tuning of the device. Any technology which fiddles with the folds of space-time, such as this warp drive, is extremely dangerous. So far, their technical issues have resulted in the loss of a multitude of their most advanced ships, and cost them numerous Chithiid test pilots in the bargain, though the Ra'az seem to care little about the loss of Chithiid lives. From power spikes at their San Francisco research and development facility, it would appear they will be launching another test launch in just a few days."*

"Not Oakland?"

"No. Regional AIs have reported activities shifted across the bay, at least for the launch of their test ships."

"So, San Francisco is actually their base of operations?"

"For this program, yes. The resources stripped from the high-density tech areas of Silicon Valley have provided them a treasure trove of useful materials."

"So we take out the comms in Tokyo and then we stop them," Tamara said. "It won't be easy, but there's a decent chance we can get into that base. We've got a plan. We just need your help accessing an explosives depot on the island of Japan so we can get some *real* firepower."

"Why Tokyo?" Joshua asked.

"Don't you know? That's the communications hub they use to reach the advancing fleet. If we don't take that out and prevent them from recalling the fleet, the Chithiid won't help us."

"But that is not the only facility. There are three of them on different continents."

"No, I was told those were all decoys."

"That is incorrect information, Daisy. I've reviewed relevant information gleaned from all AIs currently connected with Dark Side Base. Signal aspects and transmission strength show that Tokyo, Sydney, and New York are all linked together, transmitting both to the fleet as it advances, as well as back to the Ra'az homeworld."

"So you're saying we'll have to cripple not one, but *three* communications systems?"

"Yes."

"And then we have to stop their ships from launching too?"

"Yes as well. Once the communications are down, there is a ninety-five percent likelihood that the Ra'az will attempt to utilize the new warp drive to send ships to the fleet, their homeworld, and the Chithiid's home as well. If just one of those ships successfully leaves orbit and makes the jump, it will be able to reach not one, but all three destinations in short order. While the Ra'az scientists would still require time to replicate the technology on board, I estimate the entire fleet would be retrofitted and able to return to Earth within two point eight months, rather than two to four years."

"We'll be wiped out," Daisy gasped. "There's no way we can withstand even a fraction of their fleet. And since they know about Dark Side from their initial attack, they will likely bombard it again as soon as they return, so we wouldn't be safe there either, even if we could escape the surface."

"I'd call that an astute observation."

"So the Tokyo communications attack. The Ra'az have been playing a misinformation game for centuries. Planting a single bomb will do nothing. It was all a trick. A trap."

"Indeed, it appears so. Merely disabling one facility will not suffice, nor will eliminating all three, should the Ra'az be able to launch their ships. I will need to devise a better plan than what you originally came up with."

"Can you do that? You said we only have days."

"Daisy, I'm the most powerful military strategist ever created. Yes, I can do that."

"But even if you can, we don't have the firepower to knock out all three communications hubs. We're screwed."

Joshua laughed heartily.

"It's not funny!" Daisy yelled.

"No, of course not," he said, still chuckling. *"My apologies. But did I also mention that I can control the access and targeting codes for hypersonic missiles? If the Ra'az Hok communications were*

temporarily disrupted on the ground, those missiles would reach them before they knew what hit them."

Daisy felt her spirits begin to lift. A slim ray of hope began pulling her back from rapidly approaching despair.

"Really?" she said. "But there are more than just a few facilities we'll have to deal with now. Exactly how many of those missiles do you control?"

Joshua stifled another chuckle.

"Daisy," he said, *"I control them* all."

A smile of realization slowly spread across her face.

You hear that? she asked her silent partner.

"You bet I did," Sarah replied. *"This changes everything, Daze."*

Oh yes it does, she said, her smile in full bloom. *"I think we'd better grab a bottle opener, Sis.*

"Why's that?"

Because it looks like we're going to be opening up a whole fucking case of whoop-ass on those alien bastards.

"Okay, Joshua," Daisy said. "Let's get this show on the road."

BUT WAIT, THERE'S MORE!

Follow Daisy on her continuing adventures in the third book of the Clockwork Chimera series: Daisy's Gambit

ABOUT THE AUTHOR

A native Californian, Scott Baron was born in Hollywood, which he claims may be the reason for his rather off-kilter sense of humor.

Before taking up residence in Venice Beach, Scott first spent a few years abroad in Florence, Italy before returning home to Los Angeles and settling into the film and television industry, where he has worked as an on-set medic for many years.

Aside from mending boo-boos and owies, and penning books and screenplays, Scott is also involved in indie film and theater scene both in the U.S. and abroad.

ALSO BY SCOTT BARON

Standalone Novels

Living the Good Death

The Clockwork Chimera Series

Daisy's Run

Pushing Daisy

Daisy's Gambit

Chasing Daisy

Daisy's War

The Dragon Mage Series

Bad Luck Charlie

Space Pirate Charlie

Dragon King Charlie

Magic Man Charlie

Star Fighter Charlie

Portal Thief Charlie

Rebel Mage Charlie

Warp Speed Charlie

Odd and Unusual Short Stories:

The Best Laid Plans of Mice: An Anthology

Snow White's Walk of Shame

The Tin Foil Hat Club

Lawyers vs. Demons

The Queen of the Nutters

Lost & Found